THE MONEY CLUB

THE GOOD LIFE HAS ITS DARK SIDE.

FIONA LOWE

PRAISE FOR FIONA LOWE

"A gripping tale about greed, the price paid for ill-placed trust and the lessons that come with having it and losing it all … Ultimately, **The Money Club** is about hope." — *Weekend Australian*

'**A Family of Strangers** is a glorious, heart-warming tapestry of a novel.' —*The Herald Sun*

'Rich, thought-provoking, and extremely absorbing, **A Home Like Ours** is yet another incredible read from the very talented Fiona Lowe.' —*Better Reading*

'An insightful, warm and engaging story, **A Home Like Ours** is another fabulous novel from award-winning Australian author Fiona Lowe.' —*Book'd Out*

'Fiona Lowe's ability to create atmosphere and tension and real relationship dynamics is a gift.'
—*Sally Hepworth, bestselling author of The Mother-in-Law, on* **Home Fires**.

'Part-Liane Moriarty, part-Jodi Picoult, **Just an Ordinary Family** is a compelling drama about a seemingly 'ordinary' family that implodes after a domino effect of lies, betrayals, disappointments and regrets ... set to be the next Big Little Lies.' —*Mamamia*

'Lowe weaves character development and complexity with stunning finesse ... this story is not a light read, but it is one that proved difficult to put down.' —*GLAM Adelaide* on **Just an Ordinary Family**

'Fiona Lowe is the undisputed queen of Australian small-town fiction ... a moving character-driven tale that steadily draws you into its thrall.' —*Canberra Weekly* on **Just an Ordinary Family**

'A complex story that seamlessly intertwines many story lines. It is full of interesting characters that reveal more and more as the story progresses. It is raw, incredibly engaging and reads beautifully.' —*The Big Book Club* on **The Family Inheritance** (previously published as *Birthright*)

'Distinctly Australian with its power to evoke grit and tenderness, joy and bleakness, tragedy and comedy, all at once.' —*Better Reading* on **The Family Inheritance** (previously published as *Birthright*)

'Lowe is a master at painting believable characters with heart and soul that contribute to creating such an addictive read.' —*The Weekly Times* on **The Family Inheritance** (previously published as *Birthright*)

'A sweeping Australian novel of lost love and tangled family secrets.' — Australian Country on **Daughter of Mine**

ALSO BY FIONA LOWE

Daughter of Mine

The Family Inheritance

(PREVIOUSLY PUBLISHED AS BIRTHRIGHT)

Home Fires

Just an Ordinary Family

A Home Like Ours

A Family of Strangers

The Money Club

The Accident

For a free novella, **Summer of Mine**; the prequel of **Daughter of Mine**, please join my VIP Readers newsletter. You'll also be the first to hear about new releases, book sales, competitions and giveaways. Register at

fionalowe.com

Did you know BookBub has a new release alert? You can check out the latest deals and get an email when I release my next book by following me at

www.bookbub.com/authors/fiona-lowe

First Published by Harlequin Australia in 2023
This revised North American edition published in 2023 by Fiona Lowe
© 2023 by Fiona Lowe
www.fionalowe.com

THE MONEY CLUB
ISBN 978-0-6456187-9-2

Cover Design by Barton Lowe

Published by Fiona Lowe

To my dear friend Norma, who goes above and beyond supporting me with my writing.

He who loves money shall never have enough.
—The Living Bible, Ecclesiastes 5:10

'How did you go bankrupt?' Bill asked.
'Two ways,' Mike said. 'Gradually, then suddenly.'
—The Sun Also Rises, Ernest Hemingway

PROLOGUE

Izzy Harrington's three matching suitcases sat by the front door, their air somewhat embarrassed. A tattered Qantas tag clung tenaciously to the handle of the medium-sized case as if to remind Izzy she was letting the team down—Louis Vuitton luggage was designed not only to fly but to be seen. None of the three cases had graced the cargo hold of a plane in months. They hadn't even breached the cattle guard at the gate of Villefranche recently, let alone left the town limits of Glingilly, but today was the day.

The late afternoon sun streamed into the entrance hall, raising the temperature to that of a Pacific island, but instead of waving palm trees Izzy saw dust motes dancing. The waiting suitcases mocked her. Rather than holding in a few bikinis, sarongs, linen dresses and strappy sandals, the zippers bulged from Izzy forcing half the contents of her closet and tallboy into them. The rest of her clothes had been unceremoniously dumped into two-dollar-shop carry bags. Izzy imagined the cashmere sweaters flinching as they lay against the rough woven plastic.

She spun the large diamond ring on her finger. It was a looser fit than the day Brad had presented it to her, yet it had quadrupled in weight. She checked the time again. He was late. She'd expected him to walk through the double front doors over an hour ago. Should she load the suitcases into the car? She'd left them in the foyer as concrete proof she was leaving, and as an instant conversation starter for a topic that could no longer be avoided.

It won't make it easier.

Izzy knew that. Despite months of unhappiness and her suggestion they seek couples counseling, Brad's response continued to be one of two things: buy her something expensive, or sex. Once, something sparkly, a luxury vacation and mind-blowing sex had been enough—more than enough. Izzy knew that women envied her. Hell, her old self had envied her. So how had exhilaration and excitement turned into this hollow feeling that dogged her days and nights? The sparkling dream that had rolled out in front of them thirty months earlier—a golden road promising a future together of wondrous and endless possibilities—was now unrecognizable.

Even so, she wanted to limit the hurt. But was that possible when only one person wanted to walk away?

Her fingers pulled at the hair on the back of her head. She blew out a breath and contemplated a drink. She could have one gin and tonic and still safely make the two-hour drive to Geelong.

Yes! Have a drink, write a note and go.

But as tempting as it was to leave now, Izzy couldn't do to Brad what her mother had done to her and her father. Izzy's nine-year-old self had vowed she'd never take the coward's way out and inflict that sort of pain on anyone. If Brad wanted an explanation as to why she was leaving, she'd give it to him. Perhaps this time he'd hear it.

She sighed. He'd probably only hear that her leaving today meant she wouldn't be hosting Saturday's Elite function.

A loud noise split the air and her body jerked before she realized the jangling sound was the landline. It rang so infrequently it always made her jump. Two years earlier, when they'd moved into Villefranche, she'd suggested they get rid of it.

"It's only scammers or charities. Everyone else uses our cells."

"The olds will use it," Brad had said. "Plus, you can't depend on your cell during fire season."

Izzy, who'd been born and raised in Melbourne, had found this detail unsettling so the phone stayed. And Brad had been right—when it rang, if it wasn't a scammer, it was his parents, his aunt or one of his many uncles.

She heard the machine click on. *Brad, it's Jack Essen ...*

For a brief moment Izzy considered picking up and telling Jack he'd hit the wrong number. But a call from Jack would only further delay Brad.

It's about the club, Jack continued. *Give us a call back as soon as you can, eh, mate? Ta.*

Beeps followed, then silence. The walls of the cavernous entrance hall closed in on Izzy. She needed fresh air.

Pulling open the double doors, she ran down the sandstone steps and onto the circular drive, the gravel crunching under the soles of her quilted sneakers. The glare of the low afternoon sun collided with the fire-red glow of the turning maples as Izzy squinted down the long tree-lined drive, willing Brad's car to loom from the ripple of haze. She listened with unusual keenness, hearing the rustle of falling leaves, the harsh but mournful calls of the crows, the desperate bleat of a lamb. But as much as she willed it, the low throb of a diesel engine was absent.

Where was he?

Had he told her he was meeting someone? Going somewhere? Had she been so consumed by her own plans to pack up her life that she'd missed hearing his arrangements for the day over breakfast?

Izzy pulled her phone out of her pocket—no missed calls. No voice mail and no messages. Should she text him? But asking *What time will you be home?* just so she could leave him before it got dark seemed callous.

She couldn't predict how Brad would react to the news. Once, she would have bet on him turning on a charm offensive, but there'd been times recently when he'd been so distracted and distant she was convinced he'd left her despite being physically present. Other times, he almost suffocated her with attention.

That's a brave decision.

She flinched. She'd overheard Brad using that phrase on the phone with his clients many times before hanging up and saying, "Iz, why do people fear the thing they want the most?"

Izzy's thoughts swerved away from the question as Thor, their Jack Russell, raced up to her, his brown eyes filled with the excited anticipation of a walk. Her heart tore in a different way from the pain it was experiencing leaving Brad, but taking the dog would be an act of war she wanted to avoid.

Thor was only one of two joint possessions—the other being a beachfront apartment on the Sunshine Coast that Izzy had never set foot inside. When she'd suggested they spend a few weeks in Noosa, Brad had replied, "Babe, it's an investment, not a vacation house."

She'd glanced around the ostentatious Villefranche. "We live in an investment property so why not vacation in one?" she'd asked.

Brad had laughed and kissed her. "Because we deserve somewhere far more exotic than Noosa."

Perhaps that was when Izzy should have told him she yearned for a night away from luxury—to stay in a beach shack with sand on the floor, and sea breezes blowing through the cracks between the boards. But he probably wouldn't have believed her.

Thor barked, bringing Izzy's attention back to the here and now. "Is it Brad?" she asked the dog, peering down the drive.

The shape of the vehicle's lights and grille told her it wasn't and she stepped back as the sports car pulled to a stop on the circular drive. She immediately recognized the driver—Mike Essen. He was a good friend of Brad's father and, unlike some of the men she'd met via the club, he was polite and kept his hands to himself.

Mike levered himself out of the low car. "Hello, Isobel. Brad about, is he?"

She shook her head. She was wondering why he was using her

formal name when she remembered Jack Essen's unexpected call on the landline.

Why was Mike here?

Although the Elite members came to Villefranche to socialize—parties that often appeared to be networking and unofficial business meetings—Brad never took anyone into his office, refusing to conduct formal business inside their home. Instead he met people at their house or in a private space at the Glingilly Social Club.

Izzy caught a bouncing Thor by the collar seconds before he jumped and landed muddy paws on Mike's chinos. "Did you and Jack have an appointment with Brad?"

Mike grimaced. "I want one."

Brad had been complaining about Mike for weeks. "I know he's Dad's best mate, but he's driving me nuts." However, Brad's special skill in business was making everyone feel as if they were his most important consideration in that moment. If Mike was still here when Brad got home, he'd usher the older man inside and that was the last thing Izzy needed.

"I'm sorry you've come all the way out here to be disappointed," she said. "Brad's been flat out since he got back from Ireland. I'll get him to call you."

"Yeah, right."

The tightly spoken words whipped Izzy and she stared at him.

"I'll wait if you don't mind," he added. The usually genial man had vanished under a coat of implacability.

"Actually, I do mind. This is our home."

"Fine. I'll wait in the car." Mike walked back toward it.

"That's not the point," she called after him. "I'd like you to leave."

Thor suddenly barked and she and Mike turned to see the dog tearing off down the long drive. Mike immediately followed.

Shit! Izzy's mind raced. Should she run past Mike to get to Brad first? She was thirty years younger and much fitter so she could easily beat him. And then what? Tell Brad to say no to a meeting with Mike? That she needed to talk to him about something important? But Brad would never slight a client even if they were difficult. Perhaps the best plan was to go back inside and move the suitcases out of the entrance before they tripped up the two men.

She was about to turn back when she realized there were three vehicles pulling up and none were Brad's SUV. But it wasn't Alan Lumsden's Tesla or Oscar D'Angelo's Ferrari that surprised her—it was the Ford Ranger with distinctive blue and white checks. Why were the police here?

Her mind instantly raced to disaster scenarios—Brad's Merc crumpled against another vehicle. His lifeless body slumped on the airbag.

You won't have to tell him it's over.

Stomach acid washed to the back of her throat. *Shut up! He's not dead. He drives the safest car on the market.*

An image of the new cardiac defibrillator they'd recently donated to the region's emergency helicopter filled her mind, along with an unconscious Brad connected to life support and being airlifted to a Melbourne hospital. Her breathing kicked up.

You can't leave him now.

Am I his next of kin?

The thought momentarily stalled her catastrophizing. Was she? He was hers, because her father was dead and her mother was who the hell knew where, whereas Brad spoke to his parents most days and they only lived three miles away.

Izzy automatically reached for her cell to check for a message from Brad's mother, Judy. Nothing.

She suddenly remembered Brad's parents had left early that morning for a health retreat in northern New South Wales. Brad had been ticked off because they were missing Saturday's Elite function. The timing was odd—Bevan and Judy rarely missed an Elite or a Fortune function—and it was an unusual vacation choice. Izzy couldn't picture Brad's parents giving up their evening glass of wine or three, or Bevan doing yoga and eating vegan food. Would their cell phones even work up there?

Desperately fighting the urge to hyperventilate, Izzy was vaguely aware that the three men now stood beside the police car.

"Ms. Harrington?"

She blinked, trying to bring the officers into focus. She immediately recognized Brooke Riglioni, who she'd got to know on the Irish festival committee after Brad had asked her to join in his place.

"I'm happy to be the major sponsor," he'd told her, "but I don't have time for the meetings. Besides, it's a good way for you to get involved in Glingilly."

So Izzy had dressed to cover her shyness and forced herself to attend. Brad had been right—it felt good to be involved in something outside of the business, and she and Brooke always shared some laughs.

"Isobel," Brooke was saying, "this is Detective Mitchell from Warrnambool." She indicated the man next to her who was dressed in chinos and a polar fleece.

Izzy blinked as the word "detective" penetrated her panic. "Is Brad injured?"

"He should be," Alan muttered.

"She says he's not here," Mike said in a disbelieving tone.

"Where is he then?" Oscar demanded.

Izzy barely heard them and kept her gaze on Brooke. "Has Brad been in a car accident or—" she gulped, "—worse?"

Brooke shook her head and gave Izzy's arm a reassuring pat. "No, it's nothing like that."

Relief shuddered out of her. She might be leaving Brad but she didn't wish him injured or dead. With her panic receding, her chaotic thoughts reassembled into something closer to order. If Brad wasn't injured, why were the police here?

"Is it the speeding fine?" Izzy asked. "Because I've got it in my calendar to pay next Tuesday, which is a day before—"

"It's not the speeding fine," Brooke said firmly. "May we come inside for a chat?"

Izzy had no reason to deny the request, yet she heard her father saying, "Don't invite trouble in." She shook it off. Just because the police were here didn't mean trouble.

Really? And when was the last time they dropped in for a chat?

Izzy gave the unhelpful thought the metaphorical bird. Brooke had visited a couple of weeks ago to talk about the festival and to give her the direct debit details for the committee's bank account.

"Is this about the sponsorship money? Brad said he's transferred it—"

"I bet he did," Mike said.

Izzy whirled around to face him. "I don't know what your problem is today, Mr. Essen, but I've already asked you to leave. This time I'm telling you."

The three men stood shoulder to shoulder and folded their arms.

"We're not leaving until we've talked to Brad," Oscar said.

Izzy swung back to the police. "I didn't invite them so that's trespassing, right? Please tell them to leave."

"Gentlemen," Brooke said, "did any of you receive an invitation to visit today?"

"You know why we're here," Alan said. "We're not leaving until we have answers."

"Once you made it a police matter it's out of your hands and in ours," Brooke said firmly. "You need to let us do our jobs."

A police matter? Izzy's gut cramped. *What the hell was a police matter?*

"We'll wait just outside the gate," Oscar said.

"If you create a traffic hazard I'll have to charge you," Brooke said drily.

Mike sighed. "Let's go to the club. You never know, he might just show and have a reasonable explanation."

"He bloody well better." Alan trudged toward the Tesla.

The roar of engines scattered the magpies and the cars departed.

Izzy's relief was so great that when the detective said, "Ms. Harrington, shall we?" and indicated the front doors, she walked inside without thinking.

Detective Mitchell closed the doors behind them and the bang echoed around the cavernous entrance hall. He immediately spotted the suitcases and his brows rose. "Going somewhere, Ms. Harrington?"

She didn't want to tell Mitchell or Brooke she was leaving Brad before she'd told him and returned the engagement ring. "Just visiting a friend in Geelong."

Mitchell's gaze settled on the two-dollar bags. "Looks like you're moving in with your friend."

Izzy laughed and thought fast. "I've had a wardrobe clean-out. Whatever she doesn't want can go to the thrift shop."

"Is Brad in Geelong?" Brooke asked.

"No," Izzy said.

"Where is he then?" Mitchell asked.

"I don't know," she said honestly. "I expected him home an hour ago."

"I think you know where he is." The detective pointed to the suitcases. "And you're going to join him."

"What? I—"

"Do you know if Brad took his passport with him?" Mitchell asked.

Izzy stared at him, not following his train of thought. "Why would he do that? He only arrived home yesterday."

"Can we see your passport?" Brooke asked.

What the hell was going on? Did she have to show them? Was not showing them worse? Izzy's head spun, giving her nothing, so she fished the little blue book out of the document holder in her backpack.

"So you *are* on your way to the airport." Brooke's words rode a sigh.

"You take your passport with you when you visit friends in Geelong, do you?" the detective asked.

"What? Wait! No!" Sweat dampened Izzy's palms and pooled under her arms. "This Isn't—"

"You're not going to Geelong, are you?" Mitchell said. "You're flying out to meet Brad in a tax haven or somewhere we don't share an extradition treaty."

Izzy stiffened—she really didn't like the detective and she refused to be pushed around. She straightened her shoulders and tried to anchor herself. "I've got no idea what you're talking about. He'll be home soon and when he arrives I expect an apology."

"You'll be waiting a long time for that, sunshine," the detective said.

Brooke traded an enigmatic look with him before returning her gaze to Izzy. "I understand you want to protect Brad, but he's the focus of a police investigation."

Was this a joke? How could Brad possibly be the focus of a police investigation? But the serious look on Brooke's face underpinned her words—this was real.

Suddenly, the marble floor beneath Izzy's feet tilted and she sat hard on the bottom step of the stone staircase. The cold chilled her adrenaline-fueled body, racing shivers across her skin.

"Am I part of that focus too?" she asked.

"You're a person of interest," Brooke said. "We can come back with a warrant to search the house or you can make it easy on yourself and tell us where Brad is."

This isn't happening. Ordinary people didn't find themselves being disbelieved by a local police officer they considered a friend. Yet Izzy was circled by the surreal sensation of starring in a television police drama.

Pressing her palms against the stone step, she registered its cold hardness. It was real. This situation was all very real. Panic surged, pounding blood against her temples, and she tried desperately to sort through the horrifying information.

Brad was the focus of a police investigation. She was a person of interest! None of it made any sense, but a lack of logic didn't stop icicles of dread forming in her veins.

Where the hell was Brad?

And more immediately, what the hell situation had he left her in?

CHAPTER ONE

SEVERAL MONTHS EARLIER

"Luce, Rigby's in the car and you know how he gets. Let's go."

Lucy Essen heard the impatience in Jack's voice and took a quick last glance in the mirror—she'd fiddle with the flower on her hat when she arrived at the racecourse. She tucked her gloves into her clutch, added a sewing kit, first-aid kit, shawl, water, umbrella, face-mist spray and a spare pair of shoes to Rigby's backpack, then walked into the foyer.

Jack stood at the open door leading to the garage and an admiring and appreciative look crossed his face, immediately followed by a frown. She caught the moment his dark eyes dimmed with the realization that she'd spent money on her ensemble.

"You look good, Luce," she said, rolling her hands to encourage him to say the words.

"You look amazing, but how much did it cost?"

Lucy walked into the garage and got into the car. "We're going to see the horseys," she said to her son in a singsong voice. "What do horses say?"

"Neigh," three-year-old Rigby announced proudly. "Want to see a horsey. Now!"

Jack backed up the car, then pressed the remote control to close the garage door. "How much did you spend?"

"Hardly anything!" Lucy sucked in a breath and tried to sound less defensive. "I went to three different thrift shops for the dress, the gloves and the hat. I've borrowed the clutch and the shoes from Jamie at work, and Emma helped me alter the dress. The only new things are the buttons and the flower on the hat."

Jack sighed. "Tell me the whole outfit cost less than fifty bucks."

She placed her hand on Jack's thigh, still surprised by her manicured nails, and gave his leg a gentle squeeze. "Almost. Fifty-eight seventy. But you can bet everything we own that Izzy Harrington won't be wearing a pre-loved dress to the Glingilly Cup or be in borrowed shoes."

"Yeah, but you're not her."

Lucy didn't need reminding of that. "Please be happy. I could have spent a fortune, but I didn't. I've worked really hard pulling it together so it looks brand new instead of rescued."

"You could have worn something from your closet."

"No, I couldn't! This year's different, Jack. We're members of Elite now and we need to look like we belong. Besides, we've been making money all year—"

"To pay off the house."

"I know, but today's special to your mom too. Billabong's running in the Cup and I thought it might help things along if I entered Fashions on the Field. You know, show an interest in something Birdie loves."

When Lucy and Jack had first met on a tram in Melbourne—he was the lost country boy and she was the city midwife on her way to work—she'd never set foot on a racecourse, let alone placed a bet. Now she had more than a passing interest in all things racing.

Jack sighed. "The way Mom carries on you'd think she's the sole owner of Billabong instead of sharing him with a hundred and fifty others."

"I thought she owned him with the Quinns and their friends?"

"She's in a syndicate that's costing her more than her winnings."

"Still, it gives her a hobby and she loves the social side of things," Lucy said.

Her mother-in-law was a conundrum of frugality and largesse. One minute Lucy felt judged for buying furniture and crockery for their dream home, and the next Birdie was suggesting everyone in the family place a bet on Billabong.

Jack slowed behind a line of cars paying to enter the course. The previous year rain had rendered the track heavy and the grounds a quagmire—Lucy had worn gumboots and a Driza-Bone coat. But today the sun shone from a fluffy-cloud-studded sky and the beautifully clipped grass glowed emerald. No wonder the famine-stricken Irish had settled here in the 1840s, planted potatoes and tried to replicate the west country. Their love of all sports, including horse racing, had come with them. A hundred and eighty years later it still infused the district in a sweeping triangle from Camperdown to Glingilly and south to Warrnambool on the Southern Ocean. Lucy loved the family atmosphere of the Glingilly Cup and she had a soft spot for the heritage-listed grandstand with its decorative wrought iron and ornate Victorian posts.

"Horsey! Horsey!" Rigby pointed excitedly to a horse being led by a groom.

Jack grinned at his son through the rear-view mirror. "You're going to see a lot of them today, mate."

Warmth spread through Lucy and she squeezed Jack's thigh again.

Discovering she was unexpectedly pregnant two months into their relationship had been her worst nightmare. For a week after seeing the two lines on the pregnancy test she'd played out every scenario in her head. Jack asking her to terminate the pregnancy. Jack leaving her to raise a child on her own. Jack reluctantly staying with her then leaving, and replicating for their baby her own childhood of being bounced between two parents who specialized in acrimony and bitter regret.

After five days of Lucy dodging his calls and texts, Jack had arrived at her door, his face pinched with worry. Even the flowers he clutched had drooped.

"What's wrong?" he'd asked without preamble. "You look shi—are you sick? Is that why you're ignoring me? Luce, tell me what's going on. You're scaring me."

When she told him she was pregnant, he'd picked her up and spun her around until she'd almost vomited. He'd proposed on the spot.

"We've got this, Luce," he'd said, grinning down at her. "It's gonna be great."

Almost four years later, "great" was open to interpretation. Jack worked as a fly-in fly-out engineer at the Mt. Tom Price mine in Western Australia. The FIFO work took him away from home two weeks out of every four. When he was at work, Lucy worked day shifts; and when he was at home and could parent, she worked nights. She adored her job, loving how it gave her a professional space where she could be Lucy Essen midwife, rather than Rigby's mom, Jack's wife and Birdie and Mike's daughter-in-law. Not that she didn't love the first three roles—she did. And she justified the tough night-duty tours as short-term pain for long-term gain. Once they'd paid down the mortgage to a manageable level, Jack would quit FIFO and take a lower-paying job in the district, be the soccer dad he longed to be, and they'd have another baby. Since joining Elite their dream was closer, but as far as Lucy was concerned, it was still too far away.

She unsuccessfully stifled a yawn. God, she was tired—she'd been exhausted for three and a half years. Could she keep this pace up for two and a half more? Although she'd agreed to their plan, the fact that Rigby might be five or six before he had a sibling now bothered her. It seemed an age gap too big to bridge, which was why she'd asked Jack about another financial strategy.

"Are you going to talk to your dad today about a loan?" she said.

"I've asked Brad to talk to him first."

Lucy thought about her conservative father-in-law who, apart from risking a twenty-dollar bet each race day, probably still had the first dollar he'd ever earned. "Really? You think your dad will be interested in Elite?"

Jack shot her a look. "You don't know Dad. Back in the day, when everyone in town was driving to Warrnambool to play the poker machines, Dad and Bevan Quinn worked out how much money was leaving town. They convinced the chamber of commerce, the lawn tennis club, the football and the lawn bowls clubs to come together and create the Glingilly Social Club – the 'GGSC'. It was a big ask for members to risk their own money to lease the middle pub and get a gaming license, but they offered returns above the bank rate. It paid off."

Lucy laughed. "Because this town will bet on anything that moves?"

Jack shrugged. "It's more about valuing community. And look what they achieved— GGSC's the heart of Glingilly. It owns the building now, and in the last twenty years it's pumped huge amounts back into the sporting clubs and the town. Our lawn tennis club is the envy of Country Week, and the Indigenous footy scholarships are why we've currently got three local boys playing in the Australian Football League."

"I can't imagine your dad convincing anyone to take an unsecured debenture," Lucy said.

"I think Bevan convinced him, and Dad respects Bev's financial advice. Always has." Jack flashed their entry tickets at the gate. "Where do you want to park?"

"Is that Brad's car?" Lucy pointed to a Porsche.

Jack squinted. "One of them anyway. Are you sure you want to be next to them? You always say Izzy's stuck-up and unfriendly. Besides, if we're next to Mom and Dad we have built-in babysitters for Rigby."

"I guess we'll see Izzy and Brad at the Elite luncheon."

"Luncheon!" Jack laughed. "Who's being lah-di-dah now? Are you sure you're entering Fashions on the Field for Mom or to impress Izzy?"

"I'm hardly going to impress her in a revamped vintage dress from the thrift shop when she'll be wearing some overseas designer."

"You sure you only spent fifty-eight seventy?"

"Yes! Meanwhile everyone else in Elite's spending their money. Why can't we?"

"We are spending it," Jack said tightly. "On the mortgage."

"I know, but no one can see that! Just this once I want to look like we fit in. It's hard enough that, apart from Brad and Izzy, everyone in Elite is older than us and has more money. The last dividend-day party I wore Target jeans and sneakers because Brad said it was a barbecue."

Jack gave her a bewildered look. "It was a barbecue, and Brad and Izzy didn't dress up. Her jeans had holes in them."

Lucy groaned. "Oh my God, I love you, but you're clueless." She waggled her fingers to make talking marks. "Izzy's 'old' jeans cost three hundred and twenty-five dollars. Her sneakers cost almost the same and I don't even want to think about the pendant. It was probably worth more than one of our mortgage repayments."

"Jeez, even if we had money to burn, promise me you wouldn't spend it on jeans." Jack parked next to his parents' car and killed the ignition before leaning over and kissing her on the cheek. "Luce, we'll get there. Once the house is paid off we'll have some jam in the budget, but better than that, we'll have time. But we're never going to be like Brad and Izzy so don't try to keep up."

"Why not?"

"Because we're not that sort of people."

Lucy didn't know if she was offended or not. "What do you mean? We have just as much right to a comfortable life as they do."

"Of course we do."

"What then?"

Jack ran his hand through his hair. "Don't get me wrong. I respect Brad. Hell, I'm grateful he invited us to join Elite, but do you reckon he and Izzy are happy?"

Lucy stared at Jack as if she didn't recognize him. "Well, let's see. They live in a mansion, they don't have the responsibility of kids, they've taken five vacations in the last year, and when Brad travels for work Izzy goes with him. Oh, and unlike us, they go to bed together most nights of the year. Why wouldn't they be happy?"

Jack grimaced as if regretting raising the topic. "Brad wants kids. He has for ages. Has Izzy said anything to you?"

Lucy snorted. "What do you think?"

"You're a midwife and a mom, so I thought she might have asked for some advice. You know, if she's having trouble getting pregnant?"

Lucy thought of the cool and aloof woman. How she always seemed slightly detached and, unlike the matrons of Elite, never made a fuss of Rigby. Did Izzy find it hard being around children because she was struggling to conceive? The idea that there might be a reason for her coolness that had nothing to do with Lucy was reassuring.

"I'll drop a few hints today and see what I can find out," she said.

Birdie was bearing down on the car and Lucy took a deep breath, reminding herself that today was about having fun. Today was her chance to relax. Today she and Birdie had a common interest in the Cup and the fashions. Lucy would ask all the right questions about horse racing and Billabong, and keep the critical version of her mother-in-law at bay.

And if that didn't work, there was always champagne.

CHAPTER TWO

SEVERAL MONTHS EARLIER

When Billabong came across the line barely a nose behind the winner, Birdie Essen screamed in public for the first time in her life. Then she hugged her best friend, Judy Quinn.

"Oh my God! I think my heart stopped there for a second."

Judy laughed. "It's all part of the wild ride."

"Thank you! I don't think I've felt this alive in years."

And she hadn't.

Birdie considered herself sensible, responsible, prudent and practical, and for years she'd prided herself on these attributes. When she and Mike had married, they'd owned two beanbags, two director's chairs, a bed, a fridge and nine casserole dishes. They'd eaten dinner on their laps watching *The Muppets* or *M*A*S*H* on a secondhand television with a screen that favored green. With careful scrimping and saving, they'd bought a house, raised two kids and sent them out into the world. Then, with only themselves to provide for, she and Mike had paid off the mortgage and concentrated on contributing the maximum allowed to their retirement fund.

For years Mike had insisted he was retiring at sixty. By then, there would be enough money to give them a modest retirement lifestyle.

When Mike turned sixty-five, the pension would kick in as a backup. After all, they didn't need a lot, and what Birdie was craving was time with Mike.

A year before Mike's sixtieth birthday, the wind-farm company he worked for offered him a two-year contract at a higher hourly rate.

"The money's too good to refuse, Bird, and it'll top up the retirement fund. I reckon I'll push out retirement one more year."

It had taken Birdie a while to let go of her disappointment, but she'd finally channeled it into planning their long-anticipated, "Trip of a Lifetime" around-Australia. The moment Mike retired, they were taking off.

She did her due diligence—joined online forums, read reviews, and made the two-and-a-half-hour drive to Geelong to the travel trailer and camping dealership. She'd finally settled on a small all-terrain trailer, but she wasn't throwing money at it. She'd wait for the run-out sale that would inevitably happen prior to the release of the new model.

The day before the sale email finally pinged onto her cell phone, Mike was offered another generous contract.

"We want to keep his experience in the business as long as possible," his boss had told Birdie at the dinner she'd expected to be part of Mike's farewell.

She'd held onto her screaming frustration until they were home and then it had exploded out of her like lava. "This isn't what we planned! The trip's all organized. We're going west first, then north and east and south, until we circle back to Glingilly in two years time."

Mike had laughed. "You'll never survive two years without seeing Rigby and Jack."

"I will."

She'd said it so curtly that Mike's head had jerked up from the iPad, a frown creasing his weathered face.

"You okay, love?"

She'd sighed. "I love the kids, but I've done my bit. I've been the pre-school and school mom, the footy mom, the taxi mom and the dutiful daughter caring for my mom. I've done what's expected of me, but now it's our time. Our adventure's well overdue. God, we've been talking about this trip since we got married!"

Mike put his hand on hers. "And it's gonna happen, Birdie, I promise. But while I'm still enjoying work and they want me, it seems crazy to walk away from this sort of money."

Birdie had thrown every argument she had at him, but Mike just shook his head and said, "The numbers don't lie, love. We deserve a comfortable retirement and this will give it to us. But I promise you—no matter the money, the moment I stop enjoying the job, I'm out the door."

"Yes, but when's that going to be?" She'd hated the pleading in her voice.

"When the time's right," he'd said with infuriating insouciance.

The change of plans had left Birdie lost and directionless. Life toddled on as unchanging as it had for years. She minded Rigby a few times a week; she gardened, and she added volunteering at the tourist information center to the mix. If she couldn't travel, she'd help those who could. She and Mike continued to meet Judy and Bevan for Friday-night dinner and drinks as they'd done for years, but Birdie craved more. She'd toyed with getting a job, but Mike wasn't keen on the idea, and anyway, who would employ a fifty-eight-year-old domestic engineer?

So on an ordinary Friday night at the club, when Judy had casually suggested over a glass of wine that Birdie join her and some other women in a part-share of a racehorse, she'd surprised herself by asking, "What's involved?"

"It's a twenty percent share, which means we're responsible for twenty per cent of the costs and we share twenty percent of the winnings. For you, it means a thousand dollars upfront and then about a hundred dollars a month."

Mike spluttered into his beer and looked at Bevan. "Surely as a financial advisor you don't recommend this?"

Bevan laughed. "As a financial advisor, I say it's very high risk. As a husband, I say, 'Of course, my darling, have some fun.' As your mate, I say, 'Whatever it takes for marital harmony.'"

Judy laughed too and shot Mike a look. "Bev's right. Birdie deserves some fun after you torpedoed the great adventure. Twice."

Birdie smiled at her friend, appreciating her support. "What do I get for my money?"

"It works like this," Judy said. "I'm the syndicate manager for this one—"

"This one?" Birdie asked. "Do you have shares in other horses?"

"Three. It's her midlife madness," Bevan teased.

Judy elbowed him. "You can't talk. You've got your own pony."

Mike asked Bevan a question about the fuel consumption of the new Mustang and Birdie tried not to sigh. They'd known the Quinns for over thirty years and Judy and Bevan had always had more disposable income than her and Mike. Sure, they lived in a slightly bigger house, drove slightly more expensive cars and Judy's fingers flashed with a few extra diamond rings than Birdie's did, but they didn't flaunt their wealth and they'd never made Birdie or Mike feel uncomfortable. Their financial differences had never been an issue until recently when Bevan had bought the Mustang. It was the first time Birdie had seen envy scrawled on Mike's face.

"As the syndicate manager," Judy was saying, leaning closer to block out the men's car discussion, "I've registered it with the Victorian Racing Club and the gaming board. There's a dedicated bank account and everything's done by direct debit. You pay monthly and I pay the stables and distribute the winnings. Oh, and the good news—There's no tax on winnings."

Judy took a sip of her sparkling wine. "That's all the boring details. Now for the good stuff. We get regular updates on the horse, and as we're close to the stables, you can watch training now and then if you fancy getting up before dawn. We rent a small bus and go to all the country race meets. It's so much fun, and as an owner you get in for free and you can bring a guest. We get to drink at the trainers and owners" bar and you meet some fascinating people from all walks of life. The girls are an absolute hoot and there's nothing like having a flutter and watching your horse run."

A flicker of excitement flared in Birdie's belly. "Who are the other women?"

"My sister and her friends from Melbourne." Judy glanced around to check no one could overhear. "And a special few from Glingilly. That's why I want you."

The eddies of discontent that had been swirling inside Birdie for a couple of years slowed. Was this what she needed? A new interest? Something fun that was just for her? She thought about the money she'd squirrelled away for the expensive special-occasion events on their trip—swimming with whale sharks on Ningaloo Reef, the small-plane flight to the Tiwi Islands, the eco resort in the Daintree. Mike kept telling her the money he was earning now would give them a more comfortable retirement. As he'd already delayed their trip twice, and was likely to do it again, perhaps her little pot of jam could be used for more immediate enjoyment.

She picked up her cell and brought up the bank app. "I'm in. Send the account details and I'll transfer you the money now."

Judy clapped. "I'm so glad! Bevan, stop talking cars. We need a bottle of Möet and four glasses. Birdie's joined the Fascinators."

Birdie ignored Mike's incredulous look and his flash of hurt that she hadn't discussed her decision with him first. Tough. He hadn't discussed his change in retirement plans with her—just presented them as a *fait accompli*. Joining the Fascinators was a chance to shake up her life—to experience it rather than treading water and waiting. It felt like she'd been waiting years for something to happen.

And now, twelve months later, it had finally happened. Billabong had placed in his first big race, far beyond their expectations.

Birdie turned from Judy to Mike, who was standing with her at the railings holding Rigby. "Now do you get it?"

He grinned and pulled her in for a hug. "It's bloody exciting."

Birdie kissed him, then Rigby. "I can't believe how well Tessa rode him. She was looking boxed in and then in the final straight—"

"I'm hungry," Rigby announced.

Mike tousled his hair. "So am I, mate."

"Can you take him back to the car?" Another thrill ran up Birdie's spine. "I'll join you after I've collected my winnings."

Mike glanced around. "Where are Jack and Lucy?"

"They're having lunch with Brad," Bevan said. "Judy and I are just heading over to the marquee now. You two should come."

This lunch was the only thing her daughter-in-law had talked about for two weeks. Even so, shock had swooped through Birdie when Lucy had arrived on the course wearing an expensive-looking frock along with all the traditional race wear accessories that belonged at the Melbourne Cup.

"Luce is embracing Billabong's big day," Jack had said as he'd kissed Birdie hello.

"I can see that." But she couldn't look at Lucy without calculating how much money she'd spent on an outfit she was unlikely to ever wear again.

Birdie brought her mind back to Bevan's suggestion. "I thought lunch was invitation-only?"

"It is." Bevan smiled. "And we're inviting you."

"Are you sure?" Mike lowered the little boy into the stroller. "It means Rigby comes too."

"No problem," Bevan said. "Hopefully he'll inspire Brad and Izzy to get cracking on giving me grandkids."

Judy slapped Bevan's arm. "Let them get married first. Although if Izzy got pregnant that might speed up the wedding plans." She sighed. "Those two spend too much time overthinking everything and calculating the risks instead of just getting on with it."

Birdie thought about Jack and Lucy, who seemed to live their lives thinking after the event and never calculating a risk until it hit them smack between the eyeballs. Their enormous mortgage was a case in point. If that wasn't bad enough, Lucy's constant spending on unnecessary homewares and knick-knacks couldn't be helping their bottom line. Why couldn't they just wait and save like she and Mike had? Birdie came out in a cold sweat whenever she thought about how much Jack and Lucy's new and enormous leather sofa must have cost them. And Rigby didn't need a racing-car bed, but Lucy had refused her offer of Jack's old twin. Money ran like sand through that girl's fingers and it wasn't just on things for the house. Whenever Jack was home, they went out to breakfast. Everyone knew young people's coffee and avocado addiction was keeping them poor, but they—

Stop it. She gave herself a shake. Today was all about having fun and a day off from worrying about the kids. That could happen again tomorrow.

Birdie noticed the other Fascinators were already walking toward the bar. "Aren't they coming to the lunch?"

"As much fun as they are, the invitation doesn't extend to them. We'll catch up again at Fashions on the Field." Judy slipped her arm through Birdie's. "Come on. Izzy spent ages agonizing over the menu and Elaine from Paddock Providore's the caterer."

"Oh, I love her arancini balls," Birdie said, excitement fluttering at the exclusive invitation.

"And I love the Veuve Clicquot."

CHAPTER THREE

BIRDIE DIDN'T KNOW what she'd been expecting, but a white marquee with two topiary cumquat trees in white pots at the entrance wasn't it. Neither was the sight of Sam Vili, the town's buff and broad-shouldered arborist, dressed all in black.

"G'day, Mrs. Quinn." Sam's gaze took in Birdie alongside Judy and he ducked his head as if he was embarrassed.

"It's okay, Sam," Judy said easily. "Brad knows the Essens are a last-minute addition to the list."

Sam nodded and stepped sideways so they could enter. That's when Birdie realized Sam was working as a bouncer. She tried not to laugh. A bouncer at a marquee at a country race meeting? Who on earth was going to gatecrash a lunch? But then again, Brad Quinn was as pretentious with his wealth as Bevan was understated.

She followed Judy inside and was immediately met by a young woman holding a silver tray supporting a forest of champagne flutes. They were filled to the brim with fine bubbles rising in continuous motion. As Birdie accepted a glass, she noticed the decor. White cloths covered tables decorated with tasteful runners of racehorses, evocative of the day. The ceiling of the marquee was softened with clouds of chiffon, and comfortable sofas were scattered in groups so people could chat. Large plants fostered a sense of privacy between the areas.

Izzy Harrington was beautifully dressed as always and she glided over as if she was skating on ice rather than navigating grass in six-inch heels. She leaned down to kiss Judy on the cheek before saying hello to Birdie. "I hear you both had an exciting race three."

"Did you see it?" Birdie asked, reliving the thrill. "I thought my heart might stop!"

"Sorry, no." Izzy's fingers touched the back of her head as if checking her hair. "I'm on duty here today."

Duty? Izzy must have caught Birdie's confused look.

"Today's all about Brad's—our guests," she explained. "I'm making sure things run smoothly so everyone can relax and enjoy the event."

A waiter presented a tray of smoked salmon and caviar on rounds of sourdough.

"Oh, I think I can definitely enjoy one of these." Birdie popped it in her mouth and sighed. She'd only had caviar once before and the second time didn't disappoint.

While Izzy answered Judy's questions about the flowers, Birdie studied the small crowd. She recognized everyone although she didn't know them very well. A few lived on Ranelagh Street—the most expensive property in town. Others, according to Glingilly gossip, had recently renovated or installed a pool or bought a new car. Gaylene Hewitson, a long-time acquaintance through the social club, who lived in a similar size home to Birdie, now had grandchildren at boarding school in Geelong.

"How wonderful they both won scholarships," Birdie had said when Gaylene told her.

"Actually, Jim and I are paying," Gaylene said smugly. "It's the least we can do."

Birdie had gone home and asked Mike if he knew how the Hewitsons could afford that sort of money. Especially when Jim hadn't worked in two years and Gaylene had a part-time job at the pharmacy.

"Perhaps his mother left him something," Mike had said. "Or they invested wisely."

"This is Jim we're talking about," Birdie had scoffed. "He bets on the dogs and drives a beat-up truck."

Mike shrugged. "Everyone chooses to spend their money differently. I think it's great he's helping out with the grandkids' education."

Today it struck Birdie that the odd ones out in the marquee were Jack and Lucy. Those two lived payday to payday with nothing behind them. She supposed they'd been invited for the same reason she and Mike had—friendship. The Essen kids and Brad had grown up together courtesy of their parents' friendship. Not that it always meant the children would go on to be friends beyond childhood, but in Jack and Brad's case they'd remained good mates.

Birdie followed a waiter with a tray of arancini balls, popped three on a napkin, then found Mike. He'd parked the stroller next to Lucy and Jack. She gave her grandson one of the cheese balls.

Jack's grin was that of a man who'd imbibed a few drinks. "Whaddya reckon, Mom? Pretty swanky, eh?"

Birdie laughed. "It's certainly flasher than the picnic I packed."

Lucy stopped a waiter and picked up another glass of champagne. "I could get used to this."

Birdie swallowed the words "beer income and champagne tastes." Instead, she said, "Enjoy today. Sadly real life returns tomorrow."

"Real life can be whatever you want it to be," Brad said, joining them.

He tousled Rigby's hair and asked him if he was enjoying the arancini balls. Then he straightened up and leaned in to kiss Birdie and shake Mike's hand.

"Thanks for coming. I hear you had a win on race three," he said.

Birdie smiled. "Billabong did us proud."

"Excellent. Well, you're in the right place here. You're surrounded by winners."

A speaker squealed and everyone turned. Izzy was gripping a

microphone for dear life and for a split second she looked rattled. Then she ran her hand down the back of her hair and smiled—all grace and style.

"What a glorious day!" she said. "How blessed are we with this weather?" Murmurs ran around the marquee. "Mind you, it wouldn't dare rain on Elite's Glingilly Cup celebration, would it, Brad?" Her tinkling laughter followed.

Brad stepped up and slid his arm around her waist as she passed him the microphone. "It's only raining cash on Elite, right? What an awesome year we've had."

A couple of men, including Jack, cheered, then everyone clapped. Birdie looked at Mike for clarification, but he shrugged so she turned to Judy and Bevan. Their gazes were fixed on Brad, pride bright in their eyes.

"Today I want to toast you all for the belief you've shown in the program," Brad said. "I can't thank you enough for taking a leap of faith with your hard-earned cash."

Jack raised his glass. "We should be thanking you!"

"Hear, hear," someone said.

Brad gave a self-deprecating shrug. "Mom and Dad raised me to share what I have and that's what Elite's all about. A select group of people taking advantage of an opportunity while giving back to the community. So give yourselves a round of applause because last week Elite made an anonymous donation of 25,000 dollars to the hospital."

Everyone cheered and clinked glasses and then Brad encouraged people to "enjoy the day." He turned off the microphone, the music returned, and the waiters did another food and drink circuit.

"So you know what this Elite is?" Mike asked Jack.

"Yeah. We've been part of it from the start."

Birdie stared at Jack, wondering why today was the first time that she and Mike were hearing about Elite from him, and also from their best friends.

"How can you afford to donate large amounts of money to charity when you're barely keeping up with your mortgage?" she said.

"Mom," Jack said tightly. "Keep your voice down."

"Sorry, but—"

"Elite's helping us," Lucy said.

"But you're not a charity case!" Birdie spluttered in horror.

Lucy's face tightened and she turned away to check on Rigby.

Jack groaned. "How about I get Brad to explain it." He waved him over. "Mom and Dad have got a few questions about Elite."

"Great!" Brad smiled at them. "When I told Dad I was expanding, he said you two might be interested."

"Did he?" Mike sounded uncertain. "He's never mentioned it."

Brad called his parents over before outlining a program that a bookie from Ireland and the UAE had used with some success. He explained how he'd tweaked it and increased its performance. It took in the parentage, age, weight and height of a racehorse and matched it with the conditions of the course and the other horses in the race. Then it calculated the risks and probabilities of placing and generated the best price of a bet.

"It means using a pool of money. That way we can make multiple bets in each race with the odds in our favor," Brad said.

Bevan took in Mike's doubtful look. "I know what you're thinking, but Brad's set up inherent safety nets. Not all the pool is bet so losses are buffered. But the system's remarkable." He slapped Brad proudly on the back. "Just ask anyone here if they've made money this year."

"Jack?" Mike asked.

"We made forty percent on our investment, Dad. I wish we had more money to invest."

Champagne shot out of Birdie's nose.

"Sorry, but that sounds too good to be true," Mike said. "Fantastical even."

Jack sighed and threw out his hands. "*This* is why I didn't tell you."

"Mike's wise to question," Brad said. "I'd be worried if he didn't. Elite prides itself on being open and transparent. We only want members who are fully informed and who trust in the program, because the best returns come when we work as a team. It's why we're cautious about who we reach out to. Joining's by invitation only and outside of our gatherings, we refer to Elite as 'the club.'"

"Isn't that confusing?" Mike asked. "Because of GGSC?"

But Birdie wasn't listening. Her mind was stuck on the fact that the Hewitsons had been invited to join Elite ahead of her and Mike. She turned to Judy, trying to hide the hurt twisting inside her.

"And you and Bevan are part of this Elite club?" she asked.

Judy nodded and brushed Birdie's hand in a reassuring pat. "It's not what you think. This isn't like a flutter on the races or the fun we're having with Billabong. It's big money. Before we invited you to join we needed to be a hundred percent confident of the returns. The thought of you losing money at our suggestion ..." Judy shuddered. "Our friendship comes first, Birdie. It's too important to Bev and me to ever risk it over money."

"I invited Jack," Brad said, as if reading Birdie's thoughts. "If you and Mike are interested, I'd be happy to sit down with you both, talk you through the system and show you the spreadsheets and the bank account."

Birdie thought it all sounded a bit too perfect, yet everyone here was involved. Surely they wouldn't be if Elite didn't earn them money. She shared a glance with Mike, but she couldn't read his face. Did he want to explore the offer further? Did she? Her thoughts drifted to an education fund for Rigby, before pulling back fast. There was no point in daydreaming. Information was power and they needed a lot more of it before they made any decisions.

"But before we sit down together," Brad was saying, "I want you to chat with Jack and Lucy, and Mom and Dad, and anyone else here you know and trust. Ask them about their experiences and if they recommend joining." He gave a resigned smile. "Because there's no point proceeding to a meeting if you're not absolutely open to hearing about it. I'm not here to twist anyone's arm."

He pulled out a business card and gave it to Mike. "It's a hundred percent up to you and Birdie. If you decide you want to meet, give me call. If I don't hear from you, Uncle Mike, no drama. It doesn't change a thing and there's no need for any embarrassment when we run into each other in High Street or at Mom and Dad's Christmas party, okay?"

"Excuse me." Izzy appeared next to Brad. "I'm sorry, but I need to borrow Brad for a few minutes."

"No worries, love," Mike said. "By the sounds of it, Rigby's ready to get back outside."

Izzy gave Rigby a cautious glance as if he was radioactive rather than a frustrated three-year-old sick of being contained in a stroller.

Lucy leaned down to release her son, but Jack said, "I've got this. You don't need a greasy handprint on your dress for Fashions on the Field."

"That would be tragic given the effort—" *money*, "—you've gone to," Birdie said tightly.

"Oh, that's right," Brad said. "Izzy and Lucy are in the finals. Shouldn't you both be heading over?"

Izzy nodded. "I'll be back in time for afternoon tea. It's being served at 3:30 after the Fashions on the Field announcements and the running of the Cup."

"Dad and I can stay and make sure everything's good here," Judy said to Brad. "You need to watch Izzy on the catwalk."

"Thanks, Mom, but we all need to watch her. That's why we hired Elaine so we can leave for an hour and be confident everything runs smoothly." Brad kissed Izzy on the cheek, then did the same to Lucy. "Good luck. The judges are going to have a hard time choosing between you two."

"Izzy will take out Lady of the Day again for sure," Lucy said quickly.

Izzy's lips tightened. "There are no guarantees."

"No, of course not. I just ..." Lucy put down her glass. "I better freshen up."

"There's a mirror here if you don't want to risk the crush of the ladies," Izzy said.

Lucy gave a wan smile as if the offer was both a relief and a burden.

"Thanks, but I need to go anyway. I think you lose points if you cross your legs."

"We'll be there to cheer you on," Jack said. "Rigby's already practicing, right, mate?"

As Lucy exited the marquee, Birdie wondered at her daughter-in-law's manner. She was always so full of confidence and she certainly looked like she belonged in Elite—the girl had no problem spending money like water. But apparently Isobel Harrington sapped some of her savoir faire.

Rigby's yells reached antisocial proportions and Jack released the brakes on the stroller.

"Can we walk and talk?" Birdie asked.

"About the club?" Jack said.

"This club, not GGSC," she clarified.

"We can in here but not out on the course," Jack said.

Birdie huffed and gave Rigby his toy horse in an attempt to settle him. "It sounds like a secret society."

"It is in a way. Only instead of riding goats like the Masons, we make money," Jack deadpanned.

Mike laughed.

"Is it legal?" Birdie asked.

"Of course it's bloody legal! Jeez, Mom. Give me some credit. No one's forcing you to take part. But it's an opportunity. I thought you might be interested so Dad can finally retire and you won't have to depend on the pension in ten years time."

"How much money do you put upfront?" Mike asked.

"It depends. I think the absolute minimum is 10,000."

10,000 dollars! Jack and Lucy had risked money they couldn't afford. Where had they found it in the first place? Questions burned on Birdie's lips but sensing her son's ire, and remembering they were out in public, she managed not to ask them. But she'd be asking later.

"That's a chunk of change," Mike was saying.

Jack sighed. "I know you two think Brad's a bit flashy, but you trust

Bevan and Judy so talk to them. And I s'pose as long as you don't tell anyone, you could test the waters by putting some money in with mine. That way you get to see the returns for yourself but with a smaller stake."

"Or the losses," Birdie said.

"That's the spirit, Mom." Jack swung the stroller abruptly toward the entrance. "I have to go and watch Luce."

Mike patted Jack on the arm. "Thanks for thinking of us, son."

As Jack walked ahead of them, Birdie linked her arm through Mike's. "Are you seriously interested?"

"I'm always interested in secure opportunities, but I'm not going to be seduced by all this." He waved his arm to indicate the stylishly decorated marquee and the French champagne. "But if we could help Sienna and Jack and Lucy get on their feet, wouldn't that be a good thing?"

"No one gave us a hand," Birdie said mulishly.

"Only because no one had any spare cash."

"Was it just that though?" Birdie pondered, thinking about their parents. "We didn't expect a handout so we worked hard and saved for the things we wanted, then bought them. None of this Afterpay nonsense. I thought we'd taught the kids the same thing."

"Okay, boomer," Mike teased as they walked out onto the course.

"I'm *not* a boomer, thank you very much. You are."

"And that two-year age gap makes all the difference." He laughed, then sobered. "Life's different now. The kids grew up being told the world's their oyster and they could have it all. There's no concept of delayed gratification anymore and we're part of the problem."

"How?"

"Because we've had more disposable income than our parents and we spent it on them. Hell, I didn't have a decent set of headphones until I was fifty, but we gave Jack a pair for his eighteenth."

"So it's *our* fault he didn't save anything until they bought the house?" Birdie asked.

"Who knows. But you can't fault him on not working hard. He's always done that, but FIFO's tough. Wouldn't you like to help him so he could take a job where he was home every night to put Rigby to bed?"

Of course she wanted that for Jack and Rigby, but Lucy's spendthrift tendencies ruffled her feathers. "I think they'd value it more if they earned the money. I don't want to give them a handout, but I'd consider a low-interest loan so their plan happens sooner. But it's a moot point because we don't have much spare cash. All our money's tied up in retirement fund for when you retire. *If* you ever retire!"

"Perhaps this," Mike glanced around and dropped his voice, 'club' is a way of generating more cash so we can help the kids."

Something that wasn't quite envy but wasn't contentment either lodged itself under Birdie's ribs. Other people were benefitting from Elite. Perhaps it was a way to help the kids as well as a solution to Mike finally retiring.

"Judy told me they've waited until now to invite us to join because they wanted absolute confidence in it," Birdie said. "But if people like the Hewitsons are making money, then we deserve to!"

Mike rolled his eyes. "You and the Hewitsons again."

She huffed. "You know exactly what I mean. I have more class in my little finger than Jim Hewitson does in his whole body."

"So even though we're both wary and seeing flags, you're saying we should investigate further?"

Birdie chewed the inside of her cheek. "If it was just Jack and Brad suggesting it, I'd say no. But you've always said Bevan's spent his life making good financial decisions."

"He's got a nose for comfortable risks that's for sure," Mike said. "Without him, there'd be no GGSC and that was the best risk Glingilly ever took. We did okay out of it too."

Birdie took a deep breath. "Then let's talk to Bev and Judy at afternoon tea. If we're reassured, we can take up Jack's offer before we meet with Brad. I'll happily risk my Billabong winnings as a test case. After all, an hour ago I didn't have that thousand dollars."

Mike laughed. "My Birdie, the risk-taker."

"Hey, I risked life with you."

"And look how well that turned out." He grinned. "If this club pays half as well, you'll be a happy woman."

"Yeah, right." But she kissed him with a promise of how they'd celebrate together later that night.

CHAPTER FOUR

Izzy lay in the deep clawfoot bath in one of Villefranche's bathrooms surrounded by warm scented water and the glow of candles. The original owner had been a Francophile and he'd commissioned a house that paid homage to everything French Provincial on a grand scale, along with—for some reason—a medieval turret. The combination of the harshness of a medieval stone fortress and the pampering luxury of an 1800s palace made the house anything but cozy, but the view from this bathroom and the privacy it offered made it Izzy's favorite room.

She gazed out of the full-length glass doors and into the night. Gossamer wisps of cloud drifted across the darkness, barely denting the sparkle of the stars. Izzy's eyes sought the constellations she'd learned about since moving to the country. Out here, the night sky was a revelation to a woman born and raised in a city of 5 million, where streetlights and neon signs confused the birds so they chorused at 3:00 in the morning. Brad teased her about being addicted to stargazing and he was right. There was something about the vastness of the night sky and the celestial lights that kept her centered amid the unexpected and phenomenal wealth that once again surrounded her.

She couldn't believe her luck.

I wish you were here, Dad.

Her fingers strayed to her hair and she pulled them away, splashing her hand under the water. *Stop it. Today was a good day.*

The problem was, these days every day was a good day so why did she still reach for her hair? She needed to stop—the milliner who'd made her hat for the Glingilly Cup had noticed the tiny patch of baldness and asked her about it. Izzy had told her she'd had a biopsy recently, then immediately asked her a question about the hat to distract her.

Izzy breathed deeply and slid under the water, slowly releasing her breath and relaxing into the sound of the bubbles jetting around her. As she surfaced, she heard the door click.

"Hey, Lady of the Day," Brad said. "Are you getting out or am I getting in?"

She opened her eyes, smiled and reached out her arms. He gripped her hands and she rose out of the water, bubbles clinging to her skin. As she navigated the high edge of the tub he wrapped a fluffy towel around her. Then, after drying her, he draped her Lady of the Day winner's sash over her naked body, pulled her into him and kissed her.

She sighed into his mouth and opened herself up to his kiss. It lit up her body, harnessing the good parts of the day and driving out the bad, like it always did. His hands dropped to her waist, turning her toward the open doors—Brad loved sex outside—but she'd been standing in heels all day. All she wanted was the comfort of a mattress. She took control of the kiss and Brad's body, navigating him toward the next room and the king-sized bed, the cloud mattress topper and the fifteen-hundred-thread-count Egyptian cotton sheets. He only hesitated for an instant, then groaned and conceded.

As they reached the bed, he turned so he would fall back first, taking her with him. This time it was her turn to concede. After a successful day, Brad loved her on top, riding him home just like his horses had ridden in first, second and third.

Izzy didn't mind and she happily crawled up his body.

His brown eyes glittered in anticipation. "You know me so well."

She smiled down at him. "I really do."

She lowered her lips and her body to his, surrendering and taking, connecting and separating. She lost herself to the building sensations—wild, raw and all-consuming—before gladly flying out of her body and far away from herself.

Slowly, she became aware of Brad's panting chest and she pushed herself off him. He flung out an arm and rolled her in against him, her ear on his chest listening to the strong and solid beat of his heart.

"Good for you?" he asked.

"Good for me. You?"

He laughed. "Never in doubt. A great end to an awesome day. You were amazing today, Iz. I couldn't do all this without you, you know that, right?"

She pressed her lips to his skin. "I love that we're a team."

She'd never told him how she needed the help of valerian on days like today. How standing up in front of a crowd made her heart race as fast as a hummingbird's and that her worst nightmare was being the center of attention. They were a team, and sometimes that meant doing things outside her comfort zone for the benefit of the business.

When they'd first met in Melbourne, Brad was just starting out on his own and barely had enough money to pay his bills. When she'd found out, she'd almost stopped dating him—she didn't need to relive the difficult parts of her childhood. But despite not having much behind him fiscally, he wasn't in debt. He was educated and well dressed, functioned as an adult, was loved and believed in by his parents, and he was undeniably sexy. But mostly there was something about him that reminded her of her father—his enthusiasm and optimism eddied around her in an intoxicating whirl of excitement, pulling her in and promising her the world. She'd pushed aside all nagging doubts and jumped in feet first.

Brad stretched, then ran his hands through her hair. "And now the Brad and Izzy dream team are making the big bucks."

Brad was making mega bucks. Izzy was making less, because her childhood memories of boom and bust cautioned her. Each dividend day she paid her bills, donated a percentage to charity and held a small amount in reserve. Brad would have a fit if he knew her rainy-day reserve was in the bank. She could hear him saying, "Babe, the interest rates suck. You may as well bury it in the backyard."

But despite Brad's lean year when he'd left the secure fold of his father's financial services business, he'd never known financial hardship. Whereas Izzy would never forget her eighth, twelfth and sixteenth years, when her security had vanished and she was dependent on the goodwill of landlords, the food bank, teachers at school and the local thrift shop.

"What do you want me to bring you back from Dubai?" Brad asked. "I was thinking a Tiffany diamond watch."

The fizz of joy she usually experienced at the prospect of a new trinket flatlined under his surprise destination. "When are you going to Dubai?"

"Tomorrow."

She sat up fast, the sheet falling to her waist. "What do you mean, tomorrow?"

"Sunday," he said, as if she didn't know the day of the week. "Kurt's flying me to Melbourne at 10:00 so I make the 3:00 o'clock flight."

"But we always travel together."

"And I love that we do, but Tadhg called this meeting while you were wowing them at Fashions on the Field. Anyway, you've got the Irish festival committee meeting this week."

"I could miss it."

His brows rose. "Not a great look when Elite's sponsoring it. Besides, don't you have a uni assignment due?"

"Yes ..."

"So you need to be here." He kissed her on the forehead. "I'll only be gone four days. Five at the most."

Izzy slumped under the covers and snuggled back into him, needing his body heat more to soothe her disappointment than to ward against the evening chill. "I knew I shouldn't have gone back to uni."

He rolled his eyes. "It was your idea, remember."

She sighed. "I know."

When Brad started the Australian arm of Elite, he'd invited her to work with him. "The social side of things complements the business and you're so much better at all that than me," he'd said.

She'd happily quit her event management job and moved from Melbourne to Glingilly, but she'd found life in the country town slow and a touch mind-numbing. It wasn't like when they traveled and she could while away an afternoon in the souks of Dubai or at the Trinity College Library being awed by the *Book of Kells*. In Glingilly, she spent a lot of time alone in a house that echoed with emptiness.

Judy had kindly invited her to some social occasions, but there were only so many morning teas, lunches, games of tennis and local charities Izzy could endure. As she wasn't a matron or a mother, she didn't easily slot into the roles on offer. The women in town who were her age weren't exactly welcoming. During conversations about the weather, house renovations and childcare issues, they glanced sideways at her with a mixture of admiration and envy. They complimented her clothes, adding, "you can tell you're not a mom."

Even though she worked as Elite's events manager, the women judged her. They considered her a trophy wife without the benefit of a marriage certificate. Although not being married didn't bother Izzy, it seemed to provide a loophole in the social mores, acting as an open invitation for other women. Brad's past girlfriends, previous tennis partners—hell, even his high school English teacher—flirted outrageously with him.

Brad's response to these overtures was his usual urbane congeniality. He took a genuine interest in everyone he met, but often during these conversations he'd call Izzy over, slide his arm around her waist and introduce her.

The other woman's face would tense into a stiff smile and she'd excuse herself with something like, "I really must catch up with ..."

Brad would always say, "It was great seeing you." And Izzy knew he meant it. Just as she knew he loved her.

But after a year living in Glingilly and being Elite's events manager she was bored. She needed a challenge So on a dismal cold and wet afternoon, after a particularly stultifying conversation about whether lemonade scones were really scones, and a message from Brad saying he'd been held up in Melbourne, Izzy had enrolled in a graduate diploma of business administration. This was her entry to taking on a bigger role in Elite.

When she'd told Brad, he'd been silent for a few beats before smiling and kissing her. "Is this a surprise or haven't I been listening properly?"

She'd shrugged. "I've been thinking about it for a while. I really want to help you grow Elite."

"You're already doing that. We're a team and we work to our strengths, right?"

"Right." Only she knew her strengths lay way beyond choosing the best canapés and cool or warm lighting. "But I've got some other strengths that need flexing."

"If you're happy I'm happy." Brad stroked her face with his thumb. "I'm just being selfish. I hate the idea of uni tying you down so you can't travel with me."

"It won't change anything," she'd reassured him, thinking of her mostly empty days. "The lectures are available online so it's all very flexible."

Tonight, her words came back to bite her. Sure, uni was flexible, right up until she was faced with a deadline and a lecturer who wouldn't consider a junket to Dubai a good enough excuse for an extension. But even with her assignment to complete, the days and nights without Brad would be long and lonely.

Thinking of a way to fill them, she ran her hand down his sternum. "The dividends are due on Friday. I can prepare the statements for you."

"Nah, I'll do them on the plane."

"Are you sure?"

"Totally. Gotta pass the fourteen hours somehow."

"You know, you could always watch a movie and relax."

He laughed and she joined him. Brad struggled to keep still watching a movie—squirming and fidgeting like a kid desperate to leave the table.

"Besides, you know what relaxes me." He wrapped his arms around her and suddenly she was under him and gazing up into twinkling brown eyes.

She cupped his face. "Sex and money."

"And you, Iz. Always you."

CHAPTER FIVE

RIGBY'S SQUEAL PIERCED Lucy's slumber and a shot of adrenaline hauled her fast from a deep sleep—alert, scared and ready to rescue her son. Then she heard Jack's deep rumbling voice and she sagged back onto the pillows, groggy and confused. It took her a moment to remember it was Sunday afternoon. She'd worked a twelve-hour shift the night before, staying with a young mom until her baby was born. The only redeeming feature of night duty was the money and the lack of admin staff. The rest sucked, including trying to get a decent sleep.

She looked up and read the time. Damn. It didn't matter that her limbs felt lead-lined and were pinning her to the mattress or that her head was a fuzz of fatigue—it was time to get up. At least she wasn't working tonight so she only had to survive until Rigby was in bed, then she'd tumble in straight after him.

As she swung her feet to the floor, she remembered that Birdie and Mike were coming for dinner. *No* ... She dropped her face into her hands, recalling her conversation with Jack over breakfast after she'd stumbled in from work barely able to see straight.

Around Rigby accidentally knocking his milk and cereal onto the floor then sobbing inconsolably because there were no more cornflakes to replace them, and her burning frustration at finding the coffee pod container empty and Jack's seeming lack of concern that he was yet to do the grocery shopping, he'd said, "I've invited Mom and Dad around for dinner tonight."

"What?! Why?"

Normally on the night before Jack flew out, they spent the evening running through the admin of their lives before cuddling on the sofa.

"Because if we don't ask them tonight, we'll have to wait another two weeks."

"Why can't we go over to Cork Street like we usually do? Your mom doesn't work and she has the time to cook. I'm utterly wiped, Jack."

He'd hugged her. "I know you are, but you're always great after a sleep. And Mom and Dad won't care what we eat. Tell me what to buy and Rigby and I will give you some peace to sleep by going to the shops."

Oh God! He thought he was doing her a favor.

"We could talk to them on Zoom later in the week," she said.

His eyes widened, filling with shocked surprise. Then he'd laughed. "Good one, Luce."

"I'm serious. Let's do it on Wednesday after Rigby's in bed."

"Come on," Jack said gently. "You know that's not how my family works."

Once again, the stark differences between their families hovered between them. Apart from her graduation and wedding, Lucy struggled to remember a time when she and her parents had been together in the same room. As a child of divorce she was used to dealing with her parents separately, whether it be on the cell phone, by text or, less frequently, face-to-face. Moving to Glingilly hadn't changed a thing. Unlike her parents, Birdie and Mike were country people, they'd been together for decades and they didn't consider a phone call a catch-up—it had to be in person. That's why Jack, Lucy and Rigby had dinner at the Essens' once a week.

"I can't ask them for a loan over Zoom," Jack said. "And it doesn't seem right asking them at their house with Mom rushing around feeding us."

"Okay," she said on a sigh. She was so tired she'd have agreed to almost anything if it meant she could crawl into bed faster. "Buy chicken thighs. I'll make a curry."

"Dad's favorite. Good idea."

She'd speared him with a look. "And you have to tidy up and clean the bathroom."

"Too easy." Jack kissed her. "But you'll be up by one though, right?"

She hadn't replied and now, going by the noise reverberating through the house, he'd taken her silence as a yes.

Pushing through her sleep-deprived fog, she padded toward the shower and reminded herself that tonight was just another step in the plan for the future they both wanted and deserved.

"Great curry, Lucy." Mike wiped the remains of the golden liquid from his lips. "Birdie, you should get the recipe."

"Thanks, Mike, but it's pretty easy. Even you could make this one," Lucy teased. She was always more relaxed around Jack's dad than she was around Birdie.

"Recipes aren't always shared, Mike," Birdie reproved. "It might be Lucy's mother's best-kept secret."

Lucy laughed. "Actually, it's Dad's. He taught me everything he knew about cooking, which is this chicken curry and lemonade scones."

"And I taught her the rest." Jack grinned.

"Your mother wasn't a cook?" Birdie asked, a small frown between her brows.

Lucy took a breath. It wasn't the first time Birdie had sounded as if she disapproved of her parents. Then again, Birdie prided herself on being a career wife and mother. She didn't understand the juggle of being a working mother with a demanding job.

"My mother was a single parent working full-time," Lucy said. "It didn't leave much time or energy for gourmet meals."

She didn't mention how the repetitiveness of her mother's meals—taco Tuesdays, fish Fridays and omelet Sundays—had worn thin, or how she'd vowed never to do that to her own children.

Birdie picked up her and Mike's empty bowls and studied them closely. "Goodness! New bowls."

Lucy was about to mention the unexpected find on Facebook Marketplace and how the bowls filled the gap in their main dinner setting, when Birdie added, "I'm surprised you've got room to store them given the size of the new setting you just bought."

A flash of red lit up behind Lucy's eyes and a defensive comment rose to her lips, but Jack's hand brushed her arm, reminding her of tonight's purpose. No matter how uncalled-for Birdie's comment was, Lucy had to rise above it.

"Have a seat, Mom," Jack said, refilling his parents' glasses while Lucy cleared the offending bowls. Then he pulled up a chair between Birdie and Mike and placed three printed pages annotated in different colors on the table. "Before we have dessert, I thought you might want to see this."

"What is it?" Mike put on his glasses.

Jack pointed to a figure. "This is the fifteen hundred dollars you gave me to—"

"Fifteen hundred?" Birdie gave Mike a dark look. "I thought we agreed on a thousand?"

"Mom, you can have that argument later, but you probably won't need to." Jack's finger moved to the pink highlighting. "These are the races Elite bet on in the last two weeks—"

"There aren't that many races in Victoria in a week," Birdie said.

"Elite bets across the country," Lucy said. "It's a vital part of Brad's strategy."

"What's that number highlighted in blue?" Birdie asked.

"Mom, I need you to hold the questions until I've finished my explanation, okay." Jack's voice was tight with frustration.

Birdie's mouth pursed but she stayed silent.

Lucy stifled a sigh. Jack had spent a lot of time creating the chart and tables, hoping to impress his parents. If they had a hope of selling them their proposal, they needed Birdie and Mike on side, and experience had taught Lucy that if Birdie was in a huff, she wouldn't listen.

Under the table, Lucy ran her foot up Jack's shin in a gesture of support. "Birdie, the number in blue is the Elite pool of money, right, Jack?"

Jack nodded. "It was the total pool for the week, and the orange represents the percentage that was risked."

"Holy—" Mike said. "That's a lot of money."

"It is and it gets bigger each week. This is what was earned, this is what is held in reserve, and this," Jack tapped the figure in fluorescent yellow, "is your profit."

Birdie gasped. "But that's—"

"Remarkable." Mike peered at the figures. "It's a fifty percent increase."

Jack winked at Lucy. She smiled at him and harnessed her hope and anticipation to ward off sleep that tugged at every part of her.

Jack pulled out his cell phone and showed his parents a screenshot. "I transferred the original fifteen hundred and the profit into your bank account."

"Thanks, son." Mike raised his glass and looked at Birdie. "I'd say that was a successful test, wouldn't you?"

Birdie laughed and kissed him. "Okay, you're forgiven for the extra five hundred. What's the other page, Jack?"

He shared a "This is it" look with Lucy. "It's what we've earned from Elite in the past year. As you can see, some months are better than others, but there's never been a loss."

Birdie blinked at the figures. "I had no idea ..."

"Yeah, it's like working a couple of extra days a week. All the profits go straight into the mortgage," Jack said.

"We're only investing what we can spare," Lucy said, wanting to make a point.

Jack nodded. "And that's what we want to talk to you about. At the moment we're still a few years off from owning the house. But if we had some extra cash to invest, then this time next year I could give up the FIFO."

Mike took off his glasses. "Are you asking for a loan?"

Jack squirmed. "Just short-term, Dad. A year tops. Twenty grand would be great, and of course we'd pay interest."

"20,000?" Birdie scoffed. "We don't have a spare 20,000."

Disappointment curdled Lucy's stomach. Jack had been certain his parents had a rainy day cash account, especially as they hadn't bought the travel trailer Birdie had prattled on about last year, which would cost far more than 20,000. Lucy knew asking her in-laws had been a long shot and they had every right to say no, but she was desperate to change her and Jack's lives. To not be so bloody exhausted all of the time. To not be a single parent two weeks out of every four and enduring long, hard and lonely days. Was it too much to ask to be a normal family and have her husband home every night?

"Fair enough," Jack was saying. "We just thought it was worth an ask."

Mike was back studying the figures, his brow creased in concentration. As he did mental arithmetic, he was mumbling percentages to himself. A few moments later he straightened the papers into a neat stack.

"Your mother and I have been waiting to see how this little experiment panned out and I think it's proved a point."

Mike turned to Birdie, as if seeking confirmation. She gave him a curt nod.

It's over. Tears threatened and Lucy blinked rapidly, desperate not to cry in front of her in-laws and add another reason for Birdie to find fault with her. God, what had they been thinking asking for a loan?

The stress caught up with her and she craved bed and the oblivion of sleep. She was about to plead exhaustion and excuse herself from the table when Jack said, "What point does it prove, Dad?"

"We'll talk to Brad about joining Elite. We don't have a lot to risk, but any dividends we earn we'll share equally between you and your sister."

Jack stared at him, shocked delight bright on his face, then he hugged him. "That sounds bloody marvelous. Thanks, Dad!"

Relief pierced Lucy's exhaustion. She was adding her own thanks when her mother-in-law cocked one brow at her in a challenge.

"It's a gift that can only be spent on the mortgage."

The implication that Lucy had other plans for the money bit hard. At that moment, Lucy hated Birdie.

CHAPTER SIX

BIRDIE WAS TAKING a moment for herself, relaxing on a garden seat hidden behind the hedge in a nook of the French garden at Villefranche. The buzz of conversation carried on the breeze, punctuated by laughter and the delighted squeals of children playing in the lake. She closed her eyes and savored the minutes before she fulfilled her promise to mind Rigby while Lucy and Jack competed in the tennis round robin.

A familiar tinkling laugh rained over her and she opened her eyes. "What's the joke?"

Judy lowered herself onto the teak bench seat. "Just how alike we are. I didn't know you'd discovered my hideout."

Birdie smiled. "I found it three months ago at our first official Elite event. You're the only person to catch me."

"Don't worry. Your secret's safe with me."

Birdie felt compelled to explain. "Don't get me wrong, I love these occasions—"

"But they can be pretty full-on. Especially when the boys get competitive."

Birdie laughed. "Boys is right. I see Oscar D'Angelo's bought a Ferrari."

Judy rolled her eyes. "He was determined to outdo Rick Lester's Mercedes sports. Honestly ..."

Birdie wondered what amount of money needed to be invested in Elite to buy a car worth the value of a small house. She and Mike were making pocket money in comparison. She fought a wave of disquiet. For reasons she didn't fully understand, she often came away from the Elite events feeling unsettled, which was crazy because they were fun and a real treat. She reminded herself that she and Mike didn't need an expensive European car. And, to dispel her flash of jealousy, she recalled their recent vacation—the most luxurious they'd ever enjoyed.

"Our week with you and Bev at Dolphin Sands was wonderful. I've had trouble settling back into real life," she told Judy.

The Quinns had recently bought a villa in an exclusive beach-side resort on the New South Wales north coast and they'd invited Birdie and Mike as their first guests.

"Me too," Judy said. "Let's do it again as soon as the schools go back."

Birdie hid her disappointment. "That's a lovely idea, but Mike doesn't have any more leave."

Judy shot her a sympathetic look. "He's ruining all our fun. We really must get that man to retire."

"I've given up asking."

"Bevan's virtually retired now. He's handed over most of his clients to Vishal and only kept his favorites. Even so, I think he'll finish up completely by the middle of the year. We're both desperate to live somewhere warmer."

"You're moving?" Birdie couldn't hide the horror from her voice.

"That's the plan. It's why we bought at Dolphin Sands."

"But what about being close to the grandchildren?" Birdie asked, clutching at straws.

Judy sighed. "Brad's keen for kids but he hasn't even proposed to Izzy yet. He says he's planning the perfect moment. Honestly!" She threw out her hands in frustration at Gen Z's need to make everything a production. "Then Izzy will take months to plan the wedding of the year so it's immaculate from the dress down to the font on the invitations. There's no way she'll be a pregnant bride—it would seriously limit her dress options—so there goes another year. When they finally get around to giving us grandchildren we'll divide our time between here and the coast. Meanwhile, I'm not wasting two years waiting."

Something close to panic skittered through Birdie as she imagined her life without Judy at tennis, in book club, GGSC and their Friday-night dinners.

"But you'll still come down to watch Billabong race?" she said.

"He's going to race at Randwick soon. I think the Fascinators should have a week in Sydney."

Birdie thought about the costs involved—flights, fancy hotel, meals, drinks, outfits. Although there'd been occasions in the last few months when she'd sensed a shift in her friendship with Judy, this time she felt it keenly.

"I'm not sure I can afford that."

Judy frowned. "But you and Mike are making jam every week from Elite."

"We're giving it to the kids."

"All of it?" Surprise flitted across Judy's face. "Why?"

"Mike wants to help Jack with the mortgage and Sienna with a deposit. House prices in Melbourne are ridiculous."

"So once again Mike and his ethics are the problem," Judy teased. "Can't you convince him to keep some back for you to play with?"

"There's really not that much," Birdie admitted a little reluctantly.

"Lucky Elite's the solution."

"How? We're already investing the spare cash we have."

"But Mike's sixty, right?" Judy mused. "He can draw on his retirement fund."

"Can he?" Birdie left all the financial stuff to Mike. "I don't think he'd want to."

Judy gave her arm a squeeze. "Don't get me wrong. I think it's admirable that Mike wants to help the kids, but you raised them and now you deserve a break from budgeting and counting coins. This is your time, Birdie, while you're fit and healthy. Who knows what's around the corner? You should be able to fly up to visit me in Dolphin Sands whenever you want, or have a week away with the girls without worrying about the money or feeling guilty. We're planning a shopping trip to Hong Kong in a few months to get our wardrobe for the Spring Horse Racing Carnival. You *have* to come. I need you there to buffer some of the Fascinators."

The push and pull of Birdie's reality and her wants tugged hard. "I'd love to be able to do all that, but—"

"No buts." Judy raised her hand like a stop sign. "Come on, let's find Mike, Bevan and Brad and we'll crunch the numbers."

"But Jack and Lucy are playing tennis and I promised to mind Rigby."

"Izzy can mind him."

Birdie thought that was unlikely. "I think they're playing against Izzy and Brad."

"Perfect." Judy stood. "Mike and Bevan will watch the match with us and afterwards, we'll chat to Brad."

"I didn't think Brad liked to do business at social events?"

"He'll make an exception," Judy said. "After all, you're as close to family as it gets."

Over a glass of champagne, Birdie and Mike congratulated Brad and Izzy on their win.

"It was anyone's game," Izzy said.

Brad grinned. "Right up until we nailed the tie-break."

"You had us all on the edge of our seats," Bevan said.

"Luce and I know you've been missing the Elite tennis trophy," Jack said to Brad. "But look out. It'll only be spending a year with you."

Lucy muttered something about lack of sleep and handed a fretful Rigby to Jack. "It's been a fabulous day, Brad, but we need to get going. I've got work tonight."

"Can you spare fifteen?" Brad asked. "There's something new I want all the Essens to hear about first."

Lucy glanced at Jack, who nodded.

Judy reached out her arms. "I'll take Rigby down to see the ducks so you can listen uninterrupted."

"Brad!" Oscar D'Angelo joined the group. "Can we talk privately? I've got a mate interested in joining."

"Da-ad!" One of Oscar's kids tugged at his hand. "You promised you'd teach me how to row."

Brad shot the kid a smile then looked at Oscar. "Today's about family fun. We can chat tomorrow, yeah? I'm free all afternoon."

Oscar nodded. "Of course. Sorry, Brad. I let my enthusiasm get ahead of me. Great day as always, Izzy."

When Oscar walked away, Brad turned to Izzy. "Can you hold the fort for a bit? Maybe run the sack race so people stay outside?"

Izzy's eyes widened momentarily and she touched her hair. For a split second Birdie thought the young woman looked panicked, but she must have got that wrong because Izzy was saying, "Of course. Too easy."

As Brad ushered them inside, a skitter of excitement shot through Birdie. As far as she was aware it was the first time any Essen had been invited into Brad's office. When she and Mike had met with Brad, it had been in one of the GGSC function rooms. And Jack had told them Brad always came to their house as it was easier to keep Rigby entertained at home.

"I wonder what this is about," Mike said softly.

Birdie decided against mentioning her conversation with Judy. "Did Bevan say anything?"

Before Mike could answer, they almost ran into Lucy who'd

stopped just inside the office. Unlike the rest of the house, which was decorated in the French Provincial style, this seemed to be medieval from the suit of armor in one corner and the shield and sword in another. The surface of a dark wood desk—the size of a single bed—was only touched by a sleek computer screen, a leather-bound book and a Montblanc pen. There was a four-seater green leather Chesterfield sofa and two plump chairs upholstered in tapestry, but neither softened the space. It was both impressive and soulless. Birdie thought it would benefit from a seascape on the wall.

"Grab a seat," Brad said, taking an easy chair next to his father and facing the Essens.

"Feels like a job interview," Mike joked.

Brad laughed. "Well, it's an opportunity. I've been tinkering with Elite's program and running some experiments with Dad. I didn't want to risk anyone else's money in case it tanked, but for six months we've been consistently earning sixty percent returns."

"That's better than Elite," Jack said.

"How?" Lucy asked.

"Good question," Bevan said. "It's the same one I asked him six months ago."

Brad leaned forward, his face animated. "First, it's a smaller pool of money so there are fewer dividends to share. Second, I've been working with the guys from the UAE and Ireland and exchanging data. It means I've been betting outside Australia and it's working a treat." He handed around some charts. "The blue line is what I earned inside Australia and the green is outside."

Mike's outward breath whistled between his teeth.

Brad grinned. "I know, right? This is why we want to offer you first in on this exclusive deal. Fortune is only ever going to be small. Twelve investors tops."

"Sounds great," Jack said. "So we stop investing in Elite and transfer to Fortune?"

"No, mate, you need to invest in both so the hoi polloi don't get wind of it."

Jack's face fell. "That puts Luce and me out of the race."

Brad gave Jack's shoulder a squeeze. "Sorry."

Mike returned the charts to Bevan. "Thanks for thinking of us, but we can't manage both either."

Bevan handed them back. "Mike, what's your retirement fund growth been over the last two years?"

"Twenty percent."

"If you invested even half your retirement fund in Fortune you'd be laughing," Brad said.

"More importantly," Bevan added, "you'd be able to give Birdie what she wants."

"I don't need anything," Birdie said quickly. She wasn't prepared to put pressure on Mike to invest in Fortune for something as frivolous as a girls' week away.

Bevan laughed. "I thought you wanted him to retire?"

"Oh! Well, yes." She patted Mike's knee. "That's no secret."

"Problem is, love, there's a financial penalty for withdrawing retirement fund," Mike said.

Birdie's hopes flatlined.

Then Mike gave her waist a squeeze. "But judging by these numbers, if I took out a chunk to invest, I could retire in three months." He looked at Bevan. "Have I calculated that right?"

"Don't doubt yourself. You're right on the money."

Excitement tangoed with caution. "Bev, is Fortune as reliable as Elite?" Birdie asked.

"That's been our experience over the last six months."

"But all investment comes with risks," Brad said. "Horses can be injured—but I'm not telling you anything, am I?"

"Not at all." Billabong had a suspensory ligament injury and had missed his last race.

Lucy was tapping on her cell phone. "Damn. We could have accessed our retirement fund for the house deposit, but they won't release it for mortgage repayments unless you're about to lose the house."

"Don't wish that on yourselves," Birdie heard herself say and immediately regretted it.

Jack shot her a dark look.

Lucy stood, her manner brisk and no-nonsense. "Thanks for thinking of us, Brad, but we have to get going or I'll be late for work."

Brad shot to his feet. "Thanks for listening. I'll walk you out."

When they'd left the room, Mike said to Bevan, "Birdie and I should probably chat about this privately. When do we need to let you know?"

Birdie faced Mike. "What's to talk about? Elite's been reliable, and you just said if we invested in Fortune you could retire in three months."

"She's got you there, mate." Bevan grinned. "Besides, Judy will shoot me if I allow you to let this opportunity slip. She's got plans for the Quinns and the Essens to book out some island on the Great Barrier Reef."

"You mean Haggerstone?" Birdie said. Judy had shown her the stunning photos of the island with its pure white sand and clear turquoise water. "You really think we could afford a vacation like that if we invest in Fortune?"

Brad had returned and he slid in behind his desk. "If you're talking about Mom's dream island, then absolutely."

Ignoring the Quinns, Birdie looked straight into Mike's familiar brown eyes. "Are you sure you're ready to retire?"

He stroked her face. "Yes, love. I've only been hanging on so we're comfortable and have the retirement we deserve."

Her breath hitched and her heart seemed to stall. "So we're really doing this?"

"We're really doing it. I'll contact the retirement fund tomorrow and set the wheels in motion."

Birdie punched the air, then kissed him.

CHAPTER SEVEN

LUCY STOOD STARING into the fridge, slowly coming out of the fug of her pre-work nap. Returning to night shift after a break was never easy, but on the back of a full day of sun, food and wine at the Elite party, it was even tougher. Especially if her concentration was already so shot she couldn't find the meal container she was sure she'd packed pre-nap.

When they'd arrived home from the Elite dividend picnic day, she and Jack were both tired and disappointed. Their soaring elation at Brad's invitation to join Fortune was inversely proportional to the crashing low when they realized they couldn't afford it. Rigby had been overtired and overstimulated, uncooperative and playing his parents off against each other. Lucy had played the work card, left Jack to deal with a screaming child and taken a nap.

Now, with well-honed logistics skills, she reorganized the fridge shelves then rubbed her eyes—still no red container. Something made her glance at the sink and there, washed and drying in the rack, was her empty lunchbox.

"Jack!"

"What?" His voice drifted in from the family room.

"What did you have for dinner?"

"I heated up the leftovers."

"In the red container?"

"Yeah."

Fatigue frayed her patience and she threw herself into the luxury of anger. "Jeez, Jack, thanks a lot! That was my 3:00 A.M. meal. What the hell am I going to take now?"

Jack ambled into the kitchen, his face filled with contrition. "Sorry!"

He reached for her, but she wasn't ready for a hug.

"You know I use the red container for work."

He rubbed the back of his neck. "I forgot. You know Rigby was wired, and by the time I calmed him down and got him to sleep I was starving." He opened the fridge and peered in as if that would conjure a healthy meal. "There'll be something else."

"There isn't!" To her horror, tears prickled her eyes and spilled over. She swiped at them, hating the way they betrayed her. "I hate this, Jack. I hate it."

He closed the fridge door and gave her a cautious look as if she was an unexploded bomb. "That I ate your dinner?"

"Yes! No! I hate that we don't spend any time together!"

"Um, we just spent the day together."

"Not that! This!" She extended her arm to encompass the room.

"But I thought you loved the kitchen?" His tone was increasingly wary.

"Not the kitchen or the house. God, Jack! I hate that after a lovely day I have to go to work. I hate how night duty makes me feel nauseous and jet lagged. I hate that when you're home, I'm not. I should be cuddling with you on the sofa, not getting ready to walk out the door."

He pulled her in for a hug and stroked her hair. "You know the first night back's always tough. Then you find your rhythm."

She pulled her face out of his chest and sighed. "But it's getting harder. I just wish we could fast-track the plan."

"Yeah." He sighed into her hair. "I was thinking the same thing while you were napping."

"Any brilliant ideas?"

"Maybe." Jack stepped back and switched on the coffee machine before pulling the makings for a sandwich out of the fridge. "We could get a loan."

"How?" Lucy sat on a stool at the kitchen counter. "The bank won't extend the mortgage."

He passed her the latte. "From a loan company."

The glass stalled halfway to her lips. "Isn't that risky?"

"Yes and no." He slapped slices of smoked ham on wholewheat bread before adding mustard and salad fixings. "I've done some sums. Want to see?"

"Sure." She took over cutting and wrapping her sandwich while Jack brought up a spreadsheet on his laptop.

"This is the situation with a secured loan." He pointed to a row highlighted in pink.

She gulped. "The interest rate's rugged."

"It's higher than the bank for sure, but when you compare it with what we're earning from Elite ..." He opened a chart. "We still come out ahead."

She peered at the graph. "Even on the thinner weeks."

"Exactly." He grinned at her. "And there haven't been many of those."

"And more importantly, we've never gone backwards."

"Plus, you factor in the numbers Brad showed us today, Fortune earns more than Elite."

"But did you factor in the overseas betting?"

Jack's brow creased. "What's that got to do with it?"

"Here, if a horse is scratched we get our money back. But I did some research too. According to Google, if you're betting on a futures market and the horse is scratched, you lose your money."

"One step ahead of you, Luce. I checked with Brad and it's just like here. The bets are made on the day by his partners."

Lucy latched onto the wave of reassurance riding through her. "Have you got a copy of what Brad showed us?"

Jack clicked his mouse and brought up another document. Lucy read it, then rechecked Jack's figures twice just like she did with the drug dosages at work. Her figures matched his.

She thought of their aging car. "Would they accept the car as security?"

"Probably not, but we only need fifty thou, not seventy, so we won't need it. Luce, it's a short-term loan. With Fortune, we can easily manage the higher interest rate."

Lucy's stomach churned at the outrageous figure. She recalculated. Jack was right.

"We'd be able to triple our mortgage repayments," she said.

He grinned. "I can stop FIFO in a year and you can give up night duty. Hell, you could probably give up work if you wanted."

She squealed and threw her arms around him. "We can start trying for another baby in three months!"

He pulled her onto his lap and kissed her deeply. Her body lit up.

"We can start now if you want," he said.

She checked the clock. "No time."

He shot her a boyish grin. "Me and my swimmers can be quick."

She gave his shoulder a gentle push. "Me and my eggs deserve some effort."

"Fair enough." He nuzzled her neck. "I'll ask Mom to mind Rigby tomorrow afternoon."

The temptation to call in sick pulled at her, but she resisted by sliding off his lap. "You're on. Maybe ask Birdie if she can take him in the morning so you can do the loan application."

She read hesitation on his face. "What?"

He screwed up his mouth. "Let's not mention the loan to Mom and Dad, okay?"

He didn't have to convince her, but she was intrigued. Normally Jack was happy to tell his parents everything. Staying quiet about Elite until his parents joined had almost killed him. "Sure, but why?"

He shrugged as if he was conflicted about voicing his reason. "You know what Mom can be like. Treating us as if we're clueless."

She cupped his face. "Just because we do things differently from her doesn't make us clueless."

Gratitude filled his eyes. "I know. We've got a track record with Elite."

"And we've done our due diligence on Fortune and checked the figures." She dropped her hands. "But if you don't want Birdie and Mike to know we're part of Fortune, you're going to have to ask Brad not to mention it to anyone."

"Good point. Now about this loan ..." Jack brought up the website of the company and indicated the logos at the bottom of the page. "The *Financial Review* gave them a Most Innovative award."

Lucy pointed to the consumer awards. "Those are more reassuring. Means it's a trusted company."

"So, we're doing this?" Jack checked. "You sure you're sure?"

She thought about the baby and kissed him. "So sure. This time next year we won't know ourselves."

Bringing up a countdown app on her cell, she flagged today's date in the following year. She ignored the fact it was the thirteenth—she wasn't remotely superstitious. In this instance, thirteen was their lucky number.

CHAPTER EIGHT

As Izzy PUSHED AWAY from the computer, her fingers drifted up to pull at her hair. Unlike the pain in her temples that was radiating across her brows, the short sharp sting of yanked strands was soothing. She wasn't certain if her headache was due to the stress of the looming deadline for her uni assignment or if she needed glasses. Either way, it was interfering with her ability to interpret the Elite betting sheets. She'd studied the rows and rows of numbers for over an hour, comparing them with an online betting app, but she was yet to fully understand them.

She left her office and walked to the kitchen. The idea of a glass of wine tempted her, but given her snail's pace on the assignment she'd be pulling an all-nighter to get it finished. As she reached for the paracetamol instead, the 1800s French Provincial floor clock in the entrance chimed eight. She wondered if Brad's meeting was over and if she should start warming the grill for the ribeye steak. Current international time zones meant his thrice-weekly meetings with Dubai and Dublin took place at 7:00 at night.

A minute later Brad appeared in the kitchen, his eyes rimmed with dark shadows. Recently he'd been up at 5:00 in the morning and in bed at midnight as Fortune went live to investors. Three nights ago she'd read until late, forcing herself to stay awake until he came to bed. When he had, she'd queried his need for such long days.

He'd rolled his eyes. "You know how much hand-holding there is with a new client and I've got twelve all at once."

Izzy didn't understand. "But everyone in Fortune comes from Elite."

"Yeah." There'd been an edge to his voice. "But it's new and you know they're always needy at the start."

She'd snuggled into him, feeling his tightly coiled tension pushing against her from head to toe. "Perhaps I can help?"

"Thanks, Iz. I sure as hell need it."

Then he'd kissed her and it wasn't until later, when he was snoring gently beside her and she was staring wide-eyed at the ceiling in post-orgasm alertness, that it hit her. He'd interpreted her offer to help with the business as them having sex so he could relax.

Now she asked, "Good meeting?"

"Excellent." He slid his arm around her waist and kissed her. "The long days have paid off. Fortune's first official week was da bomb. Everyone's thrilled and you're a few thousand dollars richer."

She returned the kiss. "Thank you. Can you transfer 2,000 into my account. I want to buy a Maticevski dress."

His brows rose. "You'd be better off reinvesting it."

His reaction surprised her and she pouted. "I haven't bought anything since the Glingilly Cup and that was months ago. Besides," she ran her fingers up his sternum, "you always say you like me to represent the brand. I promise you, this dress screams Elite."

He laughed. "You should absolutely buy it on our next trip to Dubai."

The thought of a vacation buoyed her. "Ohh! Good idea."

He grinned. "That's me. I'm full of good ideas. In fact, you should go the whole hog and book a personal shopper. Dresses, shoes, handbags, the works."

"When are we going?"

"As soon as we've got a clear week." He glanced around the kitchen. "Do you want me to grill the steaks or make the salad?"

Fifteen minutes later when they sat down to dinner, Brad asked, "So how was your day?"

"Yeah, okay. Your mom and I had coffee and I spent some time brainstorming ideas for the next dividend day party. What do you think about a Renaissance vibe? Could be fun for everyone?"

"What sort of games would there be for the kids?"

"I was thinking this time we could let our hair down and have an adults-only event."

Brad shook his head. "We've always made dividend day a family affair and I don't want that to change. People are investing in Elite because they want to give their kids all the opportunities." He put down his fork and laced his fingers into hers. "Like we'll do for ours one day."

Izzy's throat tightened and the urge to pull her hair almost tugged her hand out of his. "I guess we could open the hedge maze. We've never done that before. Oh! We can have apple bobbing and a coconut shy."

"And archery," Brad said, not appearing to notice she'd dodged the topic of children.

While he slipped a piece of meat to Thor, she quickly changed the subject. "And this afternoon I've gone around in circles with my assignment."

"The business analysis presentation?"

She nodded. "It's worth fifty percent of the mark for this unit. I was wondering if you could help me make sense of the data."

"Sure. I've got some free time first thing before I meet with a prospective Fortune investor at 10:00."

Izzy wondered why he was meeting a prospective investor when all the places were filled, but she couldn't afford to be sidetracked. "I'm presenting at 9:00 tomorrow morning. Can you help me now?"

He grimaced and poured himself a glass of wine. "I'm knackered, Iz, and you promised uni wouldn't get in the way."

Guilt and chagrin sparred, turning the tender ribeye hard in her gut.

"It's not like we had plans tonight," she said.

"Speak for yourself. I thought we could kick back and replicate the infamous scene from that movie everyone's talking about."

She tilted her head and gave him what she hoped was a sultry smile. "I promise your help will definitely get me in the mood to play the role of the grateful and submissive wife."

He grinned. "Now you're talking. Go grab your laptop, because the sooner we nail this assignment ..."

When she returned, Brad and Thor were settled on the sofa. As she sat next to him, Brad put out his hand for her computer. "So what sort of business are you looking at?"

"Elite."

"Why?"

His snappy tone disarmed her. "I thought it was a good opportunity for me to understand more about the business."

"You know plenty about the business."

"Not really. And these betting sheets are a perfect example. I've compared them to a betting app but I can't get them to add up."

Brad grunted and moved the mouse, checking the Elite file date. "Well, there's your problem. This is from November."

"Really?" She peered at the screen, unable to believe she'd made such a stupid mistake. No wonder the numbers didn't make sense. "How can it be November's? It's the most recent one I've received."

Brad shifted on the sofa as if he was in pain. "Remember the shitstorm with Trig Barker?"

"Vaguely."

At the time she'd been organizing the Cup event and all she remembered was Brad yelling on his phone, ending the call and throwing the device onto the sofa. He'd called Trig every name under the sun plus a few she'd never heard before. She'd never seen Brad so furious—she hadn't thought him capable of such an extreme.

The moment had unsettled her and vignettes of her father's zero-to-high-octane explosions had returned, threatening to take her back to times she wished to forget. To help hold those memories at bay, she'd deliberately not asked Brad for specifics. Instead, she'd drawn on experience and given him time and space to calm down.

He'd gone for a run and returned an hour later apologetic and grateful. "Thanks for not giving me the third degree, Iz. You're the best."

Now he was saying, "Since Trig gave Elite's betting sheets to another syndicate, we no longer email them to members. I'm more than happy to go through them with anyone who wants to see them, but apart from Mike Essen, no one's asked. People are happy sitting back and watching their stake grow."

"Can you give me this week's sheets so I can finish my presentation?"

He sighed. "I could."

She ignored the unspoken "but" hovering between them. Dealing with a "no" the night before the presentation wasn't an option.

"Great. If you log into the cloud you can download them straight into my uni folder." She buried her face in Thor's coat. "Look, no password peeking."

"Iz, sit up."

She righted herself, but something about the set of Brad's mouth and the accompanying fatigue lines sent disappointment scudding through her. She gave it one last shot and tried teasing. "I thought the S and D game started after you explained the charts to me?"

He ran his hand through his hair. "Look, I'm honored you want to use Elite for your analysis presentation, but showing this comparison to a class is as bad as Trig sharing it."

"No, it's not. And honestly, I'll be lucky if a third of them show up."

"Even if only two of them show, they're business majors and this is their catnip. Think about it, Izzy. Elite is its name: special, exclusive, and limited to people we know and trust. I've—we've worked too hard to open it up to just anyone."

Intractability was written all over his face and she couldn't keep the panic out of her voice. "Then what am I going to do? I've only got twelve hours before I have to sound like I know what I'm talking about."

"Draw on your own strengths," he said easily. "You've got heaps of data from when you worked with Melbourne Pro Events."

She did, but the whole point of this assignment was to learn more about Elite.

Perhaps Brad sensed her disappointment because he added, "Hell, Izzy, be proud of yourself. You threw some serious A-grade shindigs before I lured you away to work for me."

His words fell like stones and it was suddenly important to call out the distinction.

"With you."

He gave her a blank look. "What?"

"You said I work for you, but I work with you."

"Jeez, Iz, now's not the time to split hairs! I'm bloody exhausted and I have to help you out of the hole you've dug yourself."

A mess of emotions poured through her, with frustration and panic leading the pack. "All I want is to understand Elite better and contribute more so you're not so bloody distracted all the time!"

"I'm not distracted! I'm building a business. God!" Anger rose off him like steam. "Where the hell is all this coming from, Izzy? You say you're doing this bloody course to help me, but if it was teaching you anything useful you'd understand how important it is to build on success. That's what Fortune's all about. *Our* success. *Our* future." He stabbed the air between them. "But it takes time and energy, so sue me if I can't focus on you one hundred percent of every second of every day."

"I don't expect or want that," she said. "I just want some life-work balance like we used to have. At the moment you're all work."

"Sorry." He grabbed her hand and tugged her gently toward him. "I'm here now and I'm all yours. Besides, you promised me some role-play."

And you said you'd help me.

She pulled her hand away and stood. "I did and I'll honor it after I've finished the presentation."

He sighed. "Okay. I'll watch a movie." As she reached the door, he said, "Come and get me when you're done."

She turned back, unable to tell from his voice or his face if he was teasing her or not. "I meant tomorrow afternoon! I'm going to be pulling an all-nighter. Even then I might not get it finished."

His caramel eyes flashed. "Shit, Izzy! It's been a huge week. You know I have trouble getting to sleep without you."

You know I need you, Izzy. Her father's voice popped unbidden into her mind and her hand rose to the back of her head.

Pushing away the memory and objecting to Brad's pressure, she said snippily, "What happened to 'if you're happy, I'm happy'?"

Brad's eyes dulled. "I think it went the same way as 'uni's all very flexible.'"

"It is," she ground out, anger tensing her jaw. "And I wouldn't be starting from scratch right now if you let me use Elite!"

He lurched to his feet. "You are not jeopardizing the company for a fucking assignment!"

She flinched at the word—not because it offended her, but because in all their time together Brad had never sworn at her. Never yelled at her. Never disrespected her. But before her fuddled mind could find words, Brad had picked up Thor and stalked out.

The slam of the front doors echoed off the stone.

A chill washed over her and with it came the memories of her mother walking away. Leaving her and never coming back.

CHAPTER NINE

"Any more questions for Isobel?" Cooper Barsky, Associate Professor of Business Management, scanned the lecture theater for any final raised hands. "In that case, we're done for the day. See you all next time."

As people drifted out of the room, Izzy unclasped her tightly laced fingers. Unable to stop herself, she let them find a strand of hair to pull —the relief was instantaneous. Her thumping heart slowed and she breathed more deeply.

She was disconnecting her computer from the data projector when Cooper said, "Great job, Isobel."

"Thank you." She moistened her lips. "Actually, I prefer Izzy."

"Right. Sorry." Cooper's mouth settled into a wry smile. "It's one of the downsides of a mostly online course. Why didn't you mention it at our first face-to-face?"

Izzy's cheeks burned. "I don't always find it easy to talk in a group."

His green eyes filled with surprise. "That certainly didn't come across in your presentation. Had it been more than a pass–fail assignment, I'd have given you an A."

Relief rolled through her. "I'm just glad I got through it without throwing up. I'd planned to do something completely different, but late yesterday there was a last-minute change and ..." She realized she was babbling and her lecturer wouldn't be interested or impressed by her all-nighter.

As she shoved her computer into its satchel, her stomach rumbled as loudly as thunder. Horrified, she wanted to sink below the floor. "Oh God. Sorry. I couldn't face eating anything before the presentation."

"Not even coffee?"

She laughed. "I confess there's a couple of lattes sloshing around in there."

She didn't mention the energy drinks she'd consumed last night to keep her awake so she could finish the presentation. She'd fallen into bed at 4:00, relieved to see Brad had finally returned to the house, but he hadn't stirred. Despite missing his body heat, she'd stayed on her side of the king-size bed, justifying she didn't want to wake him. In truth, she wasn't ready to have sex with him before they'd deconstructed their argument and he'd apologized.

When her alarm rang that morning, she'd woken to a cool and empty bed. The fridge's electronic message board was empty, Brad hadn't answered the intercom, and she'd checked her cell ten times between 7:00 and the start of her presentation. No texts from Brad. No texts from anyone.

"Out of curiosity," Cooper said, resting his backside on the table, "what was your original plan?"

No one in Glingilly ever asked Izzy about her studies and the genuine interest on his face overrode her normal hesitancy. "Analyzing the wealth growth of my partner's company. He's developed this awesome program and I thought a deep dive would help me understand it better so I can contribute more to the business."

Cooper nodded. "Going by your solid interpretation of the figures you presented today, I can't imagine it was lack of understanding that made you change your mind."

After the compliment she was loath to admit that she'd struggled to make sense of the Elite data. "Brad was worried about confidentiality issues." She heard the words coming back at her and realized they were likely to offend. "Oh God, sorry. I didn't mean—"

"All good," Cooper said easily. "I get it. We do insist on commercial-in-confidence here, but occasionally things slip out. And after all, ultimately your partner will either want to float the company or sell it to the highest bidder, right? Until then he's best to keep things in-house with those he trusts."

Relief that she hadn't upset Cooper swam through her. "That's what he said."

His lips curved into a teacher's smile—mild and encouraging. "And you're in his trust circle so you can still do the deep dive and achieve your goal. Judging by what you presented today, and your other assignments, he'd be lucky to have your opinion."

Was this bloke trying to charm her? But while she was trying to read him, he'd walked to the door.

"Enjoy the rest of your day, Izzy." With a wave, he was gone.

As she crossed the parking lot, Izzy checked her cell for a text from Brad—nada. She checked her voice mail and email too. Silence.

You haven't contacted him.

He owes me an apology.

But Cooper's comment about not sharing the data held up her own behavior for scrutiny. She'd put her own needs ahead of the company, then taken it personally. Brad had a right to be upset. But they'd never yelled at each other before. Never gone to bed angry or woken up and not eaten breakfast together.

Unwelcome memories of her father's erratic moods pushed their way forward again. She shoved them back. Brad reminded her of the sunny, optimistic side of her father—the part she'd adored. Thankfully Brad lacked the dark, depressive side. He was probably giving her space to concentrate on her presentation. Now it was over, they'd debrief, apologize and enjoy make-up sex.

Her cell phone pinged and Judy's name appeared on the screen. *I'm bringing lunch to Villefranche at 1:00. It's important. JQ*

What? Izzy had deliberately left the day free to spend in

Warrnambool. After the last twenty-four hours she deserved to relax with a browse in the bookshop followed by lunch at the café next door. She had no plans to return to Glingilly before 3:00.

She punched out a stabby text—*Sorry, I'm not free for lunch*—but her finger hovered over the send arrow. Why was Judy bringing lunch to Villefranche? In the eighteen months Izzy had lived in Glingilly, whenever Judy suggested lunch it was always at GGSC.

Izzy's mouth suddenly dried. Had Brad talked to his mother about their argument?

No. He wouldn't do that.

Why not? You know he's overly close with his parents.

She immediately heard Brad's voice in her head: "I have a very normal relationship with my parents." Whenever he said it, it was always code for "It's not my fault your family's dysfunctional."

Was dysfunctional. It was hard to have a family when you were an only child, both parents were dead and your cousins lived in other states.

Izzy's body clenched. Oh God—if Brad had spoken to his mother, was this lunch an intervention? Judy loved to share relationship wisdom—with or without a flute of champagne in her hand. At various times in the past she'd told Izzy things like: if a man's happy at work, he's happy at home; never go to bed on an argument; and behind every successful man is a woman. Then she'd leaned in close and added, "Brad couldn't do what he does without your wonderful support." At the time, happiness had fluttered inside Izzy. Now, all she could hear was Brad saying, "I hate the idea of uni tying you down."

She was between a rock and a hard place. If she canceled lunch to avoid an uncomfortable conversation with Judy, it would add fuel to the fire of her unresolved fight with Brad.

As much as she wanted to speak to Brad in person, she called him. It went straight to voice mail. She tried to remember what he'd said about meeting someone and checked his calendar. It was surprisingly blank. She was just texting him to ask if they could meet when her cell rang.

"Judy," Izzy said, hoping she sounded less resigned than she felt.

"Oh good, you're there," Judy said. "I was getting worried when I hadn't heard back."

"I'm in Warrnambool—"

"Really? On a Thursday?"

Izzy swallowed a sigh. Hadn't she told Judy and Bevan about the presentation? Probably not. Every time they met Brad's parents, the conversation inevitably turned to Elite. The discussions ranged from possible new members to function details and the varied investment options for dividends. It didn't leave room for talking about much else.

"I'm calling about lunch," Judy said.

"I really need to talk to Brad—"

"He's in Geelong."

This time Izzy was the one saying, "Really?" Why did Judy know this ahead of her? "His calendar has 12:00 till 2:00 marked free."

"Sorry, Izzy. Blame us. An old client of Bevan's is very interested in Elite and Brad had an opening today. Don't worry, we'll have a lovely lunch without him. See you soon." The line went dead.

On the drive back to Glingilly, Izzy got caught behind a herd of cows crossing the road and arrived at Villefranche ten minutes late. As she drove toward the garage she was surprised not to pass Judy's car. Perhaps because Judy brought food, she'd parked closer to the house?

Izzy parked, then walked through the rose arbor toward the house. She stopped at an enormous red wooden arrow pointing down toward the lake. A chalk sign hung off it with writing in Judy's distinctive scrawl: *Lunch in the maze.*

Izzy groaned. Why did the Quinns make simple things complicated? And if Judy wanted a heart-to-heart about Izzy's relationship with Brad, why did it need to happen in the maze? She and Brad had only walked it once and got utterly lost. She had no desire to replicate those sixty minutes.

She called Judy. It went straight to voice mail.

With a sigh, Izzy kicked off her heels, pulled on her gardening shoes and strode out of the garden and across the grass to the maze. In the distance, sunlight pranced across the lake, dazzling her, and she paused to savor it. She loved this view. When the ostentatious house that couldn't decide if it was a 1400s castle or an 1800s chateau circled her in stark cold loneliness, the only place she could breathe was out here, under the wide sky. Day or night, she could rely on the view for a reassuring reality check.

At the entrance to the maze there was another sign: *Be Gretel.*

It wasn't until Izzy noticed hunks of bread trailing on the ground that she worked out what the message meant. She laughed—obviously Judy didn't know the modern dating definition of the word breadcrumb. But at the rate the seagulls were eating the bread, Izzy needed to get going or she may not have a trail to follow in, let alone out.

"Be there soon," she called.

There was no reply. Oh well, the only way to solve the mystery was to walk.

Memorizing the turns for the Renaissance day fair, she took a left, two rights, three lefts and a right. Suddenly she was no longer surrounded by tall hedges, but bright sunlight.

"Ta—" she began, but the "Dah" died on her lips.

A four-sided white and gold tent was pitched in the square, its contrasting curtain sides bunched over the poles and secured with gold tassels. Under the dome, large and brightly colored cushions were scattered around the edges of a generous rug, and in the center was a low table. A silver champagne bucket held a gold-foiled bottle elegantly draped with a white linen napkin, and beside it two flutes decorated with strawberries sat ready on a silver tray. The rest of the table was covered in a smorgasbord of meats and cheeses, crackers and bread, mini tarts, fruit and nuts. There was also a distinctive cake box from Glingilly Patisserie and a silver tea service. It was a scene straight out of a British-India period drama—the only thing missing was the punkah wallah pulling the fan. It was typical Brad—elegant luxury.

Brad saw her and jumped to his feet. He walked toward her, his eyes the decadent color of melted chocolate, and his face wreathed in a wide smile that was focused one hundred percent on her. It was as if they'd never argued and he'd never stormed out.

"Hey, gorgeous. You made it."

Izzy's astonishment was fading fast and questions popped like corn. "I thought you were in Geelong."

He gave her a wink and stretched out his arms. "All part of the ruse to get you here for your surprise."

Everything looked so lush and amazing, and the look in his eyes drew her forward like a magnet, so she didn't fully understand why at the very last moment she dodged his hug.

"Was you walking out last night part of the surprise too?"

His grin faded, replaced by contrition. "No, and I hate that you think that. I'm sorry, Iz. I was tired—and before you say it, I know that's no excuse for acting like a jerk. Please let me make it up to you."

He held out his hands again, but he didn't take the final step to close the gap between them. The fact that he was asking rather than assuming lessened the low-grade agitation stirring her gut.

"I'm sorry too. I should have understood about business confidentiality. It's just I'm so proud of what you've achieved that I want to—"

But he was swallowing her words in a kiss. She gave herself up to the sensation of being adored, letting it wash through her, needing it to smooth out the dents from the night before and reassure her.

They fell onto the cushions and she laughed, throwing out an arm to indicate their surroundings. "I'm dressed more for an office fantasy than this. I should be wearing a sari."

"Doesn't matter." He nuzzled her neck and his hand roved under her corporate-style skirt. "You're not going to be dressed for much longer."

She wasn't and neither was he.

. . .

Later, wrapped in a spare blanket, Izzy noticed a business card tucked under the wooden platter. "Do you think all of Maharani Tents' customers have sex on their rugs?"

"I hope so." Brad grinned, angled the champagne bottle away from them and popped the cork. It flew into the air and landed in a hedge. He poured the glasses and handed her one before raising his. "To us."

She clinked the glass and smiled. "To more afternoons like this."

She was suddenly starving and she dived onto the cheese, putting the first hunk into her mouth without bread. Then she built herself a taste sensation of runny brie, quince preserve and salad leaves on fresh crusty bread.

Brad laughed. "You poor starving orphan. When did you last eat?"

"Last night. I was too nervous this morning."

His smile faded. "Shit, your presentation. Sorry, Iz. The moment I saw you, everything else fell out of my head. How did it go? I bet you nailed it."

She grinned and raised her hand for a high-five. "Cooper said it was an A."

"Cooper?"

"The lecturer."

She heard Cooper's voice—*you're in the trust circle*. Was now the time to ask Brad about the betting sheets for her own education? Of course it was—Brad could talk about Elite ad infinitum. But here, in this luxurious fantasy setting, she was second-guessing herself.

So much of Villefranche is fantasy.

While she was arguing with herself, she realized Brad was talking. "Sorry, what?"

He was refilling her glass. "Try the caviar."

"There's caviar?" Her mouth watered. "How did I miss that?"

Her eyes scanned the massive platter of food—far too much for two people—seeking a pile of black treasure. Just as she said, "I don't think —" she caught a glint of something gold in among the grapes. She lifted a bunch and found a small Indian brass jar with a lid. Both were intricately decorated with etchings of interwoven delicate flowers and leaves.

"Fancy!"

"Well, it's caviar." He lifted a brow. "Save me some, okay."

A guilty laugh bubbled up as she remembered the time she'd scarfed the lot. "I promise."

She lifted the lid, but inside there was no caviar. Instead, nestled on rich maroon velvet, lay a ring. As the light caught it, the large central diamond's crisscross cut glittered. It set off a parade of sparkles in the surrounding brilliant diamonds before radiating along the line of baguette diamonds that trailed down the sides.

Izzy gasped and her heart slammed so hard against her ribs it almost hurt. She looked at Brad, who was plucking the ring off its velvet bed and picking up her left hand.

"I love you, Iz, and we make a hell of a team. Let's make it official and spend the rest of our lives making money and babies." He slid the ring onto her finger and kissed her.

Thoughts tumbled through her head so fast she couldn't catch them, let alone get her mouth to form them into words.

You want this. Say yes.

Babies!

OMG, this ring! Worry about babies later.

She tilted her hand left then right, dazzled by the prisms of light. The ring was so incredible she couldn't believe her eyes. Couldn't believe that the girl who'd once been dependent on a food bank now carried over two carats of diamonds on her finger. The weight of the ring combined with the slightly loose fit caused it to slip, knocking into her middle finger.

Brad raised his phone, snapped a photo, then showed it to her. Her blue eyes—wide and shocked—stared back at her. Then his fingers were flying across the screen and the cell emitted a whooshing sound.

He pumped the air. "I love that you had no idea today was the day I'd pop the question."

She couldn't haul her gaze away from the ring. "Where did you find it?"

"I bought the diamonds in Mumbai and got the ring made in Melbourne. I've had it for months, but I've been trying to come up with the best way to propose. Paris is cliché, and that sandstorm in Dubai nuked my desert plans. Besides, I thought you'd expect me to do it somewhere exotic, but I wanted it to be a total surprise. Stun you speechless."

She laughed. "Mission accomplished."

He stroked her cheek with his thumb. "I love that we'll always associate Villefranche with our happiest memories."

Pushing last night's argument far away, she kissed him. After all, in the grand scheme of things, one silly fight when they were both tired and stressed was nothing. All couples argued—it didn't mean he was going to leave her. And their fight was barely a blip compared to her parents' arguments. Nothing had been thrown and no one was giving the other the silent treatment for days.

"So the reason you were on edge last night was because you were worried I might say no?" she teased.

"Nah, you were never going to say no." He squeezed her waist. "Anyway, I only got the idea this morning. I took advantage of you being out and the company helicoptered everything in and set it up." He kissed her again. "Make-up sex and a proposal. It's win-win."

Her delight bubbled up into a laugh. "I think we need to celebrate again." She let the blanket fall and, naked except for the ring, crawled into his lap.

He quickly pulled the blanket back over her. "Get dressed, Iz. People will be here any minute."

Panic gripped her and she reached for her hair. "What people?"

"Mom and Dad."

"Oh God!" She frantically grabbed her clothes. "Tell me they haven't been waiting close by while we ..."

He laughed. "Of course not."

"Thank God."

But the relief was short-lived. Facing her future in-laws with bird-nest hair and smeared lipstick that screamed sex was one of her worst nightmares.

Brad's cell phone beeped and he checked the message. "The Essens are coming too. Well, Mike and Birdie." The phone beeped again. "Oh, and the Hewitsons and the D'Angelo's. Possibly more."

Her fingers stalled on the zipper of her skirt. "You ... you *invited* people?" *To our private moment!*

"Of course. I knew you'd want our close friends here to share our news. But don't worry," he said easily, "we'll throw a proper engagement party soon. It will be huge!"

Friends? Izzy's mind flailed on the word. Everyone Brad had mentioned were either friends of his parents or members of Elite and Fortune. Even if Jack and Lucy Essen had been free to come, Izzy would hardly call Lucy a friend. Brooke Riglioni? Maybe, but outside of the Irish festival committee, she and the police officer didn't spend much time together. Was there anyone in Glingilly she called a friend?

"Iz!" She barely heard Brad over the roar in her ears.

He'd opened her handbag and was pressing her make-up bag into her hands. She breathed deeply, trying to still the tremble in her fingers so she didn't scrawl lipstick pencil halfway up her face. With the aid of lipstick, face powder and a brush, she reassembled herself. There was no need for blusher—her cheeks glowed pink.

Brad stepped in close and rebuttoned her blouse. "There you go. You look amazing."

"I look like I just had sex!"

He grinned. "We look like the winners we are, and everyone loves a winner."

"Brad! Izzy!" Judy rushed through the opening of the hedge, quickly followed by Bevan, and Birdie Essen.

Brad slid his hand under Izzy's left palm so her fingers interlaced with his and the ring tilted forward—big, bold and beautiful. Then he whispered in her ear, "Showtime!"

The ring suddenly weighed a ton.

CHAPTER TEN

BIRDIE WAS SITTING in the sunroom, enjoying the sunshine and tackling a cryptic crossword, when she heard, "Do you fancy lunch at the club?" She looked up to see Mike standing in the doorway, wearing some of his new clothes.

"What's the occasion?"

He stretched out his hand. "Can't a man take his wife out on a whim?"

"Absolutely!" She stood and kissed him, loving this new retired lifestyle.

Long before Fortune came into their life, their plan had always been to buy new cars and a travel trailer when Mike retired and they'd done it, upgrading both. While they were waiting for their custom trailer to be built, they were spending time putting things in order for their extended vacation. The first few months of retirement had been consumed by life administration. They'd created a self-managed retirement fund. They'd written new wills and organized powers of attorney. They'd invested in a wardrobe makeover—lots of linen for warmer climates—and Mike was tackling the long list of home maintenance jobs.

In between tasks, they'd enjoyed some luxury mini-breaks—a couple of nights at the hot springs resort at Warrnambool, and a week with Judy and Bevan at Dolphin Sands. But it was the four glorious nights in Melbourne at the five-star Langham Hotel that had cemented Birdie's belief they were now rich. Each time she thought about how the luxury hotel had welcomed her as if she'd stayed there many times before she sighed in bliss and filled her diffuser with the hotel's signature scent. She was planning a return visit for Mike's birthday.

Since retiring, Mike started every morning telling her how much they were worth. Their fast rise in wealth made her giddy, as did the amount Mike said they could now afford to spend on discretionary items. He'd surprised her with a VW Golf R, which she felt he loved more than she did. He certainly drove it a lot. She'd expected him to buy a classic Mustang like Bevan, given how much he coveted the vehicle, but he'd chosen a dual cab ute with all the extras instead.

"We need it to tow that fancy trailer you've ordered," he'd told her.

With the wait for the travel trailer dragging on, Birdie was currently toying with taking a cruise to the UK then doing the grand European tour. They could always do the round-Australia trip the following year.

As they walked out to the car, Birdie noticed the paunch around Mike's middle. The weight had snuck onto both of them since his retirement, courtesy of numerous meals out with Bevan and Judy, and the Elite and Fortune events. She hadn't thought anything could eclipse the Elite events, but the Fortune "club" took things to another level. Brad had chartered a plane and flown them to the outback Birdsville Races—Birdie was still pinching herself at the bucket-list trip. The champagne had flowed all day and Brad had invited Jack and Lucy too, even though they weren't part of Fortune. He was a kind and generous man and Birdie didn't know why she'd ever thought him flashy.

She was secretly looking forward to Brad and Izzy's wedding, which according to Judy was going to be a destination event for a select few.

"They both love Fiji and Bali so I wouldn't be surprised if it was either of those, but the Seychelles are gorgeous too," her friend had told her. "Of course the Essens are on the guest list."

When Birdie had pressed Lucy for more wedding details, her daughter-in-law had shrugged. "You know more about it than I do. When I asked Izzy, she said they'd been too busy to think about it."

"Well, it's going to happen and when it does, you'll need a passport," Birdie said.

Lucy had traded a look with Jack that Birdie couldn't decipher. Was it envy or smugness? Although what Lucy had to be smug about, Birdie had no idea. She was just thankful Jack and Lucy were in Elite and reducing their eye-watering mortgage. Just like Birdie and Mike needed to reduce their ballooning weight.

"It's such a gorgeous day," she said. "Let's walk to the club."

They chose a table with a view of the beer garden and sunshine streaming through the glass.

When Mike had placed their orders and returned with their drinks, he said, "I think I've finally settled on which computers to buy." He'd spent hours investigating his-and-hers laptops.

"So you can check your Fortune account every day no matter where we are and see how much it's grown?" Birdie teased.

He didn't laugh. "Absolutely. It's a big responsibility being a self-funded retiree. When the trailer arrives, I'll install a wi-fi hotspot. That way I can move money around and stay on top of things."

"What do you mean, move money around?"

"I'm going to use some of our Fortune dividends to buy shares."

Birdie thought about the figures Brad and Bevan had mentioned at Birdsville a couple of weeks earlier. "But I thought the reason we're investing in Fortune is because the returns are so much better?"

"They are, but it's never wise to put all your eggs in one basket."

"You've got money in Elite too."

"Yes, but it's a similar basket. We're using Fortune to generate money quickly so we can enjoy it and use it for long-term investments in other companies."

Her stomach clenched at the thought of losing the exclusive social life that came with being a Fortune member. "But you'll always have some money in Fortune?"

"Absolutely. It's a license to print money."

The spasm in her gut relaxed. "While we're on the subject of money ..." She floated the idea of driving around Europe. "There's a tax scheme where you lease a new car for the time you need it and they buy it back from you at the end."

Mike frowned. "I thought you had your heart set on going around Australia?"

"I do, but I'm going a bit nuts waiting for the travel trailer. I just want to do *something* that makes me feel retired. And Australia's not going anywhere. Let's do Europe first."

"Not sure Europe's going anywhere either." He sipped his beer thoughtfully. "Besides, we've just spent a shirt-load of money."

"I know, but we'd always budgeted to buy new cars and the van when you retired."

"We upgraded."

"Only because we have the money. I'm not talking about spending any more of our capital, just dividends." She gave him an arch look. "I mean the money's growing every week and you just said it's there to enjoy."

He was quiet, pondering her words, then he smiled and raised his glass to her. "You're absolutely right. Paris, eh? I've always fancied seeing those cancan girls."

Birdie rolled her eyes. "There's far more to Paris than showgirls. There's architecture, art—"

"I want a limit on the number of art galleries."

"And car museums," she shot back before bringing up a costing sheet on her cell phone. "If we act soon we can get a great deal on airfares."

He put on his glasses and studied the numbers. "If you want, we could go first class."

She opened and closed her mouth, momentarily speechless that

Mike had made the suggestion. "But that's an insane amount of money! Just because we have it doesn't mean we should waste it."

"True, although is it a waste when it takes twenty-four hours to fly to Paris? I'm sixty-one, I've worked hard and I deserve to be comfortable." His eyes twinkled as he handed back her phone. "Everyone else in Fortune does it. Even the Hewitsons."

She knew he was winding her up, but that didn't prevent a snake of FOMO slithering through her, fast accompanied by another fear. Did her prudent attitude to money mean she didn't really belong in Fortune? The thought unsettled her.

"In that case, we're definitely flying first class there and cruising home!" she said.

Mike grinned. "Sounds like a plan. I'll talk to Brad and get him to transfer half the vacation budget now and the rest halfway through the trip. No point missing out on big returns."

Birdie rose and kissed him. Mike laughed and swatted her on the backside and they both knew how they'd celebrate later. Afternoon sex was another wonder of retirement that she'd fully embraced.

Lunch passed in a whirl of plans, working out exactly where the cruise stopped so they didn't replicate those places on their land tour. Apart from insisting on a night at the Moulin Rouge and visiting the Leaning Tower of Pisa, Mike was happy to let Birdie create the rest of the itinerary.

After coffee, as they made their way to the exit, they were stopped numerous times by people they knew. Sometimes Birdie thought driving to Warrnambool was worth the effort just so she could stand up and leave a café without offending anyone. But today she was full of excitement and happy to tell anyone and everyone about their big trip.

She was about to launch into details about the cruise—Queen class, which meant a large stateroom with a balcony, a butler, and an exclusive restaurant and bar far away from the general public—when Mike applied gentle pressure to her arm. She turned and caught his warning look. In her excitement, she'd forgotten that she wasn't with the Elite crowd, where chatting about spending large amounts of money was as normal as breathing. She was talking to Leanne Kennedy, who worked in childcare and spent her annual vacation nearby, camping at Wye River.

Birdie retreated fast from the topic. "Oh dear, listen to me boring you. Sorry!"

"No worries, Birdie. The whole town knows you've been waiting a long time for Mike to retire."

"Thanks, Leanne." She appreciated the woman's indulgence of her runaway mouth.

"Can't quite picture you and Mike on a swanky cruise though," Leanne added.

Indignation whooshed through Birdie and she tilted her chin. "I'll send photos."

As they walked away, Mike said quietly, "Smile and wave."

"I can't wait to get out of this small-minded town," Birdie muttered. "No wonder we socialize more with Elite now than at GGSC."

Mike let her rant unabated until they were walking through the small, but historically significant, botanic gardens.

"Isn't that Brad?" he cut in.

She glanced around. "Where?"

"There." He pointed to a sprawling Morton Bay fig.

A man sat under the tree, nestled between two enormous buttresses and with his back against the trunk. As he gazed up into the foliage, he looked tiny in comparison.

"There's no way Brad would risk his tailor-made pants sitting in dirt," Birdie said.

The man suddenly shot to his feet, brushed down his trousers and strode toward them, a smile on his face and a laugh on his lips.

"It's my spirit tree," Brad said. "Isn't it a gorgeous day?" He greeted Birdie with a kiss and reached out to shake Mike's hand. "Aren't you glad you're retired and able to enjoy it?"

Mike laughed. "Work's a mug's game for sure."

"Lucky I love my job," Brad said.

"Lucky for us you do or I'd still be working." Mike gave Brad an appreciative slap on the back.

"We've been planning our trip to Europe over lunch at the club," Birdie said.

"I hope you've got walking the Cinque Terre on your list. Izzy and I loved it so much we almost stayed."

"Oh, that's something to think about, Mike." Birdie laughed. "All that exercise will offset the pasta carbs."

"Add in cycling the full length of the Canal du Midi so you can indulge in French cheese and cakes," Brad said.

"Next you'll have me joining Elite's Lycra Lads on Thursday mornings," Mike said.

"Dad enjoys it. I think he's got as much love for his Pinarello as he has for the Mustang."

"I'll have to up my fitness a bit first." Mike patted his belly. "I'm glad we ran into you—it saves me a phone call. Can you transfer 20,000 into our account today so Birdie can pay some deposits?"

"That's a brave decision," Brad said.

Birdie glanced at Mike, who was frowning. "What do you mean?" he asked.

"This weekend's the Galway Races."

"In Ireland?" Birdie checked, having heard about the racing carnival.

Brad nodded. "Yeah, and it's their biggest event. Taking money out of Fortune just before it isn't the wisest investment decision. But of course if you need the money, send me an email with your instructions so everything's above board."

The idea of losing money ate at Birdie. "Mike, there's enough in the current account to pay the deposits."

"You're married to a wise woman," Brad said. "Better yet, if you can wait until dividend day you'll maximize the Galway Races and the New Classic in Florida. Everyone's got their eye on that one."

"Sounds like we should wait then," Mike said. "I'll be interested in the results of the new race."

"You're not alone there. There's some mighty horseflesh running." Brad's cell rang and he silenced it. "Just Izzy. I'll call her back."

"How are the wedding plans coming along?" Birdie asked, hoping for some new intel.

Brad tapped his nose. "Izzy wants to keep it all under wraps so it's a big surprise."

"Well, if it's anything like the Great Gatsby engagement party, it will be amazing."

Brad's cell phone rang again and Mike took Birdie's arm. "Let's leave the man to do his job."

"Our job," Brad said. "I'm working for all of us."

"And we're very grateful," Birdie said, but Brad had already turned away. As he gave a backwards wave she heard him say, "Mate! How the hell are you?"

"Busy man," Birdie mused. "I wonder how he juggles everything?"

"The important thing is that he does and we're benefitting." Mike slid his hand into hers. "Let's go and book that cruise."

CHAPTER ELEVEN

LUCY WAS ready to run away from home. Glingilly was caught in a never-ending low-pressure system with persistent rain and flood warnings and the occasional hailstorm, making being outside ugly. Rigby was fractious with a heavy cold, which of course he'd got the moment she'd started her days off, and to top it off it was day ten of Jack's work rotation. Right now, she wasn't certain she'd survive another four days of single parenting.

Rigby rubbed his snotty nose into her chest. "Want *Bluey*."

Lucy didn't bother reminding her son he needed to say please—she was ready to do almost anything to not have him clinging to her like a limpet. She settled him on the sofa and switched on the show. He immediately laid down on the cushions, put his thumb in his mouth and stared at the screen. When *Bluey* was on, a bomb could go off and Rigby wouldn't notice.

She returned to the kitchen, filled the kettle and eyed her cell. For the last hour she'd been arguing with herself over whether or not to call or text Birdie. When Jack was away and Lucy was scheduled to work out-of-day-care hours or on a weekend, her mother-in-law minded Rigby. But Lucy knew asking Birdie to mind him just so she could get out of the house was a request that could open her up to criticism. On the other hand, if she didn't get an hour to herself today she might just lose it. She didn't even want to think about how she'd cope when her in-laws left on their vacation.

Her cell pinged with a text from Jack.

> I thought the allen keys were in the laundry? Borrow Dad's? Ask him to assemble it? Jx

But Lucy wanted to assemble the flatpack bookshelf she'd bought for Rigby herself, then fill it with books. It was a commitment to her son that stories and reading made life richer.

Ask Mike to mind Rigby! The simple solution to avoiding Birdie's pursed mouth and disapproval filled her with delight.

Mike was old school so she rang his cell, hoping that despite the weather Birdie had still gone to the tennis club and was enjoying coffee, cake and gossip.

"Hello, Lucy," Mike said, sounding genuinely pleased to hear from her instead of surprised. "How are things?"

"Actually, that's why I'm calling. Rigby's not a hundred percent and I need to run some errands. Any chance you're free sometime today to mind him?"

"Might be easier if I come to you, eh?"

She couldn't believe her luck. "Oh, that would be wonderful. When suits? I know you're busier than ever now you're retired."

Mike laughed. "Usually I'd be at golf, but this weather's put the kibosh on that. I'll be round in fifteen."

He cut the call and Lucy realized she had just enough time to dive through the shower.

She was making sandwiches when Mike arrived. "Lunch for you and Rigby," she said. "And help yourself to whatever's in the tins."

"You didn't need to do that," Mike said.

"It's the least I can do and the baking's all Birdie, not me. We're going to miss you two when you're away."

"Thirty-five days and seventeen hours to go," Mike said.

Lucy couldn't hide her surprise. "That's precise."

Mike laughed. "Birdie's made a countdown pad and every morning she insists we rip off the page together. To be honest, I was never that keen to travel overseas, but Birdie's so excited it's worth going just to see that."

"And the Ferrari and Mercedes museums," she teased.

He grinned. "Not to mention Lamborghini and Porsche."

"Well, Jack and I are a little bit green. Especially about the cruise." She sighed. "Rigby would love kids club and Jack and I could have one long continuous date."

Mike patted her arm. "Your time will come soon enough."

"I know." She almost said, "Fortune's doing so well," but thankfully remembered their secret. "Elite's had an excellent streak these last two months so instead of leaving half the dividends in as capital, we're going to withdraw all of it and put it on the mortgage. If things continue this way, we'll own the house this time next year."

"That's great news."

She smiled at his enthusiasm. "Thanks. And thanks again for your contributions from Elite. It all helps. One of my jobs today is to call Brad and ask him to transfer the money."

"You need to email him so he has it in writing."

"Really? I've always just called him and he's moved it over almost immediately."

Mike wriggled his mouth. "What amount?"

"It's only ever been a couple of thousand, but this time it's more."

"Well, he told me requests for anything over 5,000 need to be in writing. Which reminds me, I sent him an email yesterday for the final payments for the trip. I wonder if the money's dropped in." Mike pulled out his phone and checked his banking app.

When Lucy turned back from putting the sandwiches in the fridge, Mike was frowning. "Not there?" she asked.

"No."

"If you don't bank with the credit union, it can take a few days. I know it shouldn't, but it does."

His face cleared. "Yeah, that'll be it. Now where's the little fella?"

Despite the wet, the wind and the cold that made dashing between stores a *Survivor* challenge, Lucy was enjoying the freedom of shopping without hauling Rigby in and out of the car seat. Having ticked off all the boring jobs, she'd saved the best for last. She stepped into the bookshop, paused and sighed. God, she loved this place. She breathed in the woodsy scent of new books and let the quiet calm of the store wrap around her like a giant soft blanket.

With a wave to Michelle, who was on the phone, she made a beeline for the children's section. Rigby loved picture books but he was also starting to enjoy longer stories so she planned to buy a selection, including her childhood favorites. She picked up *Possum Magic* and *Magic Beach* and then found *Harry and His Bucket Full of Dinosaurs*.

She was browsing the longer stories when she heard Michelle say, "Did you read my mind? I was just about to text you."

A woman laughed and the sound made Lucy peek around the shelves. Izzy Harrington stood in the shop, as beautifully put together as always but there was something different about her. Lucy couldn't quite put her finger on it, but if asked she might say she looked relaxed. No, that was pushing it. Less uptight than usual? Maybe. Perhaps now Brad had put that indecently enormous ring on her finger and removed any ambiguity about their relationship, the woman could relax. And Brad obviously saw warmth and love in Izzy Harrington that Lucy struggled to see.

Then again, except for having a child, Lucy didn't have anything Izzy wanted or needed, so the woman had no reason to be anything more than barely polite. It was something Izzy excelled at. Even though her role in the club appeared to be event-hostessing and arm candy, Lucy wasn't naive. Women like Izzy wielded power from the bedroom, so staying on her good side was as important for Lucy and Jack as their involvement in Elite and Fortune. The last thing Lucy wanted was for Izzy to feel slighted by her and bitch to Brad.

She sighed. Staying hidden in the tiny children's section and risking discovery probably wasn't an option. She quickly added *Tashi* and *Charlotte's Web* to her book pile, then strode the length of the shop, arriving at the counter as Izzy was tapping her credit card.

"Hi, Izzy."

"Lucy." Izzy pulled at a curl, tugging it behind her ear with a jerk. "Hello," she said coolly.

Izzy's obvious displeasure at seeing her stung like a slap. Lucy heard herself saying inanely, "I'm buying books for Rigby."

One shaped brow rose. "I see that."

Lucy bitterly regretted coming out from behind the shelves. As she handed her own credit card to Michelle, she asked Izzy, "What about you?"

"Textbooks."

The phone rang and Michelle answered it, giving them both an apologetic wave as they took their bagged purchases and moved away from the counter.

"I didn't know you were studying," Lucy said.

Izzy shrugged as if she didn't care if Lucy knew or not. "Business studies."

"Really?"

Izzy stiffened. "Yes. I'm more than capable of helping Brad run the company, or does that surprise you?"

Jack kept telling Lucy that all Brad wanted was for Izzy to be barefoot and pregnant. But considering the pounding waves of animosity rolling off the other woman, Lucy didn't mention it.

"I ... it's just ... um ... no." A bead of sweat broke on Lucy's hairline. *Think!* "I thought you'd be busy planning the social event of the year."

Izzy gave her a blank look.

"The wedding."

Izzy's thumb touched her ring then dropped away as if stung.

"There's not much to plan. When it happens, it will be very low-key. Just immediate family."

Lucy laughed, unable to align "low-key" with a man who only ever entertained on a grand scale. "You're marrying Brad Quinn."

"I'm aware."

The tight words whipped her. "I just meant ..." God! Why was every conversation with this woman like tiptoeing through a minefield? Lucy glanced around, checking no one was listening, then switched the topic to something she hoped was safer. "Actually, I was about to call Brad, but as you're working with him now, I'll tell you. Jack and I want to withdraw 10,000 dollars from Fortune—"

"Okay."

Lucy blinked at the unexpectedly straightforward answer. "So you don't need us to put it in writing?"

"It's probably good practice. I've been suggesting Brad do that for ages, but you know what he's like."

Lucy wasn't sure what Izzy was implying. The man was charming and handsome, and whatever he touched turned into money.

"He believes in old-fashioned friendship and loyalty," Izzy finished.

"Isn't that a good thing?"

Izzy shifted her books to her other arm. "It is," she said slowly, "but it also leaves him wide open to being taken advantage of."

Was Izzy taking a shot at her and Jack, Lucy wondered. When they'd asked Brad to keep their names off the Fortune communications so Birdie and Mike didn't find out they'd invested too, he'd said, "Parents, eh? I totally get it. Not a problem."

"He needs a better system," Izzy continued, "to keep everyone accountable."

Who wasn't accountable? The foundation members of Elite and Fortune were all close friends of the Quinns, and they in turn had introduced their own family and friends into the circle. Lucy found the interconnectedness reassuring. The only breach of trust was Trig Barker, and Trig had never been a team player—in fact, she'd been surprised Brad had accepted him into the club. After Trig betrayed the group, he'd learned fast that as much as Glingilly protected its own, it excommunicated anyone who inflicted harm. He'd moved to Port Fairy soon after, citing family reasons, but everyone knew it was because he was no longer welcome anywhere, from GGSC to the musical society. Fortunately, the incident hadn't impacted on the club's earning capacity.

"Has something happened?" Lucy asked.

But Izzy's cell was ringing. She didn't even look apologetic when she turned away from Lucy and took the call with a brusque "Hello."

Lucy thought Izzy's prickly personality was likely to cause far more problems in the club than anything else. With a sigh she left the shop, hating how once again her mood had sunk to below the floor after spending five minutes in Izzy Harrington's company.

CHAPTER TWELVE

When Izzy opened Villefranche's front door on her return from Warrnambool, Thor tore down the stairs, hit the marble and skated sideways. Then he powered his little legs forward and threw his thickset body into her legs, before leaping and trying to lick her hand.

Almost dropping her books, she laughed at his exuberance. "Hey, buddy. What a welcome. I love you too."

He barked, then ran to the door and barked again.

"Didn't you get a—" She swallowed the "W" word, knowing if she said it Thor would become even more insane and she'd have to grab the leash and head out. Surely Brad had taken him for a run? He did it every morning unless he had an early meeting. According to his schedule, today's meetings were in the evening.

"Thor, come!" she said sternly.

Thor's frantic circles ceased and his ears drooped—a dog's version of a sigh. After a long look at the door, he slowly trotted behind her, his nails clacking on the stone floor, into the kitchen.

"On your bed." Izzy pointed to the cozy collection of blankets and toys in the corner.

The dog looked at her, then laid down beside the kitchen door, hope lingering in his big brown eyes. Izzy wanted to laugh but held back, knowing if she gave an inch, Thor would take a million miles.

"Thor, on your bed."

The dog paused by his water bowl, took a few sips, then strolled to his bed as if he'd been planning on going there all along.

Izzy switched on the kettle and lifted a mug from a drawer. Brad's cars were all in the garage so he was home and likely somewhere in the house. It was so huge they used the intercom to find each other rather than wandering from room to room. She was about to hit the button when it beeped.

"Good, you're back," Brad said.

Izzy tried not to bristle, knowing that the intercom's static flattened nuances, but a hello would have been nice.

Since their engagement two months earlier, Brad had been frantic with work, which wasn't very different from their pre-engagement life. What had changed was the number of times she'd felt more like his housekeeper than his fiancée. Less of a business partner and more of an employee. She was still consulting with him and organizing the club events, but otherwise they seemed to be living parallel lives. She was studying the theory of how to run a business and he was actually doing it. Every time she tried talking to him about increasing her involvement in the day-to-day running of Elite, Brad was either "expecting a call," "too tired," or "just heading out, Iz. Later, yeah?" Only later never came.

She'd stopped trying to discuss it with him in bed, because she never got beyond saying, "Can we ta—" before he was doing wondrous things to her then falling asleep.

Today she was going to talk to him in his office—a place she never ventured because she never knew when he was in the middle of a Zoom meeting or taking a call. But, unlike all the other rooms in the house, the office oozed work so chatting about the business was a natural segue. She'd bought an Irish apple cake from the bakery—just like the one his grandmother used to make—and over tea and cake they'd talk. She wasn't leaving the office until things were back on an even keel and she had a guaranteed position inside Elite that wasn't event planning.

She spoke into the intercom. "Hi, Brad. I was thinking—"

A loud crackle sounded and she heard, "Bring an espresso to the bedroom."

The brisk words whipped her, but her hot retort faltered on both the type of coffee at 3:00 in the afternoon and the destination.

"Did you say espresso?"

"And something to eat. I missed lunch." The light on the intercom vanished along with Brad's voice.

Izzy seethed. The moment Brad's blood sugar returned to normal levels they were definitely having this overdue conversation. He got irritable when he was hungry, but then didn't everyone? Except she'd never noticed it with Brad until recently. Perhaps she should suggest he have a check-up with his primary care doctor?

An image of Brad's reaction flashed in her head and her fingers tugged on her hair. Lately, the list of difficult conversation topics grew by the hour.

While she plated some fruit, cut a hunk of cake, made the drinks, loaded a tray and carried it upstairs, she pondered how she could get Brad into the office.

When she walked into the bedroom, he was pitching socks and jocks into a suitcase.

Her mind ran through his schedule and drew a blank. "What's going on?"

"Hello, Miz Harrington." He crossed the room, relieved her of the tray, then kissed her long and deep as if he hadn't seen her in days.

The usual quiver of desire arrowed through her and her libido sat up as smart and fast as Thor hearing the "W" word. She and Brad hadn't had sex in over a week, which for them constituted a drought.

A thought blazed in her head—Brad loved a role-play seduction. Was his terse tone on the intercom and demand for food all part of a scenario? He'd never played the boss and the secretary, or the boss and the maid, but perhaps today was the day. And as past experience had proved that they couldn't have a serious conversation in the bedroom, she may as well play along. When Brad was fed, sated and in a good mood, she'd get him into the office.

"Hello, Mr. Quinn."

But Brad had turned to the tray. He downed the coffee, then shoved the cake in his mouth.

Okay then. Not exactly sexy yet.

"I can see you're a very busy and important man."

He grinned. "Damn straight. Where are my cufflinks?"

"I think Sir left them on top of the tallboy."

He threw her his best twinkle smile and packed them. "You picked up those new shirts, right?"

She stepped in close and ran her fingers up his sternum. "Will I get into trouble if I didn't?"

His eyes burned with familiar fire and she smiled, hoping he'd suggest a mutually satisfying punishment. Her mind was spinning off in anticipation when he said, "I got a call."

All ideas of sex tumbled out of her head, replaced by a different type of heady anticipation. "I got a call" was their code for "we're getting on a plane, baby," and it had been months since she'd last used her passport.

Thinking about her long overdue shopping trip, she clapped her hands and gave a squeal of delight. "Dubai!"

"Singapore."

"Oh, okay!" It was unexpected, but the shopping in Singapore was awesome too. She ran to the walk-in closet, rose on her toes and reached for her largest suitcase. "I can get that Maticevski dress and—ouch!" The suitcase brought a smaller one down on her.

"Iz?" Brad appeared in the doorway. "You okay?"

She laughed and rubbed her head. "All good. I think the suitcases are overexcited. It's been so long since they got on a plane."

He kissed her on the forehead, then picked up the largest case and returned it to the shelf.

"What are you doing?" she asked.

"Putting it back."

"But I need it."

He shook his head. "I'm the one going to Singapore."

"No." She refused to give in to the disappointment roaring through her. "I'm going too!" She tried reaching around him for the suitcase.

"You're acting like a toddler," Brad said.

Her disappointment twisted into anger. "I'm an adult and I'm coming to Singapore."

"You can't."

"I can! This is the fifth trip you've taken without me—"

"Because you've had commitments."

His reasonable tone fanned her outrage. "This time I don't and I'm coming! I'll pay for my own ticket!"

"Izzy, please ..." He pulled her rigid body in for a hug and buried his face in her hair. "I'm sorry. I've completely stuffed this up. Of course I want you to come."

"Good." She steeled herself against the tantalizing scent of his cologne that was tickling her nostrils and reminding her of how good they were whenever they were wrapped in each other's arms.

He tilted her chin so she had to look straight at him. "But this time, it's not up to me."

She squinted at him, trying to read his face. She came up short.

"Remember Wei Chan, Dad's mate?"

She nodded. "No one could forget that hotel or the ten-course banquet."

"Yeah." Brad smiled at the memory. "Wei called an hour ago and he's got me a meeting with a bloke who's interested in investing in the development of an Elite app. But it's not just a meeting, it's a three-day event at his place, on his yacht and at some wilderness lodge in Borneo. You know how those guys are."

She did know, but her brain was snagged on "app." "Won't an app mean Elite loses its exclusivity you say is so vital?" she asked.

He laughed. "It's not the sort of app just anyone can download. It's only for our members and there'll be privilege levels, banking information, dividend reports, that sort of thing. The potential is huge and, most importantly, it'll free me up from a lot of the admin so I can focus on the stuff I enjoy."

Betrayal cut into her, stinging and burning. "But I've offered to help with the admin. I showed you my dividend system—"

"And I appreciate it, but that's just a tiny part of the app's capabilities. If you really want to help, grab those shoes so I can finish packing and then focus on giving you a proper goodbye."

He kissed her again, this time with a promise of how they could say farewell. He pulled away and grabbed two shirts. Clinging to her frustrations, she tucked the shoes into a bag and followed him.

"Brad, I'm serious about expanding my involvement in the business. I've been serious for months."

"I know and I want it too, but let's be realistic. There's a lot of training involved and you won't have the head space until you've finished your course. Anyway, you've already got more than a full load with uni, the club events, the Irish festival and the wedding." A familiar goofy grin crossed his face—the one he always got when he mentioned the wedding. "What's the update on that?"

Her thumb briefly touched the band of her engagement ring and flicked away. *Update?* Brad used that word when they discussed events. Their engagement party had been a 1920s-themed affair with a champagne fountain, a jazz band and every other bacchanalian excess attributed to Jay Gatsby. Brad had invited everyone he'd ever met, both in and out of the district, and reveled in every moment. Izzy had finished the evening feeling a lot like Zelda Fitzgerald—struggling to find her place under the dazzling sun that was her fiancé. Since then, every time she thought about the wedding, the full length of her gut burned. Mostly she avoided thinking about it altogether.

But right now, Brad's attention was exclusively on her, his face expectant. A thought slammed into her so hard she almost swayed. They never wanted to talk about the same things anymore.

"You don't have time for a detailed wedding conversation," she said quickly.

"I've got time for a quick update and action points."

She swallowed a sigh and faked enthusiasm. "My ideal wedding is small and intimate on Turtle Island. Just us and your mom and dad."

His grin vanished. "We are *not* sneaking off to get married!"

His words pushed at her and she felt herself leaning back. "A beach wedding with your parents on an exclusive Fijian island is hardly eloping."

"Izzy!" Exasperation circled him like a helix. "People like us don't do understated."

People like us? She had no idea what he meant, but before she could ask he was saying, "I love you, Izzy, and you deserve the best. I want to stand up in front of everyone who knows and loves us and show them how committed I am to you."

Her heart rate picked up at the thought of four hundred people at the wedding. "But you already did that at the engagement party."

"By the time I made my speech, half of them were tanked."

"And you think everyone will be sober at our wedding reception?"

"I'm not talking about the reception. I want the gravitas of a wedding where everyone hears and sees how much you mean to me. Hell, these days the only point of getting married is to make a big splash. A public commitment."

Her racing pulse leaped into the next zone. "I thought I was the only one who needed to hear your commitment?"

Brad plowed his fingers through his hair, his face the same as a bewildered child whose popsicle had just fallen off its stick. "Why are you being like this?"

I'm being me.

"Being like what?"

"Difficult!"

She shook her head as if it would shift his words. "You know crowds stress me out."

He gave a dismissive wave. "You say that, but at all the events we've thrown, not once have I seen you stressed. People comment on how cool and calm you are. Besides, I've never asked you to face a crowd alone. I'll be there beside you like I am at every event."

And this was the problem. "It's not an *event*. It's our wedding!"

"Exactly! And I get a say on how it happens. Hell, I'm paying for it!"

She opened her mouth to hurl, "I'll pay for the wedding I want," when Brad's cell buzzed. Of course he checked it.

"Bloody Mike Essen," he muttered. "they say like father like son, but he's nothing like Jack. I'm seriously regretting letting Dad talk me into letting him join." His fingers punched the screen. "Dad can deal with this."

Izzy sat on the bed, thankful for the interruption. These days there were too many topics that landed them in choppy seas, making her seasick. She steered the conversation toward calmer and less contentious subjects.

"That reminds me, I met Lucy in the bookshop. I said you'd transfer 10,000 into her account."

Brad's cell phone flew towards her. "Jesus, Izzy! Why the hell did you say that?"

She jumped sideways, dodging the phone, then crossed her arms to stop herself from shaking. "To save you from another unnecessary phone call—"

"They're not unnecessary!"

"Then why are you always complaining about them?"

"I don't."

"You do. You just did."

"Mike Essen is in his own league."

Incomplete thoughts spun in her head. "If you involved me more in the business, this would never have happened."

"So you telling Lucy something you know nothing about is my fault? Get real, Izzy." His incredulous look hardened. "And if you had a head for business you'd know that. Sure, Lucy can have ten grand this week, but she and Jack will miss out on Fortune's double dividend."

Guilt crawled all over her, leaving agitation in its wake. "I didn't know. I'll fix it. I'll call and explain."

"No! Leave it. I don't need you making things worse."

Unwanted tears threatened and she tugged at the hair on her crown. "I'm sorry."

Brad huffed out a long sigh, then sat down next to her, resting his head on her shoulder. "Me too. You were trying to help."

"But I didn't."

"No, you didn't, but what I said was unfair. Sorry, Iz."

He looked so hangdog that her natural inclination was to hug him and tell him it was okay. But he'd thrown a cell phone at her and that wasn't okay.

"What's going on, Brad? This angry man isn't you."

The corner of his mouth tweaked up ruefully. "Wedding nerves."

Izzy couldn't laugh. Instead relief fluttered. "Let's wait then. It's not like we need to rush into it."

"I'm joking! Of course we're getting married. Let's fill in the forms and the moment the four weeks are up, we'll do it."

Her breath suddenly came short and sharp and she frantically fought for a rescue plan. "A month's not long enough to pull together the big wedding you want."

"So we'll do it on the island with the Fortune mob, then throw a big party when we get home." He grabbed her hand. "You're my world, Iz. You keep me sane."

You won't leave me, will you, Izzy?

Unwanted memories of her father clutching her hand hammered at her. As she pushed them away, she was aware of her engagement ring heavy on her finger.

"Brad, what's going on? You seem all over the map. You're irritable and strung out and we can't talk about—" *anything*, "—the wedding without arguing."

His brows rose, clearly stating that their arguments about the wedding were her fault. "Iz, the only thing that's changed about me since we met is I love you more today than I did then."

Her throat tightened. Oh God, was she the problem? She loved him, of course she loved him. Didn't she? But lately that wasn't enough to prevent a hollowed-out feeling every time she thought about the wedding.

Who was she kidding? That feeling had arrived the day they got engaged and had only intensified.

Brad may not think he'd changed, but Izzy was certain he had. Lately, she was never sure which version of him she'd meet at any given moment of the day. The distant and preoccupied businessman who yelled and today had thrown a cell phone. The overly intense "Izzy, you're my world, I need you" man, or the optimistic and fun guy she'd fallen for. He seemed deaf and blind to the list of issues that lay between them and multiplied daily. Or perhaps he hadn't changed and she really was the problem?

She twisted the ring as her ears throbbed with her heartbeat. "Maybe we ... perhaps we should see a couples counselor."

He threw his head back and laughed in a way she hadn't heard in a long time. "Oh, Iz, you break me up."

"I'm not jok—"

But he was kissing her and tumbling her back onto the bed.

Stop him! Make him hear you.

But a weary desperation settled over her. Giving in to her body's desire was so much easier than dealing with their never-ending circular arguments about the wedding and the business. So she wrapped her legs around his waist and welcomed him in, hot and fast—needing the fire that burned between them to forge them back together so they were the united couple they'd been during their first year.

When Brad regained his breath, he stroked her cheek. "I know things have been a little rough lately."

He'd never admitted that before. She gazed into his eyes, hope soaring.

"When I get back," he continued, "we'll go to Melbourne for a few days. Just us. No distractions. I promise."

Although they'd recently traveled to Birdsville, Sydney and

Melbourne, they'd never been alone. Judy and Bevan were *always* there, along with other members of the club. Was time alone all they needed? Time away from the constant interruptions—a space where they could hear each other and rediscover their rhythm?

The idea buoyed her and she splayed her hand on his chest. "I've got a better idea. While you're at your three-day business meeting, I'm happy to play on my own in Singapore. After that we can fly to Langkawi and fill our days lazing on the beach and in bed." *And talk.*

He linked his hand through hers. "As amazing as that sounds, I really need you here holding down the fort."

Excitement made her sit up fast. Holding down the fort meant looking after the business. He'd finally heard her, or perhaps he was making amends for his hurtful outburst. Either way, she didn't care because the outcome was the same.

"Are you sure?"

"Absolutely!"

She hugged him, more than happy to give up a shopping vacation for this opportunity. While he was away, she'd create the new payment system to prove she could do it. By the time he got home, there'd be a fully tested, automated email system for off-dividend withdrawals ready for him to activate. All she needed was the passwords to the accounts and—

She suddenly realized Brad was talking and in her excitement she hadn't registered what he was saying. "Sorry, I was lost in my own head there for a bit."

He gave her an indulgent smile. "I was saying Crash Forster's finally replacing the leaky shower in the upstairs bathroom. He's coming tomorrow and so is Hi Tech. They're installing the new security and intercom system, and a bigger office safe."

Her euphoria collapsed. This wasn't an offer to be more hands-on in the business. It was domestic management.

"Their timing sucks," she said flatly. What had her father called it? Murphy's Law. They'd been waiting weeks for the tradespersons to fit them in, so of course it was happening when Brad was away. One of them needed to be at Villefranche to field the inevitable questions and make the unanticipated decisions.

"But wait, there's more." Brad's eyes sparkled the way they always did whenever he was about to give her something. "I've got a surprise. You know that secret garden and daybed you've wanted for ages down by the lake?"

Her brain stumbled, trying to recall any references she'd made about a garden or a daybed. All she could come up with was her request for an even surface for her telescope. A hidden spot with a daybed sounded like something Brad wanted so they had yet another place on the property to have sex outside.

"I wanted that?"

He laughed. "You know you do. Patrick's coming at 8:00 tomorrow with some design ideas. Choose whichever you want and he'll start. We'll christen it when I get home." He checked his watch. "Hell, I have to get going. I'll miss you, gorgeous, but book a suite at the Grand Hyatt for next weekend."

He kissed her and bounced out of bed looking more like his normal self than he had in days. Of course he did. Sex and spending money were his catnip.

Once they'd been hers.

Izzy fell back onto the pillows, uncertain they were enough anymore.

CHAPTER THIRTEEN

BRAD's three days in Singapore were followed by four days in Dubai and now he was in Ireland. Due to the time differences and their various commitments, Izzy had only spoken to him twice. The second call was an argument.

Brad had sent an email asking her to arrange two events—one for Elite and one for Fortune—on the dates she'd booked the Grand Hyatt for their special weekend together. The weekend she'd already moved twice because he kept extending his trip. The weekend where they would talk and iron out all the kinks in their relationship. Who was she kidding? It was way beyond kinks. It was a massive chasm that needed a bridge longer than Melbourne's West Gate to emotionally reconnect them.

Incandescent with rage, she'd reached for her cell phone without checking the time overseas. "You promised!" she'd screeched without preamble when he'd answered the call.

"What?"

The blood pounding in her ears had deafened her to the sleep in his voice. "You promised we'd have a weekend in Melbourne on our own and—"

"Why the hell are you waking me up at 3:00 in the morning about this? I thought Mom or Dad must have died!"

"I feel like part of me is dying!"

"Jesus, Izzy, what's wrong with you? Take a breath. Take four or five and calm the hell down."

"I don't want to calm down!" She'd marched back and forth across the oversized entrance hall that could house a family. "I want you to hear what I'm saying!"

"I'll listen to you when you're being fair and reasonable, but I'm not listening to a premenstrual rant at 3:00 in the morning." He'd hung up on her.

It had taken every ounce of restraint not to hurl her cell phone, but stone was very unforgiving. Instead she'd taken Thor for a run, then driven to campus and worked in the library, because sometimes the silence of Villefranche was too much.

She didn't ring Brad again and he hadn't called her. She'd replied to his email as she would for any client, outlining her plans for the two events, including cost estimates, and she'd requested the okay to send the invitations. A one-line reply came back: *You're the best!*

A couple of days after the angry phone call, Judy invited her for coffee at GGSC. "I thought you'd like the company," she'd said, but once they were at the club it became obvious Judy was on a fishing expedition about the wedding.

Izzy tried steering the conversation toward Brad, hoping to hear that his mother held similar concerns about him. "Brad's been ..." *Moody, irritable.* No, that sounded like she was complaining and Izzy knew that Judy would defend her son ahead of her. "I think he's working too hard. Spreading himself too thin. I'm worried about him."

Judy laughed. "Darling, you're wasting precious energy. You know as well as I do that Brad thrives on a challenge. You'd have more reason to worry if he was bored or not out there seeking the next big thing." She patted Izzy's hand. "Are you sure this isn't more about you? I think you've been a bit lost for a while now and you're ready for a new challenge."

Relief surged, filling the empty spaces inside Izzy. Someone had finally noticed and understood. The fact that it was Judy, who Brad respected and listened to, was a gift. With Judy in her corner, she might finally make some headway with Brad and the business.

"You're right, Judy. I'm so ready for a challenge, to take that next big step. Together, Brad and I will make E—"

"Amazing parents. Everyone knows that, darling." Judy leaned in and dropped her voice. "To be honest, Izzy, it's not work that's stressing Brad, it's you. You're dragging the chain on this wedding and he's champing at the bit to be a dad. Please just set a date and get on with it."

Brad had spoken to his parents about her? The heat of betrayal seared her, and she raised her hand fast from her lap to reach for her hair. But with Judy's gaze fixed on her, she curled her fingers into a fist and forced her hand back under the table. She took a long, deep breath.

"A date to get pregnant?" she asked coolly.

Judy laughed. "Start with a date to get married first. But yes, hopefully you'll be pregnant by the end of the same day."

Izzy forced a smile, finished her coffee, kissed Judy goodbye, then sat in her car and tugged out ten strands of hair. Feeling calmer, but unable to face Villefranche, she drove to Warrnambool and studied in the university library.

Two hours later her stomach ached with hunger so she walked to the café. She was holding a plate of sandwiches and waiting for her latte when one of her lecturers walked in.

"Oh, hi, Izzy," Cooper Barsky said. "Late lunch?"

She gave a wry smile. "I've been trying to beat an essay into submission."

"Are you winning?"

"I'm not sure." She was struggling to zero in precisely on her argument. Two days earlier she'd emailed a draft to Brad asking him for comments and suggestions. He hadn't got back to her.

Cooper indicated an empty table. "Do you want to talk about it?"

"That would be great, but are you sure you have time?"

"I can spare you five minutes while I drink my coffee." He pulled out a chair for her then sat opposite. "What's the problem?"

"Corporate governance. When is it overreach?"

Cooper laughed. "Take ten people and you'll get ten different opinions. It exists to protect all stakeholders and when it works well no one complains or even notices it. Basically, it comes down to the integrity of the board of directors, and to some degree the expectations and demands of the shareholders."

"By the shareholders, do you mean that they keep the bastards honest?"

"Pretty much. You only need a couple of people on the board willing to bend the rules and collude for that culture to trickle down. Private partnerships, fraud, hiding losses and environmental disasters bring companies to their knees. There have been some pretty spectacular falls from grace at annual general meetings."

Izzy had done her research and was aware of some of the infamous cases overseas, and more recently closer to home in Melbourne.

"Everyone thinks of corporate governance in terms of the big companies," she said, "but really, accountability, transparency, fairness and responsibility should be the guiding force of any business whether it's got one or 1,000 employees."

Cooper nodded. "Exactly. Sounds to me like you've got a handle on it."

"Thanks." She gave a rueful smile. "It's transferring that understanding onto the page in a coherent and logical manner that's the hard part."

"Sorry! Can't help you with that." He stirred his coffee. "How's work?"

She had no idea what he was talking about. "I think you're confusing me with another student."

"I don't think so. You work in your partner's IT firm and you did a deep dive on the analytics." He was looking straight at her now, brows raised, gaze expectant. "Did it prove useful?"

"Oh, yes, absolutely," she lied, not wanting to admit that the only things she did for Elite were arranging a few events each month and picking up Brad's shirts from the dry cleaners.

It suddenly hit her that if she sat here any longer Cooper might start asking more detailed questions that she couldn't answer. Circles of panic rippled and she stood quickly, leaving the remaining half of her sandwich. "Thanks for listening, but I need to get back to the office."

"Congratulations."

"Sorry?"

He tilted his head toward the engagement ring. "I think that's new since I saw you."

Inexplicably her panic ramped up. "Oh, right. Yes, um, Brad proposed the day of the presentations."

"Way more exciting than your pass," Cooper joked. "And if it isn't gauche to say, that ring says business is booming."

"We're very lucky," she said faintly, almost as if convincing herself.

He gave an exaggerated sigh, but a smile lifted his lips. "And here I was, hoping I'd taught you and your fellow students that good business outcomes are dependent on far more reliable things than luck."

"Don't worry, Professor." She did her best to mimic him. "Data is king and the numbers don't lie."

"Damn straight." He grinned and raised his coffee cup to her in salute.

Whenever Izzy arrived home, Thor raced to greet her, his whole body quivering in doggy excitement. Today, when she entered the kitchen by the side door, his bed was empty. Thor was past his naughty puppy phase, but she always confined him to the kitchen just in case he decided to fight a cushion or worse. She dumped the shopping on the kitchen counter and noticed the door to the entrance hall was ajar. Damn. She must have forgotten to close it. The dog could be in any of the seventeen rooms.

"Thor!" she yelled into the void of the silent house, then listened for the clack of nails on stone. Nothing. She sighed. She'd stow the cold food in the fridge then go and look for him.

She was just straightening up from loading the crisper with vegetables when Thor snuck under her arm.

"There you are." She ruffled his ears and stared into his eyes. "Please tell me you weren't destroying things?"

"He wasn't."

At the same moment she screamed she knew it was Brad. She swung around, her heart thumping.

"Surprise." He pulled her in for a hug. "Sorry. I didn't mean to scare you. Anyway, why are you so skittish? You know this house has all the security under the sun."

While her body was sinking in relief, her mind was leaping and stalling, trying to absorb the fact that he was in the kitchen.

"I wasn't expecting—weren't you coming home tomorrow?"

He shrugged. "I moved things around so I could get home earlier. Thanks for holding the fort. Oh, and great idea getting the safe installed behind the fake books. I've tested it and it's all good. Did I ever tell you how amazing you are? God, I missed you."

As he leaned in for a kiss, his cell rang.

She pulled away. "Sounds like other people missed you too."

He sighed. "Ray must have dropped into the club for a drink and mentioned he'd picked me up."

"When I was in town yesterday, a few people were asking when you were back. Before you flip out, I didn't promise anyone anything."

He shot her his most charming smile. "Of course I'm not going to flip out. I'm just sorry they bothered you, especially after I'd sent them the dates." The phone buzzed again. "At least I got a quiet hour to unpack. My dirty laundry's in the hamper, the suitcase is away and my passport's back in the filing cabinet ready for next time, which I'm hoping is our honeymoon."

She left the topic of the wedding well alone and pointed to the buzzing phone in his hand. "Aren't you going to call them back?"

"Don't you want your present first?"

Once she'd have danced with excitement at the prospect of a gift, but she'd bet her last dollar it would be another bottle of perfume to add to her growing unopened collection. Each bottle represented a trip he'd taken without her. She glanced around for the post-trip duty-free bag, but Brad was reaching into his pocket then pressing a familiar aqua box into her hand.

She waited for the surge of anticipation, the thrill and the magic that always preceded the opening of a jewelry box. Nothing broke the bleak flatness that stuck to her like glue.

Brad rested his forehead on hers. "Sorry I was gone for longer than expected. I promise you, this will make up for it."

I promise you.

Suddenly the connection between all the gifts he'd bought her shone as brightly as a spotlight on a dark stage. There were the earrings when he'd asked her to organize the first Elite party. The bracelet when he'd asked her to move to Glingilly and work with him. The watch after his first trip away without her, and the numerous trinkets he'd brought home after the many solo trips that followed. With the exception of her engagement ring, every gift was either to convince her to do something or an apology.

Was the engagement ring part of convincing her too? The thought sawed through her like a blunt knife.

"Come on, gorgeous." Brad was looking at her expectantly. "Open it."

Forcing her fingers to cooperate, she prized the edges of the box apart. A pair of diamond-studded horseshoe earrings lay on either side of a matching pendant, its fine gold chain forming a V on the white cushion.

"When I saw these, I just had to buy them." His smile twinkled in his eyes. "They're so perfect for Elite, I was tempted to get my ear pierced. I've put in an order for all the women in Fortune, because the moment you dazzle them with yours, they'll all want a set."

If he noticed she was silent instead of squealing in delight, he didn't comment. Instead he fastened the pendant around her neck and whispered in her ear his fantasy—her lying on the new daybed in the new garden wearing only diamonds.

She forced a smile. "That would have worked in Dubai but it's cold out there and raining. I'll get hypothermia."

He grinned. "There's always the outdoor heater."

For the first time she could remember, the idea of sex with Brad didn't light her up. There wasn't even a tiny spark waiting to be fanned by his clever mouth and knowing fingers. All she could hear—all she'd heard for days—were Judy's words in her head: *You're the problem.*

Suddenly she was fighting to stay upright as a barrage of incidents battered her. Brad's insistence she wait until she'd finished her course before joining the business. His broken promise about their weekend in Melbourne and, worse, his lack of concern about breaking it. Hell, he hadn't even offered her an excuse. She knew there was no point in asking for one—Elite was why. He'd just raise a brow and give her a look that implied she was stupid.

A wave of anger rolled through her at his lack of response to her requests for help with her assignment. It was suddenly glaringly obvious that his comment "Don't let uni get in the way" and his petulant storming out when she'd pulled an all-nighter to finish her presentation were connected. He'd never wanted her to study.

Cooper's words came back to her: "That ring says business is booming."

That Brad loved money was a given. Hell, she loved money too. Who didn't? It eased the way, making life far more enjoyable than just surviving. But there was something else about Brad and money that she hadn't put together until now. Brad not only wanted money, he also wanted to be admired. It was why he'd invited people to Villefranche the moment she'd said "yes" to his proposal—he'd needed them to ooh and ahh over the ring and his ability to purchase it.

It was why he wanted a huge wedding.

And a baby.

Her heart flattened itself against her ribs. Oh my God! She wasn't an equal partner in any of this. She'd never been an equal partner. Brad said he loved her, but did it even matter to him what she wanted?

"You okay, Iz?" Brad's voice sounded a long way away. "You've gone as white as a sheet."

"I—we—"

"Yoo-hoo!" Judy let herself into the kitchen, followed by Bevan, and crossed straight to Brad. "Hello, darling! You got a tan!"

She hugged her son, then turned to Izzy. "How lovely to have him home again. Now we have both of you in the same room, we're not leaving until you've set a date for the wedding."

"I'd get married tomorrow if we could," Brad said.

Izzy turned away and, with a trembling hand, poured a glass of water. She knew exactly what she was doing tomorrow.

It was the complete opposite of marrying Brad.

CHAPTER FOURTEEN

BIRDIE RIPPED the day's page off her countdown calendar and laughed. She felt like a kid with an advent calendar.

Mike had left for golf, so after doing the usual morning tidy-round she made coffee and fired up her laptop, excited to be tackling the list of vacation-related jobs. Each time she ticked off a task, it gave the trip shape, taking it from a pipe dream to reality. The night before, she and Mike had agreed on which of the cruise's onshore tours they would take. Today, she'd book and pay for them in advance, saving almost the full price of one excursion. She'd also convinced Mike to do a walking trip in Tuscany that took them past Roman ruins and into vineyards.

She opened her inbox and a barrage of emails tumbled in—final payment requests for their flights and the car lease, along with a lovely email from their house-sitter. They'd decided to get one to take care of the garden. Jack had offered, and although Birdie knew he'd do it, she was concerned about the two weeks a month he was away for work. Plants could die in that time and Lucy was unlikely to be as committed as Jack. Their own garden was testament to that.

Even though Birdie and Mike were doing their European tour first, it was the big finale—sailing home—that gave Birdie the biggest thrill.

The thought of weeks of being pampered, and knowing that her biggest decision would be what meal to choose off the menu, made her giggle like a child. She planned on doing every activity the cruise offered at least once. She might even get Mike to learn ballroom dancing.

Clicking on the cruise website, she selected the tours and triple-checked her choices. Then she moved on to payment, filled in the details and, with a rush of excitement, clicked the big green button. The messages *please wait* and *do not click again* appeared.

While she waited, she stood and refilled her coffee. When she returned, she was surprised to see the words: *your payment was unsuccessful.*

"Damn it, Mike!"

Two days ago at breakfast she'd asked him to transfer the money into the special vacation account with a different bank that refunded all the international currency conversion fees. After thirty-five years of marriage she should have known better than to remind Mike of anything before he'd eaten his muesli and read the paper, even if he did nod his agreement.

She could transfer the money herself but that wasn't the point. As she'd done the bulk of the planning and organizing of the trip, Mike's job was making sure the funds were in the correct account. She'd already spent over half an hour selecting and triple-checking all the tours. With a to-do list as long as her arm, she just wanted the job done so she submitted the details of their flexi account and pressed pay. They'd be charged a conversion fee, but so be it. It was less than a late fee and it wasn't like they couldn't afford it.

Fifteen seconds later a new screen appeared—a photo of the cruise ship with fireworks exploding above it.

"Yes!" Birdie pumped the air. It was official. They were really going to have a butler for a few weeks!

Her computer pinged as the confirmation email hit her inbox. She opened it, scanned it briefly to check their names and the dates were correct, then filed it in the vacation mailbox. Ninety minutes later everything was paid in full, including a night at the airport hotel, and she'd booked Ray to drive them to Melbourne Airport.

She was just stretching her back when she heard the wire screen door squeak, then voices and the pounding of little feet.

"Grammy! Guess who?" Rigby announced his arrival in his usual way and immediately followed with, "It's me!"

Laughing, she walked into the kitchen and gave him a hug. "It's you."

"And Daddy and Gramps."

"So I see."

"I'm hungry." Rigby ran to the pantry.

"So am I, mate." Jack grinned and dropped a quick kiss on his mother's cheek. "Pre-school duty's hungry work."

She was happy to see them both, but since she'd minded Rigby for a few hours yesterday so Jack could get some jobs done, she hadn't expected to see them again today.

Mike walked in behind them. "So's golf. Is lunch ready?"

Birdie was busy floating on the high of knowing that in less than a month she'd be landing in Paris, so instead of saying "you know where the food's kept," she opened the fridge and pulled out the fixings for sandwiches. "Mike, you make the drinks."

She made Rigby's sandwich first, telling him he could have jam slice after he'd eaten it, and then she whipped up roast beef sandwiches and salad for the adults.

"In a few weeks, you'll be making your own lunches," she said to Jack. "Has Lucy found childcare for when we're away?"

Jack snagged a piece of meat from the chopping board. "The problem's her shift work. No one wants to start at 6:00 in the morning so she's asking her boss about working afternoon shifts for three months. That way the sitter can pick Rigby up at 5:00, do bath, dinner and bedtime, then sit on the sofa for two hours until Lucy gets home."

"And if the hospital says no?"

He shrugged. "She might have to drop a few shifts."

"Can you afford that?"

Jack's mouth pursed. "How about you let us worry about that, eh?"

"Steady, Jack." Mike carried the sandwich platter to the table. "It's just the grandmother guilt talking."

"I do have the right to take a vacation," Birdie said crisply, wiping her hands on a cloth before sitting down. "But I'm sorry it's making things tricky for you."

"We're adults, Mom. We'll sort it out. Actually, we're planning a vacation ourselves. A few weeks away will solve half the childcare problems."

"We're going to a beach with palm trees," Rigby announced. "And a water slide."

"That sounds exciting, sweetie." Birdie looked at Jack. "And tropical."

"As Brad's flying us to Fiji for the wedding, we thought we'd stay longer and take a vacation."

Disappointment swept through Birdie. "So they've announced the date and it's while we're away?" Why hadn't Judy told her?

"All I know is Brad told me to keep July free." Jack bit into his sandwich.

"So you've spoken to him?"

Jack nodded. "Last week."

"When he was in Ireland?" Mike confirmed.

"Yeah."

Mike grunted. "Lucky for some."

"I ran into Ray on the way here and Brad got in yesterday. I'm sure he'll be in touch soon," Jack said.

"Good, because the report's late," Mike said.

"By a day, Dad. Chill. He'll sort it today, he always does."

"Your father's addicted to checking the Fortune balance," Birdie teased. "He gets withdrawals when he can't see the numbers."

Jack grinned. "You should try it, Mom. It's pretty exciting watching them climb. What's it up to now?"

Mike put down his sandwich and reached for his cell. Birdie would have said, "No devices at the table," but her mouth was full of food.

Mike was staring at the screen, a frown carving deep between his eyes. "Is the internet down?"

"Turn off Wi-fi and use your data," Jack suggested.

Mike swiped screens and tried again. "It's still not loading."

Jack pulled out his cell phone and Birdie said, "Surely this can wait until after lunch?"

"It'll only take a sec. Once we get the app, we won't have these issues," Jack said.

"Jam slice, please." Rigby handed Birdie his now empty plate.

"You can have it when Grammy's finished—"

"I can't get Elite to load either," Jack said. "The server must be down."

"Phones away then," Birdie said. "Let's have some conversation. Ask me what I did this morning."

Mike reluctantly placed his cell phone on the table. "What did you do this morning?"

Exhilaration bubbled inside her. "I paid for the vacation."

Mike's frown deepened. "I thought you were doing that tomorrow."

She blew out her frustration that he didn't listen. "We're going to Melbourne to see that play tomorrow, which is why I told you I was doing it today."

"But the money isn't in the account."

"So I discovered. I used the flexi account. What we lose on conversion fees, we save on credit-card fees." Mike had picked up the cell again. "Mike!"

But he ignored her shrewish tone, his attention fixed on the cell. "Damn it!"

"What?"

Mike was pushing back his chair. "The Fortune deposit still hasn't arrived. I don't care if Brad's jet lagged, I'm calling him."

"Tell him about the server." Jack was refreshing his phone screen. "He might not know."

Birdie sighed and gave up on a convivial lunch. She cut Rigby some jam slice before switching on the kettle.

Mike had walked into another room and although she couldn't make out his words, the agitation in the low rumble of his voice was clear.

Mike reappeared and paced. "Brad's not answering his cell phone so I left a message. Then I called the bank who just gave me the usual 'it can take three days' schtick."

"Brad's probably taking a nap." Birdie still couldn't wrap her head around the fact that it took twenty-four hours to fly from Dublin to Melbourne.

Jack rolled his eyes. "He's not ninety, Mom. More likely he's taking a well-earned day off and enjoying a big welcome home from Izzy."

Mike muttered something about other people's money, then asked abruptly, "Bird, do you have Izzy's number?"

"No. I've never needed it. Why—"

"Jack, do you have Izzy's number?" Mike demanded.

"Probably." Jack scrolled through his contacts, then frowned. "Maybe I put her number with Brad's." He scrolled back the other way, then shook his head. "Why do you want it?"

"Because she'll either be with Brad or she'll pass on a message."

"But you've already left a message," Jack said. "Give the bloke some space."

Mike grimaced. "Call Lucy then."

"I doubt she has it. She and Izzy are hardly BFFs."

"Why is that do you think?" Birdie mused. She had her own thoughts but was interested in Jack's take.

"Just call Lucy, okay?" Mike said.

"She's asleep, Dad," Jack said firmly. "And she'll kill me if I wake her up without a good reason."

A vein bulged in Mike's neck. "This is a bloody good reason!"

Jack threw Birdie a look that combined confusion with exasperation, then looked back at his father. "Why are you freaking out? Brad will call you when he can. If half the club members are losing their sh—reacting like you, he'll never get the server sorted."

Jack's and Mike's cell phones pinged.

"He's just sent a text about the server being down," Jack said.

"I don't care about the bloody server!" Mike said. "It's the money."

Birdie placed her hand on Mike's arm, wondering why he was so het up. "Take a breath, sit down and drink your tea. You know the bank sometimes takes longer to release the payment, but if it's going to send you into a tailspin like this, perhaps we need to open an account with the same bank as Brad."

Mike sat but his leg jigged up and down. "What if it's not the bank?"

"Of course it's the be—"

"What are you really saying, Dad?" Jack asked tightly. "Is this another go at Brad?"

"I'm saying that getting money out of Fortune is like getting blood out of a stone."

"We haven't had any trouble," Jack said.

"You're not in Fortune," Mike said.

"Oh, yeah, right." Jack hit his forehead with his palm.

Rigby copied him, then looked surprised. "That hurt. Why you do that, Daddy?"

Jack laughed and tousled Rigby's hair. "Daddy's silly."

Mike stood again. "Whenever I ask for money above the dividend amounts, Brad's always got a reason why I shouldn't withdraw it."

"To be fair," Birdie said, "it's so we don't miss out on an opportunity."

"Yeah, Dad. Brad can't win. You'd be pissed if he wasn't looking after your best interests."

"Maybe." Mike's mouth hardened. "But there's no point having the damn money if we can't access it. When I emailed Brad and asked him to transfer the vacation funds he replied, 'Sure, no worries.' The money never showed up. I've emailed him three times since. First he replied apologizing for forgetting in the rush of going OS. The second time he blamed the bank. He hasn't replied to the one I sent yesterday."

"Like Jack said, he's busy sorting out the server issue," Birdie soothed. "I'm sure he'll call tomorrow, and if not you'll see him on Saturday at lunch. Judy said Izzy's planned a—"

"If he hasn't called by 5:00 today, I'm driving out to Villefranche," Mike said.

"Jeez, Dad, that's a bit aggressive! And it puts me in a tricky spot if my father and my best mate aren't getting along. Tell you what? When I get home, I'll give him a call. He'll probably pick up for me."

"Good luck with that," Mike muttered.

Birdie rolled her eyes. "I think Gramps needs to take a nap with you, Rigby."

The little boy's eyes widened at the idea of his grandfather needing a nap. "He's too big for my bed."

Mike's cell phone rang and he grabbed it, read the screen, then slumped. "It's Oscar."

"Didn't you just see him at golf?" Birdie asked.

"Nah, he was a no show. Oscar!" Mike rose and walked out of the room.

Jack was fiddling with his cell phone again and Birdie lost all patience. "I'm not a café with free wi-fi!"

Jack didn't respond.

"Jack!"

He glanced up, clearly confused. "Sorry, Mom. I just saw something I thought Lucy had—doesn't matter. I'll check with her when she wakes up. Thanks for lunch. I better get Rig—"

"Something's up." Mike returned to the kitchen, plowing a hand through his hair. "Both Oscar and Alan are waiting on money too."

"Yeah, well, everyone is. Dividend day's Saturday," Jack said.

"No, I mean ex gratia," Mike said. "Nah, that's the wrong word because it's our bloody money!"

"Who do Alan and Oscar bank with?" Birdie asked.

"Same as the club," Mike said. "They're not subject to the same delays as us."

"What are you saying?" Birdie asked.

"I'm saying we can rule out the bank as the problem."

"There'll be a reasonable explanation." Jack tapped his phone. "It's probably connected to the server going down."

"And I'd agree, except that only happened today. Like me, Oscar and Alan have been chasing money from Brad for weeks."

Birdie rolled her eyes. "This isn't a conspiracy theory. The boy's been overseas."

Mike glared at her. "He's not a boy, Birdie, he's a businessman and we live in a global world. There was nothing stopping him transferring money while he was away. All he needs is the internet. You can't tell me that's impossible to find in Singapore, Dubai or Ireland."

"Rigby, sweetheart, you can get down and go watch *PAW Patrol*," Birdie said, wanting him out of the room.

"Yay!" Rigby raced into the other room.

When the familiar tune of the show started, Birdie said to Mike, "There's no need to use that tone with me, thank you very much. Surely if there was something wrong, Bevan or Judy would have told us. Call Bev and ask."

"They flew to Coolangatta this morning, remember? Judy's dragged him to some eco-health spa next to a national park and there's no cell phone reception."

"I'll ring the retreat. Surely they'll pass on a message," Birdie said.

Jack was pressing his cell to his ear and muttering, "Pick up, pick up."

"Brad isn't taking Oscar's and Alan's calls either," Mike said grimly.

"Luce, sorry to wake you but it's important." Jack rubbed the back of his neck. "No, he's fine ... yes ... we're at Mom's. It's about the last mortgage payment ..."

Birdie could hear Lucy's voice, but she couldn't make out the words.

Then Jack was saying, "Yes, but I thought ... Right. Okay. Yeah. Sorry ... Sorry! I'll sort it. Go back to sleep."

Birdie heard a screech of fury from Lucy as Jack hung up. He immediately made another call, but quickly sighed and turned to face them.

"It turns out our transfer hasn't come through either, and calls to Brad's number go—"

"Straight to voice mail," Mike said. "I know."

Four failed bank transfers? Birdie's gut loosened and she pressed her hand to her belly. "There'll be a good reason. Technology fails. Perhaps Brad—" Mike picked up his keys. "Where are you going?"

"To the club. I'm meeting Oscar, Alan and Jim and we're ringing all the Elite and Fortune members. We want to know if it's just us or if other club members have asked for above dividend monies and not received them. And what line Brad's spun them."

Birdie's mind raced. "And what if there's more than you four?"

"We talk to the credit union and rule out any problems their end."

Agitation skittered along her veins and her stomach gave a violent lurch. "Just talk to Brad."

Mike's jaw set hard. "I've compared notes with Al and Oscar and none of us believes a word that comes out of his mouth. Oscar wants to go to the police."

"The police? That's crazy!" Jack said. "It's one time he's been late with a request."

Mike shook his head. "It's not one time. Your mom and I've been asking for the vacation money for weeks and each time he's given us a reason not to pay. We've believed him but not anymore. Now it's smelling seriously off."

Birdie didn't want to think about what that meant so she concentrated on the consequences of the group going to the police. "Brad's family. He only has our best interests at heart. If you go to the police before talking to him—before talking to Judy and Bevan— they'll never forgive you."

Forgive us.

Birdie looked to Jack for support. "Tell your father Oscar's overreacting as usual. Tell them they all need to calm down."

"Brad needs to talk to the club and explain whatever the hell this glitch is," Jack said. "I'll come too. Mom, can you mind Rigby until Lucy's awake?"

Birdie was suddenly torn. "Surely I should go to the meeting too, if only to be the level head!"

"You have Dad representing you. I need to be there for me and Luce."

Birdie gave a distracted nod and looked straight at Mike. "You're all jumping to ridiculous conclusions. There's a reasonable explanation for the delay. There has to be."

He gave her an agonized look. "Let's hope like hell there is."

CHAPTER FIFTEEN

THIS ISN'T HAPPENING.

Izzy sat on the cold stone stairs inside Villefranche while two police officers stood watching her every move. Her breath came short and fast as she desperately tried to leash her rising panic. It wasn't just that Brad was late home, he was also the focus of a police investigation. And she was a person of interest.

"Make things easier on yourself, Izzy," Brooke Riglioni said kindly. "Tell us where Brad is."

Izzy threw up her hands. "That's the problem. I don't know where he is."

"Come on, Ms. Harrington," Mitchell said. "That answer's getting old."

Izzy's hand made a fist, surprising her with its contained violence. More than anything she wanted to punch the detective between the eyes. "If you think Brad's gone somewhere then you know more than I do."

"Then tell us where you're going," Brooke said.

"I told you." Izzy forced the words through tight lips. "Geelong."

Brooke's brown eyes filled with resigned disappointment and distrust. "To Geelong with your passport?"

Brad, where the hell are you? Walk in now so all this stops.

Fear jabbed at Izzy. Should she tell the police she was leaving Brad? Would that make things better or worse? Right now they didn't believe that she had no idea where Brad was, so why would they believe she was leaving him?

"I can assure you everything has a logical explanation." Her voice sounded distant against the throb of blood in her ears. "I have my passport so I can prove 100 points for ID at the bank. And Brad always tells me when he's traveling, even when it's last minute, so he hasn't left the country. We share a joint calendar and I can show—"

"He was seen driving out of town at 2:00 this afternoon," Mitchell said.

"Which direction?" Izzy focused on trying to sound cool and in control against the trembling forces of adrenaline.

"Toward Warrnambool."

She snorted. "He does that every day. Last time I checked, it wasn't a crime."

"It's not a crime, it's a fact. Just like your bags being packed but not in your car is a fact. A fact that points to you waiting to be collected," Mitchell said. "What time's the taxi coming?"

"I haven't booked a taxi. Ring Ray, he'll tell you."

"It's not unusual for people to slip out of the country on separate flights," the detective said.

"This is ridiculous!" Fury propelled Izzy to her feet. "I'm going to Geelong! And why would Brad leave the country one day after he just got back? Like I keep telling you, I'm expecting him to walk in any minute."

"Unfortunately, your word's not enough proof," Mitchell said.

"Fine! I'll give you proof!"

She marched to the office, thankful that Brad always unpacked thoroughly the moment he got home. The words he'd spoken yesterday rang loud in her head: "My passport's in the filing cabinet ready for next time, which I'm hoping is our honeymoon."

She opened the bottom drawer of the wooden filing cabinet and located a document holder that until earlier in the day had rested in front of her own. She dumped the contents onto the French oak desk. Brad's birth certificate, his university transcripts and a half-completed Notice of Intended Marriage form fell out. She bit her lip against a wave of regret—she hadn't realized he'd downloaded the forms.

She shook the folder again and an expired multi-currency card joined the pile. Dread sank her stomach so fast she heard the clunk as it hit the floor. The only time Brad's passport wasn't in the document holder was when he was traveling.

He'd gone. Left without a word.

She wasn't leaving Brad—he'd left her.

The room spun around her and she gripped the edge of the desk to stay standing. Desperation made her will the empty document holder to act like Mary Poppins' bag and produce Brad's passport so she could wave it triumphantly at Detective Mitchell.

Prove to him Brad hadn't left the country.

Prove he hadn't left her without a word, exactly like her mother.

Prove she wasn't a suspect in God knew what.

Her hands ached to pull her hair and she clenched her fingers, trying to keep them by her sides. Slowly, she turned to face the detective and Brooke.

"His passport isn't here, but that doesn't—"

"Surprise, surprise," Mitchell said drily.

Earlier the detective had said, "You're flying out to meet Brad." At the time, it had made no sense to Izzy. It still didn't, but something about the words and his tone kickstarted her brain.

"If Brad got on an international flight, he'd have gone through immigration and you'd know. Are you telling me he's left the country?"

Mitchell shrugged. "We'd only know if he used that passport."

"What other passport would he use? He's only got one."

Brooke gave Izzy a look that managed to combine pity with razor-sharp suspicion. The police knew something, but what? Sweat broke out on her palms.

"So he's still in the country?" she said.

"You tell us," Mitchell said.

"I've told you the truth! I expected him home by now."

Keep it together. She tugged on her hair and concentrated on breathing slowly.

"Brad's really close to his parents. I can text them. They might have heard from him."

"We believe they've left town too," Brooke said.

It took her a second to remember. "Oh! Yes, of course. They flew out this morning to a retreat in northern New South Wales."

"Convenient," Mitchell said. "Odd that you weren't invited."

"What?" Izzy looked at Brooke, who returned her frantic stare with an impassive one. "Why would I be? I don't vacation with Judy and Bevan."

"According to Mike Essen, Alan Lumsden and Oscar D'Angelo, you were recently in Birdsville, Sydney and Melbourne with them," Brooke said.

"Yes, but they were work functions. Not a vacation."

Mitchell's bushy brows rose. "We're obviously in the wrong job, Officer."

Izzy wished she had gone on retreat with Judy and Bevan and then she wouldn't have the police in her home treating her like a criminal.

The retreat. Her stomach dropped so fast, she thought she might vomit. It had seemed such an odd vacation choice for Judy and Bevan. Neither of them was the type to "go off the grid" and they enjoyed their wine too much to cheerfully give it up for a week.

Her mind bounced between conversations, unable to verify if they were truths or lies. Judy insisting on a wedding date. Last night's argument between Brad and his parents about them missing the Elite event. Had it been staged? But why? Incomplete thoughts whirled in her mind, none making sense.

"Are you implying that Brad and his parents have left the country together?" she asked Brooke.

"We're not implying anything. But we believe you're the key to unlocking the mess they've left behind."

"What mess?" She knew she sounded inane parroting back questions, but she had no idea what the hell was going on.

"No need to play coy, Ms. Harrington," Mitchell said. "To quote an interview Brad gave to the *Standard* at the Glingilly Cup," he made quotation marks with his fingers, "'I couldn't do all that I do without Izzy. We're a team in the true sense of the word.' So we know you know a hell of a lot more than we do."

Izzy threw up her hands. "I don't know what you're talking about."

"Tell us about your role at Elite," Brooke said in her usual even tone.

Izzy's stress dropped a notch. "I'm the events manager. I send out invitations, liaise with caterers and the party hire company, and I make sure the guests are having a good time. I don't know much about the day-to-day running of the business."

"Is that so?"

Mitchell's body language screamed "I don't believe you," and the irony wasn't lost on Izzy. For months she'd begged to be more involved in the business and Brad had refused her. Now a copper thought she knew far more than she did.

"Yes, it is so," she ground out, gripping the edge of Brad's ridiculously enormous desk. "And it wasn't from want of asking."

Mitchell ignored the comment. "And you pay the caterer and the party hire company?"

"I do."

"And where does the money come from?"

"The events account."

Their questions peppered her like shot. Brooke had flipped open a notepad and was scribbling furiously.

"And where does that money come from?" Mitchell demanded.

"From the main Elite account. All of this is just standard busin—"

"Where's the missing money, Isobel?" Mitchell asked.

The words hit like an electric current and every muscle jerked. Glancing frantically between the two police officers, she tried glimpsing something—anything—that hinted at what the hell was going on.

"Wh-what?"

"A large sum of money's disappeared and we think you know exactly where it is," Mitchell said.

Izzy's fingers prickled with pins and needles and she recognized the beginnings of a panic attack. *Not now.* She tried slowing her breathing.

"Isobel, we need you to come down to the station and answer a few questions," Brooke said.

Every hair on Izzy's body stood to attention and her mouth dried. "Are you arresting me?"

"At this stage, it's a line of inquiry."

The words did little to reassure her.

"I'm texting Brad and his parents," she said, not exactly sure why she was telling the police officers. "They'll get back to me and this whole misunderstanding will be explained."

"We don't share your confidence, Ms. Harrington," Mitchell said. "it's our experience that when a sizeable amount of money goes missing, people vanish, leaving one person behind to face the music. Looks like you're it."

A chill iced the length of her spine. "I want an attorney."

"The guilty ones always do," Mitchell said to Brooke as if Izzy wasn't in the room.

I want a friend. But the one woman Izzy may have considered for the role was hinting at a future arrest.

With her ex-fiancé missing and his parents possibly with him, she was utterly alone.

CHAPTER SIXTEEN

Lucy struggled through the back door clutching groceries, thankful it was Friday morning and she had five full days before she had to return to work. It had been a busy shift with three babies lured into the world by a full moon. She'd stayed late for a staff meeting, then stopped by the supermarket before treating herself to a latte and a quick bookshop browse on the way home. Now it was ten and she was faint with fatigue. She needed another coffee stat and something sweet to spark her up.

Coming off nights was always hard but she hated wasting a precious minute of her time off by day-sleeping. The weather was glorious so she'd bought picnic supplies for an impromptu visit to Tower Hill Wildlife Reserve and some family bonding time. After yesterday, they needed it. Jack had woken her for no good reason, then dumped Rigby on his mother so he could go and drink at the club with his father. If that wasn't bad enough, he'd left her to bear the brunt of Birdie's disapproval, which had reached out and whipped her when she'd arrived at Cork Street. To make matters worse, Jack had only got home moments before she needed to leave for work. She'd been too furious with him to have a coherent conversation and had barely managed a civil goodbye.

But today, out in the bush, they could relax and talk. Jack would apologize for his aberration and tell her to lie on the picnic blanket and relax while he cooked sausages. Then the three of them would do some koala and echidna spotting on the boardwalk. Rigby would love it, and the sunlight would help keep her awake.

"Hi, Ja..." The greeting died as she took in the scene.

Last night's dishes sat in the kitchen sink, Rigby was still in his pajamas and glued to the television, and Jack was sitting at the kitchen table, shoulders slumped and his head buried in his hands.

The residual embers of yesterday's anger flared. "Bloody hell, Jack! This isn't fair!"

He raised his head and the look in his eyes eviscerated her. She dropped the shopping and ran to him.

"Oh my God! What's happened? Who's hurt? Has someone died?"

Jack blinked frantically, but it wasn't enough to prevent tears rolling through his stubble. When he opened his mouth, no words came out, just a raw and primal sound.

"Daddy?" Rigby shot to his feet, ran to Jack and tried to crawl onto his lap.

Lucy's mind whirled. If either of his parents were sick or worse, someone at the hospital would have told her. Unless it had happened in the last half an hour.

She opened her mouth to ask again, but Jack shook his head—*not in front of Rigby.*

Oh God. One of his parents was dead a month before their trip of a lifetime.

Rigby touched Jack's damp face. "Are you sad, Daddy?"

Jack's body shuddered and he sucked in a steadying breath. "I just banged my funny bone."

Rigby scrambled down and kissed Jack's elbow. "All better now," he announced.

"Thanks, mate." Jack's voice was strained. "You go back to *Bluey.*"

"Okay." He ran back to the screen.

Jack stood, took Lucy's hand and tilted his head toward the study. Once inside she pulled the door to so she could still hear the television, then sat facing him, their knees touching. She placed her hands on his thighs and braced herself.

"Is it Birdie or Mike?"

Jack spoke so softly she strained to hear.

"Sorry, what?" she asked.

"It's gone."

"What's gone?"

"The money."

"Money?" Her mind, which was racing along the road of illness and death, suddenly screeched on the brakes and threw a U-turn. "What are you talking about?"

He swallowed, his Adam's apple bouncing wildly. "The Elite and Fortune bank accounts. They're empty."

Time stood still as her brain fumbled to decode the words, then immediately fought their meaning.

"That's not even possible," she said firmly. "You're only talking about the betting account, right?" She chewed her lip. "I mean, we always knew this could happen. It's why Brad keeps a reserve in case of a disaster like this."

"Brad's gone."

"Gone?" The word only added confusion to her already struggling mind. "As in gone on another business trip?"

Jack shook his head. "He's left town. No one knows where he is."

Lucy saw the agony of betrayal written in the sag of Jack's mouth and in the lines around his eyes. Her latte lurched to the back of her throat.

"Are you saying he *stole* the money?"

He shrugged. "I honestly don't know. In the thirty-two years I've known him, I've never seen him steal a thing, but the evidence is stacking up. It's not looking good."

"What do you mean?"

"He got home from Ireland on Wednesday afternoon and by Thursday lunchtime the Elite server was down and he wasn't answering his cell phone. By the time we involved the police, the bank accounts were empty."

"You've known since yesterday?" Jack's uncharacteristic behavior suddenly made sense. "Why didn't you say anything last night instead of letting me get all bent out of shape and stomp out to work angry with you?"

He gave her a rueful look. "I didn't want to worry you. Not until I knew for sure."

"Oh, Jack." She wanted to both shake him and hug him.

He rubbed his face, the action a mixture of bewilderment and exhaustion. "Yesterday, I was hoping like hell Dad and Oscar were wrong. And to be honest, you being pissed at me for a few hours was a hell of a lot easier than dealing with the possibility my best mate was ripping off half the town."

Her gut spasmed so hard she doubled over. "Your parents' retirement fund!" A gray tinge washed over Jack's face and she moved to reassure him. "The police will find Brad and Izzy and the money. Even if they've left the country—"

"Izzy's still here."

"What? Why?" It was another disorienting piece of information added to a growing pile.

"All I know is Dad spoke to a journo from the *Standard* and he told him when the police arrived at Villefranche, Izzy's bags were packed and she was leaving."

A tiny beam of pleasure penetrated Lucy's shock. "Nothing says guilt like Gucci luggage. Why didn't they leave together?"

"I don't know! And I don't bloody care!" He suddenly pushed back from her. "Fuck, Luce! We haven't just lost the dividends, we've lost our ten K, the 50,000, the lot. It's all gone!"

A violent shiver tore across her skin—as sharp and as painful as an ice storm, chilling her to the bone. She shook her head hard, but she wasn't certain if the action was to warm herself or to disagree with Jack.

"We have the house," she said, desperately seeking something positive they could cling to.

"Only if we meet our mortgage repayments."

She ran familiar numbers through her head. "We can do that. It will be like before we joined Elite when we were only paying the monthly minimum."

Jack grimaced. "It's not just the bank, remember? We owe the finance company 50,000 dollars."

This time her stomach contents reached her mouth. "We'll talk to the bank. We're ahead on the mortgage. Surely they'll let us pay a lower monthly rate."

"I don't think there's a 'surely' about anything to do with the bank. We can't afford the loan repayments *and* mortgage repayments, even if they're reduced."

The reality settled over her like cling wrap—tight and suffocating. "At twenty-one percent, if we miss any loan repayments it will balloon out to 100,000 in no time flat."

"You think I don't know that?" He raked his hands through his hair. "We'll have to sell the house."

"No!" Panic gripped her. After spending her childhood shuttled between acrimonious parents, her Glingilly house was the first place that was truly home. "We can't. We're so close to owning it."

"We're not," Jack said firmly. "We've added 50,000 dollars to the mortgage."

Her heartbeat thundered as fast as a baby's. "We'll run the numbers when we're less stressed."

"What do you think I've been doing all night? It doesn't matter which way I come at it, we're screwed."

"There's got to be a way, Jack! We'll talk to the bank."

"Sure." But he sounded utterly defeated. "If delaying the inevitable makes you feel better—but the answer will stay the same. We have to sell the house."

"But this is *our* dream home. We've worked so hard and poured everything we have into it. We don't deserve this. There has to be another way!"

He put his hands into hers. "Luce, if we do nothing and miss a loan repayment, we'll be bankrupt by the end of the year and they'll repossess the house. If we sell now, we can pay off the finance company and the bank."

Bankrupt? Her mind shied away from the horrifying reality, seeking something less terrifying.

"If we sell we'll have money leftover, right? Enough for a deposit on a smaller house?"

"That's the plan. The property market's buoyant and who wouldn't love this house?"

"But it's our home." Tears burned her eyes, but then her sorrow was swamped by volcanic rage. "I freakin' hate Brad and Izzy. When they find him, I'm going to kill him."

Jack hugged her. "You'll be at the end of a very long line."

CHAPTER SEVENTEEN

FEAR KNITTED ITSELF INTO BIRDIE, making her throat so tight that swallowing was impossible. She flattened herself against the rough brick wall and risked a glance down the dark alley. The orange flare of a lighter illuminated the silver flick of a blade. Everything inside her turned to water. She felt a drop of dampness on her thigh.

Suddenly she was underwater, unable to pull air into her lungs. Panicked, she looked at the air gauge on the scuba tank. The black arrow flickered just above zero.

Move! Go! Up!

Frantic with panic, she kicked her legs. Her lungs burned. Her head throbbed. She looked up, calculating the distance to the surface, but she was no longer underwater. For a brief moment she dared to relax, thankful to be on solid ground, until the pain of sharp stones digging into the soles of her feet made her look down. Her toes were curled tightly around a crumbling ledge.

She gasped, horror streaking through her already adrenaline-soaked body. There was nothing below her but air—tens of thousands of feet of it. She was teetering on the precipice of a mountain.

Step back! Slowly. Do it slowly.

She was carefully uncurling the toes of her right foot when a whoosh of moving air made her look up. A crow—its inky darkness broken only by its bead-like yellow eye—scolded her harshly then flew straight at her. Instinctively she lifted her arms to protect her face. Her toes uncurled. The stones slipped under her soles. She screamed, the sound eddying around her as she fell.

Birdie's eyes flew open, her skin slick with sweat. Her nightie was tangled tightly over her chest and the bedsheet covered her face. Panting, she threw it off and sat up. Rays of sunshine lit up the room and very slowly she recognized the floral curtains, her dressing table and a pile of Mike's discarded clothes on the floor.

Just a nightmare. Her heart rate slowed and her breathing steadied. She was home. She was safe.

The other side of the bed was empty and as she glanced at the clock—8.45 A.M.—the horror of the previous days rushed back so fast she gagged. She'd woken from one nightmare to face another. All of their retirement fund and savings had vanished in a flash, as if a magician had waved a wand over the balance and sucked it out of existence.

Brad had vanished too, and Judy and Bevan were still either uncontactable or refusing to return their calls. Isobel Harrington had locked herself in Villefranche and was refusing to talk to anyone other than her mandated interviews with the police.

Birdie's eyes closed under the unrelenting weight of her new and hideous reality. Wanting to hide, she was sliding back under the covers when she heard the click of the back door closing and the heavy tread of feet. A long sigh rolled out of her. If she didn't get up, Mike would come and find her.

A few minutes later when she walked into the kitchen, Mike was staring at the coffee machine as if it was a completely unfamiliar piece of equipment that had landed on the counter from another galaxy.

"You're up," he said listlessly.

"So are you." She switched on the machine and ground coffee beans.

"I couldn't sleep." His tone was accusatory, as if her four hours of slumber were a crime. "So I went for a walk."

She frothed milk. "Did it help?"

"Nothing's going to bloody help," he snapped. "We've lost all our retirement fund and you spent our savings on a freakin' vacation!"

She fought both choking guilt and the desire to throw coffee at him. "I didn't know that a lying cheating prick was going to steal all our money! And blaming me isn't helping."

Mike sat hard, his body half-falling into the chair, then he propped his elbows on the table and supported his unshaven chin. When had he last showered? Probably Thursday morning when their world was still on an even keel.

"Sorry, Birdie. It's just that if you'd waited we—"

"'If only' won't change a thing," Birdie said briskly, desperate to move on from the circular conversations of the last day and a half. "We need a plan. We've paid for the vacation so we should take it."

Mike stared at her as if she had two heads. "Have you lost your mind? We don't have any spending money. Hell, we hardly have enough for groceries and fuel."

"So we change the flights and just do the cruise. At least they feed us!"

"No!" Mike thumped the table with his fist. "We're canceling the trip."

To be this close to their trip of a lifetime and not go was inconceivable. "But we'll lose eighty percent of our money!"

"Leaving twenty percent we need." He shook his head. "You don't seem to understand. We have nothing, Birdie. Nothing!"

Thinking about their bank balance terrified her so she'd been doing her best to avoid it. "We own the house."

"And thank God for that, but it won't feed us. Tomorrow morning I'm calling Brett. I have to get my job back."

His words bit hard, reinforcing the loss of all their money, their retirement plans and associated dreams.

"How could *he* do this to us?" She refused to say that fraudster's name.

Mike grimaced. "The returns were too good."

"No! We saw the money in the bank accounts. Saw the figures on the spreadsheet."

"Who the hell knows what he was showing us? I should have listened to my gut."

"You listened to Bevan!"

A blast of fury made her spill her coffee. When she'd mopped it up she reached for her cell. No missed calls from Judy. No texts. Another wave of overwhelming disorientation hit her.

"Why haven't they called? That boy was always a bit too slick and charming, but not Judy and Bevan. There's no way they set out to destroy our lives. We're their—" tears spilled and she choked on her words, "—best friends!"

Mike made a growling sound in the back of his throat. "I don't fucking know! You know I don't know, so stop asking!"

She flinched, as much from his lack of patience as the swearing. In all their years together, Mike had rarely sworn. His usual way of dealing with catastrophe was tight silence while he churned through all the scenarios and their options. Birdie was the one to talk it out, trying to weave together a loose understanding. When their two different approaches crossed, they argued. They'd done more yelling in the last two days than in all their married life.

They drank their coffee in taut silence, broken only by their cell phones beeping almost simultaneously. They looked at each other, hope clear in their eyes.

"It'll be the police," Birdie said. "They've found *him* and the money."

Mike nodded. "And I'll take a great deal of pleasure in being a witness for the prosecution. He'll rue the day he ripped off the town that raised him."

They turned their phones over, but it wasn't the police. Nor was it Judy or Bevan.

"It's Jack," Mike said flatly.

They hadn't seen Jack since the night their world imploded. A part of Birdie had expected—hoped—Jack and Lucy would visit to check that she and Mike were okay. Check they hadn't done anything stupid now that their house was the only thing that lay between them and destitution. But perhaps Jack and Lucy had been giving them space to —what was the jargon these days? Process. Birdie huffed at the thought. It would take them longer than the rest of their lives to bloody process this catastrophe. The money was one thing. The betrayal was something else entirely.

She read the text: *Can we come over?* She tapped a reply: *Bring lunch*

Jack sent back a confused emoji that Birdie ignored. She was beyond cooking. Hell, they could barely afford to feed themselves, let alone their adult children.

Mike looked up from his phone, his face drawn—he'd aged a decade in two days. Had she? A random thought hit, eviscerating her with the truth. She could no longer afford the cost of having her hair colored every few weeks.

Birdie pulled her thoughts back to Jack and Lucy, needing to focus on something positive. "At least we can be thankful for one thing," she said.

"What's that?"

"The kids only had a few thousand dollars in Elite. Thank God they couldn't afford Fortune."

Mike nodded. "And they've both got good jobs and their house is almost paid off."

"After all the help we've given them, I hope they can help us."

Mike stood abruptly. "Bloody hell, Birdie! We're not begging for money from our kids!"

She wanted to hurl, "There's no need to speak to me in that tone," but instead she said as calmly as she could, "Where are you going?"

"To call Brett about a job."

"But it's Sunday."

"And tomorrow's Monday, which is a good day to start work."

"Ring Bevan too," she called to his retreating back. But she knew he'd already rung him so many times the number was burned onto the phone screen.

Birdie forced herself through the shower, blow-dried her hair and brushed blush onto her cheeks. When Jack and Lucy arrived—without lunch—she looked like her normal self even though she felt a million times removed from it.

To stay standing, she kept her mind fixed on the minutiae— making cups of tea, helping Rigby with a puzzle, and dumping a container of dip, some crackers and cherry tomatoes in the middle of the table.

Jack eyed the offering, clearly disappointed. "You okay, Mom?"

She'd never been aware of her blood pressure rising before, but she felt the lift that almost blew off her head. "In which universe can you possibly imagine I'm okay?" Her voice rose. "We've lost all our retirement fund and our savings. We've paid for a vacation we can't take and your father's going back to work instead of enjoying a well-deserved retirement!"

Jack took a step back. "Right. Sorry, Mom."

Lucy pulled an iPad out of her voluminous tote bag, swiped the screen and gave it to Rigby along with a snack box. "Go into Gramps' office and watch it, okay?"

Rigby's eyes lit up as if he couldn't believe his good fortune.

"Don't make a mess!" Mike said curtly. "And don't touch the computer."

Rigby stilled, his entire body wary. He'd never heard his grandfather sound cross before. "I won't, Gramps," he said quietly.

"It's okay, buddy." Lucy gave Rigby a gentle push toward the study. "When you've watched two *Blueys* come back and get your drink."

Once Rigby had left the room, Jack said, "We wanted him out of the way while we talk."

"He already knows something's up," Lucy said. "He woke up last night for the first time in months."

Birdie didn't understand why Rigby would be upset. "Surely you didn't tell him we've lost all our money?"

Jack shook his head. "No, of course not. But he—"

"There was a moment ... when the full situation hit Jack." Lucy widened her eyes at him. "Rigby saw his distress."

A wave of emotion—part relief, part gratitude—washed over Birdie. Jack understood. He had empathy for their situation and for their total wretchedness and devastation at losing their retirement fund.

She reached over and hugged him, uncertain who she was reassuring more. "Dad and I will be okay."

Mike was blinking rapidly and he cleared his throat. "Your mother's right. Things are bad, but I've spoken to Brett. He's offered me a twelve-month contract and I start back tomorrow."

Relief moved across Jack's face. "At least that's some good news. It will tide you over until the police recover the money."

"*If* they recover the money," Mike said bitterly. "Don't hold your breath, son. God knows where the Quinns have run off to."

"You honestly think Judy and Bevan have gone too?"

"No," Birdie said uncertainly at the same time Mike said, "With every passing day I think it's more likely."

"Don't you think it's strange Izzy got left behind?" Jack said.

Mike shook his head. "I think it was all very carefully staged. Each of them left town at different times and with different reasons so no one was suspicious. Isobel was obviously the last to leave and got unlucky—"

"Unlucky?" Lucy shrieked. "It was karma! And thank God for that."

"The Quinns love Izzy," Jack said. "They're not going to hang her out to dry. Eventually, they'll slip back into town to get her and the police will be waiting to question them."

"Come back and get her?" Birdie scoffed. "That's holding them to a higher moral code than they're capable of!"

Jack frowned. "You're talking about your oldest and dearest friends."

Birdie felt a shell hardening around her heart. "Friends who haven't called us. Friends don't steal, Jack. Not from us or half the town. They knew what they were doing."

"Are you saying Elite was a set-up?" Jack sounded incredulous. "A two-year long game?"

"I wouldn't put it past them," Mike said tightly.

Jack's shoulders slumped. "I can't believe they'd do that to us. To anyone."

"Well, they did. And they played us well. I bet they're laughing at how gullible we were." Birdie spat the words.

Jack was staring at her, his look clearly stating not only that he didn't recognize her, but it hurt to believe her. Birdie hated his naivety and understood his pain. For two days she'd circled the truth of what the Quinns had done to them—what Judy had done to her. Judy, who'd been more of a sister to her than her own and more of an aunt to the children. A woman who'd shared the highs and lows of life with her as they'd juggled marriage and motherhood. Had it all been a hoax? Surely not? Only the evidence was mounting.

"Think about it, Jack," she said, needing him to understand the depth of the Quinns' betrayal. "Brad got to you first. He didn't need to gain your trust because he's had it from the sandpit. Then Judy and Bevan came to us saying they'd tested Elite for a year because they never wanted money to come between friends." Birdie's stomach churned acid and the burn bored through her. "They stole from us and half the town without even blinking! I wouldn't put it past them to abandon Izzy and let her rot in jail while they're off living the high life somewhere!"

"Do the police know if they've left the country?" Lucy asked.

"They're not saying," Mike said. "Oscar wants us all to club in and hire a private detective."

"That sounds expensive," Lucy said. "I'm not sure—"

"I reckon we leave it to the police," Jack said. "Brooke Riglioni's no slouch, and I wouldn't want to be on the wrong side of that detective. Besides, Brooke said some big shot from the fraud and extortion squad's coming from Melbourne. I doubt a private investigator would have that sort of reach." He dipped a cracker into the hummus. "Besides, there still might be a logical explanation. Maybe Brad's actually protecting our investment and—"

"Grow up, Jack!" Mike said.

Jack winced. Lucy rubbed his arm.

Birdie nudged Mike under the table.

Mike frowned and pulled his leg away. "Sorry, son. But I think it's time you took off those rose-colored glasses you've always looked at Brad through, especially the last couple of years. I know I've crushed the ones I've worn for Bevan."

Birdie looked straight at Lucy and Jack. "The only good thing to come out of this mess is that you two couldn't afford to invest in Fortune."

Jack paled. "Yeah, about that. It's why we want to talk to you."

"It's okay," Mike said. "You don't have to worry about us. We own the house and I've got a job. You don't need to lend us money."

Jack rubbed the back of his neck. "O-kay, but that wasn't what I meant. Mom, Dad ..." He cleared this throat. "There's no easy way to tell you this. Please don't yell. We're part of Fortune too."

"What?" A painful prickle washed over Birdie inside and out. As Mike said, "How?" she added, "I don't understand. You didn't have the money."

Lucy slid her hand into Jack's and he licked his lips. "We looked at the returns and did the sums," he said.

"We did them every which way," Lucy added, looking directly at Birdie. "And they were sound."

"It didn't look like a risk," Jack said.

"And?" Mike's voice was tight.

"We ..." Jack swallowed. "We took out a personal loan."

"You did what?" Birdie's shriek bounced off the walls and returned to her like a slap.

"For how much?" Mike demanded.

"Fifty," Jack said, so softly Birdie strained to hear.

"50,000 dollars?" Mike's hand thumped the table so hard they all jumped. "Of all the stupid, asinine—"

"What have we always said about personal loans?" Birdie stared at them, incredulous. "We said—"

"I know! I know!" Jack raked his hair. "But like I said, we did the math—"

"And the Fortune dividends covered the loan repayments *and* doubled our mortgage repayments," Lucy said, her voice firm. "It was working well. It was savvy investing."

"Savvy?" Birdie wanted to shake her. "You—"

"And now?" Mike's voice could cut glass.

Lucy shrank back and Jack said, "We can't meet the mortgage repayments and the loan."

A wail of grief rose to the back of Birdie's throat, but she pushed it down. Later, when she was alone, she'd moan and rock for all of them. Right now she needed to be the parent—the practical problem-solver. "What's the interest rate?"

Jack laced his fingers as if the pressure would force out the reluctant words. "Twenty-one percent."

"Jesus bloody Christ, Jack!" Mike's face had reddened so deeply, his skin was almost purple.

Birdie understood his reaction—she was a hundred versions of furious with Lucy and Jack too—but she didn't like the way a vein was bulging in his neck.

"Mike, don't blow a gasket."

He ignored her, his focus fully on Jack. "I can't believe ... What the hell were you—" Mike suddenly grimaced and his right hand gripped his left upper arm, pulling it tightly against him as if it was broken. "Th ... thinking?" He gasped out the final word like he couldn't catch his breath.

"Calm down and drink some water." Birdie pushed a glass toward him and noticed beads of sweat pooling on his forehead. Why was he hot when it wasn't a warm day?

Mike's puce complexion rapidly paled to gray. "Hurts." His voice sounded strangled.

"What hurts?" Birdie asked.

"Arm. Ch—" He slumped forward.

"Mike!" Panic engulfed her, followed by paralyzing fear.

"Dad!"

"Jack! Move!" Lucy shot to her feet. "Help me get him on the ground."

Jack grunted as he heaved his father off the chair and lowered him carefully onto the kitchen floor.

"Mike!" Birdie yelled, using the tone that always made him roll his eyes and say, "Yes, ma'am."

He didn't respond.

Lucy kneeled beside him and shook his shoulder. "Dad? Mike? Can you hear me?"

Without waiting for a response, she pressed two fingers against his neck. A second later she moved them, pressing more firmly.

"Is he okay?" Birdie asked, ignoring the scene unravelling in front of her.

"Possible AMI." Lucy ripped open Mike's shirt.

Birdie looked at Jack. "A what?"

"Heart attack," Jack said hoarsely.

He kneeled by his father's head and Lucy started chest compressions, counting loudly.

Seeing Lucy's small hands rhythmically pumping Mike's chest rained the truth down on Birdie. Mike's heart wasn't beating. Or if it was, not properly, otherwise why would Lucy be thumping his heart? Without a heartbeat, a person was—

Birdie fell to her knees by Mike's feet and gripped his ankles so tightly her fingers hurt. "Don't you dare die on me! Don't you dare!"

Lucy called out, "Thirty."

Jack blew two breaths of air into his father's mouth, then lifted his head. "Mom! Mom! Listen to me!"

Through the blur of tears Birdie saw Jack's mouth moving, but whatever he was saying sounded muffled, like it was coming from the far end of a tunnel.

"... call triple zero. Call the ambulance. Mom! Now. Go!"

He blew another breath into Mike's mouth.

Torn between leaving her husband laid out on the floor like a corpse and getting help, Birdie pushed to her feet and grabbed her cell phone. Her fingers trembled so much she struggled to unlock it. When the screen finally opened, she jabbed the emergency code and waited.

Come on! Ring!

The deafening silence was suddenly broken by a long ring. Then a woman's voice was asking calmly, "Police? Fire? Ambulance?"

"Ambulance. It's urgent!" She forced the words out against rising panic. "My husband's unconscious."

As she tried to answer the dispatcher's questions—she stumbled over her street number—she heard Lucy call, "Change." Birdie turned to see Jack taking over, his hands pushing down on Mike's chest. She'd had no idea her son knew how to do this, but was thankful that he did.

The dispatcher kept asking her questions about Mike and as she relayed the foreign acronyms Lucy was telling her—AMI, CPR—she kept her gaze fixed on him, willing his heart to beat on its own.

"The cardiac paramedics are on their way in the car," the dispatcher was saying. "They should be with you in twelve minutes and the ambulance will follow."

Birdie didn't understand. "But he needs the ambulance!"

"The cardiac paramedics will get there faster this way," the dispatcher was saying when Mike suddenly groaned.

Lucy called, "Stop," and her fingers checked for his pulse. "Mike?" She gently shook his shoulder. "Can you hear me?"

His eyes fluttered open and Birdie heard a strangled sob—hers.

"Yeah, love," Mike managed and closed his eyes again.

"Mike!" Birdie sank to her knees next to him. "Open your eyes!"

He turned his head toward her, his gaze unfocused. She grabbed his hand. "Keep looking at me. The ambulance is coming."

"Good." He took in a breath. "Feel like ... death ... warmed ... up."

Birdie caught the look that passed between Lucy and Jack and she knew that Mike had just spoken the truth.

Within three minutes of the cardiac paramedics bursting through the door, Mike had oxygen prongs in his nostrils, a blood-pressure cuff on one arm and a needle in the other, along with pads and wires on his chest that attached him to a machine that scrawled his heart rate across a screen. Somehow all of the equipment made the situation almost more terrifying than seeing Mike prone on the floor with Jack pounding his chest.

"We're giving you something for the pain, Mike," the paramedic said.

"Thank God," Mike managed then closed his eyes.

"Mom." Jack gave her shoulder a gentle squeeze. "Lucy and I have been talking. We think it's best if she goes with you to the hospital. You know, to translate all the medical jargon so you understand what's going on. She thinks Dad will be transferred to Geelong and—"

"No!" Fury drove the word out of Birdie's mouth like a bullet.

Jack blinked, clearly confused. "But Geelong's got the cardiac surgery—"

"I know that!"

Jack took a deep breath and when he spoke again he sounded like he was talking to Rigby. "Then why are you saying no?"

"Lucy's a midwife. Anyway, Rigby needs her."

"Rigby will be fine with me," Jack said tightly.

Ignoring his hurt expression she said, "I'm not making any decisions until I've spoken to the doctor."

And when she did, the last person she wanted with her was Lucy. The girl's greed and irresponsible behavior had lost Jack their money and almost killed Mike. Birdie would risk seeing the doctor alone rather than have her daughter-in-law anywhere near her.

CHAPTER EIGHTEEN

Izzy sat halfway up the staircase cuddling Thor. The faces of strangers stared down at her from the portraits the interior decorator had chosen—insisting "They suit the house perfectly." Brad had wanted giant photos of their parents on the wall, but when Izzy had refused to have her mother up there, he'd said tetchily, "That will throw off the symmetry." But Izzy preferred the faces of strangers to a photo of the woman who'd abandoned her, and the impasse had never been resolved. Right now she regretted that Judy's and Bevan's portraits weren't on the wall—she'd have taken great satisfaction in pulling them down and slashing them with a knife.

The doorbell rang for the fourth time in quick succession. Izzy tensed, amazed it was still possible after days of constantly being on high alert. Thor squirmed in her arms, barking indignantly at not being able to race to the door.

"Isobel," a male voice called out. "It's Connor Greyson from the *Standard*. Are you okay?"

For a brief moment she allowed herself to believe that the journalist was concerned for her. Then she remembered the headlines of previous days. The district was out for blood and Izzy was the only available quarry.

She kept getting flashes of the Battle of the Alamo—she and Brad had visited the famous Texan site—although in this instance her house wasn't circled by the Mexican army but by journalists and angry Elite members. Izzy had tried to hire a security guard for the gate—she'd made ten calls—but no one in town would work for her. This morning she'd called the police station and an officer she didn't know had asked if she felt under threat.

"Would you feel under threat if people were outside your door yelling, 'Give us the money?'" she'd said.

"Well, it is their money ..."

She'd pulled at her hair. "I'm here alone and they're trespassing. They've tried all the doors!"

"We'll send an officer."

Izzy had assumed he'd meant straight away. Half an hour later, the police were yet to arrive.

Since Brad had vanished her days lacked all the familiar structures and situations of her normal life, rendering them so completely unrecognizable that she wasn't certain she'd experienced them. Villefranche had never been a cozy home, but now it felt like a prison.

"Isobel," Connor Greyson called again. "You deserve the opportunity to give your side of the story."

She did! She seriously did. She constantly vacillated between staying hidden inside the stone walls of Villefranche and stepping out to address the mob of angry men and women. But would it exacerbate or ease the situation? Her desire to be believed told her it would help. But memories of the media's treatment of other victimized women cautioned her to stay silent.

This new sense of self-preservation grew after each daily police interview where the questions left her feeling that she was the one with the questionable morals. The one who'd broken the law. There were only so many ways to say, "I don't know," and she'd said them over and over to the implacable faces of the police, whose looks screamed, "We don't believe you."

Brad hadn't just allegedly disappeared with all of the Elite and Fortune money, he'd stolen Izzy's power, leaving her alone, terrified and quaking.

Hating the feeling of being under siege, she stood abruptly, then had no idea what to do next.

Like a pack of dogs, the people outside sensed movement.

The doorbell rang again. Another business card slid under the door, joining the collection Izzy was ignoring. Until she had the evidence to prove her lack of involvement in the money side of Elite, there was no point talking to anyone. No one was going to believe her.

Her cell phone beeped and her heart rate soared as it did every time the device emitted a sound. Since her life had imploded there hadn't been a single text from anyone in her contact list, so all incoming messages came from unknown callers. Days earlier, few people in town had known her cell number and she wondered who'd shared it far and wide. Surely not Brooke?

Izzy had taken to reading the text messages backwards, hoping to see a name or a nickname that might tell her it was Brad. Or Judy. Or Bevan.

She wasn't one hundred percent convinced that Brad had stolen the money. She struggled to reconcile that act with the man she'd first fallen in love with, and a tiny part of her was holding out hope there was a reasonable explanation. However, as each day passed, that belief grew increasingly unstable.

If the money was safe and the Quinns hadn't abandoned her, then how could they justify their silence? It seemed impossible that Brad had worked out she was leaving him, but if he had, was this the ultimate payback? She grappled with the idea, because even with his recent evasive and erratic behavior regarding Elite, she'd never thought him vindictive.

Would you even know? Perhaps you've been living with a sociopath. What if he's been stealing from the start?

Her gut ached. Was the money in her bank account the proceeds of crime? The police were certainly keen to prove that it was.

Her cell beeped again, reminding her there was an unread text. She opened it and read the last two words—*Connor Greyson*. Then she read the message.

> Do you want to comment on the fact your father filed for bankruptcy twice?

The riff of anger underpinned by anxiety made her shake. How dare the journalist bring her father into this! He'd been dead for six years! Hell, his financial history had *nothing* to do with Brad. Why was she being attacked from all sides when she was innocent of all wrongdoing?

Except willful naivety.

She shied away from the truth—the warning signs she'd ignored. Navel-gazing wasn't going to get her out of this mess. She needed to prove something—anything—that removed her from being implicated in Brad's business. The fog of shock that had descended over her the moment Brooke and the obnoxious detective had arrived at Villefranche for the first time still lingered, but there were moments when it cleared. This was one of those times.

Releasing Thor, she gripped the stone rail, jogged down the stairs, turned left and took the next flight down into Brad's office. She shuddered as the cool air of the underground room gripped her.

The first thing the police had done was to obtain a warrant and seize Brad's computer, but Izzy knew he kept more information in the cloud than on the device. She just needed to crack his password.

She heard a derisive laugh and realized it was her.

Just! The task was up there with looking for a needle in a haystack.

She snagged her bottom lip with her teeth. If she'd been hiding the movement of money she'd have used a complicated auto-generated password. But would Brad? She knew he had a password lock on his computer that he typed in pretty quickly. Did that point to it being easy or well-remembered?

She uncapped Brad's Montblanc pen, pulled out a piece of Elite stationery and started writing everything she could remember about him: his date of birth, favorite color, schools, favorite sports teams, first car, first home—anything that might be part of a password. Then she opened her laptop.

Half an hour later, strands of her hair lay on the keyboard and she still wasn't inside the cloud. Frustrated, she pushed back the chair and stared blankly at the bookshelves.

"We want our money!" loud voices outside demanded. The stone walls muffled the sound but not the anger.

She suddenly remembered the newly installed safe. She slammed the heel of her hand into her forehead. *Stupid!* Why hadn't she thought of it before? The safe was where the money was hidden—piles of hundred dollar bills bundled together and stacked high. Cash that proved Brad hadn't stolen the money. Cash that declared Brad was protecting the best interests of Elite and Fortune members. Cash that proved she hadn't spent two years obliviously living with a thief and a conman.

Then why isn't he here with you?

Shut up!

Izzy couldn't—wouldn't—think beyond opening the safe.

She carefully removed the fake books she'd organized to hide the sleek black cube from view, then slid her fingers under the handle and pulled. It didn't yield.

Of course, it was locked, but had Brad changed the password she'd created when the bloke from Hi Tech had taught her how the safe worked?

Well, duh. He hid everything to do with the business from you.

Willfully disregarding the unwanted voice in her head, she stabbed in the code and held her breath.

The safe made a soft whirring sound. She clapped. "Thor! It's opening."

The Jack Russell danced around her feet, matching her excitement.

Visualizing the money stacks, she pulled open the safe. The immediate space in front of her was empty.

Her world teetered again and her chest cramped so hard she gasped.

Had she ever known Brad?

But the question was far too terrifying to consider, let alone answer, so she leaned closer as if that would change the view.

At first she chastised herself as ridiculous, but then she noticed an envelope camouflaged by the white shelf. She picked it up and returned to the desk. With a shaking hand, she slid the letter-opener under the seal and sliced.

She pulled out a single sheet of paper. It took her a few moments to recognize it as the title of her and Brad's investment apartment in Noosa. The last time she'd seen it was when they'd signed the sale papers, so why was it in this safe and not in the safety deposit box at the bank?

She read it again, this time more slowly, and that's when she noticed the change. Brad's name was no longer on the document—only hers.

She blinked but it didn't change what she was seeing. According to the title, she now owned the apartment. Welcome relief rolled through her. Whatever else was going on, Brad had made sure she had somewhere to live.

Once again, the question that had plagued her for days rose in her mind—had he really left her?

It felt completely out of character for him to do so, but then again, was it? As egotistical as it was for her to believe he loved her too much to leave her, when she reflected on his behavior over the last few months it threw a thick and heavy cloud over that belief. Once she would have said she trusted Brad implicitly, but now everything to do with him was like walking on a frozen lake. It looked safe, but underneath truth and lies swirled, eating away at the ice and making every step a gamble.

Why had he put the title in her name? Was it part of his plan for their future together?

A future she'd let go of before he'd disappeared.

She realized she was shaking her head. Even though the apartment was beach frontage, it was only one bedroom and came with one car space—not Brad's style at all. From the moment they'd bought it, he'd been insistent it was purely an investment.

Why hadn't he told her he was removing his name from the title?

He hasn't told you anything in months!

Suddenly her relief crashed into the jagged rocks of fear. What if he hadn't made sure she had a safe place to live? What if he'd left her with a whopping great mortgage?

Her heart pounded, fizzing panic into every tiny cell. When was the last time she'd looked at the mortgage on the property? She'd been paying her share to Brad each month, even though he'd insisted she didn't need to. Had he been making the payments or just pocketing the money?

She pulled at her hair, only this time the tiny pricks of pain didn't reassure her. Why, when she knew what it was to be stony-broke, had she let Brad make all the investment decisions and handle the money?

You had no reason to doubt him.

And she hadn't. From the moment they'd moved to Glingilly he'd deposited her salary into her bank account every Thursday afternoon.

She returned to her laptop, logged into the bank and checked the mortgage account. She refreshed the screen three times, but it never changed the fact that a seven-figure payment had been made the day Brad disappeared. A sum that paid off the mortgage.

She slumped in the huge chair, unsure of exactly what she was feeling. Most of her urged it to be relief, so she could cling to welcome calm. But, like the ominous pewter sky that preceded a violent storm, a sense of foreboding circled her like a noose.

Had Brad used Elite money to pay for the apartment?

Well, duh! You own a proceed of crime.

No. He wouldn't do that to me.

Stop being so freakin' trusting! Protect yourself.

Her thoughts spun and she picked up the Montblanc pen again and scrawled bald facts devoid of any emotion.

At least 20 million dollars was missing.

No one had heard from the Quinns in days.

She owned an apartment in Noosa.

She was still in possession of an expensive engagement ring that she'd torn off her finger and shoved in her sock drawer the night Brad went missing.

She was alone in Glingilly.

Elite members and the police considered her complicit. If the police discovered a money trail leading to the apartment being paid in full, she was toast.

Her head dropped onto the desk. The why of what had happened was immaterial. What she desperately needed was something that pointed the money away from her.

Think! Think! Think!

As she raised her head, she noticed the bank of drawers on either side of Brad's massive desk. She reached out and tugged on one. It didn't budge. She tried the other seven. Every drawer was locked and therefore demanded to be opened.

Running her hands under the edges of the desk, her fingers felt for a key. Nothing. She got down on her hands and knees and using the flashlight app on her cell phone scanned the dark corners for gold or silver metal. Nada.

Pushing to her feet, she slowly moved her gaze around the room, staring at the ominous medieval decor and willing it to give up Brad's secrets. Without thinking, she found herself crossing the room to the suit of armor. She opened the visor. *Bingo!*

"Now we're getting somewhere, Thor."

She peeled the old-fashioned key from the inside of the metal visor. With a flutter of excitement, she slid it into the lock on the first drawer. It opened with a satisfying click.

"Yes!" She pulled out the drawer and her gut swooped in disappointment. It was empty save for a few paperclips.

The key fitted the locks on the other drawers and she systematically worked her way through opening them. Some were completely empty; others contained nothing worthy of protecting.

Pinning her hopes on the final drawer, she said, "This will be it."

Thor's button brown eyes gazed at her, bright and happy, and he wagged his tail in full support. Izzy turned the key, pulled and the drawer shot out fast, stopping just short of falling from its housing.

"Shit!" It was empty. Why had Brad locked eight empty drawers?

Frustrated, she shoved it shut, but instead of rolling gracefully closed, it stopped halfway. Jiggling it, she tried to align the runners, but it remained stubbornly stuck. She pulled it back again—more gently this time—so she could remove it completely and start over. When she tipped the drawer forward to disengage it, she heard a rattle. She lifted it up and out. It didn't seem overly heavy, but she shook it again. It rattled a second time.

Was the bottom of the drawer fake? She tried to prize the wood up with the letter-opener, but it was too close a fit so she upended the drawer onto the desk. There was a tiny hole in the base. What could she push into it? She remembered the long nail she thought had been abandoned in one of the other drawers and retrieved it.

Pushing the nail into the hole, she watched the wood rise to the point where she could lift it. Underneath the fake bottom lay four cheap cell phones. Burner phones? Yet again she had a surreal moment of feeling like she was inside a television drama.

She reached for a phone, but her newly activated sense of self-preservation stopped her.

As she crossed the cavernous entrance hall to the kitchen, the doorbell chimed. She grabbed a pair of latex gloves and dashed back, ignoring another chime of the doorbell before re-entering the office. Working methodically, she switched on each phone. None contained SIM cards.

She quickly removed the other drawers from the desk and turned them over. All had fake bottoms. She repeated the process with the nail, finding SIM cards and more burner phones. As none of the phones had been used she wasn't certain what they would prove to the police, except that the average businessman didn't normally have fifteen cell phones.

She suddenly heard the roar of car engines and her breath stalled. Dear God, were they going to ram the house?

She dropped to the floor and crawled under the desk, hugging a reluctant Thor tight to her chest. Holding her breath, she tried listening over the boom of blood in her ears. It took a few seconds to realize the sound of the engines was fading rather than gaining volume.

Her cell beeped with a text and she let go of Thor and crawled out to retrieve it. The message was from Brooke.

> Isobel, we have moved people on. We suggest you padlock your gate. We will be at your front door in five minutes and would appreciate you letting us in

Izzy checked the time—it was almost two, which meant the daily interview. At least this time she could show the police the burner phones.

Don't get ahead of yourself. Where's your proof that Brad bought them and you haven't just planted them?

God, she hoped his fingerprints were on them.

Has Brad ever been fingerprinted?

Sweat beaded her top lip. Proving her innocence was a never-ending nightmare.

Her cell rang, short-circuiting her spinning thoughts. She checked the screen, but instead of a phone number there was a familiar name. Her gut turned to water and it took her tingling fingers two attempts to answer the call.

Her voice quivered with anger and tears. "Where the hell are you?"

CHAPTER NINETEEN

LUCY WISHED JACK WAS HOME, but it was his two-weeks away for work. One thing FIFO had taught her was that the universe often saved up the bad stuff and dumped it on her to deal with alone when Jack was away. This was one of those times.

She checked her watch and mentally urged Tiffany, the realtor, to speed up her inspection or she'd be late for work. The agent was the third to visit the house this week and Lucy had been underwhelmed by the previous two. She was hoping Tiffany's pitch would be perfect so she could sign the agreement papers today. As much as Lucy had railed against the idea of losing the house, now she just wanted it sold. And sold fast, so their debt was negated and she could sleep again.

This month they had no choice but to miss a mortgage repayment—paying the personal loan took precedence. Each time she thought about defaulting, acid reflux burned the length of her gut. But one missed payment was forgivable, wasn't it? Especially if they could show the bank the house had sold and the mortgage would be paid off in a few months—hopefully no more than three.

Tiffany crossed the deck, slid open the glass doors and stepped back inside. "Wow!" she said. "It's unrecognizable from when I sold it to you."

Lucy laughed. "I don't miss the bright orange kitchen tiles or the shag-pile carpet, that's for sure."

"You've done an amazing job."

"Thank you."

Lucy allowed the glow of pride to reassure her. She'd done a lot of the painting and decorating herself because they couldn't afford it any other way. Between YouTube and some DIY workshops at the local hardware store she'd learned how to strip old furniture, stencil, hang a frieze and frame prints. Although she was losing the house, she knew she could renovate another—albeit smaller—one and make it her own.

Tiffany placed her work folder on the table and indicated a chair. "May I?"

"Of course."

Lucy sat too and listened to Tiffany's pitch—a fast and targeted sales campaign culminating in an auction.

"We have families on the books looking for something just like this," Tiffany finished.

"Can you offer it to them first?" Lucy asked, hoping for a super-quick sale.

Tiffany gave her a direct and uncompromising look. "Do you need to sell?"

A hot flush spread up Lucy's neck. The news about Elite had been splashed across the local news. Some people, like Oscar D'Angelo, had spoken publicly about their membership, but most people were staying silent, far too embarrassed to admit their involvement. While Brad and the Quinns remained MIA, the media focus was firmly on the members. The letters and text messages to the editor, along with the comments on the *Standard*'s Facebook page, were centered on words starting with G—like *greedy* and *gullible*. Apparently greedy people deserved to lose everything and the gullible needed a good wake-up call. Nowhere did it mention that Elite members had based their decisions on false information. People were positively gleeful—another

G word—that previously rich members of the community had fallen into a financial abyss. Tall-poppy syndrome was thriving.

Lucy forced herself to laugh. "Having a three-year-old and keeping the house tidy for inspections does my head in so I'd like to sell as quickly as possible. What do you think we could get?"

Tiffany named a reserve price that made Lucy's heart sing. Then she added, "Of course the beauty of an auction is you only need two families to fall in love with the property and they blow the reserve out of the water. Recently, we've seen places sell up to thirty percent over the set minimum price."

"That sounds incredible. Can we have the auction in a month?"

"Absolutely. We took care of you when you bought this place and we'll take care of you selling it." Tiffany produced some paperwork and a pen. "It would be an honor to be your agent."

Preferring to work with a woman, Lucy signed the papers and rushed off to work.

She tried calling Jack before she collected Rigby after her shift, but the call went straight to voice mail. Then the evening had vanished in a whirl of dinner, bath and playing yet another game of "hospital" with Rigby.

Although Rigby hadn't visited his grandfather in the hospital, he'd seen Mike attached to oxygen and an IV, and being stretchered into the ambulance. This image was dominating his play and as much as Lucy tried to move him back to dinosaurs, Rigby insisted on playing doctors. She knew it was his way of processing an unfathomable situation. Despite her reassuring him that Gramps would be home soon, Rigby's bed-wetting continued. Mike was Rigby's hero so the moment he was discharged, she'd take Rigby to Cork Street for a visit. Hopefully, seeing Mike at home would ease Rigby's anxiety and her happy little boy would return.

It was 9:00 when Jack finally called and Lucy outlined Tiffany's plans for the sale. When she finished talking, there was silence on the line.

"Jack?"

"Yeah?"

"Well?"

"Sounds okay," he said flatly.

Lucy stifled a sigh. Since the terrifying afternoon on her in-laws' kitchen floor when Mike's heart had quivered ineffectually for a few minutes and they'd fought hard to pump blood around his body, Jack had been unusually quiet. Even when Lucy saw him on a video call, she couldn't tell where the stress of their financial situation finished and the worry for his father started. It hadn't helped that Jack had flown back to work on the day of Mike's surgery. Leave without pay wasn't an option when crippling debt hung over their heads like a guillotine.

"Your Dad's alive because of us," she said.

Jack swore. "We're the reason he had the heart attack!"

"No!" Lucy refused to accept that sort of thinking. "The Quinns and his health are the reason he had a heart attack."

A few beats of silence passed before Jack said, "I wish I was there. You'll visit Dad for me, yeah?"

Lucy wanted to pout like Rigby and say, "Do I have to?" A trip to Geelong meant asking a friend to mind Rigby all day—and Lucy offering a reciprocal favor at another time—plus a five-hour round trip on her day off. But the anxiety in Jack's voice made her agree. "I'll go Thursday."

"At least Geelong's closer to Melbourne," Jack said. "It's good Sienna's making the effort to visit."

"It is. How did she take the news about your Dad's retirement fund?"

"I didn't mention it," Jack said.

"What?" Lucy was at a loss to understand. "But Birdie's told her, right?"

"I don't know."

"What do you mean, you don't know? Surely—"

"Jeez, Luce!" She pictured him plowing his hands through his hair. "Priorities! Right now Dad's health comes first."

Lucy thought the two were intricately connected and that Sienna should know her parents had lost their retirement savings. But she only had enough energy to deal with their own situation so she let it slide. Her sister-in-law would find out eventually, and as Sienna had inherited Birdie's straight-talking, Lucy didn't plan to be around when she did.

"Can you Snapchat me a photo of Rigby?" Jack said.

"He's asleep."

"That's the point, Luce. God, I miss him."

His melancholy reached across the country and socked her in the chest. "And me?" she said, thinking she was teasing him, but it came out needy.

"Shit, Luce, I miss you so hard. Everything sucks. We were so close to living the dream and now I'm fucking stuck with this job!"

Signing with the agent had put some distance between Lucy and the cloying darkness of their situation. Now Jack's words brought it all rushing back like a bore tide and she fought to hold it at bay.

"Tiffany said it's a sellers' market so the house will go fast. We'll push for a thirty-day settlement, sixty at most, clear the debt and then we can start again."

The line buzzed with silence.

"Jack, it's going to be okay."

It had to be okay.

The following day when Lucy walked through the doors of the coronary care unit in the Geelong hospital, a bolt of mixed emotions stalled her just short of Mike's bed. The first thing she noticed was the empty visitor's chair. At least she was being spared Birdie's dual disappointment that not only wasn't she Jack, she was a poor substitute.

Her ears tuned into the rhythmic beat of the cardiac monitor and she raised her gaze to the pattern scrawling across the screen. No ectopic beats, just beautiful, regular and reassuring sinus rhythm. Lucy let go of the breath she'd been holding, then immediately gasped.

It was the first time she'd seen Mike since she'd given him CPR. She barely recognized him. She'd always considered him a giant of a man—tall, broad and solid—but today, as he lay sleeping, he was a shrunken version of his former self. Oxygen prongs poked into his nostrils and the top of a dressing peeked out above his hospital gown. She knew it would run the length of his now wired-together sternum. Unfortunately, a stent wasn't enough to improve the condition of Mike's coronary arteries and he'd required open-heart surgery to replace all five. Even so, Lucy had expected Mike to look far more robust than this.

She was about to sit when she heard her name. She turned to find a pale-faced Birdie, dark shadows under her eyes, standing behind her.

"Hello, Birdie. You look exhausted." She regretted the words the moment they left her mouth.

Her mother-in-law clutched the strap of her shoulder bag. "Of course I'm exhausted. My husband almost died." Her voice cracked. "Did die."

She pushed past Lucy and sat in the chair, sliding her hand into Mike's.

"I'm back," she said softly. "Jack and Sienna send their love."

Mike's eyes fluttered open. "Lucy?"

Lucy was still reeling from Birdie's antagonism, but she stepped forward and dropped a kiss on Mike's cheek. "It's me. How are you?"

Before he could answer, Birdie said tartly, "Exactly as he looks. Sick."

"How's Rigby?" Mike asked, his voice concerningly breathy.

This time Lucy took a moment to formulate and audit an answer. "Missing you. He drew you this." She pulled a piece of paper from her tote bag. "I think it's the two of you fishing off the pier. Hopefully it won't be long before you're back there with him."

But Mike's eyes had fluttered closed. Lucy put the drawing on the bedside table.

"Did this morning's physiotherapy exhaust him?" she asked Birdie.

"He's not up to physiotherapy yet! You broke one of his ribs and now he's got pneumonia."

The accusatory words—unexpected and unfair—slammed into Lucy. Her hands clenched and she focused on the pain of her nails digging into her palms to stop herself from yelling, "We saved his life!" She didn't want the ignominy of being thrown out of CCU. She knew she hadn't broken Mike's rib—she would have felt it happen—but Jack, whose upper body strength was far greater than hers, could have. The stats on broken ribs during CPR ran at about thirty percent. Surely the medical staff had told Birdie that?

"Jack and I both did CPR," she said carefully.

"Jack would never hurt his father," Birdie said in a furious whisper.

The inference that Lucy would hurt Mike sliced deeply, leaving her bleeding. "Neither would I!"

Birdie's steel-tight face and crossed arms radiated shockwaves of antipathy and dislike. "I think that's open to interpretation."

Stunned, Lucy struggled to speak. "Birdie, I—"

"Excuse me." A nurse smiled at them. "I'm afraid I need to ask you both to step out while I help Mike with a wash and check his dressing. Café Go's just a short walk, and the coffee's great, not to mention the Portuguese custard tarts."

Birdie kept her gaze fixed on the nurse. "We haven't met but I'm Mike's wife, Birdie Essen. None of the other nurses have asked me to leave and I don't intend to now."

A flush crawled up the nurse's neck and she looked at Lucy. "I'm sorry, but—"

"Don't be sorry," Lucy said quickly. "I'm a midwife and I totally get it."

Ignoring Birdie, she touched Mike lightly on the shoulder. He opened his eyes.

"I have to go, Mike. I hope the antibiotics kick in fast and you're breathing easier soon. Jack and Rigby send their love, and of course I'm here giving you mine in person."

"Thanks, love." He heaved in a breath. "Drive carefully."

"I will." She turned to face her mother-in-law and forced herself to ask, "Do you need me to get you anything before I leave?"

"No."

It was a slap and yet she heard herself checking again, for Jack. "Are you sure? I could go shop—"

"Sienna organized a food delivery to the apartment." Birdie spoke the words in a tone that clearly said, "Sienna's thoughtful and you're not."

The nurse's hand was on the cubicle's curtains and Birdie was refusing to look at Lucy. Awkward and embarrassed didn't come close to describing her emotions, which were quickly overlaid with disbelief and simmering resentment. God! She'd used one of her precious days off to drive hours to visit so she could support her in-laws and she was being made to feel like an interloper and blamed for Mike's post-operative complications.

Stuff it! "I'll say goodbye then."

Birdie didn't respond.

For the first time since her marriage, Lucy didn't kiss her mother-in-law goodbye.

CHAPTER TWENTY

Izzy engaged the handbrake, turned off the ignition and released her seatbelt before reaching for the door handle. But as she pushed open the door, panic gripped her. She hastily shut and locked it.

"Stop it! It's uni. It's safe."

But the loud instruction wasn't enough to slow her racing heart or ease the pain twisting along her gut.

Today was the first time she'd left Villefranche since Brad had vanished. Not that she'd wanted to leave—she was fortunate it had taken her twelve days to work through the well-stocked pantry and freezer. But now she was out of food and no one would deliver.

She'd run the gauntlet of one panic attack already, just navigating the gate. Thankfully, Jim and Gaylene Hewitson were the only remaining Elite members camping out. They'd risen from their outdoor chairs, sniffing the air like hounds baying for blood. When she'd passed, they'd screamed words she'd never imagined would be levelled at her, making her ears throb and her heart race.

According to the news, the rest of the Elite members had relocated to outside Judy and Bevan's Glingilly house. They were in for an unsatisfactory wait—Izzy doubted the Quinns would return any time soon. Perhaps never. Yet again her mind returned to that phone call from Judy four days after Brad had disappeared. It was a conversation she'd replayed in her head for days, until she could no longer tell what was real, what was memory and what was imagined.

"Where the hell are you?" Izzy had demanded the moment she realized who was on the line.

"We told you, remember," Judy said with mild reprimand. "On retreat."

"I don't believe you!"

Izzy heard a muffled version of Judy's voice, as if she was holding her hand over the cell phone's microphone. The deep rumble of a man's voice followed and then Judy was asking, "Is everything okay, Izzy?"

"What do you think? Put Brad on!"

After a couple of beats of silence Judy said, "Brad's not here. Why would he be?"

Izzy's hand tore at her hair. "Bullshit! I know what you've all done to me."

"Take a breath, Isobel! Have you been drinking?" Judy's tone was harsh. "You're not making any sense!"

"Stop gaslighting me," Izzy ground out. "Give your prick of a son the cell. Now!"

Silence hung on the line.

"Judy, do it!"

Izzy put the cell on speaker and tapped out the message to Brooke, *Judy Quinn on phone,* on her computer, grateful the devices were integrated.

"Izzy," a male voice said and for a split second her heart stopped.

"Brad—"

"It's Bevan. The last time we saw Brad was the night before we left for the retreat. When we were all together planning the wedding."

It seemed a lifetime ago. "I don't believe you."

"Why would we lie to you?" Bevan sounded genuinely bewildered.

"If he's not there with you, tell me where he is!"

"Have the two of you had a fight?" Judy asked.

"A fight? I wish!" A hysterical laugh erupted out of Izzy. "You really want to play it this way and humiliate me further? Okay, fine. You're all dead to me anyway."

"You might be mad at Brad, but you have no right to be offensive," Judy reprimanded.

"Stop this drama, Isobel," Bevan said curtly. "You're better than that."

He'd never spoken to her like this before, but then she'd never declared the Quinn family dead to her.

She sucked in a deep breath and tried again. "Brad's disappeared."

Bevan's sigh shot frustration down the line. "Brad hasn't disappeared."

"Then tell me where he is because I sure as hell don't know."

"He told me he thought he might need to go back to Dubai," Bevan said calmly.

"He didn't tell me!"

"He thought you'd be upset that he was leaving again so quickly," Judy said.

"And he got that right," Bevan added dryly.

A whoosh of sensation shot up Izzy's spine, but she couldn't decode it. The Quinns sounded reasonable in their belief Brad wasn't missing. Then again, wasn't the art of an elaborate con the ability to keep up the performance under all circumstances? A remote retreat was the perfect ruse—it had made Judy and Bevan uncontactable. Had it given Brad time to hide millions of dollars? Time to escape?

But if their intention was to hang her out to dry, why were they calling her? What did that gain them?

Izzy floundered between opposing beliefs.

"Look, Izzy, we didn't call to get into the middle of a lovers' tiff," Judy said. "We've been released from our detox adventure and Brad's sent us a welcome back text. But when we called his cell phone we got a—"

"Turned off or out of range message," Izzy said flatly.

"Yes." Judy's tone had gone from no-nonsense to worried. "You're getting that too?"

Was the question to cover their tracks or was it genuine? If it was true that they'd just got back into range after days off the grid, their cell phones would be pinging wildly with all sorts of messages.

Go carefully.

"I haven't heard from Brad since he left Villefranche," Izzy said. "Surely you've received texts from members of Elite and Fortune?"

"Oh, I haven't read them yet," Judy said airily. "Family first!"

Izzy's free hand wrapped around the edge of Brad's desk as uncertainty circled her. Was she being used or was she about to break a mother's heart? "Google our names. We're all over the news."

"What are you talking about?" Judy said.

Izzy heard Bevan muttering and knew his big hands would be struggling to type accurately on his cell phone.

Ten seconds later, Judy's agonized scream had shattered the silence. The line had gone dead.

By the end of that day, footage of Judy and Bevan walking hand in hand into the Tweed Heads police station had been splashed across all the news channels and the internet, and their photos had been printed in the press.

Despite believing she'd done the right thing, the images of the Qunins woke Izzy each night in a cold sweat. What sort of person snitched on their in-laws?

They went to the police themselves, remember?

But I told Brooke where they were.

They're not family.

But for two years they'd been her only family and she'd trusted them. Trusted Brad.

And look where that got you. You're the focus of a police investigation!

Izzy hadn't told Judy and Bevan that she'd found burner phones in Brad's desk. Nor had she told them she'd handed the phones over to the police and was now working on breaking into the cloud.

The police were tight-lipped about what the Quinns had told them, however they'd said that unlike Judy and Bevan, they didn't believe Brad was a missing person. No cross-state application had been made by Victoria Police to extradite Judy and Bevan from New South Wales and no charges had been laid—yet.

Detective Mitchell was scathing about the Quinn's deal with a women's magazine and their appearance on *The Project*.

With Bevan holding her hand, Judy had sobbed into the television camera and made an emotional plea for Brad to come forward. "We love you, darling. We miss you desperately. Please contact us. Everything will be alright."

Bevan had added, "If anyone knows anything ... If you've seen Brad or overheard any plans to hurt him, please ring Crimestoppers. Our son is a good man. We just need to know he's safe."

They were the epitome of distraught parents—devastated by their son's disappearance and bewildered by the missing millions.

Izzy didn't doubt their love for their son—he'd always been Judy's world. But she had watched the interview with a degree of dispassion that scared her. The Quinns' vague answers to questions about Elite and Fortune made her skin prickle.

Brad and Bevan had always talked business and money—it had dominated every family dinner, casual conversation and phone call. On Bevan's advice, Brad had opened a trading account with the Australian Stock Exchange.

Izzy knew this because it had been discussed in front of her and she'd asked why. "You always say the returns from Elite and Fortune are more consistent than the stock market."

Brad had given her an indulgent smile. "And that's true, grasshopper, but a wise investor always has a diverse portfolio to soften an unexpected blow in one sector." He'd dropped a kiss on her head. "Surely they've taught you that at uni."

Before she'd managed to say yes, Bevan had chimed in with a mini lecture on the ASX. Judy had sat back, sipping her wine and beaming with pride at the men in her life.

Izzy was convinced Bevan knew far more about Elite and Fortune than he was letting on to the police and the journalists, especially as he'd introduced many clients to Brad. Did he have access to the cloud? To the bank accounts?

Judy and Bevan hadn't spoken to Izzy about the business beyond their conviction that there was no way Brad would have stolen the money. The Quinns were pushing the police to consider kidnapping, but too many days had passed without a ransom note for that to be a consideration.

The day after *The Project* interview, Judy had called her. "My darling boy wouldn't steal 23 million dollars. He just wouldn't!"

Izzy wished she could say, "I agree," but with each passing day it became harder to think it, let alone say it.

"We're disappointed you haven't spoken to the journalists, Izzy," Bevan said. "It doesn't look good when Brad's fiancée isn't publicly supporting him."

"You're casting doubt," Judy said. "It's your job to help him."

Izzy hadn't known if her blood was boiling or chilling—likely both. Either way, she could barely move her rigid jaw.

"It's hard enough convincing the police that I—" *wasn't part of his plan*, "— didn't steal the money!" she managed.

"No one's stolen any money!" Bevan said.

"Izzy! We have to stick together on this," Judy sobbed.

Izzy had lost all semblance of control. "There's no together about any of this! Brad's gone, you're in New South Wales and I'm left here on my own!"

She had expected the Quinns to rush back to Glingilly the moment they'd learned of Brad's disappearance.

"Be fair, Izzy," Bevan had said crisply when Judy was too overcome to speak. "None of this is easy on any of us, but you need to trust us. This is the best way."

"How is it the best way?" she'd asked, honestly confused.

"Wherever Brad is, he'll eventually come to one of the two places he knows he's loved," Bevan said.

For a moment she thought this plan reasonable, then doubts crowded her. Had Brad even visited his parents' villa at Dolphin Sands? They hadn't owned it all that long and— Izzy's gut had fallen like a stone. Were Judy and Bevan staying almost a thousand miles away because they were guilty? Or were they just avoiding the wrath of Glingilly?

Wherever the truth lay, it meant Izzy remained the one person in town who represented Elite and everything the members had lost. The one person to blame. She hated the Quinns for that.

Every day Judy texted the same words: *Have you heard anything?* As if Izzy would keep the information from her. But self-reproach always bit, because Izzy would only tell Judy after she'd told Brooke.

Izzy still hadn't told the Quinns or the police that she'd been leaving Brad the day he'd vanished. As no one knew her plans, and she hadn't recorded them in any format anywhere, it meant the secret kept itself. And who would believe her now if she did tell them? She was already walking a knife edge with the police—accomplice versus duped fiancée—so confessing to leaving Brad would only make things worse. And in the irrational hour between 3:00 and 4:00 each morning, it occurred to her that if she told Bevan and Judy the truth, they might think she'd murdered Brad.

Alone with a never-ending parade of questions without answers, Izzy worried she was going crazy. How she wished she could take all the unwanted thoughts out of her mind like Dumbledore in *Harry Potter* and store them in a pensieve and forget about them!

It was another reason she'd left Villefranche today and driven to uni. She was desperate to fill her mind with something far removed from Elite and the Quinns. Coming here felt a lot safer than walking down the main street of Glingilly. And it would be, if she could just get out of the car.

She raised her gaze from the steering wheel and fixed it on the smooth salmon bark of the towering gum tree in the university's parking lot. Nature was supposed to be calming but agitation skittered inside her unabated. She pulled out a strand of hair, breathing through the sting, and felt her body sag.

She scanned the parking lot. The only person in sight was already on the path and walking toward the buildings.

"Come on! Out!" she told herself. "It's easier than leaving Villefranche."

She opened the door, swung her feet onto the gravel and stood. It was a glorious day—a large blue sky hung above her decorated with fluffy clouds. Magpies chortled in the gum trees, their joyous song rising above the raucous squawks of sulfur-crested cockatoos. The day seemed blissfully unaware of the shitstorm that had engulfed her and changed her life.

Today was the first day since Brad had disappeared that the police hadn't demanded an interview, nor had there been a journalist trying to contact her. Today she was just Izzy Harrington, university student— she'd even dressed the part, knowing that her normal clothes made her stand out. She pulled her baseball cap down low, slung her computer satchel over her shoulder and walked purposefully toward the cluster of buildings. She'd deliberately picked a different tutorial from her usual, choosing one with a younger demographic and a PhD student tutor. It meant she would avoid anyone she knew, and it was unlikely any of them would have seen the news and recognize her.

Izzy slipped into the tutorial room, chose a seat and, like most students, hid behind her laptop.

Cooper Barsky walked in, chatting easily with a group of students, and Izzy's heart hurled itself against her ribs. *No, no!* This wasn't happening. He shouldn't be taking this tutorial. Desperate to hide, she slumped farther into her seat.

Cooper scanned the full room with a welcoming smile that passed right over Izzy. "A full house isn't something I often see," he said. "I feel like a rock star."

She relaxed a tad.

He pulled the lid off a marker and wrote *corporate governance* on the whiteboard. He underlined it twice before turning back to face everyone. "A full tutorial means many of you are freaking out about the assignment. So instead of discussing today's topic, hit me with your assignment questions."

Oh God! In all the chaos Izzy had totally forgotten about the assignment she'd discussed with Cooper in the café. She checked the date on her computer and realized it was due in two days. She had a rough draft that needed work, but right now nothing was sticking in her brain. Should she ask for an extension?

And what's your excuse?

Your fiancé ran off with 23 million dollars?

You now own an apartment worth 3 million?

You have a ring he probably paid for with other people's money?

The police give you sideways glances even though you're trying to help them with their investigation?

"I've got a question about ASIC," one of the students said.

"What's ASIC?" another student asked.

"The Australian Securities and Investments Commission." Cooper wrote the title on the board. "It's an independent body of the federal government that regulates financial services, consumer credit and authorized financial markets like retirement funds and insurance. It exists to protect the consumer, the investor and creditors. Basically, it's the corporate cop."

"Oh, yeah," someone said. "I read they nailed that big insurance company."

"Yes, indeed. It was investigated for fees for no service, inappropriate advice and charging fees to dead people."

"Cool!" the first student said. "So when corporate governance fails, ASIC puts the boot in?"

"Well, it has powers to investigate corporate breaches," Cooper said. "As a result there was a Royal Commission and a lot of heads rolled."

"What about when a private company rips off investors?" a young woman asked. "Will ASIC investigate that?"

"That depends on the business structure. Whether it's an individual, a partnership, trust or a company," Cooper said.

She shrugged. "My uncle invested a hundred grand with a guy and now he's buggered off with the money."

Izzy froze, every sense on high alert.

One uncle and one guy doesn't mean Elite.

"The Glingilly gangster?" someone asked.

The young woman grimaced. "Yeah."

Izzy, you're a freaking idiot! Why had she thought the university was a safe space? It was only half an hour's drive from Glingilly. And Brad's business model, which had centered around the recommendations of family and friends, meant its reach was farther than the town's limits.

"It's all about trust, Iz." The memory of Brad's voice tensed every muscle. She fought to move breath in and out of her lungs.

"How dumb is your uncle getting caught up in a Ponzi scheme?" someone else said.

Izzy had read the article one journalist had written inferring Elite was a Ponzi scheme, but the police were yet to declare it as such. Bevan staunchly refuted the claim, and Izzy had met the Dubai and Irish partners.

Unless they're a smokescreen too.

Izzy rubbed her temples, hating that everything she knew and had believed about Brad was under scrutiny, constantly changing and posing more questions than she could answer.

"He's not dumb," the young woman said indignantly. "And it wasn't Ponzi. He made money for two years before the guy vanished."

The well-dressed young man scoffed. "Well, duh, Elise. That's how a Ponzi scheme works. Suck them in then bleed them dry, right, Cooper?"

"Do you know what a Ponzi scheme is?" the student next to Izzy asked her.

"It's fraud," she said softly.

"Do you have something to share with the room, Ms. ...?" Cooper asked.

Izzy froze.

The student next to her said, "She was just telling me what a Ponzi scheme is."

Cooper looked straight at Izzy. "That's great, but Kaylah won't be the only person who doesn't know. Please share your explanation with the group."

Izzy felt the burn of twenty sets of eyes on her and wished she could cast a vanishing spell and disappear. Slowly she raised her head, knowing that even though Cooper didn't recognize her, the moment she opened her mouth he would.

"A Ponzi scheme is fraud," she said quietly. "People are encouraged to invest in a product or a money-making strategy that doesn't exist, unaware that their dividends are being paid using other investors' money."

Cooper's forest-green eyes dilated in shock.

Oh God, he knows.

Of course he freaking knows. The Standard, the Age and the Herald Sun all published your name and photo.

Izzy's fingers tingled as panic took over.

Breathe ... in and out ... in and out ...

As much as she wanted to leave, she forced herself to stay seated. Walking out now would throw up far too many questions and make everything worse.

Is that actually possible?

Kaylah was frowning. "But if no money's being made, how does that even work long-term?"

Izzy stared doggedly ahead. "It doesn't."

"It only works for as long as the con artist can convince new people to invest," Cooper said, clearing his throat.

At the term "con artist," all the students sat up, their attention fully engaged.

Cooper continued. "Every Ponzi scheme shares common traits.

The leader surrounds themselves with all the accoutrements of wealth —fast cars, high-end houses and a jet-setting lifestyle. At first they approach people who know and trust them, so that's family and friends. For Ponzi to work, trust is key. People are offered a—" Cooper used his fingers to make inverted commas, "—'once in a lifetime' opportunity to invest with high returns. Early investors benefit with the promised dividends because they're key to convincing their family and friends to invest too. They inadvertently keep the fraud going."

A memory of Brad's words crashed into Izzy. "Elite is its name. It's special and exclusive and limited to people we know and trust." Her throat tightened as every event she'd organized for Elite came into sharp and unrelenting focus. The over-the-top themes. How Brad had always insisted she wear a new and expensive designer dress and how there was always a new toy—car, property, jewelry—for her to parade in front of Elite members.

Oh God! She could barely breathe. All of it had been to tempt people to join and stay, so Brad could steal from them.

"So that's why Uncle Jim made money," Elise was saying. "He was in it from the start."

"But I still don't get how it worked for two years," Kaylah said to Cooper.

"When the original scam starts running dry, often a new one's created. It's promoted as even more exclusive than the first to tempt the high rollers."

The words hit Izzy like hail—hard, sharp and bitterly cold. Cooper had just described Fortune.

"OMG!" Elise squealed. "Uncle Jim wanted Dad to join this new super-exclusive club called Fortune, but Dad had just bought an investment property so he didn't have any spare cash."

"Your dad was lucky," Cooper said. "The new recruits always lose everything."

"Why?"

"Initially they're keeping the original investors afloat, and then, when the con ultimately falls apart," Cooper's questioning gaze fixed on Izzy, "the fraudster disappears with the money."

Humiliation merged with her shock and devastation. How had she missed what Brad had been doing? Worse, she'd been unwittingly party to it.

Just leave. Leave now and never come back.

She shut her laptop and was rising out of her seat when Cooper said, "We've taken a bit of a detour from corporate governance so let's get back to it. Izzy, you and I discussed accountability and transparency. Can you please elaborate on their importance in business?"

It was clearly a warning shot, although if he'd wanted to out her he could have called her Isobel or Ms. Harrington—the names the press always used.

She risked a look at his face, expecting condemnation, but instead it was his usual teaching face. She calculated storming out versus staying. If she left now, she had no control over the narrative—not that she had much anyway.

She slowly lowered herself back into the chair and tried to form a cogent sentence.

CHAPTER TWENTY-ONE

At the end of the tutorial Izzy made a fast exit, wanting and needing to leave campus before anyone other than Cooper put two and two together and came up with Brad Quinn's fiancée. She'd just traversed the length of the corridor and reached the external doors when someone called her name.

"Izzy. Wait!"

Ignoring the request, she pushed open the door and kept walking.

A minute later she heard the crunch of gravel behind her and risked a quick backwards glance—Cooper was jogging up the incline. She picked up her pace and when he finally caught up to her he was breathing hard.

"Hey," he said. "I've been kidding myself I'm fit."

She kept walking.

"I'm surprised you came today," he said. When she didn't slow he added, "It took me a while to work out it was you in those clothes and under that cap."

She stopped then and gave him what she hoped was a do-not-go-there look. "You chased me three hundred yards to tell me that?"

"I didn't chase—" He held up his hands at her raised brows. "Fair enough. I want to talk to you."

Warning signals ran up her spine. "This better be about the course."

"You've been working in your fiancé's business and now he's vanished with millions of dollars."

She glared at him. "And that's related to the course how?"

A look of incredulity crossed his face. "You're currently doing a unit on business ethics!"

She hated his judgmental tone. "I'm very well aware of what I'm studying."

"Then you'll understand my concerns."

"You don't have anything to be concerned about. So far I've completed each assessment task and attended the required number of face-to-face tutorials."

He shook his head as if trying to make sense of her words. "Izzy, you told me Quinn's program was awesome. That you'd done a deep dive on the analytics. It means you know the business and you saw the movement of money. You're complicit in ripping off good people!"

Fury blew through her. "You don't know anything. You think I'd be standing here if I was involved in whatever the hell he was doing?"

"I really don't know what to think!"

"That's your prerogative."

"Everyone has an opinion, Izzy, and they'll continue to have one based on what the media are saying. Every time you're mentioned, your face is splashed across the screen followed by a long shot of your mansion. They always say you're hiding out in luxury. Yet you've come here today clearly in disguise and explained to the class what a Ponzi scheme is." He threw up his arms as if the action explained all his thoughts on the situation. "Talk about mixed messages."

"And what's your message, Cooper? That I lack the morals and ethics to take your precious class?" After days of being alone it felt good to be yelling at someone, even if he wasn't the person she wanted to scream at and scratch. "Fine. I won't sully your class. I quit."

She was walking away when he said, "Where's your ring?"

"What?"

"Your engagement ring. You're not wearing it."

For some unfathomable reason she looked at her left hand as if she was surprised the ring was no longer there. The night Brad had denied her the chance to return it to him and abandoned her in this hellhole, she'd thrown it across the room. The only reason she'd shoved it in her sock drawer was to protect Thor from choking on it.

She raised her chin and looked at Cooper. "It's all part of my mixed messages."

He frowned. "Are you still engaged to Quinn?"

"That's none of your business. Besides, if I gave you an answer, would you believe me?"

He studied her face as if seeking clues. "I don't know."

She gave him a fury-tinged smile. "Judge and jury then. Good to know."

"Izzy, be fair. I'm trying to be honest here. What am I supposed to think when each time we've talked you've given me the impression you were very much involved with Quinn's business?"

His words hit with an unwanted truth. While Brad and the money remained missing would anyone ever believe her again? Was Cooper the litmus test?

Her high-octane anger at him deflated like air rushing out of a balloon, but her wariness remained. "I told you I worked with him and that's true. What I didn't tell you was I was only ever his events planner."

Cooper raised one dark brow. "So why lie to me about the analysis?"

She sighed. "It's a long story and I don't feel comfortable telling it standing in the middle of the path to the parking lot."

"We could go to my office."

"No!"

He blinked at her emphatic tone. "O-kay. We're not likely to run into anyone down by the river."

"How do I know you won't push me in?"

He gave her a wry smile. "I could ask you the same question."

"My life's enough of a mess without adding the suspicious death of an academic."

She fell in beside him, finding it easier to talk when she didn't have to look at him. "I've been an events planner for eight years, but I can do it in my sleep and I wanted a new challenge. Brad was busy with Elite and I thought if I got more involved it would help us both. It's why I enrolled in the course. To show him I was serious about the business." A bitter laugh escaped.

"And?"

The skin on her cheeks burned. "And he always had an excuse as to why now wasn't the best time for me to get involved and how later would be better. I decided that if I did my presentation on Elite I could wow Brad with my data analysis. But after I spent a day trying to make sense of the betting sheets he sent to the members, I asked him to explain them to me. When he realized I wanted to present Elite, he went ballistic and stormed out. I stayed up all night writing the presentation I gave."

"You told me he was worried about confidentiality," Cooper said.

"I thought he was." Her heart thumped hard and she risked a glance at him. "You remember me saying that?"

"Of course. I suggested you should still do the analysis for your own edification."

"You did." She sighed. "But I didn't."

He frowned. "Then why did you lie to me in the coffee shop?"

She snapped a gum leaf off an overhanging branch and shredded it, breathing in the crisp, fresh scent and hoping it would steady her. "By then Brad was blocking every attempt I made to see the numbers and he was giving me a hard time about the course. You were the only person who took an interest in my studies and I was too embarrassed to tell you that the extent of my involvement was choosing canapés and being seen in dazzling frocks."

She tugged hard at the hair she could reach through the hole at the back of the cap. "Listening to you today, and looking back over the last year, it's now so fricking obvious something was very wrong with Elite."

Cooper shoved his hands into his pockets. "His parents don't think so."

"No. They've launched a missing person's campaign because there's been no activity on his bank account. The police say that means nothing. They have a few theories. One is he's slipped out of the country on a stolen passport and followed the money he's probably been squirreling out from the start. If that's the case, they're biding their time until he eventually turns up, although it will likely be in a country without an extradition treaty. Another possibility is that he's still in the country and has opened a new account under a false name and is living his life as that person."

"Do you have a theory?"

She threw the leaf into the river and sighed. "I don't know who or what to believe anymore. I've lost the ability to recognize what's real and what's fake, so I have no idea why I'm expecting you to believe me."

She looked straight at him then, suddenly filled with a new determination. "And you know what? It doesn't matter if you believe me or not. You're just a disinterested bystander taking all your information from the media and imposing your moral superiority on me. Your opinion doesn't matter. The only people I need to believe me are the police."

Something flickered momentarily in his dark green eyes. She desperately wanted it to be dislike, but it looked a lot like pity. She hated him for that.

CHAPTER TWENTY-TWO

BIRDIE STOOD at the kitchen window, staring into the yard, and a wave of melancholy hit her. For years the view had brought her joy, but not today. The flower garden was dismal winter-bare and brown, and the only green things she could see were weeds. Some milk thistles were a meter tall, having taken advantage of Mike's illness and her weeks in Geelong. Now they mocked her—*you have no control over anything, do you?* A volcanic surge of anger vanquished melancholy. Jack should have cared for the flower garden! But he was too busy keeping his own yard immaculate to impress potential buyers because his greedy wife had wanted too much too soon.

Birdie turned abruptly away from the window. As she thumped the kettle onto its base she was aware of an ache in her jaw. This had been happening a lot since Mike's heart attack. The doctor had recommended she see her dentist, but who had the time? Since Mike's discharge from the hospital, caring for him was a full-time job.

For every day of the twenty-one he'd spent in the hospital, she'd wished they were home, but since arriving back in Glingilly she wasn't sure this was what she wanted. She was Mike's wife, carer, cook and cleaner, and responsible for all the domestic tasks. She hadn't realized how much Mike contributed until she was raking leaves, putting out the trash and filling the car with gas. Even cooking—which she could do with her eyes closed and her mind on other things—had changed. So many of her old standards and Mike's favorites had been deemed unacceptable by the dietitian. Now every meal was created with the iPad open on the counter as she learned to cook new heart-healthy recipes. Meals Mike often refused to eat.

It wasn't just the extra workload. Birdie missed the reassuring support of the doctors and nurses, who'd been on hand whenever she was overwhelmed or had questions—and that had been often. But most of all, she missed Mike.

The man she knew and loved, who'd technically died on their kitchen floor, hadn't returned to her when his heart restarted. The man who'd been discharged home to Glingilly was thinner, frailer and completely lacking in spark. There were times when Birdie thought a stranger sat in Mike's chair and lay in their bed.

Her gaze fell onto his prepackaged drug kit. Once, he'd taken a multivitamin. Now the amount of medication he needed was staggering. There were pills for lowering cholesterol, pills to stop blood clots, pills to make his heart beat more efficiently—pills that made her weep. When the pharmacist had suggested a prepackaged seven-day kit with the drugs separated into their correct doses and times, Mike had said a tight-lipped "no" to Birdie's very relieved "yes." Now she noticed he hadn't taken his morning tablets. The ache in her jaw intensified.

She made tea, then loaded a tray with mugs, a glass of water, the tablets, and a healthy heart-friendly muffin that would benefit from butter that was no longer allowed. She carried the tray into the sunroom and set it on the table.

Mike lay dozing in the recliner—he did a lot of that—and once again the tangle of fear and fury hit her so hard it almost spun her around.

"Mike." She waited, clinging to ragged optimism and hope.

He opened his eyes, but the twinkle of delight that had always resided in their blue-on-blue depths was absent, along with any sign of joy that he was happy to be alive. The kick of despair in her chest was as hard as a horse's hoof.

She tried for an upbeat tone. "I've brought tea. You forgot your tablets."

"No, I didn't."

She showed him the drug pack with the intact seal. He grunted, leaving her unsure if he'd forgotten or just deliberately not taken them. She handed him the pills and the glass of water.

"Jeez, Birdie. I'm taking the bloody things. You don't have to stand there watching."

She thought there was every reason she needed to do just that, but she stepped back, picked up her own mug, then sat.

"I thought after this we could potter in the garden for half an hour. There are some milk thistles demanding our attention and they'll pull out easily after the rain."

"I've got cardiac rehab," he said flatly.

"That isn't until this afternoon."

The community health nurse, Charys, had visited a few days after they'd got home and discussed the rehab program with them both. It involved a variety of different things, including education about diet and lifestyle, drug information and exercise.

Mike sipped his tea and didn't look at her. "I don't think weeding's a good idea. I have to protect my sternum."

"You don't have to bend or extend your arms beyond what's allowed, and milk thistles don't weigh more than five pounds."

Mike made a huffing sound. "You're always saying don't overdo it. When I'm not, I still get into trouble."

Before the heart attack Birdie had often said those words when Mike would try to fit a day and a half's worth of jobs into a morning, but this afternoon's session was hardly going to be arduous. It was a "sit and chat" with the social worker.

"The doctor said it was important to do some gentle exercise every day," she reminded him, trying to sound calm.

"Yeah, well, I'm not gardening."

Birdie rubbed her jaw. "A short walk then? We could do a circuit and rest halfway at the park."

He picked up the remote. "The cricket telecast's starting."

"It's winter!"

"It's summer in England and I was supposed to be watching the match at Lord's right now."

Birdie's chest tightened so fast she thought something inside her might snap. She wanted to tell him to stop behaving like a child. That he was the one who would suffer if he didn't exercise. That—

The image of him lying terrifyingly still on the kitchen floor crashed into her yet again, bringing with it her ever-present fears. What if he was right? What if he got too tired and had another heart attack?

The thwack of willow against leather filled the room, signaling she'd failed yet again in the battle to lever him out of the recliner. She swallowed her sigh and returned to the kitchen, bringing all of her concerns for Mike with her. They played in her head in a wild and chaotic maelstrom and she automatically picked up the phone to call Judy. She wanted a bloody good whine about husbands who didn't help themselves.

It wasn't until her finger was hovering over the green button and she saw the name and number on the screen that she realized what she was doing. She dropped the cell phone as quickly as if it was covered in anthrax, uncertain who she was more furious at—herself or Judy. Her friend—ex-friend—hadn't responded to any of the texts or voice messages she'd left before Mike's heart attack.

Back then, Birdie had thought the loss of their money and Judy's silence and betrayal was as bad as her life could get. Oh, how wrong she'd been. It was during the anxious days when Mike was post-heart surgery and critically ill with pneumonia that she'd seen the Quinns on *The Project*. Seen Judy's tears and heard her pleas for anyone who knew anything about Brad to come forward. Rage had engulfed Birdie like a summer's gale—strong, hot and dangerous—and with a trembling hand she'd snatched up the remote and turned off the set. She'd wanted to fling the remote at the screen, hear the shatter of plastic and glass and the tumble of batteries against the tiled floor of the rental apartment, but she couldn't afford to replace the device. Instead she'd screamed all the words and expletives she'd wanted to yell at Judy but had kept buried inside her.

In the years before Elite had existed and Fortune had crashed, burned and consumed all of their money, Judy would have been the one sitting beside Birdie in the hospital, providing support, food, love and a laugh. She'd done it when Sienna was twelve and had fallen off her horse, and again after the under-seventeens' footy grand final when Jack had been knocked unconscious. Not once in all their years of friendship had Birdie ever doubted Judy's love for her. When they'd been in the motherhood trenches, surviving playground tedium, coping with the exhaustion that comes with sick children, and later the worries of teens and parties, there'd been times when Birdie had felt closer to Judy than to Mike.

The knife of betrayal twisted sharply.

Birdie didn't buy Judy's television tears—they reeked of crocodile. The woman had always been over-involved in her son's life and if anyone knew where Brad was right now, it was Judy. If Birdie still had money, she'd bet on that bastard boy having slipped out of the country. He was doing a Christopher Skase, holed up somewhere tropical and sunny with his stolen money, and thumbing his nose at everyone in Glingilly who'd been gullible enough to believe his blarney. Whatever the Quinns' plan—and Birdie was convinced it was an elaborate one designed to protect Brad and the stolen money—it was just a matter of time before Judy and Bevan and Isobel found a way to join him.

Birdie realized she was grinding her teeth and quickly swiped the phone screen closed. Nothing would induce her to call Judy. She'd never forgive her for convincing them to join Elite and then allowing Brad to steal their money. As far as she was concerned, seeing Judy again before she died was one time too many. She hoped the Quinns would rot in hell for all eternity, because right now, she was in a hell of her own.

She poured a second mug of tea and eyed her laptop warily. Its shiny silver casing reminded her of the money they'd spent, and opening it only gave her grief. As part of her survival strategy she only checked her email and opened the physical mail every second day. It gave her some breathing space between the parade of bad news.

The only positive thing in the whole mess of losing their money and almost losing Mike was that they now had an official reason for not taking the overseas vacation so their travel insurance should refund the cruise and the flights. This would give them money in the bank to live off until Mike was well enough to return to work.

Birdie had dutifully filled in all the insurance forms and submitted them, but the bean counters were disputing her claim, stating that as Mike's heart attack had happened before the vacation, they wouldn't pay for anything. Birdie was currently chasing doctors for letters to support her claim, but getting past officious receptionists took time and almost more fortitude than she could muster. It was just another situation where she lacked control and she hated it.

The computer pinged with new mail and she took a deep breath. Both the power and gas companies had sent "failure to pay" notices because the bank account didn't have enough money in it to cover the automated direct debits. But it was the email with the cheery subject line, *Your travel trailer is ready for a lifetime of adventures,* that punched. With everything else that was going on, she'd forgotten all about the van.

She forced herself to open the email and a photo of their custom trailer appeared with a note about how it had been finished earlier than expected so they could "hit the road." There were accompanying instructions on how to make the final payment and arrange for collection. The sum was ten percent of the total cost, but even if it had been five percent, they didn't have the money. Hell, they barely had enough to live.

Birdie's mind betrayed her by going straight to her binder book filled with plans for their trip—a culmination of a lifetime of dreams now crushed by reality. Tears rose fast, and unlike so many times in the previous weeks when she'd held them back because she needed to be strong, today they spilled over in a hot trail. Losing the travel trailer was worse than the overseas vacation because she'd never imagined exploring Europe or taking a luxury cruise. But the trip around Australia had been decades in the planning. Now it was impossible—they couldn't afford the trailer and Mike was too sick.

She grabbed tissues, blew her nose and heaved in steadying breaths. All she'd done for weeks was deal with crap, but she wasn't dealing with this. It would only remind her of everything she'd lost and she didn't trust herself not to sob down the phone. Before his heart attack, Mike had dealt with all their finances. Perhaps this phone call to the travel trailer company could be his first step in taking back some of those responsibilities.

Decision made, she returned to the sunroom. "We just got an email. The trailer's ready."

Mike didn't mute the cricket. Nor did he say a word.

Trying to override the simmer of resentment that bubbled into her gut, Birdie picked up the remote and silenced the commentators. "I thought you might give them a call."

He didn't lift his eyes from the screen. "You do it."

"No!" She jerkily pointed the remote at the television and turned it off. "I'm dealing with the travel insurance, medical insurance and negotiating with the power and gas companies to arrange payment plans. You are more than capable of making a phone call while you sit in that goddamn chair all day!"

He looked at her then, his face a mask of fury. "The trailer and the vacation were your damn ideas so you deal with them."

"And risking all our savings in Fortune was yours!"

Not once in thirty-five years had she wanted to hit him, but right now it took every ounce of restraint to hold back. She wanted him to say more so she could scream and rant, but he stayed silent and switched the television back on.

Right then she hated him with a fury that shook her. She stormed out into the garden, and when she finally silenced the angry thoughts and got her breathing back under control there were twenty milk thistles in a pile on the grass. Weeds were choking her garden just like their financial situation was choking her life. It was a constant pressure on her chest, a continuous pain in her gut and an unceasing chant in her head. Since his heart attack, Mike had checked out, leaving the responsibility of chasing money and looking after his health on her shoulders. She'd never felt so alone in her life.

She sat on the grass and checked their bank balance. The stark number told an uncompromising truth. Thank God they owned their own home, but the idea of taking out a mortgage against it and putting themselves into more debt made her shudder.

The social worker at the hospital had suggested Birdie contact Centrelink regarding social support services, and she'd spoken to a caseworker who had outlined all the documents she must submit. The relief and hope Birdie had experienced when she'd uploaded them onto the portal had been equal to her expectations when she'd filed the insurance claim. Unlike the insurance company that had said a flat-out no, forcing her to ask for a review, Centrelink had her on a long, long string. Each time she logged onto the MyGov website hoping the new message was the approval to receive some money, it was a request for yet another document. This had been going on for weeks.

Birdie hated the way she had to expose their entire financial situation. It was like standing naked in the street and being critically examined—excruciating, embarrassing and soul-destroying. They'd been financially independent all their lives, paid their taxes and never tried to rip off the government by using creative accounting. But now when they needed help, they not only had to prove they were worthy of it, they also had to endure the judgment that they'd been greedy and it was their own fault they'd lost their money.

She shut down the bank app and looked at the pile of weeds. Her mother had always said a weed was a plant in the wrong place. Birdie gave a raw laugh—she felt like she was in the wrong place in her life. She wanted to be out of the weeds and back where she belonged.

The solution was suddenly obvious. She needed a job.

But the momentary solace of that decision was decimated by reality. Who would employ a woman who was almost sixty and hadn't worked outside of the home in decades?

No one.

CHAPTER TWENTY-THREE

THE CRISP WINTER air that tingled fingertips and noses was offset by a brilliant blue sky, making it a perfect day for a real estate auction. Lucy had been up since six, cleaning the house so it sparkled for the final inspection immediately prior to the auction. Jack had been a whirlwind with the leaf blower and the long driveway had never looked so good.

Lucy tried not to let that irony dent her positive vibes. Today was their turning point. They might have lost all their money and be forced to sell their home, but it was onwards and upwards from here. The house glowed with the promise of providing a new family with a wonderful life and Tiffany had shown it to twenty people in the previous two weeks. The agent was confident there were at least two couples who were genuinely interested in buying.

"Mommy." Rigby pulled at Lucy's pants. "Tell the people to go away!"

Guilt scratched her heart—she hated that her son's world had been turned on its head. He was too little to fully understand why he couldn't play with Mike at the moment or why they had to sell the house, and it had culminated in bed-wetting and nightmares. He woke every night screaming.

Ideally, Lucy would have preferred Rigby to be elsewhere today, but their friends were busy on Saturday mornings, ferrying kids to sports and activities. Jack had suggested they ask Birdie, but Lucy was still stinging from her mother-in-law's verbal slap at the hospital and she refused to ask her for any help.

"Aren't your parents coming to the auction?" she'd said, thinking perhaps Birdie could mind Rigby by default.

Jack had shrugged. "They haven't mentioned it and I didn't ask."

Now Lucy picked up Rigby and hugged him. "Remember what we told you? One of these people will buy the house and you, me and Daddy are going to live in a new house."

Rigby pouted. "Don't want to!"

Neither do I. "It will be exciting! All your toys are coming and we can decorate your new room with dinosaurs," she bribed.

His solemn brown eyes fixed on her face. "Like Harry?"

She smiled, feeling a win. Rigby's current favorite book was *Harry and His Bucket Full of Dinosaurs.* "Just like Harry."

Jack walked in from the garden. "It's a good size crowd. Tiffany says the auctioneer's about to start."

A dart of anxiety hit, taking the shine off Lucy's optimism. "I don't know if I can watch."

Jack grinned. "Sure you can. You don't wanna miss the excitement of hearing it sell way over the minimum price we need."

She latched onto his enthusiasm. "You're right. I'd kick myself."

"Of course I'm right." He lifted Rigby out of her arms. "Daddy's always right, isn't he?"

Rigby tilted his head as if he was considering the statement.

Lucy laughed and took Jack's proffered hand. "Let's do this."

"The rise in interest rates means the market's softened and people are looking for bargains," Tiffany told them when the only bid had failed to kickstart a bidding frenzy. "Unfortunately, today's crowd were tire kickers."

"Or vultures come to watch us squirm," Lucy said later to Jack when they were finally alone. She couldn't tell if she was furious, humiliated or petrified by the failed sale. "What the hell do we do now?"

Jack was pacing the length of the family room, oblivious to the glorious view that had been the driving force behind their purchase of the house. "We don't have a choice. We keep it on the market."

"And what? Watch our debt mount and the bank seize it when we've defaulted on the mortgage more times than their goodwill allows?"

"It will sell before then." Only his voice lacked the conviction it had held that morning.

She pressed her palms flat against the kitchen counter to stop them from waving wildly. "Jack, if it doesn't sell, it's a double whammy. We'll have nowhere to live and be in a lifetime of debt."

He paused his pacing and looked straight at her. "We can always declare bankruptcy."

Her body tingled from head to toe. "Oh my God! No!"

Jack's brows rose and he gave a dismissive shrug. "It clears the debt."

Blood pounded against her temples. "That's the only positive against a pile of awful negatives. Bankruptcy affects our credit rating for seven years! We may never get another bank loan. And it puts our names on the public record until we're dead, so no one will insure us and maybe no one will even rent to us. God, it might even affect my registration with the Nursing and Midwifery Board."

The thought made her gasp and suddenly she was doubled over and coughing. She drank some water, and as she set the glass down she noticed her hand was shaking.

"Bankruptcy is the absolute last resort, Jack. I'll do anything to avoid it."

He sighed and resumed pacing.

Lucy grabbed a pen and a sheet of paper and, even though the numbers were branded on her brain, wrote their monthly income and financial commitments in two separate columns.

"They're short-staffed at work," Jack said. "I could start working three weeks on, one week off."

Despite hating the idea of him being away for so long, she did a quick calculation. "It's still not enough to cover the mortgage and the loan."

"Can you move to fulltime?"

She'd already thought of that. "Most of the extra income would go in childcare and that's if I can even get any. Plus if you're only home for one week, how do I cover the other night-duty week?"

"Mom could help."

Tension coiled through her like a steel cable. "Your Dad's still not great ..."

"Yeah, but that's short-term. I was reading the hospital website and it says that three months after heart surgery he'll be fitter than ever."

She still remembered the shock of seeing Mike's shrunken figure in the hospital bed. "He was pretty sick."

"Yeah, but he's home and doing that cardiac rehab thing, so he can't be that sick"

Lucy hadn't seen Mike since that awful day at the hospital. She knew she should visit Cork Street, but she didn't want to deal with Birdie. Besides, when he'd been discharged, she'd been working nights so she'd thrown some meat and veggies into the crockpot and sent the casseroles over with Jack. It should have made her feel better, but all she could think was it was fifteen dollars of food they couldn't really afford to give away. To add insult to injury, Birdie hadn't called or texted to thank her.

Lucy threw down the pen. As she filled the kettle, the memory of sipping gin and tonics on the emerald lawns of Villefranche knocked into her. Those carefree afternoons seemed like a thousand years ago. God, she could do with a G&T right now, but they were out of gin and she couldn't justify buying a bottle when the cost would feed them for a few days.

Jack suddenly clapped. "I've got it!"

Hope soared. "What?"

He grinned at her—all boyish delight—just like the day she'd met him on the tram. "We rent out the house until it sells! That way, the rent covers the mortgage so we protect the house *and* we pay off the loan. It's win-win."

She stared at him, her brain part-frozen in shock and the rest struggling to follow his thought process. "And where do we live, Jack? We can't afford to pay rent somewhere and cover the personal loan."

He shot her a look that implied she was slow. "We move in with Mom and Dad."

Her hands rose as fast as if she was warding off an attacker. "No!"

He grimaced. "Luce, this is the solution."

The simmer of panic bubbled into her gut. "There has to be another way."

"If there was we'd have thought of it by now. And you said you'd do anything to avoid bankruptcy."

"Yes, but—"

"Hang on, take a deep breath and think about it. Mom and Dad lost money, but they own the house. We can sleep in my old room, Rigby can have Sienna's, and we can use the rec room as our space."

"Jack, your childhood home isn't how you remember it. Your mom turned Sienna's room into a sewing room years ago and your Dad's reverted half of the rec room back to a workshop."

"We'll make it work," he said easily.

"Your Dad's still recovering," she said, desperately trying to stall his idea.

"I know and that's part of the win." He was smiling now, as if he'd thought of everything. "Living there, we can help more. I know Mom's ticked off that I haven't been around to help with the gardens, and she's freaking out over Dad's pills so she'll appreciate your medical advice."

Lucy hadn't told Jack what Birdie had said to her at the hospital.

They had enough to deal with and sometimes Jack could be funny about his parents. As a result of her own parents' divorce, their subsequent second marriages and the birth of half-siblings who were yet to finish high school, Lucy had a far more transactional relationship with her family—a Christmas visit and birthday phone calls. Jack didn't understand this and whenever he suggested she visit more often, she hid behind their distance from Melbourne and the fact that her parents never suggested driving down to Glingilly. "The road goes both directions, Jack," was her usual reply. But hiding behind distance wasn't an option with Birdie and Mike.

"It's a big ask, Jack. They might say no." *Please God, make them say no.*

Jack shook his head with the confidence of a firstborn son. "They're not going to say no. They love us and want the best for us. Besides, they adore Rigby and we'll have built-in babysitters so we can both work more." He grinned again. "I told you I'd work it out."

She opened her mouth to yell, "This isn't worked out!", but instead the pressure of the day blew its lid and she was suddenly sobbing uncontrollably.

He pulled her into a hug and stroked her hair. "Hey, shh, it's over. You can relax. This will be win-win for everyone."

She knew it was far more likely to be lose-lose. But without a single idea to counter his, once again control roared away from her as fast as an outgoing tide.

CHAPTER TWENTY-FOUR

Izzy rubbed her sweaty palms on her activewear, then slid on her sunglasses and pulled on her baseball cap. Along with her hoodie and black running shoes, this was her new uniform. She prayed it made her look like every other woman in their thirties who'd dropped kids off at school and was now heading to the gym or coffee with friends—except she was an hour ahead of them. At 8:00 in the morning, she was hoping to navigate the IGA supermarket without meeting anyone from Elite. Last time she'd shopped, this school-run-mom outfit had saved her from being recognized by Alan and Penelope Lumsden.

Keeping her head down, she walked through the automatic opening doors, grabbed a shopping trolley and worked her way methodically down the aisles, buying all the staples she could afford so she could delay returning for as long as possible. As she grabbed boxes of long-life milk, she decided it was time to grow her own vegetables.

Steering the trolley toward the front of the store, she did a quick scan of the area. No customers and one bored teen chewing her nails. *Yes!*

Izzy smiled at the teen and started unloading her groceries. The girl managed to break the record for being the slowest scanner and the worst packer in checkout history. With each thirty-second increment, another bead of sweat pooled under Izzy's arms and on her palms. Her eyes flicked between the teen, the door and the grocery bags. The moment the girl filled one, Izzy hefted it into the trolley, readying for a quick getaway.

There were only six items remaining on the conveyor belt when the main doors opened. Izzy risked a quick glance and froze. Lucy Essen walked in wearing hospital scrubs, her rubber-soled shoes squeaking on the linoleum floor. Izzy turned quickly so her back faced the woman and prayed Lucy hadn't seen her.

The teen dropped a bunch of bananas on top of a bag of salad. "Do you have a rewards card?" Izzy shook her head. "Do you want to join the program?" the girl intoned with the world weariness of someone half a century older. Izzy shook her head again. "One hundred and fifteen twenty. Cash or card?"

"Card." Izzy was delving into her handbag when she heard the voice behind her.

"If you wanted to blend in wearing Target activewear, Isobel, you should have left the Prada handbag in the car."

The bitterness in Lucy's tone seared her and she turned slowly. "Hello, Lucy."

"You don't get to say hello!"

Izzy ducked her head and turned back to the teen, who now had a glint of interest in her eyes. She swiped her card.

"Don't you dare turn away from me!" Lucy spat.

With a trembling hand, Izzy punched in her PIN. The machine beeped.

"Wrong PIN or are you broke?" the teen asked.

"Oh, she's not broke," Lucy said. "That handbag's worth two and a half grand."

"Yeah?" The teen gave it a dismissive look. "It's a crap color."

Izzy stabbed the numbers in again and this time the payment went through. The machine laboriously printed out the receipt and she shoved it in the closest reusable shopping bag. As her hands gripped the trolley, Lucy moved in front of her and blocked the exit.

"Why are you here?" Lucy demanded.

Izzy's heart hammered and her head swam. "I needed food."

"So now you're a comedian as well as a thief? You shouldn't be in Glingilly. No one wants you here and no one wants to see your ugly face reminding them of everything you've stolen from us."

"I didn't—"

"Do you get off on other people's pain?" Lucy was gripping the end of the trolley now and leaning in, her face twisted in fury. "Because of you, my father-in-law's had a heart attack. Because of you, I'm living in one room in my mother-in-law's house. Because of you, Rigby and I only get one week a month with Jack. You fucking destroyed our lives and yet you swan around with your Prada handbag and your Chlóe Lauren sneakers as if nothing's changed!"

The words ripped into Izzy like bullets, making her sway. She longed to say that she hadn't deliberately worn the shoes to taunt Lucy —designer labels were the only shoes she owned—but even in her rattled state she recognized that would only inflame the situation.

She swallowed and tried to speak. "I didn't know about Mike. I'm so sorry. Is he okay?"

"Sorry?" Lucy's face flushed red. "You're sorry? That's it?"

"Of course I'm sorry. I understand what it's like to lose everything—"

"Oh, that's rich! Your handbag alone would go a long way toward my monthly mortgage repayment."

Izzy emptied the bag on top of some tomato tins. "Take it. Sell it."

Lucy hesitated for a split second, then shook her head. "You think you can buy me off with a measly two grand when you and your fiancé have ripped off millions from this community, leaving people destitute—"

"I didn't have anything to do with that!" Izzy was gripping the trolley so tightly, pain radiated from her knuckles to her core.

"Bullshit! That day in the bookshop you said how worried you were about Brad being ripped off when in truth it was the two of you doing it to us. You told me you ran the company with Brad."

Izzy's vision blurred and she gulped in air, hoping it would keep her standing. Why the hell had she gilded the truth? *Get real! You lied.* She shook off the uncomfortable thought.

"I said I was *capable* of running the company, not that I was doing it."

Lucy snorted. "Oh, you're capable alright. Women like you specialize in treachery. Everyone knows Brad's besotted with you and he does whatever you tell him—"

"That's so far from the truth—"

"The truth?" Lucy's hands flew into the air. "You wouldn't know the truth if it rose up and bit you."

Izzy's attempt at conciliatory vanished. "If I'd stolen the money why the hell would I still be in Glingilly helping the police find it?"

Lucy narrowed her eyes. "Because you're a piece of work. You might be fooling the police with this innocent act, but you don't fool me. We'll find the money trail, and when we do you're going down for everything you've done to me, my family and this town."

She shoved the trolley and it hit Izzy hard in the belly. As she doubled over, gasping for breath, she noticed the teen grinning widely while she held her cell phone out in front of her.

By the time Izzy reached her car, the video of her and Lucy screaming at each other was going viral.

On the five-mile drive back to Villefranche, Izzy almost calmed her heart rate into the normal zone. It leaped again when she saw a silver Audi parked outside the gates.

Her first instinct was to press down on the accelerator and drive past, but there was no guarantee the driver wasn't prepared to sit out the day waiting for her. Also, she'd left Thor inside and he'd destroy the joint if she was gone for more than an hour. The problem was, there was no way she could get out of the car, open the padlock, drive through the gate, then close it without the person in the car talking to her. Not for the first time, she wished Villefranche had a different gate.

When Brad had shown her the house, she'd commented on the unprepossessing entrance. "A house like this should have ornate and automatically opening gates."

"We're not that type of people," he'd said.

"What type of people?"

"Gated-community people. That's not what Elite's all about."

She'd almost said, "Yes it is—it's in the title," but she'd caught the serious look on his face and stayed silent.

"I want people to feel welcome when they come down the drive," he'd said as he'd pulled her in for a hug. "Then be inspired by what lies beyond a perfectly normal farm gate. I want them to glimpse the possibilities."

At that moment, her love for Brad had flooded her. His boundless generosity and drive to share his success with his family and closest friends so they could all benefit. Now, the memory brought acid rising to the back of her throat. Had everything been a sham? And if it was, how had she failed to recognize his brutal narcissistic streak?

Still wearing her cap and dark glasses, she got out of the car and walked purposefully to the gate as if she ruled the world rather than wanting to hide from it. As she slid the key into the padlock, a woman dressed in black pants, a white shell blouse and a black jacket came to stand next to her.

"Isobel Harrington?"

Izzy lifted her chin. "Who wants to know?"

The woman extended her hand. "Jodi Costadopoulos."

"That tells me nothing."

"I'm the loans manager for the Lawson Group. May I have a word?"

Izzy had never heard of the Lawson Group. "What about?"

Jodi inclined her head. "This property."

Everything inside Izzy stilled. "It's not my property."

"I'm aware," Jodi said.

"Then you'll also be aware that I'm not the person to talk to about it." Izzy swung the gate open and walked back to her car.

"Ms. Harrington, it's in your best interests to talk to me."

Something about the way the woman said the words made Izzy's hand pause on the doorhandle. At the same time, Lucy's threat roared back: "You're going down for everything you've done to me, my family and this town."

Did this Jodi woman know something about Brad? Was it information that might help the police case? Help Izzy work out what the hell was going on in Brad's head? Find the money?

It was worth a shot.

"Follow me in then," she said, "and lock the gate behind you."

Once inside Villefranche, Izzy worked hard to rise above her agitation and the desire to say, "Spit it out, Jodi! Tell me why you're here!" Instead she offered the woman a selection of beverages.

Jodi eyed the Italian coffee machine and smiled. "An espresso would be perfect. I saw the sun rise this morning."

Izzy didn't ask where she'd come from, but assumed Melbourne as neither Warrnambool nor Hamilton required a dawn departure.

She appreciated the fact that Jodi wasn't attempting polite conversation but had instead seated herself at the kitchen table and was making a fuss of Thor. Izzy carried the coffee and her own chai to the table, then instructed Thor to his bed. She finally sat and watched Jodi sipping her coffee. A moment of bliss suffused the woman's face, but by the time she'd lowered the cup to its saucer her look was all business.

"Mr. Bradley Quinn took out a loan with us for the purchase of this property two years ago."

"We're not married." The words blurted out before Izzy could stop them.

"I'm aware." Jodi took another sip of her coffee. "In normal circumstances, I wouldn't even be talking to you. But according to the press, Mr. Quinn is both missing and a person of interest to the police."

Izzy swallowed a sigh. "If you've come to ask me if I know where he is, you're going to be disappointed."

"I came because I felt it only fair to deliver this news in person."

A tingling sensation shot across her skin, raising every hair on her body. "You know where he is?"

But the moment she heard her words she knew how ridiculous they were. If Brad had been found, then it would be the police or the Quinns telling her, not a mortgage broker.

"Ms. Har—may I call you Isobel?" Jodi asked. Izzy shrugged. "Isobel, you may or may not be aware that Mr. Quinn has failed to make the last six mortgage payments on this property. Since he's now disappeared with millions of dollars, the Lawson Group are no longer able to extend their goodwill."

A low roar boomed in her ears as Brad's ever-darkening shadow lengthened over her life. "What are you really saying?"

"We're repossessing this property."

Images flashed in Izzy's mind—childhood memories. Her mother slamming the front door and never returning. Her father handing her a suitcase and telling her she could only take what fitted inside. The trailer park and the mold that multiplied and crawled down the cabin walls due to lousy ventilation.

Her thoughts swerved to her bank balance and she suddenly remembered what Jodi had said at the gate. "If you're kicking me out, how is that in my best interests?"

Jodi gave her an encouraging smile. "The Lawson Group's not heartless. We understand this is your home, and considering the situation with Mr. Quinn you're no doubt experiencing a great deal of emotional stress. We're happy to enter into a tenancy agreement with you to give you time to find your feet."

Izzy blinked, stunned by this stranger's empathy and lack of blame. It was the polar opposite to Lucy's and Glingilly's reaction. "Thank you!"

Jodi nodded and produced some paperwork. "It's all pretty

straightforward. You sign here and here and we require a bond and a month's rent."

It was standard rental procedure, but as Izzy accepted the pen from Jodi her gaze sought the figures. Her eyes stung.

"2,000 dollars a week?" she said faintly.

"It's very reasonable considering the size of the property."

Since her weekly payments from Elite had ceased, Izzy's bank balance was only going in one direction—down. Paying this sort of rent she'd run through her savings in no time flat.

You own an apartment in Noosa!

She still hadn't told the police about the apartment. She didn't want to risk them seizing it before she had clear evidence proving whether Brad had either used his own money or Elite funds to buy it.

She thought of Lucy screaming at her. Of the video that was playing out the scene over and over so people could indulge in schadenfreude.

Go to Noosa. No one knows you there.

The police hadn't charged her so technically she was free to leave the state, but what did that say? Surely it destroyed all her hard work of proving to the police she had no knowledge of what Brad had been doing? And it played into the hands of people like Lucy, who believed she was complicit and biding her time in a grand plan of deception. No, Noosa wasn't an option yet. But neither was paying thousands of dollars a month in rent.

"Can I have some time to think about it?"

Jodi pursed her lips, then checked her watch. "If I don't hear from you by 10:00 tomorrow morning, then you have seven days to vacate the property."

Izzy's well-honed survival skills kicked in. "I think you'll find you need to give me sixty days notice."

"We don't have a tenancy agreement with you, Isobel. We could kick you out today."

"That depends on the date on the Notice To Pay Rent you've sent Brad. Show it to me."

Izzy caught the slight flicker of unease on Jodi's face and schooled herself not to smile.

"You're not our client and that's confidential information," Jodi said.

"I'll take that as proof you're yet to generate the letter, which means I have at least thirty days before you can kick me out. Try it before then and you'll find the law's on my side."

"What's your email address?"

Izzy told her and Jodi typed furiously on her tablet. A minute later, Izzy's cell beeped and a notification banner read *The Lawson Group*.

Jodi stood, her look flinty. "If you don't sign the tenancy agreement, you have thirty days from 10:00 today to vacate the property."

Izzy opened the door. "Thanks for dropping by. Enjoy the drive back to the city."

"Thirty days," Jodi said, pausing in the doorway. "After that, we'll bring the full force of the Lawson Group's legal team down on you."

"Good to know."

Izzy closed the door on Jodi and heard the tick tick of the clock counting down.

She had thirty days to crack the accounts and prove her innocence.

CHAPTER TWENTY-FIVE

AT 1:00 in the morning, after systematically searching every pocket in Brad's pants, shorts and shirts, clearing out every drawer in Villefranche, and revisiting every nook and cranny in the office, Izzy sat surrounded by strands of her hair. She was no closer to discovering the password to the cloud. As frustrating as that was, she reminded herself that the police experts were challenged by the encryption too—not that it made her feel any better.

She pushed to her feet, grabbed a flashlight and walked through the dark moonless night to her telescope. As she gazed up at the endless carpet of stars, seeking the infusion of calm they always gave her, she couldn't shake the thought that even if Brad was a completely different person from the one she'd believed him to be, she'd lived with him for two years.

Unlike the police, she knew his habits and idiosyncrasies. How he unpacked the moment he got home from a trip. The meticulous way he arranged his shirts in color spectrum order, and how he never wore a pair of shoes for longer than a day to give the leather time to dry before the next wear. His multilayered electronic spreadsheet for his wine collection with tabs for optimum drinking dates, re-ordering reminders and the detailed notes he recorded after opening a bottle. The stark contrast of his use of an old-school, leather-bound and monographed diary-planner, and how it had taken her weeks to convince him they needed a shared electronic calendar for the Elite events and appointments.

She'd rolled her eyes more than once when Brad refused to write in the diary with anything other than his Montblanc pen. Fortunately, there was a special leather holder in the center of the diary for the platinum-coated writing tool. Brad always kept the diary with him—in fact it was the only thing he was proprietorial about. He'd cheerfully lend people his cars and open his home and cellar to them, but the diary and the pen were for his use only and they were rarely parted.

Izzy's hands fell from the telescope and she stepped back fast. The prized pen was on Brad's desk! Why hadn't she made this connection days ago?

She revisited the final time she'd seen Brad—how he'd kissed her goodbye as usual without a single sign he was planning to disappear with millions of dollars. There'd been no sense of urgency in his departure—no sign he'd been so distracted he'd forget his precious pen. Then again, she'd been hiding the fact she was leaving him.

Did the presence of the pen mean the diary was still in the house?

Unlikely. Because (a) Brad never went anywhere without it. And (b) if it was in the house, she'd have found it by now. She'd looked everywhere. Hadn't she?

She switched on the flashlight and half-walked, half-ran back to the house.

"Thor, other than the office, where did Brad spend the most time in this behemoth?"

The sleepy dog tilted his head as if considering her question.

"The home theater."

She ran to the room, hearing Thor's toenails clattering behind her. She switched on the lights and looked on and under every one of the twelve reclining leather chairs but found only dust bunnies. She searched the drinks cabinet—no diary—and there was nothing else in the room that could accommodate it.

Killing the lights, she said to Thor, "What about the gym?"

He gave her an enthusiastic bark and she ushered him down the hall and out to the gym that was next to the pool.

It was rare for Izzy to use the space—she preferred exercising outside—but she checked the towel closet and searched around the running machine, the rowing machine, the weights and even behind the wall-mounted television. No brown diary.

Fatigue hit her like a falling rock and she sagged. What the hell was she doing? She should go to bed and start again in the morning.

She switched off the lights, walked slowly back inside and made a mug of chamomile tea. Thor, sensing the adventure was over, trotted back to his bed and curled up.

A wave of loneliness hit Izzy. How bad would it be to let Thor sleep on their—her—bed? No, not even her bed now, but the Lawson Group's bed. It was totally bad parenting but she didn't care.

"Thor, come."

He shot off his bed and danced around her feet. As they crossed the entrance hall, he lingered by the cellar door instead of following her up the stairs.

"Come on, Thor," she called.

He didn't obey.

It was one thing to let him sleep on her bed and another to allow him to roam the house all night. When he refused to come a second time, she walked downstairs.

He barked at her.

"What?"

He barked again.

"This isn't the movies, mate."

Thor ran back and forth, his nose pressed against the base of the door. She suddenly remembered Brad often took Thor down to the cellar because he was such a good ratter.

She shuddered. "Can you hear rats?"

Izzy opened the door and Thor shot down the stairs. She switched on the stairwell light and followed, feeling the incremental drop in temperature as she descended.

At the bottom of the stairs there was an electronic screen declaring the temperature and the humidity. She glanced around the beautiful space where Brad had held regular wine tastings for Elite members. Had he used their money to stock it?

The ever-present ache intensified. Brad had been so proud of his extensive cellar, storing the bottles according to region and varietals, but she was only familiar with the champagne section. Distracting herself from Thor doing his job, she ventured deeper into the cellar, admiring the play of light on the golden oak racks. She noticed that at the end of each section Brad stored laminated wine notes in dedicated pigeonholes.

She idly ran her fingers along the dust-free bottles as she walked the length of the first wall of wine. As she turned, she tripped. Arms flailing, she somehow managed not to fall or take out any wine bottles with her windmilling.

She looked down to see what had caused her to lose her balance. "Oh my God!"

She bent and scooped up the leather diary. Unzipping it, she riffled through the pages that detailed every aspect of Brad's life from meetings and phone calls to personal appointments and journal entries. Was the key to the cloud in here?

Her agitated mind hit the fog of exhaustion. As much as she wanted an entry headed *Password To The Cloud*, she knew the chances of that were virtually non-existent, and she was far too tired to be alert to clues hidden in plain sight. As hard as it would be to sleep, she needed to grab a few hours then start fresh in the morning.

She called Thor, and for the next five hours she slept with him nestled into her back and the diary pressed tightly against her chest.

After a big protein-filled breakfast—brain food—Izzy took a large latte to Brad's office and opened the diary. There were four pages separating each month and there didn't seem to be any consistent format to what Brad recorded there. One page had sketches of rings and she recognized the evolution of her engagement ring. She was momentarily torn between regret and fury. Other pages contained sketches of horses and jockeys.

Between March and April there was a list of cryptic numbers and symbols. Excited, she worked her way through them until the computer told her she was locked out for an hour.

Frustrated, she returned upstairs and systematically read every page from January. Brad's meetings in Ireland and the UAE were always followed by asterisks and dollar signs. Elite events had plus signs, and hashtags preceded appointments with potential members. He'd drawn a tiered cake on the date of Izzy's birthday, complete with elaborate frosting.

Her cell beeped as an email dropped in. She glanced at the banner and surprise rolled in her stomach. Cooper. He was the last person she'd expected to hear from considering he didn't trust her and had judged her guilty. Her thoughts drifted back to their conversation by the river—*it doesn't matter if you believe me or not!* And it didn't matter. She'd quit the course and she never had to see him again. So why was he emailing her?

One thing was certain—it wouldn't be a good or pleasant reason. She blew out a long breath as she always did these days before opening an email.

Dear Izzy,

According to the records you're still enrolled and therefore I'm inviting you to submit your assignment. As you know, this is a hurdle requirement and failure to submit means you fail the unit, which impacts on your GPA. If you submit by 6pm Friday, it will

not be marked as incomplete. Please email me when it's uploaded
so I can mark it before the cut-off date.
  Best wishes,
  Cooper Barsky

Izzy blinked and reread it. Then she put down the phone. She picked it up again and read the email a third time. Her mind lurched and creaked as she tried to align this offer with the man who'd stood in front of her with arms crossed, grilling her about Elite with the intensity of a prosecuting attorney. University lecturers, let alone associate professors, didn't chase students. If you failed to submit an assignment or sit an exam, the consequences were on the student. So why was he offering her this chance?

She reread his email, but it didn't divulge his motivation, only his offer.

The timer on her cell phone sounded. Her hour was up—she could try the cloud again. Not that she had anything new to plug in.

Her eyes drifted back to the elaborate cake Brad had drawn to mark her birthday. It was a work of art, down to the tiny lines that represented the flares of light from a sparkler. As her gaze followed the shower of sparks, she suddenly realized that what she thought were pen marks inside the frosting curls could be symbols: % and ^.

You're imagining it because you want them to exist.

She narrowed her eyes, forcing focus. Was there an *I* and an *h* too? Her initials belonged on a cake for her, but she didn't associate herself with the symbols. Was it some kind of code?

She flicked quickly through the pages and found Brad's birthdate in March. He'd drawn another intricate cake. She squinted and found *B!-Q-* in the frosting curls. Her heart rate picked up.

Bevan's birthday was in July. His cake hid *61_bq*. Izzy almost gave herself a paper cut getting to November. Judy's frosting curls contained *(JQ-ma@)*.

Hope bloomed and she ran to the office. Using the Montblanc pen, she wrote the symbols in the order of their birthdays. Then she wrote another line using them in reverse. And then she applied an alphabetical combination starting with Bevan. She knew there were many more combinations, but she'd work on them during the inevitable lockout period.

With studied care, she forced her trembling fingers to slowly tap out $61\_bqB!-Q-I\%\wedge h(JQ-ma@)$

She hit the return key fully prepared for rejection. The computer took its usual sweet time and she looked at the second line on the paper in preparation to type it in. As she glanced back at the screen, it changed. She was staring at line upon line of figures.

It took a moment for the significance to fully register and then she was squealing and punching the air.

Thor barked and ran to her, his short legs scrabbling to reach her knees.

"I'm in, Thor. I'm freakin' in!"

Doused in adrenaline, she found it hard to control her movements and her hand jerked on the mouse. She scrolled down and the figures continued in six different columns, but other than a date they lacked any identifiers. She assumed they represented money. Were they deposits? Withdrawals? They ranged from seven figures down to single numbers. Why?

Damn it! She was in the cloud, but she may as well be in a foreign country without a phrasebook.

She stared hard at the screen as if that would make it cough up answers. Column B contained much smaller numbers than the other columns. God, was there a pattern anywhere?

She suddenly remembered her weekly income. She typed in the figure and it appeared regularly in column D. The corresponding figure in B was six. *Six?* She racked her brain. Six didn't have any connection to her—it wasn't her birthday, nor was it part of her address, email or otherwise, and it wasn't connected to her phone number.

Had she ever been paid anything else? In the early days, Brad had handed her cash, and although he'd frequently told her how much her portfolio was worth, lately he hadn't transferred over any lump sums.

She brought up her bank account and typed in a date eighteen months earlier. There was one deposit, but it was from Brad's personal account, not Elite. She searched the spreadsheet. It didn't match.

What about the house payments? There were two entries in the ballpark but neither was a match.

She reached for her cell phone to ring Brooke, but it rang, making her jump.

It was Judy, which meant Bevan too—both on speakerphone. Did she tell them she was in the cloud?

Caution careened along her veins and a favorite quote of her father's came back to her: "Keep your friends close and your enemies closer." Did that apply to family as well? Ex-family. She tugged at her hair and blew out a long breath.

"Hi, Judy."

"Oh, Izzy!" For the first time in weeks, Judy sounded like her old self. "We've got such good news!"

Her legs softened and she half-sat, half-fell onto the leather chair. It skated backwards. But as she said, "You've found him?", she wasn't convinced it was good news for her.

"There's been a positive sighting!" Judy squealed. "Someone called us and sent a photo."

Izzy's cell pinged and a photo of a man slid onto her screen. He was wearing dark clothing, a baseball cap pulled low on his head and sunglasses on his face. He was definitely the right height for Brad.

"Where was this taken?" Izzy asked.

"Maroochydore."

"So the police are looking there now?"

Judy made a strangled sound and then Bevan was saying, "This information's come privately. Judy and I are driving up today and we want you to jump on a flight. We're ninety-nine percent certain he's at the Noosa apartment."

The apartment Izzy now owned. The apartment the police didn't know about.

"How do you know about our Noosa apartment?" she asked.

Bevan's laugh—a tight, tense sound—buffeted her. "Brad tells me everything. I advised him to put it in your name for tax purposes."

Tax purposes? Her hand rose to her throat, her fingers trying to pull away the rope that was strangling her, but they only touched skin.

"If Brad told you everything, why don't you know where he is?"

Bevan's sharp intake of breath whistled down the line. "I know this is hard for you, Izzy. God, it's impossible for Judy and me, but we must trust him. Brad loves us. He has a plan and it's going to work out."

"And you know this plan?"

He was silent for a moment, as if weighing up his words. "Your job's not to question everything. It only makes a difficult situation harder."

How much did Bevan know? Far more than she did, but he wasn't making a lot of sense. None of it made sense.

"How is everything going to work out, Bevan? *Millions* of dollars are missing!"

"Don't drink the Kool-Aid! Brad's got nothing to do with the missing money."

"Then who does? Is it his partners? And if it is then why is Brad AWOL instead of in Glingilly talking to the police?"

"Isobel, business is complicated." His patronizing tone—eerily reminiscent of Brad's during the previous months—sliced into her.

"Oh, I know all about complicated. I'm being kicked out of Villefranche, or did you know that too?"

Judy sobbed.

Bevan sighed. "I thought the Lawson Group might react badly to the media reports."

"Brad will hate this," Judy said. "He adores you, Izzy, and he only wants the best for the people he loves. We're sure he's been lying low fixing things and keeping us safe."

OMG! Who was drinking the Kool-Aid now?

"Safe?" The word came out on a screech. "He's left me in a town that wants me dead!"

"Which is why you need to fly to the Sunny Coast," Bevan said, his tone so tight it threatened to break. "He's made sure you have a home there and all of us can be together."

A home? In a one-bedroom apartment? That wasn't Brad. If he wanted them to be together, why hadn't Bevan and Judy come to Villefranche or invited her to Dolphin Sands? And why now, on the back of a supposed sighting of Brad, was Bevan was pushing hard for Izzy to move states?

Despite her niggles of unease, if she looked at it from the angle of Judy and Bevan's devotion to family, it made some sense. Although usually conversations about family togetherness came from Judy, not Bevan.

"I can't imagine these last few weeks have been easy for you, all alone down there," Bevan said.

Easy? They'd knowingly left her on her own! Her niggles of doubt transformed into large iron spikes.

"I can't afford the ticket to the Sunny Coast," Izzy heard herself saying before she'd thought it through.

"Don't worry about money," Bevan said.

Her childhood roared back and spun around her like a tornado. "How can you say that? I no longer have an income and—"

"I didn't make money without a backup plan. I promise you, things will improve now that Brad's surfaced. It means he's dealt with the problem."

What problem? "But you don't know it's him."

"You have to believe, Izzy. We do. We're confident it's him. It makes sense. Once we're all together again, we can all relax. We can even take a vacation to put these worrying weeks behind us."

And just like that, the conversation veered into weird—as if Brad's absence had been like an ordinary business trip.

"A vacation?" she heard herself saying inanely as her mind slipped and slithered on all attempts at understanding. "Where?"

"I don't know. Where would you like to go? New Zealand?"

"New Zealand? Why New Zealand?"

"Because you and Brad never shut up about your skiing vacation in Europe and this way you can ski again!"

As Izzy recoiled from his heated exasperation, Bevan sighed. She pictured him rubbing the back of his neck.

"I'm sorry, Izzy, I shouldn't have snapped at you, but we're all stressed. It's been the worst few weeks of our lives and I'm sure yours too. Where we go on vacation isn't important, just that we do it together as a family. We all need to relax and regroup."

"But everything's such a mess," she said.

"It's only temporary," Bevan said gently. "Brad's been sorting things out and before you know it, we'll be back bigger and better than ever. Your job's to keep the faith, so start packing. I'll book your flight and text you the details."

"You'll love the warmth, Izzy darling! We'll see you soon," Judy said.

The call ended, leaving Izzy uncertain if she was coming or going. Prior to this call, the Quinns had insisted she stay in Glingilly but now they wanted her on the Sunny Coast. They were convinced Brad was waiting for them but he hadn't contacted her or them. They were talking about a vacation?!

She struggled to draw conclusions from any of it. Was the mention of New Zealand significant? Was the money there?

Yeah, right! You're so losing it!

The Land of the Long White Cloud was better known for sheep and famous fantasy movies than it was for hiding money. It was the Caymans and Switzerland that specialized in blind trusts and tax havens—Brad had definitely visited the Caymans, but he'd never visited New Zealand. Or if he had, he'd never told her.

He didn't tell you a lot of things!

And now she wasn't convinced that his parents were being transparent with her either. Was this missing person's hunt a charade? Another smokescreen to protect Brad?

Only Judy's spontaneous outbursts of emotion tempered the ugly thought. That sort of grief was too raw to fake so it made sense that the Quinns had no idea where Brad was. That didn't exclude Bevan from knowing things about Elite that Izzy wasn't privy to. Or from choosing which bits of information to reveal to her and which to hide.

Aren't you doing the same thing?

Her list of secrets from the Quinns was growing. She still hadn't told them she'd been leaving Brad. She should feel guilty about that when they were offering her safety and security, yet she couldn't shake the feeling she was a pawn in an unknown game.

"In a few months we'll be back bigger than ever," Bevan had said.

The pull for money and security tugged at her as hard as ever, underpinned by the fact that no one knew her in Noosa. She'd be able to walk down the street there without being screamed at by angry people. She wouldn't have to worry about money.

Go and be free of Glingilly.

No!

She slapped her cheek, embracing the sting. Leaving Glingilly would only deepen her connection to the Quinns and brighten the police's spotlight on her.

And what happened when Brad turned up? The love she'd once had for him belonged to another person and another time. The way he was dealing with this situation—leaving her alone, feeding her to the Glingilly lions—meant he didn't trust her and he didn't respect her. The last six months had more than proven that. There was no future for them, even if he was innocent of stealing 23 million dollars.

Izzy picked up the cell phone and called Brooke. "Can you come to Villefranche? I've got something to show you."

CHAPTER TWENTY-SIX

BIRDIE SAT at the kitchen table studying the jobs in the paper. She knew many were advertised online, but she liked to think companies that still used print might be more old-school and therefore more receptive to hiring someone wise and experienced.

Huh!

The job hunt was a continuous lesson in rejection hiding as ambiguity. No one had bothered to reply to her resumé telling her she was unsuccessful. Her caseworker at Centrelink had referred her to an employment agency, where someone had scanned her limited resumé and suggested courses to update her skills. Birdie had enough on her plate without adding study into the mix—there wasn't enough space in her brain for that.

The theme music of *Bluey* blared from the television. Mike's yell reverberated around the house. "Turn that bloody thing down!"

Birdie ground her teeth and a vice gripped her temples. When Jack was away—and now Jack was working three weeks out of four—Lucy allowed Rigby far too much screen time.

She glanced at the ceiling. *What the hell did I do that was so bad you singled me out for all of this?*

When Jack had arrived unannounced on the Monday morning after the auction offering to drive Mike to cardiac rehab and then take her out for coffee, Birdie had been so relieved and appreciative that she'd swallowed her comment about squandering money he didn't have. Instead, she'd embraced the brief window of escaping into her old normal. She'd happily sipped her first latte in weeks.

"We're rejigging our plans now the house didn't sell," Jack had said.

Birdie, who was surfing the bliss of caffeine, managed a "hmm" before taking another sip of the rich mocha brew.

Jack continued talking, but Birdie's mind was drifting as she soaked in the familiar noises of the café and luxuriated in the respite from people wanting, needing or demanding things of her.

"Mom? Are you listening?"

She snapped her attention back to Jack. He looked identical to Mike at the same age, although Jack lacked the cheeky glint in his eyes.

"Sorry, darling, I was just having a little daydream. It's so nice to be out of the house. Thanks for bringing me here."

Jack shifted in his chair, then looked over her shoulder before his gaze fell to the knot in the wooden table. She recognized that look—part contrition, part bravado—as she'd seen it often when he was growing up. It had always heralded bad news. Her short-lived reprieve vanished and the tension that had been her unwanted companion for months slid back into place.

Jack finally broke the silence. "For us to stay solvent, we need to rent the house. Can we live with you and Dad? It's just until the house sells. It'll only be a month. Two, tops."

The coffee turned bitter in her mouth as gut-spasming pain gripped her. *No! No, please, God, no.* But her heart said yes and the battle began.

What sort of parent said no and inflicted homelessness on their child and grandchild?

But Jack was no longer a child, even if he continued to make poor choices. And they weren't limited to all things financial. Lucy was his biggest mistake. He should have married a local girl who understood country life, but no—he'd knocked up a city girl from a broken home who demanded to have everything new yesterday. Of course Rigby was a gift, but Lucy was a lead weight around Jack's neck, dragging him under. More than anything, Birdie wanted to say, "You and Rigby are welcome," but for reasons that remained a mystery to her, Jack continued to love that woman.

"Mom?" Jack's eyes finally met hers. "We know you're struggling with Dad and his recovery. Us living with you means we're around to help take a load off."

"For two weeks at a time anyway." It came out more harshly than she'd intended.

Jack had glanced out the window again. "I'm picking up an extra week of work a month." He looked back at her. "But Luce will be here. In a lot of ways she's more help than me."

Birdie knew that was a lie.

The day after Lucy, Jack and Rigby moved into Cork Street, Jack had flown out, leaving Birdie with Lucy. Every time the woman spoke, prickles ran across Birdie's skin, making her want to tear at it. Lucy poked at her food—she was on some sort of crazy diet where she fasted twice a week, and when she did eat, it was food high in protein, low in carbs and, as far as Birdie was concerned, not enough fruit. Lucy had cooked for them once, but Mike had refused to eat the meal. Birdie had enough on her plate without making more work for herself.

Now, the sound of the television continued unabated and Mike stomped past.

"Do not yell at Rigby," Birdie said sharply.

Mike grunted. "Get the kid some headphones."

"With money from our empty bank account or theirs?"

"I'm sick, it's my house and I deserve some quiet."

She agreed with two parts of his statement. "You are not sick."

He pressed a finger to the scar on his chest. "What do you call this?"

She wasn't going there. "What time's cardiac rehab today?"

"It's not."

"Was it canceled?"

He shook his head. "I'm not going."

"What? Of course you're going."

"Keep your hair on. It's not exercise. It's just someone talking at us and I don't need that."

Birdie turned and consulted the program on the fridge. "It's the pharmacist talking about medication."

He grunted. "I take the pills. I don't need to know how they work."

She raised her brows and gave him a long hard stare. At least twice a week when she was chasing him down to take his tablets, they argued over his failure to do so.

"You're going to cardiac rehab," she said, "and I'm coming too."

"Jesus, Bird, I'm not a bloody kid."

"Then stop acting like one! You might not care if you live or die, but so help me, I do. You have to take the pills. But I think some have side effects that are keeping you—" *us*, "—from being happy."

"Like what?" he asked belligerently.

"Like the nightmares." She thought of the two times they'd attempted sex. "Your trouble getting it up."

His face flushed puce. "You're not asking that in a group!"

"Then go to group and I'll make a private appointment to ask the questions." She hated how their relationship had become a battle from breakfast to bedtime. Taking a slow deep breath she changed the subject. "Any news on the trailer?"

"What do you think?"

She counted to five, trying to keep her temper in check. "I don't know. That's why I'm asking you."

When they'd told Becky, the CFO at the travel trailer company, that they couldn't pay for it, she'd been unexpectedly understanding.

"We've got a waiting list of potential buyers so we'll offer it to them. I'm sure it will sell quickly."

For the first time in weeks Birdie had dared to hope. However, it appeared that the people on the list weren't interested in their custom design, preferring the regular models. Even though they'd dropped the price there was yet to be an offer.

Birdie badgered Mike to call each week but he resisted, saying, "Becky will contact us if there's news."

Birdie felt that Becky wasn't pushing the sale hard enough. Surely the CFO wanted the debt cleared as soon as possible? But it seemed nothing in Birdie's life was straightforward, and as much as she wanted Mike to take ownership of this one task, she knew she'd be the one picking up the phone and making the call. She added it to her never-ending to-do list.

As Mike left the room, Lucy appeared, make-up on and wearing smart casual clothes.

"Rigby's had breakfast and I've packed his snack," she said. "I should be able to pick him up at 1:00, but I'll text if it runs late."

Birdie tensed and the flare of dissatisfaction burned along her veins. "You're not working today."

"Not on shift, but I have an in-service."

"Really?"

Lucy's brows drew down. "I thought Jack told you."

"Why would Jack tell me when he's 3,000 miles away?"

Lucy hesitated and her eyes flicked around the room, avoiding Birdie's gaze. "I'm sorry Jack didn't tell you when you spoke to him last night. I have to go now or I'll be late."

Before Birdie could say, "You're the one living here, you should have told me," or "I have my own plans!" Lucy had walked out the back door. It shut with a loud thwack, as if Lucy had just slapped her.

"You little upstart witch!" Birdie was reaching for her cell phone to text Jack and tell him to pull his wife into line when she heard Rigby calling.

"Grammy, I need to poo!"

With a sigh, Birdie walked toward the bathroom.

Unlike Rigby, who could be cajoled, bribed or plain manhandled into the car, that afternoon Mike stubbornly refused to attend cardiac rehab.

"Okay, fine," Birdie shouted. "But know this! Your heart attack might not have killed you, but you're doing a bloody good job of killing yourself!"

He hadn't looked away from the television. Birdie was tempted to take it out of the house, just like Mike had done once when the kids were teens and had refused to respond to him. But unlike those good old days when you could pick up a set, this television was sixty-five inches and mounted on the wall. But she was seriously close to hiding the remote.

With rage burning, Birdie stomped out of the house, got into the car and drove to the community health center.

The receptionist directed her down the hall to a room with a circle of chairs. People were gathered around the refreshment table, and Birdie saw a plate of heart-healthy muffins next to a stack of recipe sheets. She didn't recognize the other attendees, but managed a tight smile for Charys, the community health nurse.

Birdie scrawled her name on a sticker, thrust it onto her blouse and sat down.

"Lovely to see you, Birdie. Mike parking the car?" Charys smiled at her own joke. Parking was never an issue at the venue.

"Just me today," Birdie said tightly.

Concern crossed the nurse's face. "Is Mike unwell?"

Other people were taking their seats. As furious as Birdie was with Mike, and despite her threat to embarrass him in public, when it came to the crunch she didn't want to air their private lives among strangers. Their financial life was already public—conversations stopped in the IGA, at the service station, in the library—everywhere she went.

"He had another appointment," she said. "I'm here to take notes."

"You're always welcome," Charys said. "We encourage partners to come to all the education talks. Have you tried any of the recipes from the nutrition talk?"

"I'm making the muffins."

"That's great."

A woman with pink-tipped hair groaned. "But do you eat them? I find them bland and dry."

"I find banana helps," Birdie said.

"If everyone can take a seat," Charys said, "we'll make a start. As our guest speaker has another appointment, we're tweaking the session and doing the medication talk first and our group session after the break. I'd like to introduce Gabrielle, our pharmacist, who will give you the good, the bad and the ugly about the drugs you're on and answer any questions."

Birdie opened her cell to type notes she knew would be read only by her and tried to relax her jaw.

An hour later, when the pharmacist had answered all the questions —most of them asked by Birdie—she left and everyone rose to make a drink.

Birdie slung her bag over her shoulder and was almost at the door when Charys said, "Birdie, it's only intermission. We still have group."

Irritation made her skin itch. "Mike had the heart attack, not me."

"True, but he's not an island." Charys's smile knew too much. "You're very welcome to stay. A problem shared is a—"

"I'm fine," Birdie said quickly. "I need to go shopping and get home to cook dinner. My grandson eats early."

Charys's smile faded. "Are you minding your grandson on top of everything else?"

Birdie stiffened at "everything else." Was the nurse referring to the missing money or to Mike's heart attack? "I like to keep busy," she said brusquely.

"Right. Of course." Charys smiled again, although this time it held unwanted understanding. "Even busy people sometimes need to talk. Call me anytime—I'm always here." She laughed. "Well, Monday to Friday anyway."

Birdie nodded, not wanting to say anything if it risked Charys banging on about counseling.

But the nurse didn't seem to expect her to speak and continued,

"I'll see Mike in the morning at exercises. It's spin class, which everyone enjoys."

Birdie swallowed—*good luck with that*—and left the building.

She stopped at the supermarket on her way home, cursing that she'd forgotten her reusable shopping bags. As she entered she almost fell over a stack of schoolbags. She didn't usually shop at this time of day and the store was full of high-school kids buying chocolate bars and energy drinks.

Birdie knew the layout of the shop like the back of her hand and quickly grabbed the ingredients for tuna casserole—red meat had become a once-a-week treat. The casserole was a favorites of Rigby's, although she knew Lucy didn't really like it. But to quote Rigby, "Tough cheese and wattle peas." Birdie had no idea where her grandson had heard the phrase or if he'd made it up, but she'd found herself muttering it under her breath at least once a day—usually when Mike complained about something.

Birdie returned to the front of the store. There was only one checkout open and she joined the line. The weight of the milk dragged on her fingers and as she tried swapping hands without dropping the other shopping she wished she'd grabbed a basket.

The line didn't appear to be moving. She leaned around the student in front of her and looked down the conveyor belt. The teen behind the counter was talking to one of the high-school kids. Birdie sucked in a breath and counted to five. The girl remained deep in conversation.

Birdie glanced around for the owner or the store manager, but neither were in the aisles. She dumped the milk on the conveyor belt. "You're not being paid to talk to your friends!"

Five sets of eyes turned her way and the girl gave her a mulish look. "They're customers," she said.

"Then serve them."

"Welcome to IGA," the girl said to a golden-haired boy who looked like he spent more time in the surf than the schoolyard. "How are you today?"

He grinned. "Yeah, alright. You?"

The girl picked up his pack of chewing gum and slowly passed it over the scanner. "That's two dollars fifty. Do you have a loyalty card?"

"Nah."

"Cash or card?"

The boy waved his cell phone at her and paid.

The girl proceeded to draw out the next transaction, shooting Birdie a triumphant glance when their payment wouldn't go through.

Birdie had little control over her life, but she'd be damned if a seventeen-year-old girl was going to disrespect her *and* make fun of her. She turned and marched to the back of the store, knocked loudly on the office door and opened it.

Bailey Jamieson, who'd dated Sienna in eleventh grade and had always been a little bit in awe of Birdie and Mike, looked up from a computer screen and jumped to his feet.

"Mrs. Essen. How can I help?"

"You can teach Jenna Treize some respect."

He frowned. "I don't understand."

"Right now she thinks she's back in the schoolyard hanging out with her friends instead of working."

Bailey sighed and rose. "Right. Sorry. I'll have a word."

Something about his tone made her ask, "Has this happened before?"

"A bit. Jenna works pretty well when there's other staff around, but my regulars leave at 3:00 to pick up their kids. I can't be out there as tomorrow's orders have to be finalized by 4:00 and Deidre's on vacations. We're a bit shorthanded."

"Hire me," Birdie said, surprising herself as much as Bailey.

He laughed—the sound uncomfortable.

She pushed on. "Why not? I'm reliable and you can get your work done knowing that things are running smoothly in the store after three."

"The thing is, Mrs. Essen, it's just a short-term issue. Deidre's back in a couple of weeks and—"

"By then, all your customers who shop between 3:00 and 4:00 will be lost to Warrnambool. I can't imagine David will be thrilled about that."

Bailey grimaced at the mention of his boss's name. "But Mrs. Essen, why would you want to work here?"

She looked straight at him and shot a truth arrow. "Unless you've been living under a rock, Bailey, I think you know why."

"Oh, yeah. Sorry." He gave her a wry smile. "You know, I always envied Brad and Jack. Last year I even tried to join Elite, but I didn't have enough money. I'd just saved the entry fee when Brad disappeared."

"Consider yourself lucky," Birdie said tightly.

"Yeah, I guess." Bailey raked a hand through his hair. "Can you work 3:00 to 7:00 on weekdays?"

Not once in her life had Birdie imagined herself a checkout chick or a shelf-stocker, but then again she'd never imagined losing all her money either. "Absolutely."

"I never expected to be your boss, Mrs. Essen."

Birdie studied his face—was this a power trip? Could she afford to care? But Bailey was smiling at her with the same friendly grin.

"Perhaps it's time you called me Birdie."

"Okay, Mrs.—Birdie." His cell rang and as he reached for it, he said, "Come in at 1:00 tomorrow for training and we'll sort out the paperwork then."

"No wife of mine is working at the IGA!" Mike greeted Birdie's news in a tone that implied what he said was law.

She looked at him, wondering where the man she'd loved for years without a second thought had gone. She missed him, and she didn't like this new version one little bit.

"Why on earth not?" she said.

His face twisted as he threw his hands in the air. "Because we're better than that!"

She stared down his pride, knowing their survival depended on her hurting him. "We're not! We're broke!"

"Do you want the whole town talking about you?"

"They're doing that already! And I'd rather that and pay the gas and electricity bills than beg at the food bank."

His eyes lost any hint of softness. "So you're prepared to turn our lives into chaos for eighteen an hour?"

She had no idea what he was talking about. "What chaos?"

"I'm not driving yet and I have doctor's appointments."

She bit off the comment that he'd been given the all clear to drive but had chosen not to. "You can walk to the clinic to see Malcolm, and you don't have another Geelong appointment for six weeks."

"What about dinner?"

There was a sulkiness to his voice that reminded her of Sienna when she'd been eight.

"What about dinner?"

"We eat at 6:30 and you won't be home until after 7:00."

"There's nothing stopping you from eating at 6:30."

"There is if it isn't cooked."

She counted silently to ten, trying to stall her frustration that verged on full-blown anger. Was this all she was to him? A cook, cleaner and carer?

But before she could muster a coherent sentence Mike was saying, "What about Centrelink?"

"Oh my God! Can you hear yourself? I would rather the self-respect of working at the IGA than prostrate myself at Centrelink. You'd understand that if you actually dealt with them!"

His mouth flattened into a familiar stubborn line. "What about Rigby?"

"Rigby is *Lucy's* responsibility."

He frowned. "You offered to help when Jack's away and she's at work."

Birdie had never offered—Lucy and Jack had assumed.

Mike continued. "Lucy's depending on you and it's not fair to—"

"Fair!" Birdie's breath came hard and fast. "Do not lecture me on what is and isn't fair. *Nothing* about what's happened to us is fair! If you're so concerned about your grandson's childminding arrangements then step up and start grandparenting again."

He tapped his chest. "So you want me dead now, do you?"

I want something other than this shadow of a life we're living.

Lucy appeared in the kitchen with Rigby on her hip. The boy had his hands over his ears.

"Rigby wants to say goodnight," Lucy said bluntly, her face betraying her displeasure.

"Use inside voices," Rigby said.

"Did you hear that, Gramps?" Birdie said.

Mike grunted and left the room.

"We're sorry, darling." Birdie ruffled Rigby's hair. "How about you go and choose a story? I'll be there in a minute to read it and tuck you in."

"Come now, Grammy."

"I just have to talk to Mommy for a minute."

Rigby pouted, but when Lucy put him down he ran to his room.

Birdie turned to Lucy, feeling a surge of triumph blooming in her chest. "Starting tomorrow I'm working from 3:00 till 7:00 at the IGA. That means I can't collect Rigby from childcare when you're on a late. You'll need to make other arrangements."

Suck on that, sweetheart.

As she waited for Lucy's shocked surprise and anger, glee danced inside her. She'd just made the younger woman's life difficult, which seemed an appropriate payback for all Lucy had done to her.

But Lucy's face didn't betray a single emotion. "Congratulations."

Birdie thought she'd misheard, but then Lucy's mouth carved into a small smile and Birdie knew she'd heard correctly. She didn't know what was worse. That her daughter-in-law had spoken the words her husband should have voiced or that Lucy showed no signs of distress at the spanner Birdie had just thrown into her life.

"Grammy!" Rigby's voice drifted into the kitchen.

"Coming!"

As Birdie stepped into the hall, she realized with a jolt that Lucy would have heard her and Mike's argument. Lucy had already known about the job and had absorbed the news. Birdie hated her just a little bit more for that.

CHAPTER TWENTY-SEVEN

BIRDIE'S JOB at the IGA lobbed a grenade into Lucy's life, loosening the tenuous grip she had on balancing shift work and childcare while Jack was away. The afternoon shifts were the problem as Rigby's day care closed at 6:00. Every time Lucy thought about it, rage flared high and hot. Why, when the nursing staff were predominantly women, didn't the hospital provide childcare until 10 P.M.? Hell, why didn't they provide childcare full stop?

Lucy had interviewed four family day care workers to cover the afternoon shifts, but really it was an illusion of choice—only one woman was prepared to mind Rigby in the evenings. Lucy reassured herself that just because Tarryn was a bit rough about the edges it didn't mean she wouldn't do a good job caring for him. The house was certainly set up for kids, with childproof locks and gates, and there was a reassuring planner on the fridge outlining each day's activities. Brody, Tarryn's teenage son, seemed great with the children and Rigby had mentioned him a few times. He'd been very proud that Brody hadn't found him when they'd played hidey.

Rigby was equally clingy before the drop-off at Tarryn's as he was at the day care center—he wrapped his arms and legs around Lucy and cried every time. She fought guilt and wretchedness as she prized him off her, kissed him and thrust him at Tarryn, or Cheyenne at the day care center. Surely, now he was three and a half, leaving him should be getting easier not harder.

She always rang as soon as she arrived at work and was always told, "He's playing happily." The reassuring words didn't fully banish the agonies that she was scarring him in some way.

When she'd mentioned that to a co-worker with adult children, the woman had laughed. "Oh, love, stop worrying. When he's twenty, he'll blame you for something so it may as well be that you made sure he was safe."

Rigby, who was used to being cared for by Birdie, railed at the change. He'd only just adapted to the 6:30 A.M. day care drop-off when it was time for a week of afternoon shifts. Those drop-offs were particularly fraught, because no matter how often Lucy reminded him that after lunch he was going to Tarryn's, he'd throw a tantrum—arms and legs flailing—as she tried to strap him into his car seat.

As for night duty, it was almost impossible to sleep at her in-laws' during the day with the television blasting. Lack of sleep reduced Lucy to a permanent state of jet lag, leaving her irritable and short-tempered. She tried her best to say as little as possible to Birdie and Mike to avoid saying the wrong thing. The day she got up at noon because of the roar of Formula One and Mike said, "Can't sleep?", she'd walked outside and screamed.

So when the nursing manager of maternity services asked if she'd like to cover a colleague's long-service leave in the pregnancy care clinic, Lucy accepted. It was the solution to her sanity.

"But you'll lose your night duty allowance," Jack had said. Not even the grainy video picture could hide his frown. "We're supposed to be earning more money, not less."

"It's full-time for three months, and I work a late on Tuesdays and Thursdays teaching antenatal classes. The money won't be much different."

He peered at the screen. "Have you actually done the math?"

She hadn't, and not working weekends would reduce her take-home salary.

"I'm exhausted, Jack," she pleaded. "You're hardly here, and your parents—" *won't look after Rigby.* "I need this," she continued. "Besides, by the time it finishes, the house will have sold and we can buy that empty cottage in O'Flaherty's Lane."

Jack rubbed the back of his head. "And you'll go back to nights then?"

"Yes. When I can actually sleep in my own house!"

Although she missed delivering babies, Lucy enjoyed the education component of pregnancy care, especially challenging pregnant couples to look beyond the birth to the massive change their baby would bring to their lives. The week before, she'd played a soundtrack of a crying baby as the couples arrived for class. One bloke stood up a minute after he'd sat and turned off the sound.

"You can't actually do that with a crying baby," Lucy had said. It had been the perfect introduction to the class on parenting.

Today's clinic was fully booked and she'd been ignoring her buzzing watch telling her there were messages on her cell. At morning tea, she was surprised to see a missed call from Sienna. She didn't know her sister-in-law all that well—three or four family celebrations a year wasn't enough to forge a friendship, and they didn't really communicate much outside of those events.

"Thanks for returning my call," Sienna said, sounding very much like the office manager she was.

"No prob—"

"I'm worried about Mom and Dad. With everything that's happened they really don't need the stress of you and Jack living there. You're a nurse so you understand that, right?"

It was like Sienna had reached down the phone and grabbed Lucy by the throat, stifling her breath and blanking her mind.

"Lucy? Did you hear me?" Sienna asked.

She decided to deflect. "Isn't this a conversation you should be having with Jack?"

"Hah! You know what my brother's like. He doesn't think there's a problem."

Loyalty made Lucy side with Jack. "Perhaps that's because there isn't. It's not like we just moved in unannounced. We asked and Mike and Birdie could have said no." Her fingers suddenly gripped her cell. "Have they said something to you?"

"No, but that's not the point, is it?" Sienna said briskly. "You and I both know that Mom thinks the sun shines out of Jack's ass, but that doesn't mean you can take advantage of them. Dad's sick and—"

"He's better now." Lucy embraced the steel of chagrin straightening her spine. "But you haven't seen him since he was discharged from the hospital, have you? How many weeks ago was that?"

"How much rent are you paying?" Sienna asked.

None of your damn business. "How much of the money they gave you for your house deposit are you giving back?"

"That money was a gift."

"Exactly and gifts can be returned." But something warned her not to continue down this road. "I have to go, I've got patients waiting. Talk to Jack about this sort of stuff, Sienna, not me, okay."

She didn't wait for a reply but punched the red button on the cell phone, wishing she could punch her sister-in-law.

An hour later, Lucy was in the middle of explaining to a woman pregnant with her third child why she was experiencing pelvic girdle pain when her watch buzzed. As soon as she'd sent the woman to physiotherapy for a consultation she checked her cell. Day care had rung three times.

She immediately returned the call and as it rang disaster scenarios screened in her mind—Rigby convulsing with a fever, Rigby lying unconscious, Rigby—

Someone was saying, "Big Blue Whale childcare."

"Oh, hi, it's Lucy Essen, Rigby's mom. I have three missed calls from you and—"

"Thanks for calling back, Lucy," Donna said. "We've had a bit of an issue with Rigby today and we think it would be best if you came and picked him up."

Issue? "Is he sick? Hurt? What?"

"He bit Lewis."

Lucy was trying to make sense of why Rigby would have bitten his best day care friend and was about to ask, "Did they both want the same toy?" when Donna added, "And when Cheyenne gave him a timeout, Rigby bit her too."

Horrified embarrassment burned Lucy's cheeks. "Oh my God! I'm so sorry. Are they okay?"

"Lewis's mother is pretty upset. We think it's best if Rigby had some time at home with you."

"But I'm at work and—"

"We know you've had some big changes recently what with ..." Donna's voice trailed away before she added, "And you've moved. It's a lot of change for Rigby to process."

Lucy couldn't deny any of it, but the point of childcare was to mind the child and Rigby wasn't sick. "It's the weekend tomorrow. Can't he just stay the day and then he has two days at home to calm down?"

"We need someone to collect him as soon as possible," Donna said firmly, "or we may have to reconsider his enrollment."

Could a child be expelled from day care? Lucy had no idea, but despite her anger at Donna's threat, she couldn't risk it.

"I have to organize someone to cover for me, but I'll be there within the hour."

She hung up the phone, her mind racing. Rigby had bitten a kid and he'd also bitten Cheyenne, who he adored. Why? As much as she wanted to be angry at the day care center for not dealing with the situation in a different way, she couldn't ignore what he'd done.

She called her boss and lied, saying Rigby was sick. Then she called pediatrics.

"Any chance the social worker's on the floor?"

. . .

When Lucy and Rigby arrived home late morning, she gave him a drink and a snack, then asked him why he'd bitten Lewis.

He shrugged and looked at his feet.

As far as she knew, he'd never bitten anyone before so the subject had never come up. "Biting hurts people and I know you don't want to hurt anyone."

His head shot up, his eyes glinting with determination. "Big boys bite and I'm a big boy."

Where was this coming from?

"No, Rigby, they don't bite. They use their words."

"Brody bites."

Lucy's heart kicked. "Did Brody bite you?"

Rigby jumped up from the table, grabbed a dinosaur and charged around the room roaring.

Rigby's got it wrong. Brody was probably just playing with him.

But she pushed the thought aside, knowing children who'd been abused were often disbelieved.

She caught Rigby on his second circuit and, using all her energy to sound calm, she tried again. "Rigby, did Brody bite you?"

He nodded.

"Were you playing a game?"

Rigby shook his head. "He said a bad word."

"Did he say the bad word before he bit you?"

Rigby nodded.

"Where did he bite you?"

Rigby pointed to his bottom and his thigh.

Nausea churned through her. "Did he ... did he bite your penis?"

Rigby gave her a look that implied she was a few sandwiches short of a picnic.

A form of relief tempered her horror that a fifteen-year-old boy had bitten her son. She hated that Elite had reduced them to this—being forced to leave Rigby in a place where he wasn't safe.

She pulled Rigby onto her lap. "Brody's not allowed to bite you. No one is allowed to bite you, and you're not allowed to bite other people.

It's a big rule for everyone, grown-ups too. No one's allowed to touch your bottom except to help you wipe after a poo. And your penis is just for you to touch."

He snuggled into her and said quietly into her chest, "I don't like Brody."

She kissed the top of his head to give herself time to stifle a sob. "Neither do I. You don't have to see him anymore and you won't be going to his house again."

His head shot up so fast it barely missed her chin. "Can I watch *Peppa Pig*?"

"Sure."

She tucked him up on the sofa, then went and stood in the doorway of Birdie's sewing room. Jack was supposed to have reorganized it on his first week home so Rigby had his own room, but Birdie had put him to work in the garden.

During Lucy's coffee with Daniel, the pediatric social worker, he'd suggested that Rigby needed his own room with his own toys to feel more secure.

"Three-year-olds don't have the vocab to tell us they're worried and anxious. It manifests in their behavior, like biting."

"Will it help with his bed-wetting?" she'd asked.

"Fingers crossed."

Even though Lucy knew that the biting issue had a different source, she couldn't hide from the fact Rigby was struggling with all the changes in their lives. She was willing to try anything and if having his own bedroom helped she'd do it today. Rigby in his own room would surely help her and Jack too—their sex life had been severely curtailed since they'd moved to Cork Street. It was hard enough getting in the mood knowing his parents were down the hall. It was impossible with Rigby in the room.

"Let's do this."

She stepped into the room and opened the closet. First she reorganized the shelves, creating space for the sewing machine and all the associated sharp items. Then she dismantled the large sewing table and moved the lamp, leaving a clear floor.

After lunch, she took Rigby into the garage and together they washed Sienna's single bed frame free of years of dust.

"Is this my new bed, Mommy?"

"It is."

"Can we paint it red?"

Lucy saw the white wrought iron through her son's eyes. "You and Daddy can do that."

Much to Rigby's delight, she used Mike's drill to assemble the bed, then together they dragged his mattress down the hall and heaved it onto the slats.

Lucy pushed one of the many fabric-storage boxes under the bed.

"I can do it!" Rigby said.

She smiled at his enthusiasm. "Okay then, show us your muscles."

"Arrgh!" Using his entire body, he shoved the second box into position then beamed up at her. "I'm very strong, Mommy."

"You are."

"I can look after you."

Emotion clogged her throat and she hugged him tightly, trying not to cry. He shouldn't be feeling that he needed to look after her—it was her job to look after him. A job she was failing. She should have insisted Jack set up this room a month ago.

For the first time since they'd moved to Cork Street, she unpacked Rigby's suitcase of clothes, letting him choose the drawer for his socks and jocks and another for his T-shirts. Then he "helped" her make his bed with dinosaur sheets, and while he played on it with his snugglies she curated a book basket by his bed.

"Is this my very own dinosaur room, Mommy?" he asked.

Shame poured through her as she remembered her promise before the auction: "All your toys are coming and we can decorate your new room with dinosaurs." With so little space most of his toys were in storage, but she suddenly saw how much her son needed all the things that represented his normal.

She held out her hand. "Come on, buddy, let's go and get your toys so we can finish decorating your room."

That night Rigby asked to go to bed early, and after one story he said, "You can go now, Mommy."

She laughed and kissed him. "Sleep well, sweetie."

"I will."

He said it so confidently that she dared to dream he might not wet the bed.

"Mommy's just next door," she said.

"I know."

"And when you wake up in the morning, Daddy will be home."

"Yay! And we'll paint the bed."

She kissed him on the forehead, turned on the nightlight and closed the door.

She could hear the television—when could she not—which meant Mike was still in the recliner. He'd refused her offer of dinner, saying, "I'll wait for Birdie. Thanks anyway." Lucy was never sure if this was so Birdie didn't eat alone or if Mike didn't like her cooking.

Lucy had loaded the dishwasher and turned it on before putting Rigby to bed, but the frypan she'd used to make the ratatouille was soaking. She should wash it and give the stove a wipe before Birdie got home. But it had been a hell of a day and it was Friday night, so she poured herself a glass of wine, promising she'd take half an hour for herself then galvanize into action.

She was halfway through the glass and an episode of *Bondi Rescue* when Birdie burst into the bedroom, startling her. Her mother-in-law still wore the blue and red IGA apron.

"Why is Rigby sleeping in *my* sewing room?" Birdie demanded.

"That was always the plan—"

"No, it was not."

"Sorry." Feeling at a disadvantage, Lucy swung off the bed and stood. "Jack talked to you about it when we moved in and I—"

"He most certainly did not."

Lucy eyed Birdie warily, taking in her crossed arms and taut mouth. "We discussed it and I thought he had."

"Well, you thought wrong. This is *my* house, Lucy, not yours. You cannot make unilateral decisions—"

"I didn't think I had." Birdie's face stayed as hard as granite. "I'm sorry there was a miscommunication."

"Tomorrow, you move him back in here."

"Birdie, please." Lucy hated begging, but her mother-in-law needed to understand what was at stake. "Rigby needs his own room. There was an issue today at childcare. He's not coping very well with everything—"

"And whose fault is that?" The judgment on Birdie's face reached out and scratched Lucy. "You wouldn't be in this mess if you weren't so impatient and needing everything yesterday. Who in their right mind takes out a personal loan?"

Chagrin filled her. "That was Jack's idea!"

The moment she said the words she knew it was the wrong tack. It would have been wiser to attack Birdie and Mike's decision to invest all their retirement fund in Fortune than to criticize Jack.

Birdie's look of loathing hit her with the power of a punch. "I very much doubt that."

She left the room before Lucy could manage a reply.

"Your mother hates me," Lucy told Jack that night as soon as he'd caught his breath.

He'd walked in the door just before midnight and thankfully Birdie and Mike were already in bed and not around to monopolize him. Lucy had hustled him down the hall—Jack hadn't protested—and they'd tumbled into bed, desperate to connect after three very long weeks apart.

Now he wound strands of her hair around his fingers. "She doesn't hate you."

"She does." Lucy told him about Rigby and the biting.

"Jeez, Luce. He can't go back there."

"You think!" She sucked in a calming breath. "I know he can't go back there, and we need to surround him with stability to help him cope with all the changes. Having him camping out in here with us hasn't helped." She lay her head on his chest. "The thing is, I don't understand why your mother went ballistic on me. The only reason we hadn't moved him earlier was because she had you working flat out in the garden and doing other jobs."

When Jack didn't say anything she prompted him. "Right?"

He sighed. "I never got around to talking to her about it."

She sat up fast. "Jack!"

"Sorry, but that week we moved was a blur, and I didn't want to do it on the cell phone or on a video call. I was going to talk to her tomorrow."

"Oh God, no wonder she's upset. Why didn't you tell me?"

"I never thought you'd do it on your own."

"Why not? I do just about everything else on my own."

He tensed. "That's not fair. You know I'd be here if I could."

She slumped against him and sighed. "I know. It's just now Birdie has yet another reason to hate me. I never told you, but when she said she couldn't mind Rigby in the afternoons, she was smiling!"

"Aw, be fair, Luce. She was probably just embarrassed she was letting you down."

Lucy knew that wasn't the case—she'd seen the delight on Birdie's face. It was as if her mother-in-law was deriving pleasure from making her life more difficult.

"She's gotta be embarrassed about the IGA too." Jack ran his hand through his hair. "Poor Mom. Instead of retirement she's working with Deidre the dragon. That's enough to make anyone cranky."

Lucy chose not to say that she felt sorry for Deidre—working with Birdie wouldn't be easy. Living with her was almost impossible. Every night the walls of Jack's childhood bedroom bore down on Lucy, reminding her of everything they'd lost. She needed time away from the claustrophobic house. Who was she kidding? She needed time away from Birdie.

She trailed her fingers down Jack's chest. "Let's go away for the weekend. Rigby needs time alone with us and we can easily get a cabin at Robe."

Jack caught her hand. "Luce."

"Good idea, right?" she said, ignoring his tone.

"We can't afford the gas for a six-hour round trip."

Desperation tugged hard. "Portland then. It's closer."

"It's not the destination. We don't have the readies to drop a hundred and twenty bucks on a cabin or to eat out. Every cent counts."

At that moment she hated his common sense. "Fine! But we're going on a picnic tomorrow, just the three of us."

"The forecast's crap. There's a hundred percent chance of rain."

The thought of spending the day stuck inside amid tension that could be carved with a knife almost made her sob. She could see it all as clearly as if she was living it that very minute. Mike's non-existent patience even when Rigby was playing happily. Birdie's huffing and puffing when Lucy sat reading for half an hour on a precious day off, making her feel like it was a criminal act. Birdie talking to Jack and excluding Lucy from every conversation.

Exasperated, she jerked away from him. "It's alright for you. You're hardly here, but I'm living every single day in a house where I'm not welcome! And now your sister's harassing me too. She called me at work and told me we have to move out. Part of me agrees with her!"

New lines carved in around Jack's eyes. "Ignore Sienna. I do."

"Which is why she called me!" Her voice rose and cracked and she blinked fast.

"Shh." Jack made to pull her back into him but she moved out of reach. "Aww, come on, Luce. Don't be like this. I'm only home—"

"This isn't home! My home—our home—is full of strangers and we're living in one room!"

He grimaced as if he was in pain. "I'm only back for a week. I don't want to spend it arguing."

Fury, swift and strong, streaked through her with a velocity that almost physically spun her. How dare he infer she was the problem. She blinked furiously, not wanting to cry, hating that everything in this house drained her of precious emotional energy.

"We need more space," she said slowly and carefully. "Your dad might enjoy helping you convert the garage back into a rec room. He needs something to take his mind off— He needs a project and we need the space."

When Jack didn't say anything, she nudged him. "Hello?"

A long sigh rumbled out of him. "Sorry."

She recognized his distracted tone. "What?"

"Dad. It's just I thought by now he'd be ..."

"Be what?"

"Better."

"He's improving. He should exercise more, but—"

"He's not Dad though, is he?"

Even without the moonlight illuminating his distress she heard it in his voice. "He'll get there." She sounded more confident than she felt. "This will help."

"I'll talk to him, but we can't force it if he doesn't want to. It's their house."

"You think I don't know that! Your mother told me that today." *And every other day in lots of little cutting ways.*

Jack stroked her face. "If Mom didn't want us staying here, she would have said. And today was just a misunderstanding. Apologize, and next time check before you make any more big changes."

Resentment simmered. "I didn't think I needed to check because you'd already done it!"

Jack tensed against her. "Luce, I can't be the go-between for you and my folks when I'm not here."

"You make it sound like you have been."

"Well, Mom's complaining to me that you're always hiding in here instead of being in the living room chatting to them."

"That's not true! I do talk to them, but I also need some time on my own."

He raised his brows.

"Oh my God! You're taking their side."

"I'm not taking anyone's side." He rubbed his face with both hands, then looked at her. "I know it's hard, but it's hard for all of us. Just promise me that from now on you'll check with Mom about stuff, okay?"

Betrayal stung Lucy like a thousand bees. She turned on her side and pretended to sleep.

CHAPTER TWENTY-EIGHT

Izzy was slipping her cell phone into her handbag and glancing around for her car keys when Brooke called.

"Oh, hi," Izzy said. "I'm on my way into town now."

"Sorry, Isobel. Something's come up and Mitchell and I have to be elsewhere. But the numbers expert can still attend. Is it easier if he comes to you?"

Since Izzy had showed Brooke the cloud data, they'd been waiting on the expert's analysis. Apparently he had some questions for Izzy.

"I thought the meeting had to happen at the station?" she said.

"Not necessarily. It was easier for Mitchell, but as he won't be in attendance ... Anyway, we don't technically have to be there unless you feel uncomfortable being alone with the expert."

"Should I?"

"No. He's a straight up and down bloke and he's had to pass every check under the sun to contract for us. I've never seen him put a foot wrong."

Any chance Izzy had not to be spied walking into the police station, and then seeing her photo splashed all over the Glingilly Facebook page and beyond, was a win.

"Okay. I'll open the gate." She chewed the inside of her cheek. "But in case a journo sneaks in, I want to see ID. What's his name?"

When Brooke didn't reply, it took Izzy a moment to realize the line had dropped out. She called back but it went straight to voice mail.

Half an hour later when the doorbell pealed she still hadn't heard back from the police officer, but the timing was a match.

Thor barked excitedly.

"This meeting's going to clear my name, buddy. This is my get-out-of-jail card."

Izzy opened the door and almost slammed it shut.

Cooper Barsky stood in the portico wearing boots, chinos and a fine corduroy navy jacket with elbow patches—he looked more like a professor of English than business. Thor traitorously dropped a ball at Cooper's feet and gazed up at him with hopeful eyes.

"Hello, Izzy."

"What are you doing here?" Her words came out sharp and accusatory.

A small crease formed between his eyes. "Brooke said you were expecting me."

"What? No ... I—" It suddenly hit her. "*You're* the numbers expert?"

He didn't react to her incredulity. "That's me."

"I thought it would be someone from Melbourne."

"It's a local case."

"Sure, but you're an academic."

He shrugged. "I did my time in the high-pressure corporate world before I moved down here for a change of pace. I love teaching, but contracting for the police now and then gives me the best of both worlds."

Izzy's confusion must have shown because he added, "I get to keep my hand in forensic accounting and my students benefit. May I come in, please?"

She wanted to say no, but she'd agreed to this meeting and her refusal would only delay the inevitable. She stepped aside.

He walked into the entrance hall and stopped, taking in the grand sweeping stairs, the portraits and all the stone. She was used to this reaction and was anticipating the usual "wow" comment.

"Have you uploaded your assignment?" he said.

Her brain pivoted. "Wait, what?"

"Your corporate governance and business ethics assignment." His tone was patient. "The one I emailed you about."

"Oh, right. No."

"How about you upload it before we look at the Elite numbers?"

Why was he so concerned about her GPA? She ignored him and took the stairs down to Brad's office, hearing his footsteps following.

Cooper studied the medieval decor more intently than he had the entrance hall. "Are you sure this isn't a dungeon?"

She grimaced. "One definition of dungeon is a thief's hole, I think it pretty much is."

He gave a wry smile. "How about we work somewhere with natural light?"

She sighed and turned back to the stairs.

"Bring your laptop," Cooper said.

"Why? You've brought yours."

"Your assignment's not on mine."

He was like Thor with a bone and, for reasons she couldn't fathom, it irritated her.

"So what's the deal, Cooper? You need my enrollment so your funding doesn't get cut?"

He ran his hand through hair that needed taming by clippers and sighed. "You got me."

She couldn't tell if he was serious or not. She snatched up her laptop and made her way to the kitchen.

"Enough light for you?"

This time when he looked around, his face softened with approval. "Perfect."

He removed his computer from its leather satchel and set it up on the American oak baker's table.

"Coffee? Tea?" she asked, more out of social politeness than good grace.

He cocked a brow. "Are you offering so you can delay uploading the assignment?"

She pressed her palms down hard on the counter to keep them away from her hair. "I thought you were here in your capacity as a numbers expert for the police. Not as my lecturer for a course I've quit."

"I can do both. Anyway, according to the records you haven't officially withdrawn from the course."

"You might have noticed my life's radically changed. Right now uni's not my top priority."

"It probably should be in your top three." He sounded like a career counselor. "When all of this is over you'll need the qualifications more than ever."

Despite her best efforts, a harsh laugh escaped. She thumped the start button on the coffee machine. "Why? Even when I prove I'm innocent, no one's going to want to employ me."

"You don't know that," he said mildly.

"Oh, please! Have you seen the internet lately? That stuff lives on forever. Besides, my assignment's just a rough draft. It will fail anyway."

"How about you let me decide?"

She remembered the day down by the river and the pity shining from his eyes. How it had seared her. "I don't want a pity pass!"

"Good, because that's not my style. But if you're so bothered by the possibility, I'll get someone else to mark it. Deal?"

She was suddenly exhausted. "Okay, fine."

She stomped around the kitchen counter, tapped on the keyboard of her computer, logged into the university website, selected the assignment and uploaded it. When the screen changed, declaring the submission successful, she pointed to it.

"Happy, Professor Barsky? Can we move on now?"

He smiled as if she'd just done him a favor. "We can."

Not sure if she was aggrieved or relieved, Izzy carried over the coffees then sat next to him. "Brooke said you'd looked at the figures and you have some questions."

"I do." Cooper pulled a pair of glasses out of his pocket and consulted the copious notes he'd scrawled into a spiral notebook. "Brooke said you believe that the number six in column B references you?"

"Possibly. I can account for most of the figures, but not all of them."

"Hmm." He pushed his glasses up his nose. "Thing is, I would have thought as Quinn's fiancée you'd be number one or two?"

She tried keeping her face neutral. "Brad's parents are more likely to have been assigned those numbers."

Cooper looked at her then, his green eyes serious. "If that's the case, who would be four and five?"

"I don't know." She'd expected him to ask her something about her relationship with Brad and for some reason the thought made her uncomfortable. "Another reason I might be six is ... I Googled it, and numerology sites say it's the motherhood number." She shrugged at his blank look. "Brad was very keen to start a family."

Cooper wrote that on his notes. "Did Quinn follow numerology?"

"He was interested in anything to do with numbers and horses, but until I found his diary I didn't know he had regular appointments with a numerologist. It turns out I knew nothing about everything to do with Elite."

"Do you think Quinn would consider himself number one?"

She thought about the juxtaposition that was Brad. His desire to share his good fortune and his need to be front and center.

"I do." She pointed to the numbers. "But if those figures are withdrawals, they're not very large. He told me he charged a fee for every win so they could possibly be that. Then again, considering what's gone down, I have no idea if what he told me is the truth or a smokescreen."

"He might have given himself more than one number to hide the movement of money." Cooper pointed to some highlighted figures in a different column. "Some of these numbers are big and there's a cluster of them from a few months ago. Ring any bells?"

Izzy looked at the dates, then consulted her own diary. Her stomach suddenly rolled so violently she almost threw up her lunch. Oh God. One of those figures must represent Mike Essen's lost retirement fund.

"You okay?" Cooper asked. "You've gone green."

"I ... it's just ... that's when he started Fortune." She sucked in a deep breath. "Are those the amounts people lost?"

"As big as they are, they're only part of the story. According to Jack Essen, the only way to be invited into Fortune was to also be in Elite. I've matched these three figures to three Fortune members."

"But there were twelve. Where are the others?"

Cooper pushed away a flop of hair. "With fraud at this level, very few things are straightforward. Quinn's clever. He might have told you there were twelve but there's likely to be more. I think he's used a mismatch of numbers to hide the movement of funds."

The complexity of the data spun around her and Izzy dropped her head into her hands. "Everyone thinks I'm part of this fraud, but the only thing I'm guilty of was falling in love with a man who perhaps never existed."

"You think Quinn isn't his real name?" Cooper said.

She lifted her head and managed a small smile at his literal interpretation. "I mean I never took him as someone who'd set up a Ponzi scheme and fleece his community. His parents are convinced his overseas partners are the culprits and that Brad's gone to ground to protect us while he sorts it all out."

The deep crease between Cooper's brows was back. "Protect you?"

"Those are the words his parents used, not me."

"Protect himself more likely." Cooper rose and poured two glasses of water. "What do you believe?"

She shrugged. "I don't know what or who to believe anymore so I'm sticking with my gut. Why would a man who was obsessed with getting married as soon as possible, and pushing hard to start a family, leave without a word? Why would he cease contact with his parents who he spoke to every day? And if everything with Elite was above board and it's his partners who've ripped him off, why didn't he go to the police?"

Cooper grimaced. "You won't get an argument from me or the police about any of it. More and more, things are pointing to Quinn having skipped the country on a false passport. He was probably moving money overseas from the start."

"His parents are convinced he's in Queensland."

"Everything's being investigated," Cooper said.

"And?"

"Sorry, I can't say."

"Oh my God!" Izzy tugged at her hair. "What more do I have to do to prove I'm not a suspect? I've exposed my entire financial history. I told Mitchell about the sighting of Brad in Maroochydore and how the Quinns are pressuring me to go to Queensland."

"Izzy, me not telling you isn't a matter of trust. I signed a confidentiality clause. If I break it, it voids my contract and risks me being charged. It could also impede the case."

Was he telling the truth? She studied him, trying to read him.

Hah! You couldn't read Brad so why do you think you can read this bloke?

She decided to stick with facts and learn what he'd discovered from the cloud. She pointed to a figure of 960,000 dollars and the number eight next to it in column B. "Any idea what this means?"

Cooper checked his notes. "Eight is something I want to talk to you about. When did you buy this place and do you own it outright?"

Indignation surged. "I don't own *any* part of Villefranche, nor did I have a say in Brad's decision to buy it!"

Cooper held up his hands in surrender. "Sorry. I shouldn't have assumed."

She nodded, not wanting to say, "That's okay," but wanting to acknowledge his apology.

"I'm not absolutely certain when he bought it, but it was sometime between January and March two years ago. I don't know what he paid for it, but I can tell you he's defaulted on the mortgage. The Lawson Group's about to repossess it."

Cooper wrote down the name of the company.

Izzy, not wanting to give him an opportunity to say anything that was judgmental or sympathetic, added, "To be honest, it will be a relief to live somewhere else."

He grinned at her. "Surely you'll miss the cozy ambience?"

She snorted. "It's ridiculously ostentatious, but now I know what I do about Brad, I see that was the point."

Cooper nodded. "Jack Essen believes Quinn also purchased property in Queensland and Western Australia. What do you know about that?"

"If he bought in WA, he never told me."

"And Queensland?"

She tried not to squirm under his inquisitive gaze. Although she'd presented the cloud data to the police, she was yet to tell them about the Noosa apartment. Before she did that she wanted a cast-iron guarantee that she was no longer a suspect. But all Brooke could promise her was, "For the time being the investigation's shifted away from you."

Would owning the Noosa property swing it right back? As much as Izzy feared telling the police, she knew she had more chance of being believed if she volunteered the information. If they discovered the apartment themselves, it would raise the question—what else was she hiding?

The engagement ring? No, Brooke had seen that. Hell, the whole town had seen it.

For some reason, telling Cooper about the apartment seemed less terrifying than telling Mitchell, but even so she wished there was gin in her glass instead of water.

"There's an apartment in Noosa." She forced the words she didn't want to say around the lump in her throat. "We bought it together."

Cooper's eyes widened. "Shit, Izzy—"

Her hand flew up like a stop sign. "Before you say anything, I need you to listen to the whole story. I mean really listen and not jump to conclusions."

"I can do that." He took off his glasses and faced her.

She found the intensity of his gaze unsettling. Perhaps because this story might undo all her hard work proving to him and the police that she'd had no idea Brad had devised an elaborate con and ensnared her in it along with everyone else.

"After we moved here, Brad greeted me every Monday morning by telling me how much my Elite investment had grown. He started talking about investment properties and 'Now's the time to get a foot in the door' of the property market. I thought it was a good idea because—"

She quickly swallowed the words "I wanted security" and "my father," knowing they would only drop her deeper into the hole she was desperately clawing her way out of.

"For the first time in my life I had the funds to buy something so I started looking at apartments in Melbourne. I found a great place in Docklands but Brad pooh-poohed the idea, saying, 'There's a glut of tiny box apartments' and 'You need to look at rental and resale potential.' He found the apartment in Noosa. When I pointed out I couldn't afford it, he suggested we buy it together."

Cooper sighed. "Of course he did. Was this before or after he proposed?"

She thought it an irrelevant question. "It was two years ago. Anyway, I assumed I'd use my Elite money for my share of the deposit, but Brad insisted I was better off using my savings. He always gave me a hard time about leaving money sitting in the bank earning little interest. He said the Elite money should stay where it was and continue to grow. I trusted him so I didn't question it. I used my savings."

She rushed on, hoping to stall a raised brow. "Ask Brooke, Mitchell or any of the Elite members. They'll tell you that Brad always did his best to talk anyone out of withdrawing capital and when he did, it always made sense. Now we understand his motivation had nothing to do with altruism and everything to do with stealing."

Cooper nodded. "It's a common conman tactic. So is offering to pay the mortgage and pocketing your share of the money. I'm sorry you've lost your savings and the apartment."

She sat on her hands so they couldn't rip at her hair. "That's the thing. At the rate we were paying it off, it should have been a fifteen-year loan, but when Brad disappeared I turned his office upside down and I found the title in the safe. Brad never said a word to me, but the mortgage's been cleared." She inclined her head toward the numbers on the screen. "I searched for the payment but there isn't a perfect match."

"He probably split it into different amounts to hide it. Don't worry, I'll find it."

"It gets worse."

This time both of Cooper's brows soared. "How?"

"He's transferred the apartment into my name."

Cooper swore.

"When I asked Bevan about it, he said Brad did it on his suggestion for tax purposes. Judy says he did it to look after me."

Cooper's gaze bored into hers with the intensity of a cat watching prey. "What's your interpretation?"

Her heart pounded and she was suddenly short of breath. "When I found the title I didn't know what to think. Now, with weeks of hindsight, I think it's just another way to steal and hide 3 million dollars. Only I'm not prepared to hide it for him." The desperation that was now a permanent part of her ached anew. "Cooper, can you crack his system so I can get out from under this nightmare?"

"That's the plan." He gave her an encouraging smile not dissimilar to the one he gave in class. "But I advise it's in your best interests to tell Brooke about the apartment."

Izzy chewed the inside of her cheek. "You have to tell her, right?"

"I do. But if you tell her with me in the room then you get in first and it looks a thousand times better."

"Right." She just wished it was over. "I'll text her and ask her to come over as soon as she can. Meanwhile ..."

She stared at the dates for the figures that corresponded to the numbers four and five, trying to think of people, events—anything that might connect them. She was about to ask Cooper if he had any thoughts when she felt a wet and cold sensation on her shin.

"To your bed, Thor," she said.

He barked, picked up his ball and tried with Cooper.

"Thor!" She threw Cooper an apologetic look. "Sorry. I usually take him outside around now."

"No worries." He ruffled Thor's ears. "We could do with a break and a walk—" Thor's barking hit its highest pitch and he ran frenzied rings around Cooper's feet. Cooper raised his voice, "—might just be the thing we need for another breakthrough. You know, blow the cobwebs away."

Izzy half-laughed and half-groaned. "Even if it wasn't, now you've said the "W" word we're committed."

"Sorry. I'm not familiar with the passionate adoration and excitement of dogs. My cat specializes in disdainful disregard." Cooper grinned. "No chance of self-aggrandizing. She keeps me grounded."

"If you throw that ball, Thor will constantly demand your attention and also smother you with affection."

"I consider myself warned."

Much to Thor's frustration it took them a few minutes to pull on coats, hats and gloves to ward against the damp winter chill. The moment Izzy opened the door, the dog took off like a shot, dancing on the back patio, eager for the ball.

Cooper pulled back his arm to throw. Thor barked. As the ball soared into the leaden sky and beyond the boundary of the house garden, the dog took off, tearing through the box hedge.

"Sorry." Cooper's look was reminiscent of a kid who knew he'd done the wrong thing. "Guess I should have avoided the plants."

Izzy shrugged and started following Thor. "The garden's not my concern anymore. Anyway, I'm impressed. Even with the ball launcher I can't throw it that far. Who knew you had a bowler's arm."

"Pitcher."

"Sorry?"

He smiled. "I play baseball."

"That's not very common, is it?"

"Put it this way, it's never going to replace cricket, but its popularity's growing. Warrnambool's got a small club."

Thor barreled up with the ball and dropped it at Cooper's feet. He obligingly threw it again.

"How did you get into baseball?" Izzy asked.

"I did a year at the University of Wisconsin as part of my PhD."

As they walked, Cooper kept throwing the ball and Thor kept chasing it, and they chatted about his time in the Midwest state and the challenges of living with a lot of snow.

"There's only two seasons—winter and road construction." He grinned at the memory. "But the long summer evenings make up for it. They're perfect for cookouts and playing ball, as the locals say. Plus I fish, so there's a bit of arm movement in casting."

Izzy had no interest in fishing and was about to change the topic when she realized Thor hadn't returned in quite some time. They were far beyond the house now and she squinted into the weak afternoon light, trying to spot his stocky white and brown body.

When she couldn't see him, she circled her mouth with her hands and yelled into the wind. "Thor! Come!"

He didn't appear and she swore softly. She hadn't brought him down here since Brad had disappeared. In winter, it was easier to walk him along the road and avoid tramping across a muddy field.

"He's probably found something more interesting down by the lake." She couldn't stifle a shudder.

"You're wearing enough layers to cope with snow so you can't be cold," Cooper said. "Does your shiver mean 'interesting' isn't a good thing?"

She sighed. "Jack Russells are hunting dogs. Just in case you're queasy, prepare for the possibility of a mauled duck."

"Noted." He shoved his hands deep into his pockets. "Still, if he has acted on his baser instincts, I know a great duck à l'orange recipe."

Despite the awful possibility of a dead duck, she had a crazy urge to laugh. "Pragmatist are we?"

He grinned. "When it comes to food and wine, always."

They kept walking and Izzy kept calling Thor. She hesitated by the entrance to the maze. "If he's not by the lake, we'll check here on the way back."

But Cooper had his back to her and was pointing in the direction of the secret garden. A momentary shaft of sunshine was glinting off metal. "What's that silver thing?"

"My telescope stand."

Interest flashed across his face. "You're a stargazer?"

"Only since I moved down here. There's something about—"

"There he is!"

She followed the direction of Cooper's outstretched arm, which was pointing to the boat shed on the shore of the lake.

"His bum's up in the air," Cooper said. "Looks like he's digging."

"He's probably found a chop bone from—" Mentioning an Elite picnic suddenly seemed in very bad taste. She started walking and, when she thought she might be in earshot, yelled, "Thor! Come here!"

The dog ignored her.

"He isn't usually this badly behaved," she said. "He actually passed puppy school with flying colors."

Cooper gave her a bemused look. "Perhaps he's just channeling his inner cat."

Izzy marched over to her dog, who was diligently digging the sand under the boat shed door. "Stop that."

Thor barked and kept digging.

She reached down to grab him by the collar, but he ducked away, then doubled back and restarted digging, his paws frantic. This time when she reached for him he growled.

"Bad dog!" she admonished.

Thor bared his teeth, then snapped at her.

Cooper pulled her hand away. "Maybe you need to let him dig."

For a moment she was too stunned at Thor's behavior to say

anything. "I don't understand. He's never done anything like this before."

Thor, who was now trying to wriggle under the door, backed up and kept digging.

"Looks like he's keen to get inside the shed. What's in there?" Cooper said.

"Stand-up paddle boards and canoes. There's also a small yacht and an aluminum fishing boat. Nothing he'd want." She put her hands to her cheeks as realization hit her. "Rats."

"What?" Confusion crossed Cooper's face. "Oh, you mean there's rats in there?"

"Probably. It's been closed up for a few months." She tried to open the shed door before Thor hurt himself trying to shimmy under the steel.

"It's sticking on the sand. Want me to have a go?" Cooper asked.

Izzy appreciated he hadn't just taken over. "Thanks."

Using his booted foot, Cooper lifted the right-hand side of the door. He'd only opened it a third of the way when Thor shot between his feet and disappeared into the gloom. His frenzied barks bounced off the old steel walls, deafening them.

Cooper's eyes lit up with laughter as he pushed a rock against the now fully opened door. "At least he's playing fair and giving his prey plenty of warning."

Izzy didn't join in. "Except that's not like him either. It's like another dog has entered his body."

She peered into the gloom, her eyes adjusting to make out the paddle boards stacked on their racks on the left of the shed. Her mind immediately returned to the Elite party by the lake where Brad had asked her to organize sack races. Her stomach flipped, washing nausea through her. That was the day he'd convinced the Essens to invest in Fortune.

Thor's barking didn't let up. "For God's sake, Thor! What's going on?"

She stepped into the shed. It predated Villefranche and somehow had escaped the rest of the property's manicured design. Even on the bleak winter's day, pinpricks of light streamed through holes in the aged corrugated-iron roof, giving the space a ghostly feel.

A shocking stench hit her nostrils. "Oh God, that's disgusting."

"Smells like something's died in here," Cooper said.

"Thor! Come!" But Izzy knew it was already too late. He'd have found the decomposing fish or possum and be covered in the odor. She'd have to bathe him.

"Do you want some light?" Cooper's voice came from behind her.

Before she'd replied he'd switched on his cell phone's flashlight app. A narrow band of white light beamed along the ground. Thor was jumping up the side of the yacht, desperate to reach the deck. As Izzy took a step toward her dog, the light jerked up.

"Jesus!"

Cooper's tone froze her and she followed the beam.

Inside the boat she saw a familiar pair of heritage red Scrivani Derby shoes and the cuffs of a pair of Louis Vuitton trousers. Her gaze continued up the body to—

Her hand rose to her mouth but it wasn't enough to stifle her scream.

Izzy felt as if she was standing outside herself and her scream was attacking her—ripping and tearing into her like a jagged saw. Her arms rose in front of her face, trying to ward off the unimaginable and grisly scene and the old memories that were thundering back. She wanted to run, flee as fast as she could, but her feet rooted her to the spot.

The scream kept coming. The shoes and clothes said the body was Brad, but her horrified mind recoiled from the rest of the stark facts.

Someone was touching her—an arm rested against her shoulders, turning her with gentle pressure.

"Izzy. Come away."

She realized it was Cooper, but she couldn't move her feet.

"Lift one foot," he said. She stumbled and he caught her. "I've got you. Try again. That's it, and another."

It took an eternity, but she finally reached the door. The moment she was outside she fell to her knees and vomited. Cooper pushed clean tissues at her before handing her his water bottle. Then he helped her move onto the grass. The entire time Thor barked.

Cooper shrugged off his coat and wrapped Izzy in it, but not even two layers of goose down could temper the violent shakes racking her body.

He sat next to her and produced a tin of mints from his pocket. "You're in shock, Izzy. You need sugar. Put these in your mouth."

But her fingers shook so much she couldn't pick up the candy.

"Stick out your tongue." He put three in her mouth, then wrapped his arm around her shoulders again. "Is this okay?"

She could barely think, but the pressure of his chest on one side of her, his arm on the other, and his body heat seeping into her wasn't unwelcome.

"I'm so sorry," he kept saying. "No one deserves to see that."

Izzy heard a moan and realized it was coming from her. She instinctively turned her head into Cooper's shoulder as if that would block the image of Brad's barely recognizable face, but of course it didn't. Whether her eyes were open or closed, she could never unsee it.

A thought hit and she raised her head to look at Cooper. His previously wind-pinked cheeks were now pallid gray. "You saw it too."

"Yeah." He took a long slug from his drink bottle.

They sat together in silence until he eventually dropped his arm. "I need to call Brooke."

He stood and walked a few steps away, taking his reassuring presence with him. Izzy's shakes rushed back.

As she gripped her knees to her chest, trying to steady the tremors, Thor finally stopped barking and came out of the shed. His brown eyes, usually so full of curiosity and joy, were dull and doleful. He burrowed into her lap and she buried her face in his fur, forgiving him for snapping at her.

"You knew," she whispered. "You knew he was here."

CHAPTER TWENTY-NINE

When the police arrived, Brooke squatted next to Izzy. "Do you need a doctor?"

Izzy had no idea what she needed. A complete memory cleanse would be good.

"Have you told his parents?" Brooke asked.

Izzy shook her head, aghast that it hadn't occurred to her to call them. God, how was she going to tell Judy and Bevan? "Not yet, but I—"

"Good." Brooke gave her a stern look. "Keep it that way. I want the Quinns informed by my Queensland colleagues."

Izzy's cottonwool mind couldn't grasp the reasoning. "Why?"

Brooke stood then, towering over her. "This is a crime scene, Izzy."

A crime scene? It was pretty obvious Brad had killed himself. "How? He suicided."

"Any violent death is a crime scene," Brooke said firmly. "Don't leave the property."

"Oh my God!" Izzy heard the hysteria in her voice. "You think I had something to do with this?"

"This is standard procedure," Brooke said evenly. "Considering what's gone down with Quinn, there's more than one person with a motive to hurt him."

"I didn't want him dead!"

"And at the moment no one is saying you did. But as you and Doctor Barsky found the body, you need to stay on the property until we've interviewed you both."

Not that Izzy was capable of going anywhere, but she fought for a semblance of control. "When will that be?"

"I don't know. A few things have to happen first. We need to examine the scene and notify forensic medicine. It will be a coroner's case." Brooke turned to Cooper. "You okay, Doc?"

"I will be."

"Numbers are easier, eh? Can you take Izzy back to the house and stay there."

Cooper nodded, then stretched out his hand to Izzy to help her to her feet. Worried Thor might bolt, she passed the dog to him and stood on her own.

"Izzy," Brooke said.

"Yes?"

The police officer's face had unexpectedly softened. "I'm sorry for your loss."

Guilt and grief speared Izzy so sharply it was all she could do just to nod.

Back at the house, the urge to keep moving meant Izzy paced in jerky steps back and forth across the long wide sitting room. In comparison, Cooper's movements were slow and lumbering. He'd been doing something in the kitchen for ages.

"Here. I thought you could do with this." He stepped into her path and proffered a mug. "It's Irish coffee without the cream."

"Are you trying to get me locked up?"

A baffled look crossed his face. "I'm trying to help."

"It's alright for you! You don't have any connection to Brad. I don't think I should be drinking when I'm about to be interviewed about a dead body!"

He frowned. "Izzy, do you need an attorney?"

She made a huffing sound, unsure if it was a laugh or a cry. The tears rolling down her cheeks confirmed it and all at once she was utterly exhausted. She sank onto the sofa and Thor bounded into her lap.

"I don't know what I need. I can't believe Brad would—" Her hands found her hair. "I mean, for weeks I've hated him for abandoning me in his mess while he ran away, dodging everything. But all this time he's been—" Her voice cracked. "Dead."

Cooper sat next to her and set the drinks down on the coffee table. "Suicide is a form of abandonment."

Her heart twisted, spiraling pain through her. "Maybe it's payback."

He was quiet, but when she didn't add anything, he said, "I don't get it."

"I was leaving him." The words were out of her mouth before she'd considered the consequences.

Surprise rippled his concern. "Izzy, you can't blame yourself for his death. You—"

"I meant karmic payback."

"Yeah?" He shook his head as if it would help him understand. "I'm still not following."

She stroked Thor's rough winter coat, needing the calming touch. "After the engagement, things between us deteriorated fast. If I'm honest, I can track the breakdown to the start of the year. I should never have let him slip that ring on my finger. I should have left him then, but ..." She shied away from the truth and stared out the window. "The day I decided to leave him was the day he vanished. The day my life turned to shit."

"I didn't know Quinn, Izzy, and finding him that way ... it would rock anyone." Cooper took a big sip of his coffee and stared at the intricate carving around the fireplace. "When the shock wears off and your rational self resurfaces, you'll see that everything that's happened to you is *not* payback for your decision to leave him."

He was trying to reassure her, but he didn't know her truth or how hard it pummeled her. She'd thrown herself headfirst into the intoxicating excitement of the early days with Brad, and she couldn't deny that her attraction to him had increased once he'd started making money. Hungry for gifts, not once had she questioned Brad's extravagance. She'd embraced the five-star luxury, the overseas travel to exotic places and a closet full of clothes that cost as much as some people paid in rent for a year. She'd selfishly taken it all, luxuriating in the freedom wealth gave her. Except it wasn't freedom at all.

Izzy turned to face Cooper. Care and decency radiated off him in waves, deepening her guilt.

"No," she said softly. "It's payback for staying."

Izzy continued to swing between believing Brad had stolen the money and believing he'd been used. His erratic behavior over the previous six months now hinted that he'd known he was in trouble either financially or personally or both. And the kicker—he hadn't told the police. Now he was dead and the police wanted to talk to her —again.

The first interview took place a few hours later at Villefranche, after the police had produced a new search warrant. Sitting next to Cooper, Izzy told Brooke and Mitchell about the Noosa apartment.

The second interview was the following day at the police station. To get there, Izzy had run the gauntlet of the press pack who'd returned to the gate.

Now, inside the interview room, Mitchell was grilling her about a suicide note.

"I told you yesterday, I've never found one. Nothing's changed," she said wearily. "I think maybe the apartment's his note."

Mitchell's face was thoughtful rather than disbelieving. "That he was making sure you were looked after?"

"I don't see how using stolen money to buy a house is looking after me!" She drew in a long breath as her anger tipped into grief. "But then I never thought he'd take his own life. Clearly his thought processes were muddled."

Mitchell didn't react. "Did you know he owned a gun?"

She met his gaze. "Yes."

Brooke placed a clear plastic bag into the middle of the table. "Is this it?"

Izzy made herself look at the small black gun. "Is that ... Did he use it?"

"It was found at the scene."

An image flared in Izzy's mind and her body involuntary flinched. She immediately squeezed her eyes shut and forced the rising coffee she'd drunk earlier back into her stomach.

Breathe in. Breathe out. In. Out.

"Have you seen this gun before?" Mitchell asked.

She opened her eyes, studied it, then shook her head. "Brad owns a rifle. The only time I saw him use it was for duck shooting."

She didn't add it had been an invitation-only Elite event to tempt some city investors. "We'll give them the whole country estate experience, Iz," Brad had said. She'd been surprised he hadn't included a fox hunt on horseback.

"Do you know where the rifle is?" Mitchell asked.

"The last time I saw it, it was in the gun safe."

"When was that?"

"Yesterday when Brooke removed it." Izzy glanced between the two police officers, trying to work out what was going on. "I've never touched the damn thing. I hated it."

Brooke pointed to the gun on the table. "Are you certain you've never seen this gun before?"

"I have never seen this gun before." Izzy looked away from the killing device. "He never showed it to me, never mentioned it and I never stumbled across it. When did he buy it?"

"That's what we're trying to determine," Mitchell said.

"But isn't that just a matter of checking the gun register?" Izzy said, then felt an insidious chill crawling across her skin. She heard Judy's and Bevan's voices as clearly as if they were in the room: "Business is complicated. He has a plan. Brad's sorting it out."

Had Brad been in business with international crime figures rather than businessmen?

Don't be ridiculous!

But the thought wouldn't budge.

"Are you saying Brad was murdered?"

Mitchell rolled his eyes. "Sounds like you've been watching too many police dramas."

She detested this man so much. "His parents are convinced his business partners are behind the theft of the money."

"We're aware."

"But you don't believe them?"

"There are lines of inquiry."

"Can you categorically tell me Brad shot himself?"

"I can categorically tell you we're doing our job." Mitchell stood. "Thanks for coming in, Isobel. We'll be in touch."

Mitchell hadn't given her any information, nor had he clarified anything, and now he was dismissing her? She stood, irritated, wanting to argue with him rather than deal with a difficult phone call.

"Am I allowed to call Brad's parents now?" she asked tartly.

"They haven't called you? Interesting." Mitchell opened the door, indicating she could leave. "Knock yourself out."

The phone call to Judy and Bevan did not go well.

"We're arriving tomorrow and staying at Villefranche," Bevan said.

Izzy didn't want them in the house. "Oh? I thought you'd go home."

"I n-need to be c-close to him," Judy stammered, her voice clogged with tears.

"We need to be together," Bevan added, reiterating what he'd said earlier in the week when he'd insisted Izzy fly to Queensland.

Izzy's gut cramped and she pressed her hand to her belly. Every part of her was rejecting the idea of having them at Villefranche with her. She didn't know if it was because she feared Judy's palpable grief or if she didn't trust them.

Brad's death had muted her emotions, leaving her numb. Part of her wanted to scream and rage, but guilt left her floundering. The Quinns would expect her to be bowed down by sadness, not lit up with fury. They'd expect her to be wearing the engagement ring.

When Brad's parents arrived at the house, Izzy barely recognized Judy. In the time she'd known her, she'd never seen her without styled hair and flawless make-up, and accessorized in perfect harmony with her outfit. The woman who collapsed against Izzy, her body racked with sobs, was haggard with misery.

"My darling boy. My poor darling boy."

Izzy staggered under Judy's weight, and as she brought her arms up to support her she heard herself saying, "I'm so sorry. So very sorry."

If Judy thought it an odd thing for Brad's fiancée to say, she didn't show it. Izzy understood then that Judy's grief was so encompassing that it didn't allow for anyone else's. She hated that it offered her an out.

Izzy continued to hold her, feeling the wetness of Judy's tears seeping through her blouse. She dropped her own head to the woman's shoulder, wishing she could feel something other than heart-racing anxiety. When it became clear that Judy wasn't going to step back of her own volition, Izzy raised her head and caught Bevan's eye.

He moved forward and put a hand on her shoulder for a brief moment before helping Judy to the sofa.

"I'll make coffee," Izzy said and escaped to the kitchen.

When she returned with the tray, a pale but composed Judy said, "We need to plan the funeral."

Words rushed into Izzy's mouth—*the body hasn't been released yet* —but she held them back.

"Brad would want a funeral mass," Judy said. "Father Corrigan's coming at 6:00."

The only time Izzy could remember Brad going to church was at Christmas when Judy had insisted they all attend midnight mass. When Izzy had expressed dismay, he'd said, "Just think of it as magic. Bells and spells." He'd grinned. "That's what I did at boarding school." Izzy doubted Brad would have wanted a religious funeral, but that wasn't her biggest concern.

"Have you considered having the funeral in Melbourne?" she suggested gently.

Judy's eyes widened and the look she gave her implied Izzy had grown two heads. "Why would we have it in Melbourne?"

"He went to school and uni there, and we lived there. I thought perhaps the school chapel ..."

"That's thoughtful, Izzy, but all his family and most of his friends are here."

"It's just ..." Nervous, Izzy licked her lips. "I'm not sure many people will come."

"Of course they'll come!"

Izzy wondered if this was what the magical thinking of grief looked like. Surely Judy had received angry and ugly emails, texts and calls from Elite members. From Birdie Essen.

"Judy," she said carefully, "Glingilly's angry. Do you want to put yourself in the path of furious people at the funeral?"

Judy's cup clattered into its saucer. "My son was murdered, Isobel. He was stolen from me," she said in a low, grievous tone. "We are having the funeral at St Bridget's and the bells will toll."

Izzy wanted to point out that neither the police or the coroner were yet to definitively state that Brad had been murdered, but she caught Bevan's steely gaze and remained silent.

"I know you were his fiancée, Izzy," Bevan said.

Judy wept at "were," and Bevan reached out and patted her thigh.

A sharp, stitch-like pain tore down Izzy's side. *Tell them you were leaving him.*

Before his funeral? I don't think so!

"But as his parents," Bevan continued, "we will be making *all* the funeral and burial decisions."

Izzy dropped her head. "Of course. I understand."

Bevan frowned as if he'd been expecting a fight.

Judy's hand shot out and gripped hers. "You poor girl. We're not excluding you. Of course we want you to speak at the funeral. You must."

Even if Izzy hadn't reached the point of walking away from her relationship with Brad, standing in front of a crowd was always a form of torture. With everything else hanging over her head, speaking at Brad's funeral would sink her.

"I don't think I can."

"I think you need to," Bevan said.

Izzy wasn't sure if the statement was supportive or a threat.

Izzy wore black to Brad's funeral. As she slipped the Alexander McQueen dress over her head, then shrugged into the Catherine Walker woolen coat, she had a momentary ripple of concern. *You should be wearing sackcloth, not couture.*

But as Brad had preferred her in bright colors, these were the only black clothes she owned. They were the antithesis of the clothes she'd worn to her father's funeral. Back then her only suitable outfit was her waitressing uniform of black pants and black shirt. She'd worn them because she couldn't afford to buy anything new.

You just have to get through today.

Unbeknownst to the Quinns, after the funeral Izzy was moving into a cottage close to the river. She'd arranged it all by cell, not just because Bevan questioned her any time she picked up her car keys, but because the media was back and the town was awash with disaffected people.

Gavin, the owner of the cottage, didn't seem to care who Izzy was or who she was connected to. All he'd wanted was two months rent upfront. "It's a month-by-month rental, but it comes fully furnished now Grandpa's in the nursing home," he'd told her. Going by the photos on the website, it had last been furnished in 1975.

This time, Izzy wasn't waiting to explain her plans to anyone. Yesterday, when Judy and Bevan were being interviewed by the police, she'd loaded her car trunk with her bags. If she'd had a friend in town she'd have asked them to drive her car to the cottage. But she was on her own so she'd leave straight after the funeral.

She folded her speech twice and slid it inside her clutch. It was only short, outlining her early days with Brad in Melbourne before he'd started Elite—back when they were happy, and well before she'd met Judy and Bevan. She reassured herself that by sticking to the early days she wasn't speaking ill of the dead. After all she'd been through, she couldn't in good conscience say that prior to his death Brad was a good or honorable man, or the love of her life—no matter how much she'd once believed both to be true.

The chauffeur-driven car ride to the church with Judy and Bevan was silent and cloying. As Izzy stepped out of the limousine to stand under an iron ore sky, a brutal wind whipped her. Holding her breath, she scanned the area, anticipating an angry mob, but apart from Brad's aunts and uncles the churchyard was empty.

Connor Greyson from the *Standard* stood outside the church gate with a photographer. After a week of headlines and tawdry articles about Brad, Izzy had expected more press.

Brooke Riglioni stood at the church steps wearing her police uniform. Izzy wasn't certain if she was in attendance as a member of the community or for security. Not that it looked like many people were coming. Izzy released her breath.

Bevan and Judy were greeting their relatives so Izzy slipped into the church. Despite the fact she'd prepared herself, the sight of the Tasmanian blackwood coffin and the large but tasteful spray of native flowers on top of it made it hard to breathe.

Stepping up, she placed her hand on the polished wood. It was cool beneath her fingers. "I hate it ended like this," she said softly. She'd fallen out of love with Brad, but she despaired he'd taken his life.

She glimpsed the priest out of the corner of her eye and, not wanting to talk, walked into the cloisters and pretended to study one of the many icons of Christ on the Cross. This one showed his heart outside of his body and dripping blood. Izzy shuddered and took a seat.

The family filed in, filling the first two rows of pews. Judy, pale and shaky, sat next to Izzy. Izzy knew she should say something supportive but she couldn't manage it.

Low murmurs—comments about the flowers, the chill of the church, a mutter of words Izzy couldn't decipher—rumbled on the frigid air. Her tension dropped down a level, and she was thankful for the lack of Elite members and therefore a scene. No matter how conflicted her own feelings were about Brad, Judy and Bevan, she wished them the comfort of a dignified service.

It crossed her mind that if there was an afterlife and Brad was up there watching, he'd be devastated by the small attendance.

You must have known it would all fall apart, right?

But there was no right about any of this. Perhaps Brad's need to be front and center had been a warning everyone had missed—lost under the glare of a lavish lifestyle and the promise of money.

The priest checked his watch and frowned. It was already past eleven. Ignoring Bevan, who was holding up five fingers, the priest signaled for the organist to stop.

As he welcomed everyone, the excruciating squeak of the old church door made him fall silent.

Oh God! Adrenaline put Izzy's senses on high alert, yet also glued her to her seat. This was what she'd been expecting—Elite members disrupting the funeral.

As she stared doggedly forward, people turned toward the noise.

"Who's that?" Judy whispered to Bevan.

He shook his head. "I don't know."

Izzy turned then and blinked. It didn't change who she was seeing. Wearing a suit and tie, Cooper Barsky slid into the back pew.

What was he doing here?

CHAPTER THIRTY

A BONE-TIRED BIRDIE walked in after a busy shift at the supermarket to discover the kitchen replicating an explosion. Dirty dishes were sprawled across the sink, remnants of mashed potato clung to a saucepan still on the stove, and the oven was switched on but empty. Birdie's jaw stiffened to a point so taut it threatened to crack. This wasn't Mike's doing. Since his surgery, his sole contribution to the household was taking out the trash—and that only happened after several reminders.

The chaotic mess had Lucy written all over it. The girl was used to Jack cleaning up after her, but he was away and Birdie refused to be plunged deeper into service. She turned off the oven and was about to stomp down the hall to find Lucy and demand she clean up immediately, when a shout came from the sunroom.

Mike! Panic swamped her and she ran. "Is it your heart?"

He shook his head and pointed to the television. A blue news banner ran across the bottom of the screen declaring *Breaking news*.

"They've just found Brad Essen's body."

"Wh-what?" Her knees softened and she sank onto the sofa.

Mike replayed the news report. "Doesn't say how he died. I hope it bloody hurt!"

"Mike!"

His jaw jutted—belligerent and unrepentant. "At least we might get our money back."

But she barely heard him. Her brain was spinning like a top and none of her thoughts made sense. Brad was thirty-two years old. How could he be dead? Her thoughts sped toward Judy. Poor Ju—*No! Don't go there.* She reminded herself of her best friend's betrayal and her stark silence.

"I don't think I can go to the funeral," she said.

Mike stared at her as if she'd lost her mind. "Of course we're not going. Funerals are for paying respects and we're sure as hell not doing that!"

Lucy appeared holding a limp Rigby, whose cheeks burned with the high color of a fever. "Rigby's spiked a temp and I can't find the liquid para—" Her eyes roved cautiously between Birdie and Mike. "Is something wrong?"

"That depends on your definition," Mike said.

The following morning the police insisted Birdie and Mike visit the station and they asked if they recalled anyone from Elite threatening to kill Brad.

Mike scoffed. "What do you reckon? Everyone muttered it the night we discovered he'd taken off with all our money."

Detective Mitchell was unamused, as was Birdie, especially when the detective insisted on interviewing them separately. Losing all their money to a scam was one thing. Being treated as a murder suspect gave a whole new meaning to degrading.

Birdie read every news article that week and trawled the internet for information, but it was thin on the ground. The chatter in the supermarket was impossible not to hear, but the whispered comments were louder. She felt the eyes of the town on her and sensed their questions and condemnation.

Everyone had a firm opinion—formed from the media's phrase *the death is being investigated.*

"That means suspicious, right?" Sonny Cronk said as he stood in the checkout line.

"Yeah. it's big money. Let's face it, people have killed for less." Tyson Kontelj winked at her. "Was it you, Birdie?"

She schooled her face into the blank mask she used whenever any customer referenced Elite. "That will be seventeen fifty, Tyson."

"Nah, I reckon he topped himself," the next person in the checkout line said.

"Yeah, but if he'd done that," Tyson said, "They'd say *the death's not being treated as suspicious.*"

Birdie checked the clock and wondered how she'd survive the next two hours.

Later that day, at the meeting Oscar had called for Elite members, he told them the Quinns were back. He'd flown to New South Wales a few weeks earlier, hoping to talk to Judy and Bevan, but hadn't got beyond the security gate of the Dolphin Sands complex.

"They're at Villefranche, not Garden Street," he added.

"Of course they are," Gaylene Hewitson spat. "No gates to hide behind in Garden Street."

"You wait," Alan Lumsden said. "The moment the funeral's over, they'll scarper back to New South Wales."

"The police might charge them with something so they can't leave," Birdie suggested.

"Hah!" Mike said. "They're too slippery for that."

"Oh, they'll bolt alright," Oscar said tightly. "Which is why we have to act now."

"What do you have in mind?" Rick asked.

"Isn't it obvious? We crash the funeral and demand answers," Oscar said.

Birdie recoiled as the prickle of anxiety raised every hair on her body. Perhaps it was the lapsed Catholic in her, but despite her hatred for the Quinns and what they'd done to them all, crashing a funeral was a step too far.

"Bastard Brad will have left an estate." Alan's voice, devoid of any sympathy, boomed around the room. "Money that belongs to us!"

"Yeah!" Jim Hewitson said. "It's our money, not the Quinns'."

"What if he left it all to Izzy?" someone said.

"Either way, they have to pay it back," Gaylene said.

Birdie felt the mood change—the murmurs in the room had taken on an agitated tone. She understood everyone's frustration and despair —it matched her own—but a vigilante mob storming St Bridget's had disaster written all over it.

"Let's think about this for a minute," she said. "If you crash the funeral, Brooke Riglioni will throw all of you in the lockup for the night."

"I don't care," Alan said. "I just want my money!"

"So do I, but let's be realistic. They're not going to hand over cash at the funeral and Brad's assets are part of a police investigation." Birdie crossed her fingers like a child as if it would be enough to defuse anger and promote reason. "Melbourne will send TV journalists and if you crash the funeral, the only story will be pictures of you lot being shoved into the paddy wagon. But the park's across the road and if you make banners and invite the journos over, they'll film you. Use national television to apply pressure. Let the journalists hound them in ways we never can."

Silence choked the room and Birdie's mouth dried as all eyes stared at her.

Mike eventually broke the strained silence. "Bird's got a point."

They voted to go to the park.

Birdie was thankful for the towering cypress pines on the edge of the park that shielded the view to the church, making it difficult to see the arrival of the hearse and the funeral guests. She didn't want to glimpse the coffin or see Judy. Her nightmare the previous two nights was bad enough—Judy hysterical and prostrating herself on the coffin. It had woken her at 3:00 in the morning in a cold sweat and stolen further sleep.

Most of the Elite members were angsty, peering through the trees and muttering about moving to stand by the church gate.

"We can't risk looking like an unhinged rabble or we'll lose viewer sympathy," Birdie said. "We need our message to be clear and calm."

Alan had brought binoculars. "They've all gone inside. A cameraman and journo are coming over," he reported.

"Let's do this," Oscar said.

Birdie raised her placard—she'd used Rigby's red paint to write *Give us back OUR $$$$*. Mike's declared *Quinn means thief!* All the other placards being waved around them had similar themes. Gaylene's stated *Dead doesn't mean Not Guilty*.

"Hello, everyone, I'm Samantha and this," the journalist indicated the cameraman, "is Gus."

Although Oscar did most of the talking—"If Bevan and Judy Quinn are as innocent as they claim they are, why won't they meet with us?"— Samantha spoke to everyone. After half an hour, she started glancing back toward the church, clearly not wanting to miss the moment the Quinns exited the building.

"Thanks, everyone." She slid her notebook into her bag. "I'll take your questions to the Quinns and see if we can get a response."

"Will we be on tonight's news?" Gaylene asked.

"Absolutely."

Birdie checked her watch. She hoped the group wouldn't break their promise to stay away from the church, but she didn't have time to stay and be the voice of reason.

"I'm going home to get ready for work," she said to Mike. "You coming?"

He shook his head. "I'm having lunch at the club with this lot."

Birdie should be happy he was out of the house, but all she felt was a festering fury. Whenever she suggested they go out somewhere he always refused.

"One drink," she said icily, "and no chips."

He shot her a withering look. "I'm not a child."

The jury was out on that one. Since his heart attack he demanded more of her time than Rigby did.

"I'll see you after work then."

She deliberately walked to the corner of the park as it took her away from the media scrum gathered at the church gate, and then she crossed the road and took the street that ran behind the church. She could faintly hear the organ—processional music—and she tried not to think about what it represented.

She was halfway along the church block when she tensed, thinking she could hear Judy calling her name. She blew out a breath, berating herself for an overactive imagination. Even if Judy hadn't cut off all contact, she wouldn't be on this side of the church. She'd be out the front and getting into the car to take her to the cemetery.

"Birdie! Wait!"

Shock stilled her feet so fast she almost fell over. *No. Not possible.* Even so, she turned slowly.

In the distance, she saw Bevan stepping out of the rear side door of the church. As it occurred to her that they must be using this exit to avoid the journalists at the front, Judy came running toward her, arms outstretched.

"Oh, Birdie!"

Birdie caught the other woman by the upper arms, doing her best to hold Judy away from her as the pavement tilted under her feet. She wasn't sure if that was from being knocked into by Judy or the storm of emotions leaping and spitting inside her.

Suddenly she was sixteen again, standing in front of her furious and embarrassed mother. *Bridget Beatrice O'Neill, you have a lot to learn. A true lady is always gracious and well-mannered in public. Behind closed doors is the place for true feelings, not the tennis club! I'll not be able to show my face in town after your little performance this afternoon.*

Performance was right. Birdie steeled herself to ape politeness.

"Judy. I'm sorry for your loss." She forced the words from a throat tight with anger and they came out stiff but civil.

"It's been awful. It *is* awful." Raw grief clogged Judy's voice. "I can't bear the thought of my Brad in the grou—" Sobs cut off her words.

Birdie's nostrils flared in a conflict of emotions and she dragged in as much air as possible to stop herself from screaming or crying.

"I need you, Birdie." Judy raised her tear-stained face, her eyes beseeching. "I needed you in there." She waved vaguely in the direction of the church. "You've known my Brad since he was a baby. Why weren't you there?"

The violent surge of anger that consumed Birdie blurred her vision. She stepped back and folded her hands across her chest, trying to hold everything in.

"You know why," she said with icy control. Judy stared at her as if she didn't understand at all. "Brad stole all our money."

"No!" Judy's voice shook.

"He bloody well did! And everyone in Glingilly knows it."

"He would nev—"

"Then where is it?"

"I don't know," Judy implored. "And I don't know why my best friend believes those lying pricks over me."

Potent rage forged weeks of shame, regret and guilt into a jagged nugget, then slammed it into disbelief. Birdie's mind twirled and her body shook so violently she didn't know if she was capable of opening her mouth. But then she heard a dangerous noise and she realized it was coming from her.

"Because 23 million doesn't just vanish!" Birdie was vaguely aware of the sound of running feet. "Brad stole it!"

"You can't say that! He's innocent. Nothing's been proven and the police never laid any charges—"

"Only because they couldn't find him! And you—" Birdie was

screaming now, "—you enabled him. You convinced us to invest in him and then you disappeared from our lives with our money. What sort of friend does that?!"

Judy's face was a mix of shock and confusion. "I can't believe you're saying all these hurtful things when I've only ever been a true and loyal friend! I've spent weeks not knowing where my son is, fearing the worst and hoping against hope that everything will be alright. Bevan and I have done it all alone! Unsupported by the people who should have been there for us after everything we've done for them. For you." Judy heaved in a breath. "You lost some money. I lost my son!"

"Some money?" Birdie couldn't believe what she was hearing. "900,000 dollars! Now we have *nothing*! I'm stacking shelves at IGA! Jack's losing the house and Mike almost died—"

"But he didn't!" Judy's eyes glittered with manic intensity. "Mike's still alive!"

Birdie thought of the shell of a man who'd taken the place of her husband and the last shred of her tattered control unraveled. She whipped back her arm and slapped Judy's face so hard her palm burned and the jolt radiated to her shoulder.

"You and your precious asshole of a son have ruined my life! I'm glad Brad's dead."

"Gus! Are you getting all this?" a woman's voice yelled.

"You bitch!" Judy launched herself at Birdie.

Birdie stumbled, falling back against the fence. The sharp jab of a picket knifing her in the back was followed by the stinging tear of Judy's manicured nails ripping her face. She ducked, then slammed her palms against Judy's chest and pushed. The woman's high heels tottered under her, but she came back, head-butting Birdie in the stomach.

The breath left Birdie's lungs in a painful whoosh that almost brought her to her knees. She gulped in air. "You thieving, conniving witch!" she screamed. "Where's the money?"

She was grabbing for Judy's hair when a hand caught her arm. A woman spoke her name but Birdie barely registered—her focus was fully on Judy. On inflicting pain just like Judy had done to her. She pulled against the restraining hand. It tightened and Birdie felt the pinch of nails against her skin.

"Birdie, please. It's not worth it," a woman's voice said softly in her ear.

Birdie was aware of the sudden loss of pressure on her arm and it broke the spell of her all-encompassing fury. It was like falling back to earth after visiting another planet.

Her heart slowed and her blurred vision straightened into focus. With horrifying clarity, she took in the shocked faces of all the Elite members, the soft gray fluff of the television crew's microphone boom, the back of Samantha's teal-blue blouse and the running legs of the cameraman. They were chasing a grim-faced Bevan, who was hustling a hysterical Judy and a stony-faced Izzy away from their questions.

They filmed you. They filmed everything.

"Birdie." Mike appeared next to her, his chest heaving. "What the hell?"

Oh God. Silver spots danced in front of her eyes and it took effort to breathe.

"What was that about not looking like an unhinged rabble?" Oscar asked, brows raised. "Losing viewer sympathy?"

"This will be your fifteen minutes of fame." Gaylene sounded oddly jealous.

"I'm sorry," Birdie said softly. "I'm so sorry."

"Don't be sorry," Alan said. "I'm proud of you. You just did what we've all wanted to do for weeks."

Jim rubbed his hands together. "It must have felt so damn good."

But it felt far from good. It was so far removed from anything Birdie had ever experienced before that she couldn't even name it. Shame lived, breathed and multiplied inside her, leaving no place untouched. She itched to run and hide, to shut herself away, but people were patting her on the back and shaking her hand. Their approval stung. She hated being praised for sinking as low as humanly possible and giving in to the base instincts of hitting and scratching—behaving like an animal.

She'd struck her best friend.

She's not your friend anymore. She ruined your life.

And that was the truth. But the thought of seeing herself on television—wild and out of control—made Birdie gag.

When Birdie finished work at 7:00 that night, her head throbbed and her legs ached. Apparently the footage of her and Judy brawling on the pavement outside St. Bridget's had been the teaser for the nightly news bulletin. Half the town had "popped in" to the supermarket on the pretense of needing one or two grocery items, but really to see Birdie. They either praised her or teased her, and she'd reached the point that if one more person swiped their hand in a claw shape at her and said meow she couldn't trust herself not to swipe back. If she hadn't needed the money so badly she would have taken off her apron and walked away.

Now, she surveyed her kitchen. Either Lucy had eaten elsewhere or a minor miracle had occurred and she'd cleaned up. Did this mean her daughter-in-law was finally turning over a new leaf? Birdie had told Jack in no uncertain terms it had to happen.

She opened the fridge, irrationally hopeful that the tidy kitchen gesture might also extend to a waiting casserole—an acknowledgment of her truly awful day. She stared, looked side to side, bent her knees and came up blank. She slammed the fridge door so hard the bottles rattled.

"Mike!"

But he didn't answer. Of course he didn't—he couldn't hear her over the blare of the television.

She stomped into the sunroom, immediately feeling the winter chill through the windows, and tugged abruptly on the curtains. "Why didn't you close them to keep the heat in?"

"Didn't want to miss your fight on national television."

His censure branded her. Mike believed in keeping private matters behind closed doors and Birdie had well and truly broken that rule. But it was his lack of support—his failure to see that she was the only person in this family holding everything together—that hurt the most.

"Did it occur to you that tonight might have been the night you stirred yourself to cook dinner?" she said tartly.

"You know I don't cook."

Her jaw ached. "I think it's time you learned."

The doorbell pealed and she watched him, waiting to see if he'd stand to answer it. Waiting to hear if Lucy would call out, "I'll get it." But not even Rigby's running feet stirred the air.

The bell rang a second time.

"I'll get it then, shall I," she muttered. As she walked to the door she couldn't imagine who would be visiting without warning at 7:30 in the evening. It better not be someone who'd come to take another crack at her very public meltdown.

Reluctantly, she opened the door then gasped. Two uniformed police officers stood on the faded welcome mat. Neither of them was Brooke Riglioni.

"Mrs. Bridget Essen?" one of them asked.

"Yes." A flutter of panic hit her. Had something happened to Jack or Sienna? She called over her shoulder, "Mike! Now!" before turning back to face the police. "Please wait until my husband's here."

"This is regarding a matter pertaining to you, Mrs. Essen."

"Me?"

Mike lumbered up behind her. "Officers," he said. "Is there a problem?"

"Oh God, what's happened?" Lucy called, running up the hall. "Is it Jack?"

The older police officer produced an envelope. "Mrs. Bridget Essen, this is an interim restraining order issued by the Warrnambool

Magistrates' Court after an application by Mrs. Judith Quinn against you. You are not permitted to have any contact in any manner with Mrs. Quinn."

"What?" Nothing was making sense. "Why?"

The younger police officer looked away as the senior officer continued. "After today's incident outside St. Bridget's church, Mrs. Quinn is fearful of more harmful behavior—"

"Harmful behavior!" Incensed, Birdie pointed to the long scratch on her cheek. "What do you call this?"

"If you break the restraining order," the officer continued calmly, as if he'd done this many times before, "you will be arrested. You're to attend the Warrnambool Magistrates' Court on the twentieth of this month. The summons lists the full details of the applicant's reasons behind the order. Now you have been served, the order commences immediately."

Mike's face had paled but his mouth was a flat and stony line. "Jesus, Birdie. This is all we need."

"Do you understand, Mrs. Essen?" the police officer asked.

"She understands, officer," Mike said.

The anger hit Birdie fast—a forcefield in its own right. It bubbled wildly, lashing at the police, at Judy and at Mike. How dare he imply she was the sole person to bring chaos into their lives. Especially when he'd abrogated all responsibility and retreated into himself, leaving her to deal with everything from trailers to Centrelink. Leaving her to work in a supermarket where she was the butt of everyone's jokes so they had money for food.

"Oh, I understand alright," Birdie ground out. "I only regret not calling that woman something that started with C instead of a witch!"

"Mrs. Essen." The officer's tone held a warning. "Glingilly police are aware of the order and will not hesitate to enforce it."

She peered at the officer's name tag—Sergeant O'Connor. "Are you new to Glingilly?"

"I'm from Warrnambool, Mrs. Essen."

Warrnambool? Birdie didn't understand why Brooke wasn't the

one delivering the summons. Her gut roiled with sudden awareness. If the level-headed policewoman had been consulted this summons wouldn't be happening. Instead she and Judy would have received a lecture and a stern warning for behaving in a way that was offensive to other people.

A vague memory niggled at the back of Birdie's mind—Judy passing her cell phone to show her a photo of a cute-as-a-button baby girl in a christening gown. It was her great-niece, Maeve O'Connor. Judy had talked about how thrilled her sister was that her son had finally returned to Warrnambool so she could be a doting grandmother to baby Maeve. Birdie told herself there were many Irish names in the district and this man was unlikely to be Judy's nephew. And yet ...

"I see," she said stiffly. "And would you be related to Mrs. Quinn?"

His shoulder gave a slight lift. "The magistrate issued the order, Mrs. Essen. I'm just serving the summons."

Except Birdie wasn't stupid—she'd lived in the region all her life. So often it wasn't what you knew but who you knew. She withdrew the paper from the envelope and looked for the magistrate's name. When she found it, she was unsurprised. She'd met the man and his wife a few years earlier at Judy and Bevan's party for their thirty-fifth wedding anniversary.

Game, set and match to the Quinns.

Again.

CHAPTER THIRTY-ONE

WITHOUT A SPACE TO call her own, Lucy was slowly losing her mind. Mike had agreed to the suggestion that the garage could be returned to the rec room, similar to how it had been set up when Jack and Sienna were kids, but each time Jack suggested, "Let's make a start, eh, Dad?", Mike always led with "Now's not a good time." A litany of excuses followed. As Jack was only home one week a month, this meant the delay was considerable.

More than anything, Lucy wanted to storm the garage and do it herself, but she knew what would happen if she did. This time it wouldn't just be Birdie who would erupt, but she sensed Jack would as well. At least tonight Birdie was out and the house was quiet and Lucy didn't have to worry about raised voices waking Rigby. Having his own room hadn't solved the bed-wetting issue like she'd hoped, and he continued to lurch between clingy and wild. Oh, how she missed her happy-go-lucky little boy, but until the house sold they were stuck in no-man's-land.

Since Brad's funeral and Birdie's very public meltdown, the mood in the house resembled a ticking bomb, only without a set time to explode. Tension hung hot and heavy like water-logged tropical air just before the arrival of the wet. Birdie blew up over the most trivial things —a toy left in the living room, a plate on the table, a kitchen sponge left in the sink rather than next to it. This behavior had Lucy second, third and fourth guessing every step, every word, every breath.

After the sponge episode, Lucy had called Jack. "It's official. Your mother's totally lost it."

Jack had sighed. "Be nice, Luce."

Disloyalty struck her hard between the ribs. Not for the first time she was aware of a shift—Jack's recent propensity to side with his mother. "Why would you assume I'm not being nice?"

He was silent for a beat too long. "Look, she's going through a lot—"

"Oh, and I'm not!"

"Your best friend didn't betray you."

"Yours did!"

There was silence for a moment. "Yeah, well, he topped himself so I can't deck him like I want to."

"Did he though?" she asked. Weeks had passed since the funeral, but Brad's death was still tinged with unknowns. Not that it changed anything for her and Jack or the other Elite members, but people were hanging out for a verdict from the coroner.

"Can we change the subject?" Jack said wearily.

"Can we return to your mother?"

There was a hiss of breath. "Just cut her some slack, okay? I know you're capable of that if you choose to," he'd said tightly.

Sparks had ignited behind her eyes. "I could be if she showed even a hint of offering me the same courtesy. When you're home and experiencing Birdie's full-blown irrationality, you might not be quite so condescending. Oh, wait, you're Jack, so you won't experience it!"

She'd hung up before he could reply. She hated that she'd sounded like Sienna.

The memory of that conversation raced Lucy's heart. She hated that in so many of her and Jack's recent conversations she felt like they were on opposing sides. She missed him. Missed their old life, and how when she was tired and irritable he would make her laugh. Now he treated her as if she was just another problem he had to deal with. And that ticked her off, because unlike him she never got a break. She was working, single parenting, being made to feel she was imposing on his parents ... Some days she wished she could be the FIFO worker and leave all the crap behind.

But once again she was inside Jack's old room. The urge to pull down the Wolfmother poster was strong. God, they were adults! Had been adults for a decade, but in this house they were children again, told what to do and given unsolicited and unhelpful advice.

Balancing her laptop on her thighs, she reread an email from Tiffany: *Considering the lack of an offer would you consider dropping the price?*

A surge of stomach acid rose and burned, just as it had when she'd read it that afternoon. She closed the laptop against the offending words. They couldn't afford to drop the house price. Then again, they couldn't afford not to sell the house either.

Had Jack seen the email? If he'd read it, he hadn't called her to talk about it. But that was Jack's approach to most things these days—ignore the hard stuff. If you didn't discuss it, then it didn't exist.

Discontent spurred her to her feet. Rigby was asleep and Birdie wasn't home to give her tart pout of disapproval. She stuck her head around the door of the sunroom and raised her voice above the police drama Mike was watching.

"You okay if I go out for a walk? Rigby shouldn't wake up."

Mike grunted. Without confirming, Lucy accepted it as a yes.

Escaping the claustrophobic house, she turned toward the river and immediately sneezed—the wattle was flowering, hinting at spring. It took her a few steps to realize she was tiptoeing rather than walking. Currently her life was one big tiptoe—a metaphor for living in her in-laws' house.

She extended her stride and concentrated on long, slow, deep breaths. After all, the point of leaving the house was to find a source of calm and refill her constantly diminished well. She focused on the bite of the cool evening air laced with mist from the nearby falls, the dull but constant roar of the river as it poured over the black basalt rocks, the pungent clean scent of the eucalypts—nature at its soothing best. A cloak of peace billowed around her and she raised her arms, letting it slide gently over her like silk. Then she pulled it around her and accepted its offer, in this moment, to lock out all the stresses in her life.

Lost in her thoughts, she realized she'd been walking randomly and didn't have a clear idea what street she was on. Considering the damp air and the lack of streetlights, she must be close to the river park.

She brought up Google Maps and found her location. O'Flaherty's Lane. The empty and cheapest house in Glingilly was on this road—the one she and Jack would buy when their house sold. They'd recently expressed their interest directly to the owner's grandson on a video call.

"Can we look at it?" Jack had asked.

"I'm swamped with work so I can't get down for a bit but go have a look from the outside. You'll see she's old, but solid," Gavin had said.

"But we could move straight in?" Lucy had asked.

"Oh, yeah. Easy. It's got everything you need, but you'll want to redecorate."

Lucy could handle some decorating if it meant she had a place to call home that didn't include her in-laws. If it meant they could add value to the property and ultimately sell it and regain a house similar to the one they were losing.

According to the map, the cottage wasn't far so she walked toward it. This part of Glingilly didn't have sidewalks so she was thankful for the three-quarter moon to light her way.

A dim light shining through the trees in the distance snagged her attention. She knew it couldn't be the cottage, because it was empty and had been since Paddy Whitehead had moved into the nursing home. She thought there was an empty field on either side of the house, but she could be wrong. The day she and Jack had visited, an unexpected rainstorm had hit and they could barely see through the windshield for water. They hadn't even tried to get out of the car to look around. The following day Jack had flown back to work and the next time he'd been home, Birdie's never-ending requests on his time had consumed the week.

Lucy knew there were houses at the other end of the lane so did the light mean she was walking in the wrong direction? She checked her cell. The blue arrow pointed toward the cottage so she kept going.

An owl hooted as she rounded the slight curve in the road and then the silhouette of the property came into view. A golden privet hedge grew wild, its branches protruding over an old wire gate that hung at a rakish angle. Lucy hastily reassured herself that Gavin had told them the cottage was old, but solid. Solid was the important thing. Solid was their lifeline.

Four chimneys symmetrically dotted the roof, and the moonlight reflected off a corner of the bullnose veranda. Underneath it, a dim yellow light spilled from one of two sash windows. It lit an old, curved garden seat and aged veranda boards that cried out for oiling.

Lucy tensed. Was someone living here? Gavin had told them it was empty.

Walking quickly, she reached the driveway and made out the shape of a car. She fumbled with her phone and switched on the flashlight app. The small beam illuminated the registration.

"You've got to be freaking kidding me!"

Without second-guessing a thing, Lucy stormed up the veranda steps and banged her fist on the door.

A dog barked and she heard the clacking of nails racing across floorboards. A cobweb-covered faux coach lamp switched on, barely illuminating the door, and then Izzy Harrington's voice called out tentatively, "Who is it?"

"Lucy Essen!"

The door opened and Thor rushed out, eager to greet Lucy, but she only had eyes for Izzy. The woman was dressed in flannel pajamas, the woolen coat Lucy had always coveted, woolly socks and sheepskin-lined boots. Her face was thinner than the last time Lucy had seen her, and she embraced the fizz of schadenfreude when she saw the fine lines crisscrossing the skin under Izzy's eyes.

Despite Izzy's look of uncertainty she offered, "Come in."

"I don't want to come in!"

"O-kay. But it's absolutely freezing. Are you sure you want to talk outside?"

"I don't want to talk at all!"

"Then why did you knock on my door?"

The reasonableness of Izzy's tone only inflamed Lucy's ire. "It's not your door. It's my door! *My* door!"

Thor barked at the shrillness of her voice and Izzy stared at her as if she had a kangaroo loose in the top paddock.

Lucy suddenly sagged. What the hell was she doing? As much as she was pinning her escape from her in-laws on this cottage, it wasn't hers. Right now she was behaving as crazily as Birdie.

"Sorry," she managed tightly. "I lost it there for a minute." She turned and walked fast toward the steps.

"Lucy, you must have wanted to say something."

The words pulled her back. "Why the hell are you here?"

"It's the only rental I can afford."

Lucy scoffed. "Don't give me that."

"You can choose what to believe, but it's the truth."

Lucy hated that Izzy's tone was eerily similar to how she often sounded these days—exhausted and resigned. She tried to pop the tiny bubble of sympathy. "Yeah, well, after everything that's gone down, sue me if I don't believe you."

Izzy threw out her arms and indicated the cottage. "Do you honestly think I'd choose to live in a house with dodgy wiring, no heating and what I'm hoping are possums in the roof but are probably rats?"

Lucy shuddered, then rallied. "Stop exaggerating. This cottage has solid bones. It just needs some redecorating."

Izzy's laugh could strip paint. "I'm not exaggerating and I'm not cadging for sympathy either." She pulled her coat more tightly around her and Lucy saw the fingerless gloves. "To be honest, I thought you'd be pleased I was reduced to living here," she said evenly. "After all, you think I deserve it."

Lucy chewed the inside of her cheek as the urge to blame Izzy for everything that had happened with Elite dueled with the image of Izzy looking like she hadn't been warm in a long time. Lucy's own hands were now stinging from the cold.

"I'll come in, but only to check you're not exaggerating," she said.

"Fair enough, but I can't promise you it's much warmer."

Lucy followed Izzy down the feebly lit hall lined with a faded wallpaper dado. She glanced left and right, catching the glow of an open fire in a room with a line of flying ducks on the wall. The other doors off the hall were all closed, probably to keep the heat in.

"Keep left," Izzy called over her shoulder. "There's some dodgy boards."

The floor immediately sloped downwards as they walked into the kitchen, which must have been tacked onto the house. Going by the old wooden kitchen cabinet, that had been around 1950. Lucy immediately felt the cold wind blowing in under the large gap between the sloping floor and the back door.

Izzy caught her staring as she placed a saucepan of water on the ancient gas stove. "I tried the electric kettle, but it blows the fuse so ..."

Gavin had only mentioned the dated decor in a way that had strongly hinted some paint and new curtains would do the job. Lucy tried to picture Rigby living here, but all she saw were disaster scenarios—lead paint, broken floorboards, possible mold.

A fizz of indignation tingled her gut. "It's barely habitable! Gavin shouldn't even be renting it."

Izzy spooned hot chocolate into two mugs. "Believe me, there's always someone who's desperate enough. I've lived in worse."

Lucy couldn't picture it. "No way!"

"At least this place has hot water." Izzy pulled a bottle of coffee liqueur from the shelf and held it up in question.

Lucy found herself nodding. "I thought you'd be living with Judy and Bevan," she said. "After all, you were engaged to Brad."

Izzy had her back to Lucy as she poured boiling water over the chocolate powder, but her shoulders tensed.

"How are things living with your in-laws?" Izzy asked.

"Utter crap, but it's warm."

"It's warm in the living room."

Izzy carried the drinks up the hall, placed the mugs on a chunky pine coffee table, then added another log to the fire.

Lucy sat and got the sensation she was Alice, but instead of tumbling into a rabbit hole she'd tumbled inside the sofa. She fought her way forward, balanced on the edge of the seat, and picked up her drink.

"I never imagined I'd be doing this," she said.

Izzy's brows rose. "You mean drinking alcohol-laced hot chocolate in a house that's falling down and listening to the soothing scurry of vermin?"

"Mostly sitting down with you." Lucy sipped the drink and watched Thor, who was sitting next to Izzy on alert, as if she needed protecting. "I want to believe this designer sackcloth and ashes look you've got going is just another con. You have to have money somewhere. *Our* money."

"I don't," Izzy said flatly, as if she'd said it many times before. "I lost money too."

Lucy shook her head. "There's no way Brad would rip you off."

"Why not?" Izzy's tone was harsh. "He's known—" She sucked in her lips. "He knew Jack all his life and he ripped him off. Ripped you off too and so many others."

"Yes, but he loved you. People don't do that to people they love."

"So you're a romantic? People do all sorts of horrible things to those they love." Izzy stared into the fire. "I don't think he loved me."

"Don't be ridiculous! I saw the way he looked at you. Every woman in town was green with envy."

Izzy screwed up her face. "Maybe he loved me once. In the early days. But this last year, I think I was just unwittingly part of the brand. Part of the con."

Lucy didn't understand. "What do you mean?"

"Hindsight is a bastard spotlight." Izzy sighed and pulled her knees to her chin. "Things between us hadn't been good for months."

None of these words matched the pictures in Lucy's head of Izzy and Brad. "But you got engaged."

Izzy grimaced. "And I regretted it the moment I said yes. I wasted months trying to improve things between us instead of working out why they'd gone wrong." Izzy's ringless hand reached out to stroke Thor's ear. "I'd just nailed it and was leaving him when the money vanished."

"You worked out Elite was a Ponzi scheme?"

Izzy shook her head hard. "No, I was clueless about that. I never questioned the money he was spending because I honestly thought the program was earning it. I meant I finally worked out that Brad had never been interested in what I wanted or needed unless it was something that made him look impressive and encouraged people to join Elite."

Lucy stared at her, trying hard to let the words sit rather than instantly judging them. "Are you talking about your clothes and jewelry? Your engagement ring?"

"Oh, yeah. And I fell for that ring hard." Izzy blew out a long breath, the air condensing in a white cloud around her face. "And exactly how shallow and self-indulgent does that make me?"

So much! But the sharp pain of introspection dug in under Lucy's shoulder blades, reminding her of her own failings.

"Possibly equal to the rest of us," she said. "I loved your clothes, but at the same time I hated how effortlessly glamorous you always looked."

Izzy frowned. "I loved the clothes too, but Lucy, it was an illusion. None of it was real. None of it was effortless. I hated being the center of attention."

Lucy struggled to align this information with her memories of Izzy —her aloofness, her stilted conversation as if talking to Lucy was both a bore and a chore. "But you floated around as if you were better than us."

"Did I?" Izzy seemed genuinely perplexed. "I don't remember that. If I did, I certainly didn't mean to."

Lucy rechecked her memories. They faltered under the scrutiny. "I thought you did."

A wry smile tugged at Izzy's lips. "Sorry. It must have been the mix of alcohol and valerian. Most Elite events I was barely holding it together."

Lucy thought of the cool and distant woman who'd made her feel uncomfortable in every conversation they'd ever had. Until tonight.

"Oh my God! All this time I've thought you were rude and stuck-up, but you're shy."

Izzy's eyes widened momentarily and then she laughed. "Thank you, I think."

Embarrassment dumped over Lucy. "Sorry, that was a crap thing to say."

Izzy shrugged. "You've said worse."

"That's true."

"I wasn't being sarcastic." Izzy reached for Thor. "I get anxious in social situations and maybe that means sometimes I come across as rude. It's not intentional. Mostly I'm working hard not to break out in a cold sweat."

Lucy put her mug on the table, pondering the statement. "You're different tonight."

"Am I?" Izzy poured more liqueur into their empty mugs. "Maybe it's because I'm no longer representing Elite so it's easier to be me."

Lucy got a flash of life behind the stone walls of Villefranche. "Did you feel like you were always on show?"

"That's a good description. I hadn't thought of it like that but you're right. I couldn't even go to the hardware store in my gardening clothes because of," she waggled her fingers, "'The brand'. I hate that I didn't realize earlier Brad was using me. I'm devastated I was unknowingly complicit in him getting people to part with and lose their hard-earned money."

She raised her gaze to meet Lucy's. "In a way, I was just as bad as him. I let everyone think I was far more involved in Elite than I was to make myself look—feel successful. I was kidding myself that my life had a purpose beyond being a clothing and jewelry model. I regret that I let you believe I knew more about the business than I did. I'm sorry. The reality is that I never got close to the books. Whenever I tried, Brad had a reason why that moment in time wasn't good. I had absolutely no idea what was going on. If I had, I would have gone to the police. But as it was, I learned about the missing money after the Elite members."

In the flickering firelight, Lucy watched Izzy's hands tugging at her hair and the play of anguish on her face. For the first time since their lives had imploded, she believed her.

"Do you think he—" The bald words jammed in her mouth.

Izzy spoke them instead. "Committed suicide?"

Lucy nodded.

"A year ago I would have said he'd never do something like that. But back then I thought he was a completely different person."

Lucy thought of the many recent conversations around the Essens' table. "Not that Judy and Bevan have spoken to us," she said, "but according to the media, they blame the overseas partners for the missing money. What do you think?"

"I think Judy needs to hold onto the memory of the man she thought Brad was."

That didn't tell Lucy what she wanted to know. "Did he leave you a note? A letter? Anything that explained why he did it?"

Izzy gave her a look that combined a mixture of bewilderment and anger at the situation. "If he did, I never found it. And he died without a will, so anything he owned—" She gave a bitter laugh. "Anything he *stole* goes to Judy and Bevan. But as his assets are part of a police investigation it's all moot."

Izzy seemed to give herself a shake, as if she was putting some space between Brad's death and now. "Not that it isn't lovely to see you, Lucy —in fact you're my first guest." She laughed again, the sound pained. "And considering how much the town hates me, you're probably going to be my only guest. But last time we met you tried to run me over with a shopping trolley, and tonight you screamed at me that my front door was yours, so I'm confused as to why you're here."

Lucy was suddenly hot and uncomfortable. She pulled off her coat. "It's complicated."

"Everything about Elite's complicated."

"Right." Lucy picked up the fire poker and pushed a log, watching the sparks fly up the chimney. "I didn't set out to visit you. Hell, I didn't even know you were living here. I just needed to get out of my in-laws' house and my feet brought me here."

Izzy frowned. "Odd place for your subconscious to bring you. It's not exactly on the way to anywhere."

"We have to sell our house."

"I'm sorry."

"Yeah. Thanks. But the person who should be sorry is dead." She rammed the poker so hard the log rolled onto the hearth. "When we settle our debt, this place is about the only thing in our price range. When I saw you here, I lost it. It was like you'd taken another thing from me."

Izzy met her gaze. "There's a win for you. When you buy it, you get the privilege of kicking me out."

An hour ago that would have been sweet revenge, but now Lucy saw a woman who'd been betrayed as badly as her—possibly worse. Things with Jack weren't great, but at least he hadn't screwed her over.

"As much as living with Birdie is impossible, now I've seen the inside of this place there's no way I can bring Rigby here," she said. "He's already having nightmares."

"That must be really hard."

Lucy studied Izzy's face, checking for mockery, but she only read empathy. Apart from the social worker, it was the first time anyone had shown some understanding of what she was going through.

"I'm his mother. I should be able to make him feel safe, but nothing about our life at the moment is doing that and—" Her voice broke and she gulped in a breath.

"Can I help?"

Lucy stiffened. "Got a spare million have you?" Izzy ducked her head and Lucy immediately regretted the words. "Sorry. That was unfair. I just don't see how you can help."

"Me neither. And I'm sure you have lots of childcare available with Birdie and Mike—"

"I don't."

"Oh." Surprise flitted across Izzy's face. "Well, maybe I could take Rigby to the park sometimes to feed the ducks and give you some down time, or at least a supermarket run without a tag-along."

The offer was gold, but a thought stayed Lucy's excitement. "Rigby doesn't really know you."

"Oh, right. Of course."

"Anyway, I thought you didn't like kids."

Izzy stroked Thor's rough coat. "Liking and wanting are two very separate things. I like them one on one in small doses. I'm just not certain I'm capable of caring for one for eighteen years."

Responsibility pressed down on Lucy. "Part of me gets that. I left Rigby with someone I thought would protect him, but I got it wrong and now—" She blew out a breath. "Now I'm super cautious."

"I get it. We need to protect kids from adults screwing them up." Izzy cuddled a squirming Thor. "Maybe we could just meet in the park one day. I'll bring my fur baby, you bring Rigby and it can be a play date."

Lucy heard a hint of quiet desperation in Izzy's voice. Was it loneliness? A need to make amends? She wasn't sure, and between work and single parenting she barely had time for herself, let alone keeping Izzy company. Then again, she no longer saw much of her friends—none of them really understood how much her life had changed. The truth was, she'd been avoiding them because dropping five dollars on a coffee or bringing a hostess gift to a lunch wasn't in the budget.

"I'll bring a thermos of coffee," Izzy added, as if reading her mind. "And bread for the ducks."

Lucy stunned herself by saying, "That sounds great."

CHAPTER THIRTY-TWO

When Brooke told Izzy that the coroner had declared Brad's death a suicide, she slumped in the uncomfortable chair in the police interview room. Flashes of Brad in the boat shed thwacked her and she scrubbed her face with her hands, trying to banish them. Other equally distressing images followed.

"I never thought otherwise," she finally managed, the words bald and flat.

"I know, but the illegal gun cast doubt," Brooke said. "We wouldn't be doing our job if we didn't follow all the leads."

"I still don't understand why he had an illegal gun."

Brooke raised her brows as if Izzy was dense. "Quinn ripped off millions of dollars without a qualm. An illegal gun goes with the territory."

Izzy tugged at her hair. "Oh God. I can't believe how much I didn't know."

Brooke patted her on the shoulder. "To be honest, most charismatic people like Quinn have a different style of exit plan. They usually do a runner."

Thoughts of her father drifted across Izzy's mind. "Some things you can't run from. But now we know Brad suicided, does this mean I'll no longer be getting visits from the police?"

"Not from me and Mitchell."

"That doesn't sound as reassuring as I'd hoped."

Brooke's mouth tweaked up on one side. "Now Quinn's dead, the investigation's been taken out of our hands. I can't say if Melbourne will be contacting you or not."

"Can't say or won't?"

"I honestly don't know. Like I said, it's out of our hands. There's no evidence against you regarding the emptying of the accounts, but ..." Brooke gave an uneasy shrug.

Izzy's palm hit the table. "The bloody Noosa apartment! They better be investigating the Quinns. They are, right?"

Brooke's face was as neutral as a professional poker player's and Izzy knew she wouldn't answer her question.

The police officer stood. "Speaking of the Quinns, I'm going to Villefranche now to give them the coroner's report. They have to be out of there by tomorrow morning, but you'd know that, right?"

"I do."

Judy and Bevan hadn't taken her relocation to the cottage well and Judy called and texted daily. Izzy only answered a third of the calls, because she knew how the conversation would go—begging, pleading, anger, then tears.

Once, on an icy wet day, Izzy had given in to Judy—her desire to be warm for a few hours overruling her natural caution. When she'd arrived at Villefranche, there was a police officer in attendance and an attorney supervising the Quinns as they packed. The majority of the contents of Villefranche were in dispute—the Lawson Group and the police versus the estate of Brad Quinn.

"We're here to represent Brad's best interests," Bevan had said.

Izzy had restrained herself from replying, "Don't you mean your best interests?"

The weeks since Brad's death hadn't diminished Judy's violent grief one iota and Izzy suspected she was buzzed a lot of the time. Bevan lurched between cool and dismissive, kind and concerned—the combination discombobulating. The two-hour visit had done Izzy's head in and her half-formed plan of telling the Quinns she'd been leaving Brad had vaporized in the edgy atmosphere.

Bevan had asked her what item of Brad's she wanted to "keep him close."

Izzy didn't want anything. "I have the ring he designed for me." And instead of saying she planned to sell it if it wasn't seized as a proceed of crime, she added, "Honestly, it's enough."

Bevan had suggested one of Brad's cashmere sweaters, but Judy had bolted to the walk-in closet and stood at the entrance like a sentinel.

When Izzy was leaving, Bevan had clasped her hand. As he leaned in to kiss her, he'd whispered, "Keep this for Judy," then slipped something long and cool into her sleeve. Before she could respond, he'd pushed her out the door and shut it behind her.

Izzy wished she'd thrown the Montblanc pen into one of Villefranche's hedges, but Judy's grief—so much greater than her own—undid her. Not wanting the pen in her possession or having a reason for the Quinns to contact her again to retrieve it, she'd gone straight to the post office and mailed it to Judy.

Now, as Brooke ushered Izzy outside into the spring sunshine tempered by a chilly breeze, she said, "Would you consider staying on the Irish festival committee?"

The question stunned Izzy. "I'm not sure they'd want me."

"No one from Elite's involved."

"Even so. Their relatives and friends probably are."

"Izzy, what you need to understand is that a lot of the Elite members acted like they were too good for the town. So on one level there's sympathy for them, but it's offset by the feeling that perhaps they were greedy and deserved what's happened."

"They didn't!" Izzy realized she'd shouted and she took a deep breath. "Sorry, but no one deserves to have their money stolen from them. Anyway, don't I come under the banner of thinking I was too good for the town?"

"I never got that feeling," Brooke said.

After what Lucy had told her, Brooke's compliment surprised Izzy. "Thanks, but I no longer come with sponsorship money so I'm not really value-adding."

"Your ideas do that. Anyway, we've got a new sponsor so the money's covered. What we need now is someone with the time and expertise to coordinate the festival. You've got event experience."

Izzy didn't know what she was doing tomorrow let alone in a few months. "I need a real job and there's nothing in Glingilly."

Brooke gave her a long look. "So you're leaving town?"

"I honestly don't know."

"The committee met on Tuesday and they asked me to offer you the job. It comes with a small stipend that might just cover food and rent, which means you can run the festival and finish your studies. Think of it as breathing space to work out what you might do next."

Izzy stared at her. "Why are you being so nice?"

A look that combined a hint of hurt and a dollop of resignation crossed Brooke's face. With a jolt, Izzy realized it must be hard to be both a police officer and a regular citizen in the same town.

Brooke shrugged. "I like you, Izzy, and you've had a shit few months. No one who's experienced what you've been through would be in the right headspace to make any big decisions for a while."

Could she stay in Glingilly for a few more months? Izzy was hoping Judy and Bevan would return to northern New South Wales— not that she'd asked or been told—but it would make her life easier. She thought about Lucy and their tentative détente. The park visit had gone surprisingly well, probably because they'd avoided all difficult topics and just enjoyed watching Rigby's delight feeding the ducks. They were hardly friends, but Lucy had suggested they do it again.

Now Brooke was offering her some breathing room, which was definitely a show of respect if not friendship. And spring was here, meaning warmer weather, so life in the cottage would start to improve. By the time the summer heat hit and turned it from an icebox to a sweatbox, she'd be gone. But for now ...

Izzy sucked in her lips and blinked quickly to hold back a rush of tears. "Send me the paperwork and I'll sign the contract."

Brooke held up her hand for a high-five.

Izzy was in the Glingilly library watching the lectures she'd missed, although she was struggling to concentrate. The cold and a lack of wi-fi in the cottage had forced her into town. As much as she'd wanted to drive to the university library, she had no other reason to be in Warrnambool so she was saving gas. After the heart-racing incident outside the post office when the Hewitsons had spewed their vitriol at her, she'd been tempted to turn tail and run. But she'd committed to Glingilly for the next few months so she needed to learn how to live here.

Her cell phone lit up with an incoming email. Welcoming the distraction from the dry lecture, she glanced at the banner. It was from the university advising her that results were available. Her mouth dried. With everything that had happened since Cooper had insisted she upload her corporate governance assignment, the weeks had slipped past and she'd forgotten all about it. Did she want to know her mark? All she needed was a pass and rationally she knew that. But what if she'd failed?

Her breath caught on the thought and she coughed. A few bent heads lifted from books and newspapers. Izzy sipped some water.

I don't want a pity pass. Why the hell had she said that? Right now a pity pass sounded like a great idea.

She hadn't seen Cooper since the funeral. She'd wanted to ask him on the day why he'd come—was it something to do with forensic accounting?—but she'd never got the chance because Bevan had hustled her away from the melee and into a waiting car.

Cooper had messaged her that night asking if she was okay. He'd probably seen her trying to pull Birdie Essen away from Judy, who'd been trying to scalp her. Everyone had seen that—there'd been a flash of Izzy's black coat and white face on the news. His second text had arrived the following morning.

As the days passed, Izzy told herself she hadn't replied to him because all her energies were consumed with making the house habitable. But if she was honest, she was avoiding him. She acknowledged it was rude, especially as he'd mostly been kind to her, but the problem was that whenever she recalled how much he knew about Brad's fraud and her obliviousness to it, shame walloped her. The assignment had been the final assessment for his unit, and the fraud squad had removed the case to Melbourne, so she'd reassured herself that there was no reason to see Cooper again.

If you failed the assignment you'll have to retake the class.

The thought made her drop the cell phone. As she picked it up, it buzzed in her hand and she jumped. Oh God, it was like she'd willed Cooper to call.

Was he calling to warn her of bad news?

Don't take the call. Just log in and find out.

But without fully understanding why, she walked outside and answered the call. "Hello."

"Izzy! Thank God."

There was no mistaking the relief in his voice and her heart sank. "I failed, right?"

There was a long moment of silence. "What?"

"The assignment. That's why you're calling."

"Ah, no. I passed it on to a colleague like you asked. To be honest, after everything that's happened I'd forgotten all about it."

She paced. "Then why are you calling?"

Again there was a slightly too long pause. "How are you sleeping?"

The question was unexpected and confusing. "Um ... oh, you know ..."

"Yeah. I think I do." He sighed. "That's why I'm calling."

The way he said the words took her straight back to the boat shed. Her legs jellied and she sat hard on a bench seat. She'd been so consumed by her own experience she'd forgotten Cooper had been there with her. That he'd seen what she'd seen.

Immediately afterwards at Villefranche he'd been so together, making her drinks, sitting with her while they waited for the police, nodding encouragingly as she haltingly told the officers about the Noosa apartment—a calm and reassuring presence. Then he'd left and her days had been consumed with the police, the Quinns, the funeral, moving and surviving. Not once had she stopped to think how Cooper might be coping. Or not coping.

"Do you wake up in a cold sweat?" she asked.

"So it's happening to you too?"

"At least twice a week."

"I'm in Glingilly, Izzy. Can I buy you coffee?"

In a café, the eyes of the town would bore into them and their conversation would be overheard and relayed far and wide well before they'd stood to leave.

"How about a walk at Tower Hill?"

"Really? It's pretty chilly."

"Man up, Cooper."

He laughed. "Noted. See you soon."

When Izzy arrived, Cooper was already at a picnic table, defending it from a curious emu. He rose and greeted her with a light kiss on the cheek. As her lecturer, it was wrong. As the man who'd been with her and a dead body, it was absolutely right.

He handed her a carry cup. "Latte, right?"

"Right. Lucky guess?"

His cheeks, already pink from cold, seemed to redden. "You drank one at the uni café and you made yourself one at Villefranche."

"Wow, good memory." She glanced at his boots. "Shall we do the peak climb?"

"Why not. It'll keep us warm."

As they walked to the trailhead and entered the track, she sipped the coffee and sighed. "Thank you for this. Café coffee's not in the budget and I haven't had a decent one since I left Villefranche."

She braced herself, expecting him to ask where she was living.

"You're welcome."

His serious gaze scanned her face as if he was looking for imperfections and her hand rose to her cheek. "Do I have a smudge?"

He shook his head. "You've lost weight."

She shrugged. "Being accused of stealing millions of dollars and finding a dead body will do that to a girl." When he didn't crack a smile she said, "Why were you at the funeral?"

"To support you."

Her coffee went down the wrong way and she coughed.

"You seem surprised." His words came out flat, as if he was disappointed.

"I ... it's just ... I thought it must have had something to do with the case."

He shook his head. "My only job was to study the numbers."

"Right." Three beats too late she added, "Thank you for coming."

"You're welcome." He sipped his coffee. "Not that I did much. I was hoping to talk to you but—"

"Things went crazy pretty fast."

"How are they now?"

"They're ..." But she didn't want to sink into depressive thoughts about the cottage. "I'm keeping busy working for the Irish festival committee and finishing the course."

"So you're staying in Glingilly?"

"For now."

"That's great!"

She laughed. "You sound far more enthusiastic than I feel."

His mouth curved into a smile. "I'm just happy you're taking on projects. It means you want to get up in the mornings."

"Some days it's harder than others." She stepped around a log and suddenly remembered what he'd said on the phone. "You said you're not sleeping."

"I have no trouble going to sleep. It's the recurring dream that wakes me that's the problem."

"The one that features what was left of Brad's face?"

"That's the one." He seemed to hesitate, then added, "I went to see a counselor the police recommended."

"Has it helped?"

"Yes and no. What about you?"

The trail was steep and she was breathing hard. "Have I seen someone?" He nodded. "No."

"Do you think you should? I mean, you've been through a lot."

"To be honest, just the thought of telling another person my story feels like it will sink me."

He didn't say anything for many steps, as if he was considering her words in the same minute detail he considered numbers. "You can always call me at 3:00 in the morning. I know your story and chances are I'll probably be awake."

"That's kind but—"

"Not really. I'd appreciate the chat too." He shoved his hands into the pockets of his puffer jacket, out of the icy wind. "And there's no longer a conflict of interest."

"Brooke told me Melbourne's taken over the money trail."

"Actually, I handed my bit over."

"Why? I thought you enjoyed the challenge."

"I do. But after finding Quinn, it all got a bit ..." He looked straight at her. "Personal."

A shiver raced up her spine. She couldn't tell if it was a good shiver or a warning shiver. Either way, it didn't matter—her life was in disarray. But aside from that, even if it had been the best possible scenario—Elite hadn't existed, Brad hadn't suicided and she'd broken up with him because their relationship had run its course—every self-help book, professional counselor or person with a grain of common sense would advise her she was far from ready to fall into another relationship.

She quickly reminded herself that Cooper wasn't even suggesting that. "Personal" just meant he was working through the shock and trauma of discovering a dead body. Besides, Cooper Barsky with his corduroy jackets, serious gaze and long thoughtful pauses was a very different man from the men she dated. *That* was a caution in itself.

With chests heaving and calves burning, they reached the peak. They stood admiring the view through a stand of casuarinas, across the water-filled volcanic crater and out to the Southern Ocean.

When she'd caught her breath she moved to invoke the friend zone. "You sure you want to be friends with someone who still has an axe over their head?"

He turned toward her. "The Noosa apartment? We don't think Quinn bought that."

Her hands hit her hips. "He did! We both did. I signed the papers and our names were on the loan."

"I'm not disputing your experience, Izzy," he said calmly. "But after the initial deposit, we can't find a record of him making another payment."

"What? But I paid my share every month." Yet again, Brad's actions made no sense. "He had access to money all the time. Hell, he emptied the bank accounts of millions the day before he died. Surely he used that money."

"He emptied the accounts a lot earlier than that."

Izzy sat on the seat provided for exhausted walkers. "How is that possible? The members always had access to view the accounts. They only noticed they were empty that day."

"Don't apply logic to fraud, Izzy, it will do your head in." His face was a mix of empathy and real-world experience. "Quinn was clever and he had the programming skills to make all sorts of things look real when they were smoke and mirrors."

Her mind churned and snagged as she fought yet again to understand. "Then why did he let people see they were empty?"

"Maybe he did it because he knew it was all over." Cooper shrugged and sat down next to her. "Thing is, we'll never know for sure and as tempting as it is to speculate, I don't recommend it. It's a sure-fire road to insanity."

"Yes, but—" Her chest tightened, searing her with a familiar sharp pain. When it happened, the only thing that relieved it was to pull out some hair, but that would definitely show Cooper she was already crazy. She shoved her hands under her thighs.

"If Brad didn't pay for the apartment, then surely it was Bevan?" she said.

"Just because we can't find the money trail yet doesn't mean Quinn didn't pay for it. And it's not Bevan. He's been cooperative and shown us his bank statements. His payouts were in line with everyone else's and there's no record of him contributing to or buying that apartment. Remember, Quinn had dealings with people overseas. Perhaps it was part of a deal. At this stage we just don't know enough, and tracing money overseas takes time and patience."

"It has to be connected to Brad," Izzy said, sounding like a broken record, but unable to fathom another solution.

"There's no surely about anything Quinn or those of his ilk do. Every case shares similarities, but Brad Quinn was smarter than most."

Suddenly overwhelmed, Izzy rested her forehead on her thighs. The apartment was like a tangled knot of fishing line—impossible to untie. She didn't know how long she'd been face down when she felt the warmth of Cooper's hand on her shoulder.

"Izzy? I want to ask if you're okay, but obviously you're not. What can I do to help?"

Slowly she raised her head and sighed. "Does any of this confusing mess mean I'm no longer under suspicion of stealing money?"

A smile broke his worried face. "You're in the clear."

"Seriously?" More questions doused her hope that what he said was true. "If I am, why didn't Brooke tell me?"

"She probably doesn't know. My report went direct to Melbourne and all investigations operate on the mushroom principle. They keep people in the dark until it suits them."

"So I'm really in the clear?"

"You're really in the clear."

Izzy jumped to her feet, relief flowing as fast as a flooded river. "Oh my God! I can't believe it."

Cooper laughed and stood. "Believe it."

Suddenly she was gripping his arms, as if he might vanish before she could thank him. "You have no idea what this means to me. If the police believe me, I can deal with no savings and living in an almost squat. I can even cope with Elite members treating me like dirt. *Thank you* for telling me."

"Now I wish I'd told you earlier."

Was that a shot at her for not replying to his texts? But there was nothing on his face that indicated anything other than apologetic regret.

"Well, now I know!" she said. "I just wish I could afford champagne to celebrate."

"Let me take you to dinner. It won't be what you're used to, no caviar or Bollinger, but—"

"Good." The word shot out far more harshly than she'd intended, driven from her mouth by shame and guilt. "Sorry. What I meant to say is I don't deserve an expensive dinner when so many Elite members are eating beans on toast. And to be honest, being seen out celebrating would be interpreted as me giving the Elite members the bird." She thought of Lucy. "And I don't have enough friends to lose any."

"Right." Cooper rocked back on his heels, clearly thinking. "How about this then? I have a curry in the freezer and a bottle of Australian sparkling wine I can chill."

The idea of doing something as ordinary as eating dinner with another person pulled at her as much as the cold wind chilled her.

"Do you have heating?" she asked.

He looked taken aback. "Ah, yes. I have heating. Is that a problem?"

"God, no! It's a bonus."

He laughed. "Let's hope it compensates for the fact my cleaner's been sick."

She thought of the cottage. "Oh, it definitely will."

He grinned. "Great! Let's go unfreeze that curry."

As Izzy navigated the steep descent, it was the first time in weeks that dread didn't accompany her.

CHAPTER THIRTY-THREE

EVERY EVENING WAS A JUGGLING act for Lucy—cook dinner, feed Rigby, bed routine with fingers crossed that Rigby would settle quickly, and then she was racing back to the kitchen to clean and tidy to meet Birdie's exacting standards. The last thing she had the energy for was another sponge meltdown. She wished her mother-in-law recalled the chaos of tired children and how if Lucy missed washing a frypan or left a dessert bowl on the table it wasn't a malicious act, just life.

Tonight when she walked into the kitchen, Mike was standing by the counter, his hand on the kettle.

"Cuppa, love?"

Lucy hoped she didn't look as shocked as she felt—it was the first time since she'd moved in that Mike had offered her anything. "That would be lovely, thank you. Where's Birdie?"

He threw a teabag into a mug and poured boiling water over it. "Inventory. She won't be home until ten."

"She's been working a lot lately."

"Yeah."

"That's got to be helping."

He grunted.

Lucy suddenly wondered if Birdie was choosing to work overtime as a break from Mike. She wanted to shake him and say, "We saved you so you could live your life, not just exist." Then again Lucy felt like she was just existing—waiting for Jack to come home. Waiting for the house to sell. Waiting for the rest of her life.

Mike silently passed her the mug.

"So you got any plans for your evening alone?" she asked.

He gave her a sideways look as if he couldn't quite work out if she was joking or not. "It's a toss-up between *Vera* and *Grantchester*."

Before Mike's heart attack he'd rarely sat on the sofa, but now he watched a ridiculous amount of television—so much so, he did little else. The garage was still the garage.

"Have you asked him again?" Lucy had demanded of Jack the last time he'd been home.

"Dad will tell me when he's ready."

"He's never going to be ready!"

Jack had shrugged as if that was highly likely.

To stop herself from entering into yet another circular argument that only added to the ever-growing ball of anger filling her chest, Lucy had walked to Izzy's. They'd sat on the back step in the spring sunshine, drinking tea and watching a kookaburra sparring with a snake. But the best part was Izzy listening to her vent and not even offering a solution.

"That sucks," Izzy had said when Lucy drew breath.

"It so does. Thanks for listening."

Izzy had shrugged. "It's the least I can do. Can you do the park again this Wednesday?"

Now, in the kitchen, familiar irritation popped and fizzed inside Lucy at Mike's inertia. Before she'd censored herself, she said, "So no plans then."

She'd expected another grunt or being ignored, but one side of Mike's mouth unexpectedly tweaked up. "You got something against British crime shows?"

"Not per se."

"But?"

"But ..." She thought about how the rec room would make her life in this house just that bit more tolerable. "I thought perhaps we could do something together."

Surprise flashed across his face. "What did you have in mind? Two-handed five hundred? Cribbage?"

"Last year you admired Jack's workshop set-up and I helped him do it. I wondered if you'd like a hand sorting your workbench?"

"Ah." Mike sipped his tea.

Lucy heard his stonewalling and she suddenly wanted the truth. "Mike, if you don't want us to have the garage as a living space please just tell me straight up. I'd rather know than endure this yoyo of frustration and hope."

He was quiet for a moment and then a long sigh rattled out of him. "Just pack it up, love."

"The workshop? No! That's not the plan. We just thought it would work better in the other corner. That way the garage can be a sitting space at night, but during the day it's still your workshop." Not that he'd used it for months.

He shot her a flinty look—one that said, *I know what you're thinking*—but she caught the brittle fragility around the edges. "There's no point, Lucy. Just sell the lot."

"Your tools?" she checked, incredulous at the suggestion.

"Yeah."

But not even the anticipation of the much-needed money the sale would bring in could tempt her. Despite his gruff words, she heard the heartache behind them. It created another dull ache that joined all the others. She thought of Rigby's confusion about the changes in his life and saw them mirrored in Mike's eyes—bewildered, hurt and angry. She was barely holding her own life together but something made her reach out and touch his hand.

"You planned to make Rigby a station for his train set. Can you at least make that before you sell?"

"I don't think so, love."

Not even for your grandson?

Lucy didn't know if it was fear of stressing Mike or something else entirely, but since his heart attack neither Jack nor Birdie ever questioned his constant refusal to do things. But this? She couldn't let this slide past without comment. Mike's quiet and continual rejection of Rigby's requests to read a story or to build Lego—things Mike had done willingly and enthusiastically before his heart attack—were contributing to her son's anxiety. Rigby needed his involved grandfather back in his life.

She weighed up the pros and cons. If she pushed Mike on this, what was the worst thing that could happen? He'd kick them out of the house? Part of her thought that wasn't such a bad outcome. But unlike Birdie, Mike had always had time for her so she doubted he'd give her the boot. And she knew he was physically capable of doing what she was about to ask him without any fear of sparking a major medical emergency or even a minor issue. It was his mental state that was the biggest problem.

"Are you really okay disappointing Rigby?"

Mike's eyes narrowed. "I thought you were better than that, Lucy."

She refused to allow any guilt to land. "I'm a mother, Mike, and I'm a lioness when it comes to Rigby. He's suffering because we trusted the wrong man."

"He's not on his Pat Malone there."

She gripped her mug and forced herself to keep going. "I know he's not alone, but he's not old enough to understand why his world is unrecognizable."

"Hah!" Mike slammed his hand on the table. "I'm old and I don't understand how I allowed it to happen. I mean, Christ! I'd always been so careful."

"I know," she said softly. "And Bevan was your closest friend. Of course you trusted him. He's always had your best interests at heart and he's never steered you wrong. We don't know that he did. He must be hurting too. I mean, think about it. Brad was the calculating and manipulative one. God, he probably ripped off his father as well and Bevan's too embarrassed to admit it."

"I just wish he'd talk to me." Mike sighed. "But Birdie's thrown a spanner in the works there."

As much as Lucy wanted to pile on her mother-in-law, she thought the Quinns' restraining order was over the top. Sure, Birdie had delivered the first slap, but Judy's reaction was far from that of a woman fearing for her safety.

"Don't you think that if they wanted to talk, they'd have spoken to all the Elite members by now?"

"You just said he's probably embarrassed." Mike threw out his hands. "It's a bloody mess. Not just the money, but Brad ... I wish we'd never heard about Elite."

Lucy sighed. "But we did and we can't shy away from it. I know people think we were greedy, but I don't see it that way. Is it greedy to want a home and a husband who sleeps in the same bed as you do every night?"

"No, love, it isn't."

"And Jack is away more than he ever was and that's hard on Rigby." She leaned forward. "This is not a guilt trip, Mike, this is the truth. Rigby misses you. I'm not expecting you to kick the footy, but he'd love nothing more than snuggling up with you on the recliner and reading a book."

A thick silence stretched between them and it took every fiber of restraint that Lucy had to ride it out. She expected Mike to rise any second and return to his fifth limb—the television set.

He eventually got up and walked to the door. He stopped and turned back to her. "You coming then?"

"I thought we established British crime shows aren't my catnip."

He shook his head. "The garage. If I'm going to make that station for Rigby, first we have to clean up the workbench so I can use it."

For the first time in a long time, Lucy dared to hope.

Lucy stood on the border of the sidewalk and the driveway entrance waiting for Jack. She'd asked him to text her when he was driving through Mortlake so she knew exactly when he'd arrive in Cork Street. The moment he pulled up on the ramp, she opened the passenger door and got in.

She leaned in, dodged his mouth and kissed him quickly on the cheek. "Let's go."

Exhaustion emanated from him in the gray shadows under his eyes and the slump of his shoulders. "What do you mean go? I just got here."

She saw the curtains twitch and panic jetted through her. Birdie had seen the car and they had less than a minute. "The lookout, the park, I really don't care."

"Luce, I got the red-eye, landed at 6:00 and I've driven two hundred miles from Melbourne. I just want a shower and a sleep."

"You know your parents and Rigby won't let you nap. Birdie will insist on cooking you breakfast. Your father will grill you about work and tell you the latest crazy plan Oscar and Alan have dreamed up to find the Elite money. And Rigby will cling to you like a limpet until you've kicked the footy, read him five books and played hide and seek. I need time alone with you now, not at 9:00 tonight when you'll be unconscious."

"I haven't got the energy for sex."

"God, Jack! It's not about sex." The front door opened. "Reverse, now! Go! Please!"

Her desperation must have got through to him because he threw the car into gear and backed onto the street. As he turned, Lucy saw Birdie on the front porch, her face pinched. At least Rigby wasn't with her. If he had been, the game would be up. She shrugged away her mother-in-law's displeasure, reassuring herself she was Jack's wife, therefore she came first.

Neither said a word on the short drive to the lookout. It was overcast—a homogenous gray, making it impossible to tell where the ocean finished and the sky started.

"Where's the blue sky?" Jack peered through the light mist. "Bloody Victoria. I don't miss this miserable weather."

An unwanted dart hit and the words slipped out. "I hope you miss us."

Jack sighed. "Jeez, Luce. You know I do."

Did she? On one level she did. But increasingly, she knew that by the end of his week at home Jack was relieved to be leaving again. Part of her grudgingly understood—hell, she'd leave if she could—but most of her resented the freedom it gave him, not just from Cork Street and Glingilly but from the everyday decisions that rested on her.

Before Elite had crashed and burned, Jack had managed a lot of their life admin during his two-weeks away, but now he was slow to respond. The payments she understood, because it was a constant juggle to meet all their bills on time. But the same didn't apply to other decisions, like the house. Whenever Tiffany sent them an email it was Lucy who inevitably raised the topic and pressed Jack for a response. On a video call three weeks earlier they'd redone all their sums and reluctantly dropped the price. It hadn't precipitated a rush of offers and the devastating silence continued.

She hauled a thermos and cups out of her tote bag along with a packet of German biscuits from Aldi.

Jack stared at her. "Did you turn eighty while I was away or are you back on the tools?"

"Ha ha!" She passed him a cup of tea. "Izzy introduced me to budget morning and afternoon teas."

Jack choked on his drink. When he'd stopped coughing he said, "Back the cart up. Izzy? You've been talking to Isobel Harrington?"

Lucy understood his incredulity. After her first visit to the cottage she'd told Jack that Izzy was living there and how it was barely habitable. Of course their conversation had then gone down the inevitable path of what else they could afford to buy. She certainly hadn't mentioned her visit to Izzy where she'd raged about him and his parents. Rigby had been the one to tell Jack about the park visits, but he was always so excited about feeding the ducks that he didn't mention Izzy.

"I know," Lucy said. "Weird, right? We've been catching up a couple of times a week."

"But you never liked her."

"She's different. I'm different. I don't know if we've both changed or the whole Elite bubble was the problem ..." She shrugged, unable to put her finger on the exact reason. "We're bonding over being screwed over and being poor. I gotta say, for someone used to living the high life she has enviable budgeting skills. She's teaching me a lot, including using a thermos and European biscuits instead of coffee and cake at a café. I just saved us ten bucks. You're welcome."

She expected him to say something like, "You're the best," or to tap his mug against hers, but he only grimaced.

"How's work?" she asked, trying not to sound grumpy.

"You ask me that every night on the phone."

She stiffened. "Sorry to bore you. Anyway, we haven't talked for two days and a text saying *all good* doesn't give me any details."

"I was busy and I knew I was seeing you today."

"And now you're sitting next to me and still not telling me anything!"

"I'm fuckin' exhausted!"

"Boo-hoo. Poor Jack got the red-eye and had one interrupted night's sleep," she snarled. "Well, man up, because you won't be getting a full night's sleep this week. Rigby wakes at 3:00 every morning in a wet bed."

Jack rubbed his face. "Still?"

Her anger deflated with worry. "Still. The tension in the house is awful and Rigby can sense it. I talked to your dad—"

"Oh God, what did you say? Tell me you didn't pressure him about the garage? Or anything else. Because if you did, Mom will have my guts for garters and the last thing I need is more crap like that."

Betrayal wound through Lucy like a snake ready to strike—Jack had just made this all about him. Instead of telling him about the previous night's hour spent making a start on Mike's workbench, she said, "Your father's miserable."

"We're all miserable."

"Yeah, well, this is different. He's given up. Oh wait, you know that, but you and Birdie are too scared to call him on it."

"It wasn't your father's chest we were pounding. Oh, hang on, we wouldn't be doing that because we never see your father—"

Lucy's cell phone was ringing and she grabbed it so she didn't have to listen to any more of Jack's opinions about her family. "It's Tiffany."

Jack's moody face lightened. "It might be an offer."

Lucy answered the phone. "Hi, Tiffany. I've put you on speaker because Jack's here."

"Perfect timing then," the realtor gushed. "I've got good news."

"We're all ears." Lucy grabbed Jack's hand and squeezed as hope spun the ball of worry in her chest.

"There's an offer on the table."

"Thank God!" Jack said.

Tiffany named a price that was 50,000 dollars less than the asking.

Lucy's mouth dried. "But that's twenty-five percent less than the original price."

"True," Tiffany agreed.

"But I don't understand," Lucy said. "I thought people were flocking to regional towns."

"They were, but you missed that bubble and now things have settled down."

"Surely that's a first offer and we can counter, right?" Jack said.

"Knowing what you wanted I've already pushed them to their limit," Tiffany said.

"But it's not enough." Lucy hated the childish whine in her voice.

There was a brief silence and then Tiffany said, "Certainly you can hold out for a higher price but remember this is the only offer we've had. You need to decide if you want to wait another three months, possibly longer, for another offer when there are no guarantees it will be higher. Once a property's been on the market for months, buyers know people aren't rushing to grab it so it gets a reputation as fair game. It becomes harder to secure a good price when they know the seller's already compromised at least once and there's still no sale. And just so you know, the phone's not ringing hot. I don't have anyone else on my books looking for a property of this size. To be honest, I'm having trouble selling houses on standard town blocks and they're closer to all the facilities."

Lucy flinched and the memory of the day their money had vanished roared back, filling her with the same unrelenting terror. She wanted to speak, but she had no clue what to say.

"We'll discuss it, Tiffany," Jack said. "And get back to you."

"Of course. Talk soon."

The cell beeped with disconnection and Lucy swiped up to silence it.

The trough of worry that had moved onto Jack's forehead when Elite collapsed deepened. "We're better off leaving the tenants in the house," he said firmly.

"Financially maybe."

"What other considerations are there?"

She glared at him, stunned by the question. "We can't live with your parents forever!"

"Of course not, but can we please have this conversation without you getting all dramatic?"

"Dramatic?" Her voice chilled with icy fury. "Rigby needs stability."

"He's got that at Mom and Dad's."

"He hasn't. Open your eyes this week and really look. And it's not just Rigby. I need a place of my own! We need our own space."

"Well, this price isn't how you'll get it. Hell, we couldn't even buy the cottage let alone pay for the renovations you say it needs before we can live in it."

Anxiety pumped hot agitation across Lucy's skin and she scratched the patch of eczema that was her Elite "tattoo." "It's the land around the cottage that makes it expensive. If Tiffany's having trouble selling houses in Glingilly then surely we can get a livable bargain."

Jack reached into the back seat, retrieved his tablet and brought up the real estate listings.

"When we put our house on the market there were fourteen houses for sale in town," he said. "Now there's five. All of them are out of our price range."

"So we drop some literature around town and make offers to people who might be thinking of selling."

Jack snorted. "And say what? Sell your house to us for thirty percent less than market value?"

"Jack, I can't live like this."

He turned toward her, his face tight. "You can."

"I can't."

"You seem to think we have a choice."

"We *do* have a choice. We accept this offer and sell the house."

"Then what?" His arms flew up into the air, narrowly missing the mug on the dashboard. "Squander what little money we have left on renting because you're too precious to make it work living with my parents?"

His words sparked and sizzled in the confines of the car. Not once in their four and a half years together had he ever implied she was spoilt, self-centered or unlikeable. But now, instead of the usual pride and love for her nestling in his eyes, she saw a look that was identical to Birdie's—dislike. She lurched between heartache and fury. How could he betray her like this?

"*You're* not selling? What happened to 'us', Jack? This isn't all your decision."

He shrugged. "It's the only decision that won't make things worse for us."

But he was wrong. That decision had already inflicted more damage than Lucy thought they could repair.

CHAPTER THIRTY-FOUR

BIRDIE REALIZED that for the first time in a month—the last time that Jack had been home—her jaw was less tight. Lucy, who'd been more sullen than usual at breakfast, had silently left for work early, taking Rigby to childcare on the way. When Birdie had questioned it, Jack had pointed out they had to pay for childcare whether they used it or not so Rigby was going for the morning.

"This way I get a free morning," Jack had said. "I thought we could go for a walk."

"Good luck getting your father to come."

But Jack hadn't asked Mike.

After a walk along the river path, pink with grevillea flowers, they sat in Birdie's garden enjoying a cup of tea.

"This is nice," Birdie said.

"Yeah, your roses are doing great. They don't even look like they're missing Dad's annual dose of mushroom compost."

Birdie had meant it was nice spending time alone with Jack. "Roses are tough. Give them enough water and a good prune, and they'll pay you back in blooms."

"Hopefully Dad will be back in the garden soon."

"And pigs might fly," she muttered, then drained her mug.

Jack shifted on the seat, clearly uncomfortable. Birdie almost told him how difficult Mike was to live with, but Jack was saying, "We got an offer on the house."

Relief effervesced so quickly she almost burped. But before she could express her delight, Jack said, "We're not accepting it."

She flinched as if he'd dumped ice-cold water over her. "Don't tell me," she said savagely. "This is another one of Lucy's brilliant ideas."

"She thinks we should accept it, but I don't. Right now she's pretty pissed with me."

Birdie took a slice of pleasure from the fact that Jack and Lucy were fighting. Perhaps now the scales would fall from his eyes and he'd see her true colors.

"I assume you have a good reason," she said.

"Yeah." He sounded grateful. "It's too low. When we clear our debts there won't be enough money left for a deposit."

She couldn't believe it. "Not even north of the railway line?"

"Not even there. Prices have skyrocketed."

"Then Lucy should sell her outrageously expensive dinner setting and leather sofa."

He sighed. "Mom ..."

Her ire bubbled. "What?"

"Selling our stuff wouldn't get us even close to the line. Besides, what would we sit on or eat off?"

Birdie crossed her arms. "I'm sure there's other things she could be doing."

"She's doing her best," Jack said stiffly. "We both are."

"I'm not sure her best is good enough."

Jack looked like he wanted to say something but stayed silent.

Birdie was about to press him when the significance of them not accepting the offer on the house suddenly penetrated. When he'd first asked her weeks ago if he and Lucy could move into Cork Street, he'd said, "It'll only be a month, two tops." It had already been longer and right then she knew what he was about to say. The familiar tension re-entered her jaw.

"You want to stay here longer?" She heard the dismay in her tone, but Jack was smiling so he'd either missed it or he was ignoring it.

"Yeah. Thanks, Mom. I knew you'd understand it's the best solution."

But as much as Birdie wanted to side with Jack over Lucy, this was far from the best solution for her. The future stretched out in front of her like a fog-filled road.

"And if the next offer's low too?"

He sighed. "I guess we cross that bridge when we come to it."

Already it was a bridge too far. She immediately heard Sienna's voice in her head and she closed her eyes for a moment, trying to force it away.

"Does your sister know?"

"No."

"Then tell her!" Jack startled at her shrill tone. "The last thing I need is another lecture from her on how you're freeloading."

Two red spots appeared on Jack's cheeks. "We're paying board!"

"And your wife seems to think that absolves her of any further responsibilities. If this situation is ongoing then—"

Jack's cell phone beeped and he glanced at the screen. "Shit, sorry, Mom. I have to pick up Rigby." He kissed her cheek and ran to the gate.

That's very convenient, Jack! Disgruntled, Birdie picked up the mugs and returned inside.

The house felt different, but it wasn't until she put the mugs in the dishwasher that it hit her. Unfamiliar and blessed silence pulsed between the walls. She checked the kitchen counter for a note from Mike. He hadn't mentioned going out, but since the restraining order their interactions were limited to arguing or taut silences. He lived in the sunroom and she in the kitchen. At night they stayed so firmly on their own side of the bed there may as well have been a wall down the middle.

There was a certain irony to this bed freeze. Initially after his heart attack, she'd been worried sex was too much exertion for his heart and he hadn't shown any interest. But when the doctor gave him the all-clear, he continued to lack interest. Since their one disastrous attempt, she hadn't pushed it because right now the thought of Mike touching her was enough to kill any stray flickers of desire.

"Mike!"

When there was no reply she did a quick sweep of the house. He wasn't inside. How hard was it to leave a note? It was just another example of his lack of respect for her. She picked up her cell and called him. It went straight to voice mail. How hard was it for him to turn his cell onto ring when he left the house?

She sent a curt text—*Where are you?*—even though the chances of a reply were slim to none.

Sliding her cell phone into her pocket, she opened the internal door to the garage, intending to grab the vacuum stick off the charger. An unexpected flicker of movement in her peripheral vision startled her. She screamed.

"Jesus, Bird," Mike said. "You trying to make me cut off a finger?"

She turned to face him, her palm pressed to her chest. "You just gave me a hell of a fright. I thought you were a burglar."

"Clearly I'm not."

Now that her heart rate was slowing, she realized he was standing in front of his workbench—a place he hadn't visited since before his heart attack.

"Are you making something?"

"I'm taking a crack at making Rigby that station for his train set."

Did she dare hope this was a sign Mike was slowly coming out of the blue funk he'd been in for months?

"He'll love it," she encouraged.

"That's the plan. Lucky I'd bought everything I need before we went broke."

As she walked over to look at his progress, she realized that the workbench was less cluttered than usual. A moment later she realized it was positioned diagonally opposite from where they'd set it up four years earlier.

"You moved it?" she said.

"We thought it would work better over here."

She wondered who "we" was when Jack had only been home a day. With the exception of this morning, he'd spent most of his time with Rigby.

"You and Jack?"

Mike shook his head. "Lucy."

Birdie's short fuse ignited. "This was Lucy's suggestion?"

"Yeah, and I think she's right."

"How so?" Birdie asked tightly.

"The light's better, and it's closer to the roller door so not as far to move the horse when I'm cutting timber or to sweep up the residue." He glanced around the garage as if seeing it with new eyes. "I don't know why we didn't think of it sooner."

She sucked in a seething breath. "I did, but you insisted on it being closer to the internal door."

He shrugged. "I don't remember that, but this set-up's better for the kids. Now Jack's home, he can connect the telly and if you vacuum the sofa, they'll be set."

She knew she should be happy that Mike was out of the recliner, out of the sunroom and away from the TV, but she had to actively tense her arm tight to her side so she didn't whack him with the vacuum stick.

"Let me get this straight. For weeks you've ignored every suggestion I've made and refused to come out here. But when Lucy asks, you just do it?"

Mike's mouth flattened into a mulish line. "Lucy doesn't nag."

"Nag?" The room turned vermilion. "You interpret me encouraging you to re-engage in your life, in our marriage, as *nagging?*" Her indignation bounced off the walls. "Well, perhaps if you took some responsibility for our lives, for our situation, and actually helped me instead of staring at the television all day then I wouldn't be constantly asking you to do things! But you've become as self-centered and selfish as everyone else in this family!"

He turned back to the workbench, his back rigid and his shoulders implacable. "At least I'm not shaming us in public."

"This again?" She threw up her hands. "Maybe if you stopped wallowing and actually tried to talk to Bevan—"

"I think you put the kibosh on that."

"There's no restraining order against you! But this is your new schtick, isn't it? Blame everyone else. I have no problem with you blaming Brad. I just wish you'd blame Bevan because I sure as hell blame Judy—"

"Now there's a surprise."

"Oh, very funny." Months of frustration roared. "Yes, I've made mistakes, but you're no saint either. Do you think I wanted any of this? Of course I bloody didn't, but at least I'm not lying doggo and sticking my head in the sand! I'm working two jobs, one paid and the other the unpaid drudgery of keeping this house afloat with no help from anyone. And now Jack tells me they're staying indefinitely! I'm doing everything and you can't even manage to call the trailer company once a week!"

Mike remained frustratingly silent—the way he always did when she lost her temper—and it added ire to her vitriol.

"So sue me for making sure you keep your medical appointments, for cooking you healthy-heart food and checking that you've taken your medication so you stay alive. All of which I do without a single piece of gratitude or thanks from you. But you're mighty quick on the criticism and the accusations of nagging. Well, I'm sick of being your punching bag, Mike. I officially quit."

She stormed out of the garage and it wasn't until she was grabbing for her handbag, cell and car keys that she realized she was still clutching the vacuum cleaner stick. She lay it across the hall floor so that whoever walked in had to step over it. Maybe someone might pick it up and use it. *Hah!* She was long past believing in miracles.

Once, she would have driven straight to Judy's. Depending on the time of day, her friend would have pulled out a pack of Tim Tams or the wine and sat listening to her vent. Over the years there had been many occasions when Birdie had reciprocated, but now the friendship was dead.

Birdie drove with no idea of a destination, just an overwhelming need to get as far away from Cork Street as possible. She took the road toward the wetlands, flinching as she passed the racetrack, then pulled into the sanctuary's parking lot. Stowing a water bottle into her handbag, she marched along the lakeside track, her bone-deep anger at Mike making her oblivious to the twittering birdsong and the scent of eucalyptus.

"I hate you," she yelled.

A flock of corellas took flight, squawking their displeasure.

Birdie stomped on, screaming whenever she felt like it. She was sick of being used and abused. Everyone wanted something from her. "Can you mind Rigby?" "What's for dinner?" "Have you seen my blue shirt?"—that one was code for "Have you done the laundry?"

Birdie didn't even get a break at work. Deidre—who'd held a grudge since the elementary school fair of 2007 when Birdie had been asked to coordinate the cake stall ahead of her—got her rocks off by treating her as if she was incapable of using a box cutter, let alone counting back change.

Her life felt like it was one long held breath punctuated by explosions that didn't give her the release she craved. Mostly the explosion left her feeling worse. She managed to hold things together at work, because she needed the job and yelling at Deidre was a fast track to unemployment, but at home it was a different matter. One day she'd completely lost it with Lucy over a kitchen sponge—not that she felt much guilt over that. How hard was it to wring out the sponge and hang it over the faucet?

And nagging! Mike's accusation both ignited her fury and gutted her at the same time. How had they reached this point? Birdie hadn't been an unrealistic young bride—they'd weathered some very ordinary patches in their marriage, especially making the transition from young couple to parents. But during all the lows and highs, they'd always respected each other. Things had never felt as dire as this. Right now, she had absolutely no desire to ever go home again.

She could picture it now—she'd walk in and Mike would act as if she hadn't stormed out. Jack would be staring into the fridge as if the next meal would miraculously form itself and dance onto the table like a Disney cartoon. Rigby would beg her to play Memory with him, and Lucy would either be holed up in her room or looking like she'd just sucked on a lemon.

The urge to run away and stay away burned hot in Birdie's veins.

The knowledge she had nowhere else to go chilled her.

She let out another long scream and hated the sob that tried to follow. If she started crying, she was scared she might never stop.

"Mrs. Essen?"

She looked up. A woman in activewear was coming toward her with a smile on her face. It took Birdie a second to place her—it was Charys, the community health nurse. She wanted to die on the spot.

"Are you okay?" Charys asked.

"Fine," Birdie snapped.

"Are you sure? It sounded like you were screaming."

"Last time I checked that wasn't a crime."

"Don't get me wrong. I've got nothing against a good scream—in fact I've been known to do it myself. It's just …" Charys's face filled with understanding. "I wonder if you're finding things a bit difficult after Mike's heart attack?"

"Difficult?" Birdie snorted. "That's the understatement of the year."

Charys indicated a bench seat a bit farther along the track. "Would you like a listening ear?"

Birdie had only ever confided in Judy and it felt wrong to be talking to someone else. But for all the screaming she'd done on her two furious circuits around the lake, she wasn't experiencing anything close to catharsis. She was just as angry, only with an added layer of exhaustion.

"I don't want to interrupt your run."

"I promise you're not. I was running out of puff anyway and looking for an excuse to stop and stretch. You'd be doing me a favor."

Birdie was skeptical. "Does me venting come under the banner of nurse–patient confidentiality?"

"Absolutely. Even before I became a nurse, my mother taught me to treat people's stories with the same respect I'd want them to treat mine."

The reassuring words flattened Birdie's last remaining piece of resistance and she slumped onto the seat. "I don't even know where to start."

"With the heart attack? I know you were there when Mike collapsed. It must have been terrifying."

"It was. I was bargaining with God to keep him alive but ..." A long breath shuddered out of her. "Maybe He got confused and sent the wrong bloke back, because the man living in my house isn't Mike. He's been given a second chance but he's acting like his life is over. It makes me so mad I could ..."

"Scream?" Charys suggested.

"Scream, hit, punch. I'm angry all the time. I mean, sure, our life is nothing like it was before the heart attack, but ..." Birdie's arms rose and fell as words failed her.

"It's not uncommon after a heart attack to suffer from depression," Charys said.

"The patient or the spouse?"

"Sometimes both. For the patient, it's often the first time they've faced their own mortality and that can be very confronting. And for their partner too. Do you think Mike's depressed?"

"Well, he's something, but whatever he is, he's not going to admit it to me."

"Ah." Charys nodded. "Men often find it difficult to verbalize their feelings, and if the heart attack is the first time they've confronted such big emotions, they don't always know what to do with them. That's why we have the twice-weekly group chat as part of cardiac rehab. Although I don't remember Mike saying much."

"That sounds about right."

"Do you think you're depressed, Birdie?"

She shrugged the thought away, not allowing it to land. "I don't have time! One of us has to work to keep the power on and put food on the table."

Charys frowned. "When Mike skipped the talk with the financial counselor, I assumed his heart attack hadn't impacted on your financial situation."

"Our financial situation was the reason he had the heart attack!"

"It's never one thing, Birdie," Charys reassured. "It's a mix of genes and lifestyle and—"

"We invested in Elite."

Birdie heard herself saying the words and wondered what the hell was happening to her today. It was bad enough being ripped off and having half the town know and judge her for it, but to volunteer the information to a stranger? She really was losing it.

Charys's eyes widened. "I'm so sorry. That must be ..."

Birdie appreciated the woman's struggle to find words that adequately described her situation. "Absolute shit pretty much sums it up. My son lost everything too, so he's moved back in with his family."

"The grandson you mentioned?"

"And his wife. My house is groaning with people and my workload's doubled."

Charys gave her a sideways look. "No one can put anything away, right?"

"Oh my God! Are you living in my house too?" A trickle of relief ran through Birdie. "They manage to create a mess in every room they visit, and even the ones they don't."

"My family share that talent." Charys's laugh faded. "Oh, Birdie. I'm so sorry you're facing these challenges all at the same time. You have every right to feel overwhelmed and be out in the bush screaming."

"Thank you." Tears burned the back of her eyes. "I just wish I had control over *one* thing in my life."

"I think you do."

"It doesn't feel like it. Just before Mike's heart attack, he'd retired. I was looking forward to spending time together, just the two of us. But he's shut down and all we do is argue. Instead of being off around Australia doing things together, I'm back to being tied down by family responsibilities. I love my kids, but they're not supposed to be living with us at thirty and behaving like they're fifteen!"

"And they can't afford to live somewhere else?"

"They say they can't."

"Birdie, you do have the right to say no sometimes."

"That's much easier in theory. No parent wants their child to suffer."

"That's true. But I know when I visit my childhood home it's very easy to slip into the role of being a kid again. But your son and his family aren't visiting; they're living with you so they need to act like adults. I imagine they're grieving their loss of their independence too."

Birdie huffed. "They wouldn't be in this mess if they hadn't wanted everything yesterday."

"I thought they lost their money in Elite like you and Mike?"

"They did. But we don't have a massive debt hanging over our head like they do. I blame my daughter-in-law. Mike had his heart attack straight after they told us."

"I'm sorry." Charys worried her bottom lip. "But Birdie, the timing of the news and the heart attack was a coincidence. He was going to have that heart attack one day soon with or without bad news."

Birdie chewed over the statement, not wanting to swallow it. "You can't know that for sure."

"I do. I can show you the angiogram if you like. There was so little blood getting through Mike's coronary arteries he was a ticking bomb for a heart attack. Your daughter-in-law is off the hook."

Birdie blocked the image of Lucy pumping Mike's chest and crossed her arms. "I don't think so. They took a ridiculous risk with a personal loan and we taught Jack never to do that."

"Was it a joint loan?"

"Yes."

"I'm sure if your son didn't want to take out the loan he wouldn't have."

Birdie opened her mouth to say, "Lucy probably pressured him into it," when she remembered Jack's words on that fateful day. "We did the math. We took out a personal loan." And just this morning—"I'm the one who doesn't want to accept the offer."

Jack wouldn't be talked around if he thought something was a bad idea.

The realization sat uncomfortably and Birdie tried to push it away. But perhaps it showed in her shifting on the seat or in her face, because Charys's face filled with knowing. It exacerbated Birdie's discomfort.

"When our world's turned upside down, sometimes it's easier to be angry with other people," Charys said softly.

It was like an arrow hitting a bullseye and the urge to defend herself sent hot words rushing out of her mouth. "Lucy deserves my anger."

Charys's brows rose. "But not your son? Lucy's lost her money too, so doesn't that put her in a similar situation to you?"

"Yes, but—"

"Perhaps you're really most angry at yourself."

The words fell like bricks—sharp, heavy and painful—and Birdie's volcano of fury surged again.

"Of course I'm bloody angry with myself! But I'm angry with everyone." She threw out her arms in frustrated defeat. "Why didn't one of us have the good sense to see Elite was a scam and save us from this hell?"

Charys gave her shoulder a quick squeeze. "Don't beat yourself or the family up about it when you can't change what happened.

Remember, a talented conman never gives you a reason to doubt them until it's too late."

"You got that right." Birdie slumped, suddenly exhausted. "I'm so tired of being angry, Charys. Before all this happened it took a lot for me to erupt, but now it's my default setting. I don't like who I am anymore."

Charys was quiet a while, staring out across the lake. "You talked about not having any control, and I understand that in terms of the money you lost, but you should be able to control what happens in your home. When your son and his family moved in, did you have a household meeting?"

Birdie shook her head. "It happened straight after Mike got home from the hospital. I was barely coping with his meds, his moods and the new diet so there was no space in my brain for cleaning rosters."

"Then now's the time to establish some ground rules. You're not Mom, Dad and the kids anymore—you're four adults sharing a house. Draw up a roster of jobs and make sure Mike and Jack are on it too. Share the load."

"Jack works FIFO. He's hardly home."

"That must be hard for Lucy."

"They made that decision to pay for the house."

"Doesn't mean it's easy."

Birdie was getting sick of Charys's fair-mindedness. "It's not easy sharing a house with her either."

"I don't doubt it." Charys gave her a long look. "How would you feel if she has the same thoughts?"

"Do I have to care?"

Charys shrugged. "Well, your son and grandson love her, so if you want a good relationship with them, it might be easier on you if you care."

Birdie huffed. Talking to the nurse wasn't like talking to Judy. Her friend had always sided with her no matter what she'd said or done.

"Jack says Lucy's doing her best, but ..."

"Are you?" Charys asked.

Birdie was fast regretting sitting down with this perceptive woman. "Jack knows exactly how I feel," she obfuscated.

"But does he want to?"

"Of course." But the question itched like prickly heat.

The truth was that Jack never replied to her venting texts. She'd chosen to believe those silences meant he agreed with her. But now she saw his tight face and heard his cautioning tone and long sighs whenever she criticized Lucy. Was the closeness in their mother–son relationship—something she'd always prided herself on—not really closeness at all, but bare tolerance? *Was* she doing her best?

You know you're not.

The thought that her behavior was pushing Jack away dueled with her resentment that her life was no longer her own. God! Why, on top of everything else, did she have to be the one to change?

"What if I don't want to do my best?" she said.

Charys gave a faint smile. "It makes you human, but it also makes your life harder. You said you don't like who you are right now. I won't lie to you—letting go of your anger won't be easy, but it's the first step in healing. Talking with someone will help too."

Birdie bristled. "You mean a shrink?"

Charys shook her head. "I doubt you need to see a psychiatrist. But talk to your primary care doctor about a mental health treatment plan. That means you'll be able to see a psychologist and medical insurance will cover the appointment fees. And think about doing something that isn't work or caring, cooking or cleaning. Something that's just for you."

"I can't afford to do anything!" Oh dear Lord, she sounded like a petulant child. "Sorry, Charys, I do appreciate you trying to help."

"There are loads of free activities in town. Everything from joining Friends of the Wetlands to a book group at the library."

"I used to love reading, but I can't concentrate on anything much at the moment."

"I get that. I heard that the Irish festival is looking for committee members. That will keep you busy *and* get you out of the house."

For years, Birdie and Mike had attended the festival with Judy and

Bevan, enjoying the great music and Guinness. This year they couldn't afford it and there was no way in hell they'd be going with Judy and Bevan. But if she volunteered across the weekend, she'd still be in the thick of things.

For the first time in a long time, a ray of hope filtered through her misery.

CHAPTER THIRTY-FIVE

Izzy lay in a shaking bed. The first time it had happened she wondered if it was another earthquake, but as it occurred each night around the same time, she realized it was Waring, the resident wombat, so-called because he was wearing her down. If it wasn't a nightmare waking her, it was Waring—although today he was lumbering under the house much later than usual. She should roll over and try to sleep another hour until dawn, but something made her reach for her phone.

There was a green dot next to Cooper's name—he was awake too.

Since their walk and talk at Tower Hill, they'd shared quite a few phone calls during the inky hours between two and four. Lying in the dark unable to see each other and connected only by a phone line gave their conversations an element of freedom that was missing in their face-to-face meetings. Mostly when they were together they shared an easy camaraderie, but there were moments of unexpected tension—source unknown. She'd tried talking too much as well as silence to banish the strain, but neither were reliable tactics. These moments left her on edge and more than once she'd made an excuse to leave. But on the phone, their conversation flowed.

Sometimes they talked nonsense; at other times they discussed the state of the nation. They talked about worthy books they'd found boring versus the guilty pleasure of rollicking fiction that the literati despised. They traded stories about the places they'd traveled and shared dreams of the places they hoped to visit.

Once, Izzy fired so many questions at Cooper about his corporate work and life as an academic that he'd eventually said, "I'm sweating! None of my job interviews were this intense."

She'd laughed, suddenly embarrassed. "Sorry. It's just I find it all fascinating."

"Really?" He sounded genuinely surprised. "My ex declared both me and my numbers dull and boring."

"I can only speak for the numbers. They're never boring," she'd said, surprising herself with the teasing.

"Numbers are a hard act to follow."

"You do your best."

He'd laughed. "Good to know."

She'd spent a large part of the next day wondering about his ex, and most of the evening telling herself she shouldn't be wasting her time. But she kept coming back to the issue of dull. Cooper was quiet and thoughtful—certainly nothing like the high-octane thrill of being around her father and Brad. Both had pulled her into their world, sharing its pleasures, but also demanding things of her. Considering everything that had happened—both in the past and the more recent past—was excitement overrated?

Then again, Cooper had mentioned he enjoyed fishing. Just the thought of sitting for hours waiting made Izzy squirm. But did a love of fishing make him dull or just content with his own company? Contentment was something neither Brad nor her father had known— they'd always been on the lookout for the next big thing, which was both exhilarating and intoxicating.

Right up until the moment it exploded in a ball of fire.

Surely there had to be something in-between dull and explosive?

Frustrated by her circular thoughts, she'd taken Thor for a run across the fields behind the cottage, trying to still her mind.

Now the vivid green dot next to Cooper's name called to her, but again she hesitated. This time she wasn't lying awake because she was soaked in nightmare-fueled adrenaline—she'd been woken by a wombat. But was Cooper awake post-nightmare? Probably not, otherwise he would have called her. Still ...

She continued to deliberate on whether she should call or text him, hating how much she was overthinking things, when her cell phone pinged.

> Fancy a sunrise? I'm going fishing at Killarney Beach. Will either cook you fish or buy you breakfast.

A string of emojis followed showing waves, a fish on a line, eggs in a pan and bacon.

The idea of fish for breakfast reminded her of breakfasts in Malaysia, although she doubted Cooper would have coconut rice. What tempted her most was the treat of a café breakfast in Port Fairy. Granted, she would have to endure a chilly and deathly slow time on the beach, but she'd do it for good coffee and poached eggs on sourdough bread. Besides, Thor would love tearing up and down the sand chasing gulls.

Already wearing her thermals, she rolled out of bed, pulled on a cashmere sweater, corduroy pants and a woolen beanie. She zippered her puffer jacket, made a thermos of tea, called Thor and headed out into the dark.

On a sunny day, Killarney Beach was a curve of white sand, turquoise water to rival the Pacific, and grass-covered dunes. In the pre-dawn orange glow, the volcanic rocks were jet, the water navy and the distant hills ink.

Izzy made out Cooper's silhouette on the waterline. As she walked closer she was surprised at the absence of a chair. Wasn't fishing a sitting affair?

Thor barked and Cooper turned, raising his arm in a wave. "You made it."

"I can't feel my fingers."

"I made a thermos." He indicated a cane basket.

She laughed and held up her own. "Snap! Can I pour you tea?"

"Sounds good."

As she handed him a mug, she pointed to the two enormous fishing rods stuck in holders in the sand. "I thought you sat and held a fishing rod."

"That's freshwater fishing, although not for salmon."

"Right ..."

He laughed. "Is this your first time surf fishing?"

"It's my first time fishing full stop."

He rubbed his hands together enthusiastically. "Then prepare yourself for adventure."

She glanced at the static lines. "Seriously? It doesn't look very exciting."

"That's half the fun. Surf fishing's ninety percent anticipation and ten percent exhilaration."

Izzy hugged her mug for warmth. "If you say so."

Thor, who'd raced down the beach, belted back, spraying them in sand. The dog barked and looked at Izzy, his face loaded with delight.

Cooper bent down and gave him a scratch behind the ears. "Glad you're excited, mate, but I think we've got our work cut out convincing Izzy."

Izzy pointed to the orange ball of sun rising behind the hills. It was spraying the sky peach and casting a ladder of golden light across the water, connecting the headland to the sand. "I'm impressed by the sunrise."

His mouth curved into his gentle smile. "I'm taking that as a good start."

They watched the sky lighten to blue, and the earth and sea assume their vivid daylight colors, while gentle waves rolled in against the shore.

"Is the tide coming in?" Izzy asked.

"Yep. If you don't want to get wet take off your boots and roll up your pants."

She did as instructed and put her boots and socks on the dry sand next to Cooper's. When she turned back to the water, he was reeling in his line.

"The fish are there," he said.

Izzy watched his long fingers rebait the empty hook. She tried not to flinch at the idea of handling the wet and slippery fish or the stink that would cling to her fingers.

"Is the tide important in fishing?"

"It is if you want to catch something. Best chance is ninety minutes either side of the change. Any other time you'll enjoy the beach more swimming or going for a walk. I'm going to cast, Izzy, so stay exactly where you are so I don't hook you."

"Thor, come!" Izzy called, and caught the wet and sandy dog by the collar.

Cooper picked up the rod and, raising it above his head, twisted as if he was throwing a javelin. The next moment the rod pushed through an arc and the line streamed high into the air, far out to sea, before dropping into the water.

"Wow!" Her surprise at his athleticism slipped out.

Cooper laughed and adjusted the line before placing the rod in the holder. "I'm taking that as a compliment. Do you want to have a go with the other one?"

Anticipation fluttered in her belly, then flatlined. "Do I have to bait the hook?"

"My dad would say yes, but I'll treat you just this once."

"Once? Okay, that means this will be my one and only cast."

His dark eyes danced. "I doubt it. It's pretty addictive."

Izzy thought about her father and Brad and closed her eyes for a moment.

"Izzy? You okay?"

She opened her eyes and forced a smile. "All good. Now show me what to do."

Cooper handed her the rod and stood beside her issuing instructions.

After a few failed attempts to get the line to even reach the tide mark, he said, "What if I stand behind you and hold the rod too? That way you can feel the correct position and the motion so you can replicate it."

Izzy thought replicating his effortless casting was as likely as a mosquito-free wetland, but she agreed. He moved in behind her and her cold back immediately warmed. It took everything she had not to snuggle into him and gather more of his heat.

Cooper's head was next to hers, his mouth close to her ear, and although she heard his words—"Move your hand here and angle your feet forty-five degrees to the water"—the touch of his hands on hers and the tickle of his breath on her ear stole her concentration and flooded her with sensations she hadn't experienced in months.

How the hell was she aroused by fishing?

A voice in her head laughed at her.

I am not attracted to Cooper!

There were so many reasons not to be, and yet there was no denying the race of her heart or the flush of heat streaking across her skin and diving deep to quiver between her legs.

Break contact. Break contact!

But her body was too busy luxuriating in bliss and Cooper was saying, "Relax into it, Izzy. Be at one with the rod and feel the motion."

A hysteria-tinged laugh escaped.

"Have faith," Cooper said. "You can do it. On my count. One, two ..."

At three her arms rose, her body moved as one with his and the reel streamed, sending the line out in a perfect arc. Fascinated, she watched it drop into the water.

"Good job! You put it in the gutter." Cooper adjusted the reel, then stepped back.

Izzy immediately missed his heat and gripped the rod. "I don't see any concrete so what's the gutter?"

"It's the space between two sandbars. The fish play there because the water's pushing the crustaceans off the edge and that's dinner. Stick your rod in the holder and watch the line. Any tugging and you reel it in."

"With my luck it'll snag seaweed."

"Nah, that goes against Barsky's law."

Intrigued, she faced him. "What's that?"

"Whenever we take someone fishing for the first time they always catch something."

She got a ridiculous flutter at the thought of catching a fish. "Like I said, seaweed."

"You wait," he said confidently. He started talking about drop-offs, holes and water drainage points. Then he reeled in his rod, peered into the water, walked a little farther down the beach and recast his line.

She watched him, fascinated. This was no stab-in-the-dark approach to fishing. This was tactics and military precision. She supposed it matched his love of numbers—logical and precise. Surely fish were less reliable?

Lost in her thoughts, she was suddenly aware of Thor barking and dancing around her feet. She assumed he'd dropped a stick he wanted her to throw, but when she looked down she only saw sand. Thor was now behind her, standing by the fishing rod, which was bending wildly.

She grabbed it before it pulled the holder onto the sand and braced herself against the hard tugs. "Cooper!"

He ran back to her, his face split in a broad grin. "Barsky's law."

"What do I do?"

"Start reeling it in slowly."

"I can barely hold it. It feels like it's going to pull out of my hands."

He stepped in behind and gripped the rod. "I've got it, you reel. Pull up the rod and reel. Up and reel."

She started turning the handle. "It feels like it might break."

"It shouldn't. This line is heavy enough to catch a shark."

Izzy almost dropped the rod. "I don't think I want to catch a shark."

"Don't think about what it is, just concentrate on reeling it in. That's it, keep going. Walk with me."

He moved backwards and she followed, her focus fully on the line.

Thor raced into the shallows and that's when she saw a flash of silver. "Thor! Come!"

"I'll go," Cooper said. "You got the rod?"

"Yes."

She watched him jog into the water and pull up the line. A massive fish flailed on the hook. Izzy put the rod in the holder and ran down.

Cooper met her on the sand holding the fish aloft with both hands. "Salmon, Izzy! You've exceeded Barsky's law. I reckon this baby weighs about nine pounds."

She laughed. "Can I take a photo before you put it back?"

"Sure, but it's well over the legal limit if you want to eat it."

She thought about how many meals it would provide. "What if you fillet it and we share it?"

"Sounds like a plan." Cooper put the fish into the waiting bucket and wiped his hands. "It's probably still good fishing for another thirty minutes if you wanted to keep going. We can catch and release."

"I think nature's given us enough today." Her stomach rumbled. Embarrassed, she laughed. "Besides, you promised me breakfast."

"Salmon it is."

The lure of a café breakfast called—it had been months since she'd eaten one. "How about I cook you salmon for dinner and you buy me breakfast at Rebecca's?"

His brows rose. "Oh, so this is a negotiation situation?"

Her skin tingled at his teasing and she was suddenly aware how close they were standing. "Think of it in terms of a trade."

"How are you going to cook the salmon?"

"There are a few possibilities. Pan-fried with basil pesto served on fluffy mashed potato with ratatouille and crunchy snow peas. Or oven-baked in an Asian-style marinade."

He rubbed his jaw as if he was weighing up the offer against his contribution.

"And if I cook at your place," she said quickly, "I'll throw in the washing up as well." She looked up at him and smiled. "How can you say no to that?"

"Perhaps I want to see where you're living."

Her flirting flatlined. "You really don't."

The dawn had been still, but now the ubiquitous wind the beach was famous for kicked up and Izzy's hair whipped across her face. She went to push it away and her hand met Cooper's. Together they brushed her hair behind her ears and then he was lowering his head and she heard him say, "Can I kiss you?"

"I don't know." The words slipped out before she had time to weigh up his question.

He raised his head, his face guarded. "Fair enough. I'll pack up."

"Cooper." Her hand gripped his forearm. "It's not a no."

"It's not a yes." A shadow dimmed his eyes. "Is it Quinn?"

"Sort of."

His mouth sagged. "So even though you were leaving him, you're still not over him?"

She shook her head. "It's not that, it's me. I don't trust myself. I'm terrified I'll make another mistake."

"I'm not him, Izzy." Everything from Cooper's stance to his tone of voice was serious. "I've been told there's absolutely nothing about me that's charismatic or exciting. I promise you that with me, what you see is what you get. I'm a geeky bloke who pays his taxes, loves numbers, enjoys sudoku, pottering in the garden, playing baseball and fishing."

His earnestness reached out and circled her. "Actually, it turns out fishing's pretty exciting," she said.

"It really is." His grin faded and he adjusted her beanie, which was creeping down across her eyes. "Another thing you need to know about me is that I don't rush into anything. So I don't expect you to either. Besides, a kiss is just a kiss, not a future."

She hated that her brain instantly questioned Cooper's ability to commit when she'd just said she didn't want to rush things.

"So we take it one day at a time?"

He nodded and laced his fingers into hers. "One event even. Seeing as you're so obsessed by good coffee, let's start with breakfast at Rebecca's."

"Thank you." Grateful, she rose on her toes and slid her lips quickly across his wind-chilled lips, tasting salt and sunshine.

His free hand cupped her cheek and stalled her movement away. He sighed against her mouth and deepened the kiss.

For the first time in months, Izzy momentarily left her reality in a pile at her feet and lost herself in a kiss that both surprised her and took her breath away.

Going slowly may not be as easy as she'd thought.

CHAPTER THIRTY-SIX

By 4:30, the pregnancy care clinic was showing all the signs of running over time and Lucy was fearful of late childcare fees. She flipped through her options. Birdie was at work, which was a good thing because Lucy would do almost anything to avoid asking her for a favor. Mike, who she would have called now that he was slowly taking more of an interest in his life again, was representing all the Essens at an Elite meeting and hearing Oscar's latest report.

Members were maintaining their rage and rumors flew that the missing money was definitely hidden overseas, although exactly where ranged from the Bahamas to Switzerland. Oscar was determined to find it and he had pressured Bevan at GGSC. Bevan had slapped a restraining order against him, Alan Lumsden and the Hewitsons before departing for New South Wales.

Now Brad was dead and the police investigation had moved to Melbourne—and seemingly gone quiet—all the media had lost interest. Lucy assumed the police were grinding through the numbers and any clues they'd found they were keeping to themselves. With each passing month their slowness infuriated and angered the Elite members.

Expectations of a resolution falling in their favor lay dented and rusting.

After months of railing against what had happened to her, Lucy was slowly coming to the conclusion that expecting any money to come their way was a pipe dream that created more stress than accepting their investment was gone for good. She wanted to move on, but with Jack refusing to sell the house, every day felt like treading water. For the first time in their married life she was glad Jack was a continent away in the Pilbara—it saved yet another argument. But it also meant he couldn't pick up Rigby.

Lucy momentarily considered calling one of the playgroup mothers, but picking up someone else's child late in the afternoon when their own children were likely melting from tiredness was a big ask. The late fee was looking like a reality.

Call Izzy.

You said no to her offer.

But that had been before Rigby knew her. Now, after their numerous chats in the park, Rigby knew Izzy and he loved that she pushed him on the swings for a crazy amount of time before losing interest. Lucy appreciated that too and most importantly, she trusted her. Plus Izzy's work was flexible and she drove a safe car.

What about the house?

Lucy took a deep breath and listened to her gut. Izzy would keep Rigby safe.

Between patients, Lucy called her.

Izzy didn't even let her finish her question before saying, "Of course. And don't worry how late you are. We'll be fine."

Lucy parked the car outside Izzy's cottage and noticed a string of fairy lights laced between the gingerbread fretwork. They were new since the last time she'd visited.

"Mommy!" Rigby raced out the door with Thor, their enthusiasm booming like a sonic wave. He pointed to the lights. "Look. Izzy says they're early stars."

Lucy hugged her son—he smelled of hot chips and citrus.

"Hello, Lucy."

Izzy stood in the doorway, all hostess grace and style and ringed by formality. But Lucy no longer experienced stabs of jealousy or discomfort around her—Izzy was Izzy. She started every visit wound tight and fifteen minutes in she relaxed.

"I can't thank you enough," Lucy said. "Was he good?"

"Were you good, Rigby?" Izzy asked.

He nodded, his face serious. "Thor was naughty, Mommy. He wanted to eat my nuggets."

Lucy couldn't believe Izzy had given Rigby dinner. "You fed him?"

"And bathed him."

Lucy hugged her and blinked back tears at Izzy's thoughtfulness. "Oh my God, that's above and beyond. Thank you! I owe you."

"How about signing up as a volunteer for the Irish festival?"

The question surprised her and she opened her mouth to say, "I don't think so," but instead heard herself saying, "Sure, why not. It's on when Jack's home so he can be the parent-in-charge and I can play with you."

"You'll be working."

Lucy laughed. "Believe me, compared with my paid job and single parenting, checking tickets or supervising people peeling potatoes is all play."

"That's great!" Izzy's smile was pure delight. "Thank you—it'll be fun working with you. I'll put your name on my list and I'll email you all the details. Tell me which events you want to work at and I'll give you first preference."

"So there are advantages being friends with you," Lucy teased.

In the dusk light, Rigby was happily throwing a ball to Thor.

"Do you want to stay for a drink or do you need to get Rigby home to bed?" Izzy asked.

"I'd love a wine and a whine, but I better get him home. Also, I have to clean the bathroom before Birdie leaves me another passive-aggressive Post-it note."

"Things still awkward at Cork Street?"

Lucy heard the edge of mania in her laugh. "I'd take awkward any day over toxic silences and irrational explosions."

"No more offers on the house then?"

"I'd have told you if there were."

"Really?"

Izzy's stunned face surprised Lucy. "Of course. You're about the only person who understands what living this mess is really like."

This time Izzy's laugh was tight. "In-laws and all."

"I thought Judy and Bevan were in Dolphin Sands."

"They are, but Judy likes to text, call and FaceTime. A lot."

"I guess she sees you as her link to Brad."

When Izzy didn't reply, Lucy was about to ask her if she was ever going to tell the Quinns she'd been leaving Brad when a car pulled up. A man who looked to be in his late thirties, and dressed in conservative smart casual clothes, raised his arm in a wave.

"Who's that?" Lucy asked. "He's definitely not a local."

"Cooper Barsky."

"And he's ...?"

"He was my uni lecturer last semester."

Even in the dim light, Lucy would need to be blind to miss the pink flush on Izzy's cheeks. "And what is he to you now?"

"A friend."

"Yeah, right, Izzy." Lucy punched her gently on the upper arm. "He's more than that. You've been holding out on me!"

"No, I haven't. It's just ..." Izzy tugged at her hair. "It's all so new and ... I dunno ... because of how Brad died, part of me feels like I'm disrespecting him by seeing Cooper."

"No." Lucy grabbed her hand. "You said things with Brad were over, that you were leaving him. Would you be thinking like this if he was still alive?"

"No, but—"

"There's no but, Izzy. Brad chose to end his life. It doesn't mean yours stops too."

Cooper was pulling two shopping bags out of the trunk and Lucy noticed a bunch of supermarket flowers sticking out of one of them.

"But it's fast," Izzy said. "Isn't it too fast?"

"It's not that fast. It's been months, and when you add in how long you were unhappy, that's almost a year. Anyway, I met Jack a month after I'd broken up with a guy I'd been with for a long time and now, four and a half years later—"

She swallowed the words "we're still together." Right now she and Jack were not an example worth citing. During his last furlough they'd struggled to be in the same room without arguing, and since he'd returned to work they hadn't spoken. Their few text messages had been short and to the point—life admin and studiously avoiding the topic of the house, but it hung between them ugly and unresolved.

An unwanted childhood memory hurtled back. Lucy sliding quietly out of the kitchen, desperately hoping that her parents wouldn't notice, as her mother hurled the words, "I hate you, Graeme!" at her father. His reply: "Hate doesn't even touch how I feel about you!" The crash of a glass hitting the wall. Her father swearing. The days when silence built itself into an impenetrable wall of barbed wire and jagged glass.

Their inevitable split had brought Lucy little relief as her parents used her to play off against each other, until they both met and married someone else. Then they almost forgot about her.

Lucy was suddenly breathing hard. Had she and Jack stepped onto that same road? *Please God, no.* She'd made a promise to herself and to Rigby that his childhood would be free of that kind of acrimony. That she and Jack would be happy, would respect each other and together would give Rigby the stability every child needs. But she and Jack were barely speaking.

"Are you okay, Lucy?" Izzy was peering at her, worry lines creasing her forehead.

Thankfully the gate squeaked when Cooper opened it, causing Thor to abandon Rigby and the ball. He raced across the yard, all bum wriggles and happy barking, greeting Cooper as if he was a king.

Lucy's laugh was strained. "Your dog loves him."

"Thor loves everyone," Izzy said drily. "He adored Brad, and I know he misses him because he sleeps with one of his shoes. About the only person Thor has never bonded with is Bevan." Izzy shrugged. "Then again, Bevan doesn't like dogs so it's hardly surprising Thor ignores him."

"Have you told the Quinns about Cooper?"

Izzy sighed and shook her head. "You're the only person who knows."

Lucy remembered the heady early days with Jack—they seemed a different lifetime. A sharp pain cramped her gut and almost toppled her.

"Looks like this man of yours has brought dinner," she managed.

"He wanted to cook, but it's the first time he's been here. I've tried to warn him about the cottage—you have to stay for a drink." Izzy's chin rose, giving her the aloof and chilly aura that Lucy hadn't seen since the final Elite event.

"Izzy, breathe. He's not here to judge the house or to have me play gooseberry. He's here because he wants to spend time with you. So drop your chin or you'll scare him off with your icy unapproachable look."

"Oh God!" Anxiety whipped across Izzy's cheeks. "Am I doing that?"

Lucy laughed and mouthed "Smile" just as Cooper's foot hit the veranda.

His mouth creased into a quiet but confident smile. "Hello." He leaned in and gave Izzy a brief kiss on the cheek. "You okay?"

Izzy gulped in some air. "Uh-huh."

A slight ripple of concern rolled across his forehead, but he turned his attention to Lucy. "I'm Cooper Barsky. A friend of Izzy's."

Lucy shot out her hand to meet his and shook, enjoying the firm, but not dominating, grip. "Lucy Essen." His eyes momentarily widened and Lucy added, "A friend of Izzy's."

He relaxed. "Lovely to meet you, Lucy. I think I've met your husband."

"Jack?"

He nodded. "Before the Elite case was referred to Melbourne I was the forensic accountant. Jack was very helpful." He glanced at Izzy, his eyes searching her face, trying to read what he'd walked into. "I brought a bottle of local pinot noir to go with the salmon, but I can open it now if you ladies would like to chat while I make dinner."

A man who was prepared to let two women sit and chat while he cooked sounded too good to be true. Then again, he was yet to see the kitchen. Even so, Lucy already liked Cooper Barsky. She'd always thought the way Brad had looked at Izzy was something every woman hoped for, but now, looking at Cooper, she recognized the difference between the gaze of someone who'd got what he wanted and genuine affection.

She smiled her thanks at Cooper's offer. "As perfect as that sounds, I need to get Rigby home to bed. But maybe another time?"

"That would be great." Izzy's words came out in a rush. "I caught a huge salmon. It's going to take ages to get through it so come to dinner soon and we'll cook for you at Cooper's house so you don't have to worry about Rigby and the floorboards."

Lucy stared at her friend, trying to picture her on a beach with one of those huge surf rods. "You went fishing?"

Cooper gave Izzy's waist a squeeze. "She's a natural."

Izzy laughed, and as her tension fell away she looked happier and more relaxed than Lucy had ever seen her.

"It was so much fun, Lucy! You should try it."

Lucy drove home, trying to align the woman she'd thought Izzy was a year ago—ice queen, designer-dressed, international jetsetter—with the woman in jeans and a sweater who'd just done mom duty with Rigby and had gone fishing with a bloke who looked like he'd be more at ease in the lofty air of academia than on a beach fishing. She could hardly match Izzy as the same person and she laughed.

"Is it a funny, Mommy?" Rigby asked sleepily from his car seat.

"It's a riddle, honey."

Rigby fell asleep before they arrived at Cork Street and she carried him into an empty house, transferring him straight into bed.

Weary and hungry after a long day, she walked into the kitchen planning to eat leftovers before cleaning the bathroom and falling straight into bed. She stopped short—Birdie sat at the table.

"Oh! You're home." Lucy could have kicked herself that her disappointment rang through the words.

"I usually am at 7:45."

Lucy nodded and opened the fridge, taking longer than necessary to find her container of Mexican chicken just so she could stay hidden.

As she closed the fridge door, Birdie said, "I expected the bathroom to be clean."

Lucy's hands tightened on the container but she shot for light and breezy. "I just got home too. Clinic ran late and then we had a sickie at the end. By the time I got her settled into the ward, it was close to seven."

Birdie frowned. "Poor Rigby. That's a long day for him."

Lucy found herself slamming the microwave door. "He had a lovely time with Izzy. So much so he's sacked out early."

"Izzy who?"

"Harrington."

Birdie stared, her eyes round black discs. "Have you lost your mind?"

"No. Izzy is one of the few people in my life who's actually in my corner!"

Birdie crossed her arms. "Thank you very much."

Gobsmacked, Lucy stared at her mother-in-law. "You're offended that I don't consider you in my corner when you blame me for Mike's heart attack and find fault with everything I do?"

Birdie grimaced, but her gaze slid away. Eventually, she said, "It's more about what you don't do."

"It's not that I don't do things around the house, Birdie, I do. But I get constantly interrupted by Rigby, Mike or Jack when he's home. Some days just getting the laundry done feels like a marathon event."

Birdie's brows rose. "Are they just handy excuses?"

"You tell me! I've seen Mike walk in here when you're cooking and ask you everything from 'where are my keys' to 'we're out of toothpaste,' and you stop what you're doing to help."

Birdie didn't respond so she pushed on. "When I first moved in, I tried my best, but who cleans their bathroom daily? No one I know." She threw out her arms in frustration. "And when I do what you ask me, you're impossible to please. God, not even maids at five-star hotels could match your standards."

"It's not that hard to wipe down a basin so it's clean and dry."

"No, and it gets wiped. It's not my fault someone uses the damn thing before you turn up for inspection. I'm not a child, Birdie, but living here is like school camp, only the rules aren't clear. And Jack is judged by a different standard."

"You can always leave if you're not happy."

"Oh my God, Birdie! You honestly think I have an active choice? I don't want to live here anymore than you want me here. I'm so jealous of Jack." Her voice cracked. "He gets to leave and has three weeks of freedom every month, while I'm stuck working and single parenting and feeling your hatred for me radiating off you every time we're in the same room."

Birdie stayed seated and silent, but a red flush crawled up her neck and pinked her cheeks.

The microwave beeped and Lucy turned as much to avoid looking at her mother-in-law as to retrieve her dinner. She knew she'd just crossed a line and there was no going back. Jack, who was already angry with her, would tip into furious for upsetting his mother. He'd side with Birdie. She could hear him now—"Are you determined to make our lives even more miserable?" If Izzy's guest room had been habitable, Lucy would be packing a bag and asking if she could stay a few days.

The heat from the microwave container was burning her hands. When she turned around, Birdie was on her feet with a bottle of wine in one hand and cheese in the other.

"I'll eat this in my room," Lucy said.

"I'd prefer it if you didn't."

The tightly spoken words sliced into her. Jack had told her that when he and Sienna were teens, Birdie had been militant about no food in bedrooms.

Lucy didn't hide her sigh. "The garage then."

"No."

"No?"

Birdie poured two glasses of sauv blanc. "I'd like you to eat here with me."

Lucy narrowed her eyes, uncertain where this was leading. "So you can berate me further?"

Birdie handed her the glass of wine and sat, every part of her slumping. "I'm stuck too, Lucy. Nothing about my life is how I pictured it either. I hate that I'm angry and difficult all the time. I hate that Mike is as absent as Jack, but more so, and I'm angry he's leaving me to deal with everything."

Lucy didn't know what to say so she took a slug of wine.

"I'm seeing a counselor," Birdie said.

The wine shot up her nose and Birdie gave her a wry smile. "I know, unexpected. I'm still surprised by it myself and it's been confronting. She asked me if being so hard on you was me trying to force some control over something when I have so little over everything else."

Lucy realized for the first time how the fallout of Elite had given her and Birdie unwanted things in common. "And?"

Birdie met her gaze and blew out a breath. "And I think she's right. Sharing my house with another woman isn't easy."

Lucy felt she had nothing to lose. "Especially with one you don't really like."

"Oh, Lucy, it's not that." Misery pulled at Birdie's mouth. "We're different generations. I find it hard to think of you and Jack as adults. You've always lurched from one disaster to another. First Rigby—"

"Rigby's not a disaster!" Dear God, how long was Birdie going to hold onto this? "Yes, the pregnancy was unexpected, but that was *four* years ago! And we weren't teens. I was twenty-seven. What's more responsible than committing to each other and raising a child?"

Birdie glanced down at her hands for a long time. "It's not just Rigby. Charys explained I shouldn't blame you for Mike's heart attack. That it would have happened anyway. And I'm trying hard to do that, but ..." She raised her head, her face drawn. "The personal loan rocked us to our core."

Lucy breathed deeply, quelling the urge to yell. "Jack and I made a *joint* decision based on the returns we'd been receiving from Elite. How is that any different than you and Mike investing your retirement fund? We all thought Fortune was a safe bet."

"And we were all wrong! We should never have done it. We should have protected you and Jack. God, we've got years of life experience. We should have known better. Realized it was all too good to be true."

Lucy couldn't ignore the anguish on her mother-in-law's face and suddenly things started making some sort of misguided sense.

"Oh, Birdie. You might see us as kids, but we're not. We're more than grown and it's not your job to protect us." As Lucy heard her words, the juxtaposition backhanded her, hard. "But you're protecting us by letting us live here even though you resent us being here."

"I don't resent—"

Lucy held up her hand. "I feel that you do."

A look reminiscent of Rigby when he'd been caught doing something he shouldn't crossed Birdie's face.

"Rightly or wrongly, there are too many days when I feel like I'm the only person keeping this ship afloat," Birdie said. "And the truth is, I liked having a sewing room and a garage for my car, and a quiet and tidy house. We didn't just lose all our money, I lost my freedom." Birdie spun her wedding ring. "And perhaps I'm a bit jealous of you."

"I can't see why."

"We both have to work, but you have a profession you love and it fulfils you. I have a job that numbs my mind."

As much as Lucy found Birdie difficult, and she certainly hadn't appreciated the almost gleeful way Birdie had told her about the job at the IGA, she'd always begrudgingly admired the way her mother-in-law got on with things. Especially when Mike had checked out for months.

"You deserve a medal for putting up with Deidre," Lucy offered as an olive branch.

"Hah!" Birdie sipped her wine. "Thank you."

Emboldened by this strange conversation, Lucy said, "I miss having my own house and my own space too. So much so it aches, here." She pointed to her solar plexus. "Every day I feel like a failure as a mother because we've stressed Rigby so much he's regressed. I hate that Jack and I made decisions that lost us the house and imposed us on you and Mike when you're struggling too. I hate that Jack and I can't agree on the best next step and—"

She gnawed at the cuticle on her thumb, then rubbed her face, suddenly bewildered and exhausted. "I probably shouldn't tell you this, but right now I'm absolutely terrified Jack and I aren't going to survive this. Rigby doesn't deserve so much failure. No child does."

She drained her wine glass as if it was water.

Birdie refilled it. "You're a very good mother."

Stunned, Lucy blinked, unable to find words.

"I mean that, Lucy. You are. I never had to juggle a job and children, let alone shift work. I probably should have stopped cleaning and played with my kids more. Sienna's mentioned it more than once. I think it's why that girl never dusts."

Lucy laughed, then stopped herself. "Sorry."

Birdie shrugged. "I've always liked things just so, my way. Losing everything's made me cling to that even more. The counselor mentioned OCD, but I don't think I'm that bad, am I?"

"Before we lost the house, you used to clean our place whenever you visited."

"To help you and Jack," Birdie said indignantly. "Because you're both so busy and the house was so big."

Disquiet rippled through Lucy. But as this was the most honest conversation she'd ever had with Birdie she may as well say it. "I thought it meant you didn't think I could keep a house clean. I've always felt you didn't approve of the house." *Or me.*

"Mike and I were surprised by the house. We thought you'd overextended."

"We hadn't. We had a budget."

Lucy vividly remembered the day they'd invited Birdie and Mike over to see the finished renovations and Birdie's lackluster reaction to the décor, new furnishings and crockery.

"I worked extra shifts to cover the cost of decorating the house and I hunted down bargains on Facebook Marketplace," she said. "The sofa was a store demonstration model so it was marked down and I renovated the scuffs on the leather. I didn't buy the new-season china I really wanted because I couldn't justify that sort of money, so I bought the clearance design from the outlet store."

"Why didn't you tell us that?" Birdie sounded genuinely baffled. "I thought you'd spent money you didn't have."

It was time to draw a line in the sand and show Birdie she truly was an adult.

"I didn't have to tell you, Birdie. Just like you didn't have to ask my advice about buying a travel trailer."

For a moment the only sounds in the kitchen were the ticking of the clock and the low burr of the fridge.

Eventually, Birdie sighed. "You have a point. You didn't owe me an explanation and I shouldn't have leaped to conclusions. It's going to take me time to truly learn that you and Jack aren't kids."

Lucy felt the woman's struggle and respected her for trying hard to change thirty years of mothering.

"But mostly I didn't tell you because I was embarrassed we had to be so frugal," she added.

"Oh, Lucy." Birdie sounded pained. "I don't know if it's a generational thing or something else, but when Mike and I started out, I prided myself on a quality bargain. You should too."

Lucy shrugged. "I just wanted to forget how every dollar was precious and pretend I'd paid full price. Ironic, right, given everything that's happened."

"We all have moments like that. What was I thinking when I chose Queen class on the cruise? We didn't need a butler."

"Hindsight's a bitch for sure."

They both sipped their wine and then Birdie suddenly straightened in her chair. "You and Jack ... what you said before ... He loves you."

"Right now I'm not so sure."

"Right now I'm not sure that Mike and I like who we are, but that's separate from love. At least I think it is. I'll keep you posted on that."

Lucy felt like she was in a parallel universe. She and Birdie had never spoken so openly before. It was both discombobulating and freeing.

"I think Mike's happier now than he was," she said.

"And you had a part to play in that." Birdie screwed up her face for a moment. "I'm not proud that I got angry when I found out he'd listened to you about the workshop. I'd been making similar suggestions for months."

Lucy traced a bubble of condensation around the base of her glass. "I get that. You're working really hard and Mike fell apart and he hasn't been easy to live with. We lost the house, but you lost your retirement dream and got us instead. I know how much you were looking forward to traveling."

"Thank you." Birdie reached out and touched Lucy's hand. "You never say much about your family, and I know you think we're too close to Jack—"

"It's not that exactly." Lucy had never explained her relationship with her parents because it hurt. "Before Elite crashed and burned, I loved how Rigby had hands-on grandparents in you and Mike, because my parents—well, they love the idea of Rigby more than the reality."

"They sound busy with their younger children."

"Yeah." Lucy took in a breath. "And I did appreciate your help." Birdie shot her a skeptical look and Lucy felt the arrow hit with accuracy. "Fair enough. There were times when I felt judged and I was less than appreciative."

"And as hard as it is to admit it, there were times when the judgment was there, but I hope it was less often than you believe." Birdie fiddled with the edge of the placemat. "There have been many times since the crash that I've felt taken for granted in my own home."

For the first time Lucy saw the opposing side to Birdie's anger— sorrow and sadness—and she stepped out of her own bubble of pain. "I'm sorry there were times I made you feel that way."

"Thank you. But you're not alone. Mike's an expert and Jack has his moments." Birdie leaned back. "I think it should be carved in stone that parents and adult children never live under the same roof. No one has privacy and all couples need that. But Lucy, this is where duty and the ideal clash. I apologize for saying 'move out.' I should never have said it. I couldn't live with myself if you and Jack moved and it put you under more financial strain. No parent wishes that on their children."

"But you don't really want to live with me."

"Not just you, honey. Everyone! I daydream about running away and a couple of weeks ago I did for a few hours, except no one noticed." Birdie laughed. "But I ran into Charys from cardiac rehab at the wetlands and I think it was the universe giving me a hard slap. I didn't enjoy the conversation, but I needed it. She suggested the counselor. She also suggested we have a household meeting of four adults living in a share house and work out a cleaning, cooking and gardening roster."

"I like that idea. Having set jobs with set times would be a relief."

"That's the plan anyway." Birdie's mouth curved into a tired smile. "I've got a few more sessions with the counselor and I can't say I enjoy them, but I know I need them. Otherwise I risk losing you, Jack and Rigby."

"You'll never lose Jack." Lucy couldn't completely hide the tinge of resentment, despite not wanting Birdie and Jack to fall out.

"Unless I change my ways, I think I'm close. I've done far too much complaining to him lately and that's why I can tell he loves you, Lucy. He puts you first."

Lucy started. "It doesn't always feel like it. We've argued a lot about you."

Birdie rubbed her face. "I think he's been trying to walk a tightrope of pleasing both of us."

"And failing."

Birdie shrugged. "I didn't put him in an easy position. The counselor pointed out I was lucky to have him for twenty-six years and now his allegiance is with you, as it should be. As Mike's was to me when we first got married. I always vowed I'd be nothing like Marjorie Essen, but … Mothers and sons, Lucy. You'll understand one day. As you say, you and Jack are adults and I have to step back. I'm trying hard, but it's early days and I'm going to make mistakes."

"And it's hard with us living here."

"Harder. But a mother should only want her child to be happy. And although I haven't wanted to acknowledge it lately, you and Jack work well as a team. You make him happy."

Lucy's heart tore. "Not at the moment. We can't seem to agree on anything so we've stopped trying. We haven't spoken in two weeks. Sometimes he's stubborn to the point of …" She threw up her hands, unable to think of an analogy.

Birdie laughed, the sound knowing. "Absolute frustration?" she offered. "He gets that from Mike."

This time it was Lucy who raised her brows.

Birdie laughed. "Fair enough." She was thoughtful for a moment. "You probably won't like this, but I think you and I are similar in more ways than we care to admit. We also both have husbands who've put their heads in the sand."

"I'm not sure Jack's done that."

"No? Jack knows you're unhappy living here but he's sticking doggedly to his original plan, which might see you still here in six months or a year's time."

A rush of goosebumps raced across Lucy's skin. "It's why we're arguing so much."

"Why do you think I'm working at the IGA?" Birdie asked. "I thought Mike and I would start doing things to help dig us out of this mess, but even when he was given the all clear by the doctor, he did nothing."

Birdie hacked into a wheel of cheese. "I sometimes think women deal better with a crisis than men, because we've spent years making sure our kids are fed and safe and warm. I look at the images of women with children in war zones and see on their faces what they endure trying to keep their children safe. Protecting those we love is ingrained and we're driven to keep doing it. It's why I get up every morning and just keep going."

This evening was the most revealing conversation Lucy had ever shared with Birdie. "I read somewhere once that women are the emotional heartbeat of the family."

Birdie nodded. "We are and it's time our men stepped up and valued it."

Good luck with that. Although Lucy instantly chided herself because Mike was finally showing signs of re-engaging in life—he'd finished making the train station and was puddling with making some wooden trees. He'd also read to Rigby when Lucy had suggested to her son, "Take a book to Gramps."

"Has Mike seen your counselor too?" she asked. Birdie rolled her eyes. "Right. Stupid question."

"Not stupid at all and I'm sure it would help him, but you know what he's like." Birdie shrugged. "And I can't change that. But I can change me, so that's what I'm concentrating on. Now that things with

Judy are ..." She gave herself a shake. "I need new interests. I've decided I'm going to volunteer at the Irish festival."

Lucy laughed—half-amused and half-dismayed.

"What? You don't think I can do it?"

"Oh, no, you'd be great and they'd be lucky to have you." Lucy tested the waters of this new version of her mother-in-law and their fledgling relationship. "Especially your cleaning skills."

"Ha, ha, very funny."

"There's just two things you should know before you sign up."

"Oh?"

"I've already signed up, but I'm sure we can ask to be rostered to different events. I don't want to rain on your 'me time.'"

"That's both kind and wise," Birdie said. "What's the other thing?"

"I'm just checking you know who the event coordinator is this year."

"No idea. I was going to get the number off the posters that have sprung up around town."

"It's Izzy." Birdie's face paled and Lucy rushed on. "Brad screwed her over as badly as he did us. She's sharing the old Whitehead cottage with half of Glingilly's wildlife."

"I thought she'd be living with Judy and Bevan?"

"No."

Birdie was quiet for a long time. "I never said, but at the funeral when Judy and I ... Izzy tried to help me up. She said it wasn't worth it."

"And she'd know." Lucy worried the inside of her cheek. "You know how we've been at odds? Well, I totally misjudged Izzy for two years. I always thought she was stuck-up and superior, but she's shy and finds being the center of attention incredibly stressful. She's actually kind and caring, and she's beating herself up that she had no idea what Brad was up to."

"So she's part of our club."

Lucy wasn't certain what Birdie was getting at. "As in having our lives upended by Elite? Or women being let down by men? Or ...?"

"All of the above." Birdie smiled. "Izzy always threw great events. I'll happily work for her at the festival."

Later that night, Lucy lay in bed with her mind spinning from all of Birdie's revelations. She was familiar with angry patients with chips on their shoulders, and she knew how people clung to their rage rather than choosing the hard and often terrifying path of change. But Birdie wanted to try—wanted to do things differently.

Lucy's thoughts turned toward herself. Since the crash, she'd allowed Jack to make all the decisions about the house and their lives—but Birdie was right. Not only was his plan no longer working for them, it was tearing them apart. If they had a hope of surviving their post-Elite life, they needed a new plan. But it had to be one that Jack could see working for them or he'd cling tenaciously to the old one and sink them both. All she had to do was think of a new strategy.

Hah! Hadn't they already spent hours going around in circles and pulling up blank. In the inky blackness of the midnight hour, creating world peace seemed easier than finding a new way forward.

She must have finally fallen asleep because suddenly she lurched out of it, heart pounding.

"Mommy!" Rigby cried. "Mom-eee!"

She looked at the clock: 3:00 a.m. She sighed and swung her feet out of bed. She'd bet her last dollar he was lying in a wet bed, cold and shivering.

When she opened the door she blinked twice, but the image didn't change. Birdie stood at Rigby's door.

"Go back to sleep," she said. "I'll settle him. You've got work at 7:00."

For the first time in months, Lucy wanted to hug her.

CHAPTER THIRTY-SEVEN

Izzy lay snuggled in a blanket on a picnic blanket in the middle of the field behind the cottage, looking up into the night sky. It was a crescent moon, perfect for stargazing, and although she now lived closer to town than she had at Villefranche, the light pollution was minimal.

She reached out her arm and tugged on the cuff of Cooper's chinos. "What can you see?"

"Venus."

She laughed. "I can see that with the naked eye."

"I can see Mars."

"Jupiter?"

"Hmm."

"That's bloke talk for no, right?"

He pulled his eye from the telescope and stretched out his hand to hers. She counter-tugged and he dropped down next to her. "Be kind, it's 1:00 in the morning."

When Izzy had told Cooper about her telescope and her love of stars, he'd insisted on coming out with her.

"But are you really interested?" she'd asked.

He'd cocked his head as if he couldn't believe her question. "I'm interested because you are. Anyway, you came fishing with me when you thought you wouldn't enjoy it."

"Yes, but there was a sunrise on offer."

"I thought it was the lure of breakfast," he teased.

"It totally was, but stargazing only offers the chill of the small hours."

He'd grinned at her. "Perfect. We'll have to snuggle up to keep warm."

Cooper was the first bloke she'd ever gone out with who loved to cuddle. Then again, they had started dating during an icy southern Victorian spring. Come summer, it might all change. Come summer, she'd be gone.

The weather had conveniently obliged for stargazing on a Friday night. Cooper had arrived with a portable barbecue and steaks— "Thought we could do with a change from salmon"—and Izzy had contributed the salad and baked potatoes. Full of Angus beef and a full-bodied cabernet shiraz, they'd fallen asleep on the sofa until Izzy's alarm had woken them. The nippy hike across the field dodging cow pats in the dark, along with Thor's enthusiasm for the night walk, had chased away sleep.

Now, Izzy checked her watch. "Okay, can you find Orion's belt."

He picked up her hand and pointed with it. "The saucepan, right?"

"Correct." She moved their hands down about thirty-five degrees. "That red supergiant star is Betelgeuse. It's where we watch for some meteor action."

"I'm told the Orionids move fast and are trapped in the debris from Halley's Comet," Cooper said in his professorial tone.

She laughed. "You're told?"

"I might have consulted the internet."

"Well, lie back and count."

"What about the telescope?"

"We'll use it later. The first time we can enjoy the show from here."

Izzy always found watching the Orionids to be a bit like a peripheral vision test—pinpricks of light dashing fast across the sky.

"There!" She hauled their hands to point.

"Where?"

"They're fast. Keep your eyes fixed here."

"Okay but—Oh! Magic!"

"That's two."

"Three."

Sometime later, they'd counted sixteen.

"Is that a lot?" Cooper asked, his body spooned in next to hers.

"It's up there. It's possible to see twenty in an hour, but they move so fast they're easy to miss. Want to try the telescope now you know what you're looking for?"

He nuzzled her neck. "That would mean moving and I'm quite comfortable here with you."

His words rumbled through her, detonating pockets of desire and releasing a rush of need that heated her from head to toe. She rolled into him and kissed him, reveling in the way his mouth roved over hers and lit her up.

His hand slid under her puffer jacket and found the band of her sweater and then his fingers were skimming her skin and skating along her spine and she was arching in against him. He groaned.

Without breaking the kiss, he pulled at his own jacket as she pushed at his shoulders, hating all the layers that separated them. She ripped his shirt out of his waistband and pushed her hands against his belly, soaking in his heat.

He rolled her under him and pushed up her sweater and camisole before kissing her from her collarbone to the top of her leggings. She was limp with longing and just the anticipation of his mouth and tongue on her almost made her come. When his fingers peeled back the wide band of lycra, cold air hit her and her eyes shot open. The stars blinked at her and Brad's voice—so clear and loud—boomed in her head.

Babe, there's nothing like sex under the stars.

"Stop!" Her hands gripped Cooper's forearms like vices.

Thor barked and raced to her side, a guard on duty.

Cooper's lips had left her skin even before Thor's growl. It was too dark to see his face but she heard his ragged panting.

"Sorry," she heard herself saying as she tried to banish Brad's face. "I'm sorry."

He rolled onto his back. "No, I should have checked. I thought being spontaneous under a glorious starlit sky might give me some street cred on the boring scale."

She patted around in the dark until she found his hand. "You have to let that comment of your ex's go. You're not boring. You're ..." She searched for words. "Methodical and thorough."

He laughed, the sound wry. "You're not quite selling it, Izzy."

She hated that her issue had raised his and yet she didn't really want to go into why.

"How about this then? I want to have sex with you."

"O-kay." He didn't sound convinced. "But you said stop." When she didn't say anything, he added, "If it's contraception, I've got that covered."

"You always travel with a condom?"

"Ever since you kissed me on the beach."

"So for two weeks you've thought you were in with a chance?"

"Not expecting, just hoping." He squeezed her hand. "Want to tell me what's going on inside that big brain of yours?"

She could imagine his face—serious and kind with a twinkle in the depths of his eyes. She didn't want to hurt him. "You won't like it."

"Maybe, but I need to know."

She sighed. "As much as I appreciate your spontaneous and romantic idea of sex under the stars, I can't do it here."

He was silent for a few beats. "I don't mind where we have sex, Izzy, but when you said stop, you sounded frantic. Almost scared. I need to know why so I understand."

She pulled her hand out of his and hugged herself. "It's Brad."

"Ah." Resignation filled the space between them.

Panic skittered and her blood pounded in her ears. "No, Cooper, it's not that. I told you the truth, we were over months ago. It's just ... He had this thing. I don't know if it was a fetish or what, but it became a bit of an obsession." She took a deep breath. "He got off on having sex outside, and I don't want him in my head when I have sex with you. I don't want him anywhere near us."

"That's easily fixed, Izzy. I sure as hell don't want his ghost hovering over us either. I've got enough performance anxiety as it is."

She laughed, grateful for his understanding but bemused by his concern. "Why are you worried?"

"Because you're the most intelligent woman I've dated."

Warmth flooded her and she treasured his words. Brad and her father had always told her she was beautiful first, and with Brad her looks had become a commodity she hated.

"I bet you say that to all the girls," she teased.

She saw a flash of white teeth in the dark—Cooper's grin—and then he leaned in to kiss her.

Thor growled.

Cooper groaned and pulled back. "Between Quinn and your dog, I may never be allowed to touch you again."

"Thor, sit." She stroked her dog's head, feeling the reassuring roughness of his coat. "So what now?"

"We could watch the Orionids' next show."

Disappointment slugged her. "Or we could go to your place."

"Yours is a lot closer."

"We'll have the thundering company of possums and a wombat."

"As long as Quinn and Thor are locked out and you're in the bed with me, I really don't care."

She shot to her feet and started dismantling the telescope.

The next morning, Izzy woke up in a tangle of limbs and felt the blissful warmth of a body that was longer and broader than her dog's. Cooper's breath stroked her ear and his arm lay between her breasts, the pressure reassuring as it nestled her into him as if they were two pieces of a puzzle. She sighed, content for the first time in over a year. For all Cooper's talk of performance pressure, he'd been a generous lover, putting her needs first. Delight tangoed through her as she revisited the memory.

His lips pressed a kiss to her shoulder. "Morning."

She kissed his hand, then rolled over to face him. He was all sleep-tousled hair and a white smile line was creasing through his dark stubble.

"How did you sleep?" she asked.

"Best sleep I've had in months. You?"

She stroked his cheek. "Same. No nightmares."

His mouth curved into a grin. "We might have to experiment again tonight. You know, to rule out any variants."

She laughed as desire arrowed through her. "What about the cumulative effect?"

"Now you're talking."

He kissed her long and deep and she rolled into him, wanting exactly what he was offering. This time when she came, she gave in to need and cried out.

Thor barked then whined on the other side of the door.

"It's okay, Thor," Izzy gasped, then laughed at the crazy situation.

Panting, Cooper fell back. "Right up until last night, I thought he liked me."

"He does. He's just a bit protective."

"I'll let him in so he knows you're safe."

Cooper got out of bed, fished up his boxer briefs from the floor and opened the door. Thor blasted in like a rocket and bounded onto the bed. He licked Izzy's face, then turned and gave Cooper a triumphant bark.

"We'll have a man-to-man talk later, Thor," Cooper said. "I'll make us a cuppa. Do you have any cookies?"

At the word "cookie," Thor jumped off the bed.

"In the pantry in the red tin."

Thor eagerly followed Cooper out of the bedroom and Izzy slid back under the covers, boneless and happy.

Cooper returned five minutes later with two steaming mugs and the red biscuit box. "Your pantry mousetraps were busy overnight."

"Ugh! They always are."

He'd pulled on a shirt and sweater but his legs were bare and when he got back into bed he placed his icy cold feet on hers.

Izzy shrieked. "And to think I was going to cook you breakfast."

Cooper laughed as she leaned forward to pile the covers over their feet.

"What's that?" he asked.

Izzy glanced around. Her bedroom was basic—bed, bedside table, book, lamp, water bottle, closet and a chest of drawers. She checked the cornices for spiders. "What?"

"This?"

She felt his hand land lightly on the back of her head and froze. *Stupid, stupid, stupid!* It was the first time he'd seen her without a beanie or a cap on her head, or her hair in an updo.

"God, don't tell me this house has given me lice?" Her voice quivered with the lie.

Seriously? You're hiding behind head lice? Eww!

"I don't think you get head lice from a house," Cooper said.

Izzy felt him put down his mug and then his fingers were in her hair and gently cupping her skull. Every part of her screamed to run, but where? For all its sins the cottage was her home, and she knew Cooper well enough to know that if she bolted he'd follow to check what was going on.

"I can't see any lice," he said. "It's like the hair's missing in this one spot. Does it hurt?"

"No." Shame battered her. She'd managed to hide her trichotillomania from Brad, but it had never been quite this bad.

Distract him! Tell him it was rubbed away by the cap.

That doesn't even make any sense!

Panic collided with humiliation. Everything with Cooper was all so new and shiny and this would taint it. Taint them. Mark her as unwell.

You started from a place of tarnish with him when he doubted you over Elite. He was with you when you found Brad.

As sweat pooled under her arms and her mind churned with trepidation, she felt Cooper's lips lightly brush her bald patch then stroke it tenderly. His hands fell away.

"You've been through a lot, Izzy. You should probably get it checked out just to make sure it's nothing sinister."

She sat rigid, her limbs paralyzed. Behind her she felt the mattress shift as he adjusted his position and then she heard him sipping his tea and crunching into a cookie.

"Do you have plans today?" he asked. "Or do you want to spend it together?"

He's changed the topic. You're off the hook!

She blew out a breath knowing she'd just dodged a bullet.

As she settled back on the pillows she glimpsed myriad emotions bright in his eyes—everything from lust and wonder to care and concern—and knew she was wrong. The bullet was still racing fast toward her. It wouldn't hit today, but it would eventually rip into her.

In a week or so he'd ask her if she'd had the check-up. If she said no he'd remind her it was a good idea. If she said yes and the bald patch was nothing to worry about, he'd ask for the medical explanation. In-between, he'd likely consult Doctor Google.

Despite knowing she'd be long gone from Glingilly in six months time, something told her that whatever this was between them, she'd be foolish to start with a lie that would be quickly unmasked.

"Trichotillomania." The word exploded into the air with more force than she'd intended.

Cooper blinked at the seven syllables. "A word game before breakfast? Crikey, that's hardcore."

In any other situation she would have laughed, but she was too terrified to do anything other than get this admission over with. "No.

The bald patch. It's trichotillomania. I—" She licked her dry lips. "I pull out my hair."

He set down his mug again and turned to face her. "Okay."

"Okay?" She didn't know what she'd been expecting, but it wasn't this. "It's far from okay! The diagnosis has the word 'mania' in it! I'm so crazy, I rip out my hair."

Cooper's face had turned from open to wary. She caught the moment he bit off another "okay." "You're not crazy, Izzy."

"You're not a medical doctor."

"No argument there," he said, sounding infuriatingly calm.

Agitation spun so fast inside her it burned and her breath came short and hard. Thor, ever hopeful of another biscuit, had settled on Cooper's knees, but now he crawled into Izzy's lap. Desperate to keep her hands busy and away from her hair, she stroked his fur, but it didn't soothe her like pulling hair did.

"Do you really want to tell me, Izzy?" Cooper asked quietly. "Because it sounds like you don't."

She hated how he'd recognized her second thoughts and wondered if she should accept his offer to stop now. But that horse had bolted—she'd already named her condition and it would always hang between them.

"All I want to do right this second is pull out some hair and welcome the calm it gives me," she said. "But at the same time I hate that I want to do it and I hate that I give in to it so often. I mean it's nuts. I know it's nuts, right?"

His face was a mix of kindness and concern. "It sounds complicated."

Her anger faded. "Yeah. It is."

"Will a hug help you feel calmer?"

"I have no idea."

"We could give it a shot."

She sighed and moved into his arms. They wrapped around her and his hands settled on her spine. Her agitation hurled itself against the reassuring pressure like storm waves pounding on the sand. The urge to pull at her hair stayed strong.

"Am I allowed to ask any questions?" Cooper said.

"Maybe."

"Perhaps it might be better if you tell me what you feel comfortable sharing."

A rush of emotion had her blinking back tears. "You're too nice."

"Yeah, I know." His mouth pulled down on one side. "Boring and nice. The double whammy of dull."

She pressed her lips to his chin. "I'm a new convert to those character traits. I'm starting to think they might be a lot safer for me."

He frowned. "What do you mean?"

Could she do it? Tell him?

You committed to that when you told him you have trich.

She thought she might be able to manage it if she didn't look at him so she turned in his arms. With her back against his chest, his chin resting on her shoulder and his arms cradling her, she gazed out the window, barely noticing the vivid yellow of the canola crop.

"Before I met Brad, my father was the most exciting person I knew. He had this way of walking into a room and switching it on, illuminating it with his enthusiasm. People gravitated to him, wanting to be part of his dynamic aura. He had this way of making you feel like you were the only person in the room."

Just like Brad.

"My earliest memory is sitting in front of him on the carousel at Luna Park, feeling the horse rising up and down, listening to the calliope, being dazzled by the lights and knowing he was right there, keeping me safe. Every time the ride ended I'd beg for another and, unlike my mother, he always said, 'Anything for my princess.'"

"Sounds like a wonderful memory," Cooper said.

"Yeah." It came out on a sigh. "It is."

"I'm sensing a but."

"Oh, yeah. There are lots of those. The first time things collapsed, I was eight."

She took a breath and kept going. "My dad pretty much ran away with the circus when he was seventeen. He did motorcycle stunts using fire and jumps—daredevil stuff. By the time I was born he'd left the circus far behind him and was a live events entrepreneur. Everything from circuses to magic then theater spectaculars. He brought out some big shows from Las Vegas and later he did live music events. *Rock On the River* was him."

"I have the T-shirt."

She heard the smile in Cooper's voice and couldn't imagine him at a three-day rock concert. "You went?"

"Once, when I was at uni. It wasn't really me, but I was twenty and chasing a girl. Turns out she was chasing a musician so ... Anyway, back to you."

Izzy bit her lip—she'd enjoyed the diversion. "Some of Dad's events earned him the big bucks and some lost him more money than he had. My childhood was a series of booms and busts. The booms were like living in an animated Disney movie without the scary bits—all vivid colors and toe-tapping music and endless gifts. He brought the circus to my seventh birthday."

"I'm guessing the busts weren't quite as magical?" Cooper said.

"They definitely had their own rhythm. My mother left us each time. Dad sold everything, we moved, and he fell into a mire of depression while I learned the indignities of living on the breadline, standing in line at the food bank and generally just surviving. Dad would eventually rise again, find new backers and pull off another success or three. That's when my mother returned. She always came back—until she didn't. The last time she left I was sixteen and I've not heard from her since."

"Shit, Izzy. That's ..."

"Hard? Horrible? Horrendous? It was all of that and more. I was the kid who was constantly thrown into adulthood then pushed back to being a kid and hauled out again. I hated my mother for leaving Dad when he needed her most. I hated that she was only ever around for the good times."

"Hated? Is that past tense?"

"Sort of. Lately, after everything with Brad, I've got some insight into why she left for good. I just can't forgive her for leaving me."

Cooper hugged her tightly and pressed a kiss into her hair, his empathy flowing into her. It was enough support to get her to the hardest part of the story.

"Dad brought out the Black Bears from the US and backed the Australian and New Zealand tour. He was convinced it was his big comeback, and early ticket sales were great."

Cooper stiffened behind her and she was surprised he'd remembered. Then again, the lead singer's drug-fueled diatribes and Nazi sentiments had been splashed across the national headlines.

"Wasn't Damon Leroy deported?"

"He was, and Dad shot himself at home." She had no control over the shudder that started at her toes and ratcheted up her body until she shook all over. "I found him."

"And you found Quinn. Jesus, Izzy. No wonder you're pulling out your hair."

An ugly laugh erupted from her. The hair-pulling had been her solace since her father's first bust and had waxed and waned ever since. With sudden clarity she now recognized a pattern. During the good times, when her father lavished her and her mother with presents— everything from clothes and jewelry to technology and experiences like helicopter skiing and diving—the need to pull out her hair was almost dormant, only rising again when her parents began inevitably to argue over money.

Her thoughts turned to the early days with Brad and the gifts he'd given her. How she'd believed they represented his love. How they'd made her feel secure in the relationship. She gasped, tears spilling, and reached for her hair.

Cooper didn't stall her hand but he moved in front of her. "What is it?"

The sting of her hair leaving her head short-circuited her pain and she swiped the tears off her cheeks with the hem of the sheet.

"I've just had one of those moments when I realize how much I've messed up my life."

A deep line scored the space between Cooper's brows. "Judging by what you've told me, I think it's fair to say that your parents have contributed a fair whack. I never thought I'd say this, but I've got a new respect for my stable and uneventful childhood."

He brushed her cheek with his thumb. "I'm not sure the sorts of highs and lows you've experienced are healthy, Izzy. It sounds incredibly unreliable and stressful."

She heaved in an almighty sniff, then grimaced. "Sorry. That's pretty gross."

Cooper shrugged. "I've done worse watching *Toy Story 3*."

She mustered a wobbly smile. "I think I've spent years confusing money and expensive gestures with emotional safety."

"Lucky for you there's no fear of over-the-top and expensive gestures from me," he teased. A frown followed. "Too early?"

"Little bit."

"Sorry." He settled back behind her and cocooned her with his body. "Have you ever talked about this stuff with anyone?"

"Besides you? Not really. There was a disastrous session with the school counselor after my mother left for good, but all she managed to do was exacerbate my shame about the trich. To be honest, when Dad died, I just wanted to forget and move on. I sort of managed that for a while, but since Brad ... it's all come back."

"I bet." Cooper sounded slightly distracted, like his brain was churning through facts. "My skill lies firmly in numbers, Izzy, not psychology. But when I wasn't sleeping I found talking to that counselor helped. She gave me some stress-management tips and they work more often than not." His fingers massaged her shoulders. "Maybe think about seeing someone?"

Usually the thought of baring her soul saw her hands reaching for her hair and this time was no different. Except her brain wasn't racing away from the suggestion—it was more of a slow jog.

"You mean find a better way to deal with my anxiety than ripping out my hair?"

"If you think it will improve your life, then yes, absolutely." He was quiet again for a bit. "And Izzy?"

Bubbles of worry popped inside her like corn and she had to consciously force out a "Yes?"

"I don't think you're nuts or crazy or manic, or any of those things you said. I think you've dealt with more than your fair share of trauma and you're remarkable for having survived, qualified and carved out a successful career. You should be immensely proud of that. But life can be far more than survival mode, Izzy. You deserve to be happy."

I need you, Izzy. Don't leave me, Izzy.

Both her father and Brad had always made her life about them. Their only nods to her happiness were a parade of gifts that came with demands and expectations. Yet Cooper was telling her that she deserved to be happy. No one had ever said that to her before.

Did she deserve to be happy?

God, she wanted to be.

She wanted to be free of the shame that came with pulling out her hair. Free of the need to hide her secret so she didn't see the recoil then disapproval in people's eyes. She wanted to be free of the legacy of the two men who'd professed to love her, but had loved money, the chase of it and what she could do for them more.

Gratitude at Cooper's words swelled inside her. "Thank you." It came out wobbly.

"You're welcome." He kissed her. Thor, who was now at the door, barked. "Your dog needs a walk and I'm starving. Let's walk into town and have breakfast."

"Breakfast in Glingilly is way more public than hiding out in Port Fairy," Izzy said. "I can't promise you people won't give me a hard time and make you feel uncomfortable."

"Let me worry about my feelings, Izzy."

She didn't know what to do with that so she said, "Also, you can't keep buying me breakfast when I can't afford to reciprocate."

"One day in the not-too-distant future, you'll be back on your feet and buying me the breakfast special."

It was a future she couldn't visualize. "Oh, and what exactly will I be doing?"

"Something that stretches your talents and invigorates you."

Izzy wished she shared Cooper's confidence.

CHAPTER THIRTY-EIGHT

BIRDIE WAS ABOUT to close down the till when Izzy Harrington appeared from the back of the store and stopped abruptly just shy of the conveyor belt. She was holding a bottle of milk and a can of dog food—likely an emergency food dash, because Birdie hadn't seen her in the IGA for months. Wariness radiated off the younger woman as she glanced around, clearly willing another employee to appear.

Birdie thought about what her counselor had said and readied herself to redirect any unwanted anger away from the situation, only to be surprised and thankful for the dull throb of fatalism. She thought about the hard, but beneficial conversation she'd had with Lucy. Izzy too had suffered by her association with Elite, but unlike Judy and Bevan, with their protection from the police, she'd stayed in town and faced the wrath of devastated people.

Now Izzy was rolling back her shoulders and advancing to the register, her mouth tweaked into what could only be described as a grim and determined smile.

"Hello, Birdie."

"Hello, Izzy. How are things?"

Izzy blinked. "Um, things are, um ..." Her hands fluttered toward the cap on her head before falling back to press palms down on the black belt. "Up and down. But I'm sure you're familiar with that."

"Absolutely." Birdie scanned the milk.

"How's Mr. Essen ... Mike?"

"He's ..." Birdie was going to say fine, which was her social default, but something about the solicitude in Izzy's eyes stopped her. "Physically, he's mostly recovered."

"Lucy said—" A stricken look crossed Izzy's face as if she'd just stepped into quicksand.

Birdie moved to reassure her. "It's okay. Lucy told me that you're friends now. I was shocked when I heard, but it does make a certain sense. We're all members of a club that no one else is in any hurry to join."

"Hah! That's one way of putting it. Lucy's helped me more than she knows."

"That's good to hear." Birdie scanned the dog food. "It's taken me too long to recognize her strengths."

"For some crazy reason our brains like to obsess on the negatives."

"That sounds very insightful."

Izzy shrugged. "I've just started seeing a therapist."

"Good idea. I have too." Ignoring the surprise on her face, Birdie said, "I hear you're looking for volunteers for the Irish festival. Do you think you could use me?"

Izzy's face lit up. "Oh my God, yes! You used to run the Devonshire tea tent at the show, didn't you? Would you do me the biggest favor and take on the Irish stew kitchen?"

The mention of the Devonshire tea tent instantly threw Birdie back to fun times with Judy—they'd run it together for years. This time she lost the struggle to keep anger and betrayal tossing around inside her like debris in the wind.

"I can't and won't work with Judy!"

"Oh, Birdie. No, of course you can't and I didn't mean that. Anyway Judy's—" Izzy moistened her lips. "she won't be part of the volunteer team, I can promise you that. But I can't guarantee she won't attend."

"I wish to hell they'd just move to New South Wales permanently." When Izzy didn't respond, Birdie said, "Can I choose my own team for the kitchen?"

"Sure!" Izzy's hands fluttered. "But the same works for the other volunteers."

Birdie laughed. "It's okay, Izzy. Lucy told me she's volunteering and we've already agreed that as we live together It's best not to work together."

"Sounds like a plan, but I hope you'll both come to the music marquee on the Saturday night for the volunteers' thank you."

Birdie considered her new relationship with Lucy. "We can certainly manage that."

"Awesome. It would be great if you can come to the next planning meeting, or I can meet you at the hall one day and run through things? Glingilly Country Meats is donating the beef, but I'm still chasing vegetables."

"I know Damien Doyle—I'll reach out. I'm sure he'll donate the spuds and carrots if he gets a sign and a mention in the sponsors' list."

Excitement skipped through Birdie at having a project that was nothing to do with Elite, the IGA or home.

Izzy reached around the Perspex divider and hugged her quickly, then moved back, clearly embarrassed. "Sorry. That was—"

"Lovely," Birdie said. "There was more appreciation in that hug than I've experienced in a while." She squeezed Izzy's hand. "And I need to thank you for trying to make me see reason at the funeral."

Izzy grimaced. "No, you don't. It was a challenging day."

Laughter burst out of Birdie. "That's one way of describing it. One of the hardest things is trying to reconcile the person you knew and believed was your best friend with the person who stole from you and is now hiding behind the protection of the police."

Izzy laughed, then sobered. "Oh, you're serious? You can't possibly think that the Quinns have police protection?"

"They know a lot of people and they have some influential friends with the power to protect them. I'm not the only Elite member who's been slapped with a restraining order. Oscar hired that bloke from Melbourne—you know, the one that survived that gangland shooting? The police told him to stay out of it."

"Because the fraud squad's still investigating. I'm sure that's just standard police procedure," Izzy said.

"Is it? It's taking a bloody long time and they haven't held a press conference in months. Oscar thinks Brad shipped our money overseas. I think he spent it. Either way, with the police in the Quinns' pocket it's impossible to get anything back, so I'm trying to leave it all behind and focus on the positives. And talking of positives, it's knock-off time, so give me seven dollars twenty for your groceries and I'll lock up the store."

When Birdie arrived home, the scent of meat, garlic and red wine wafted out to meet her. She found the slow cooker on the kitchen counter, top and tailed green beans in a microwave dish, and peeled potatoes resting in a bowl of water. Surprised, she glanced at the schedule on the fridge—it wasn't Lucy's night to cook, it was hers.

She heard the television fall silent, followed by Mike's footsteps. When he arrived in the kitchen he said, "Good, you're home."

The words were familiar and always came with the unspoken message of "Good, you'll cook dinner," but his smile was an unexpected addition.

Be fair. Once he always smiled at you like that.

"Is Lucy putting Rigby to bed?" she asked.

"No, she and Jack have gone to Warrnambool."

"Jack's home? He isn't due for three days."

"They flew him to Melbourne for some meetings and lucky for him they finished early. I thought he and Lucy could do with some time together so I offered to babysit."

Birdie wasn't sure what surprised her most—Mike noticing that things between Lucy and Jack were rugged or that he'd offered to mind Rigby.

"Did Lucy or Jack cook you dinner as a thank you?"

A sheepish look crossed his face. "I got Jack to show me how to do a pot roast. Turns out it's just chucking everything in the slow cooker and switching it on."

The shocks kept coming. Not knowing what to say, Birdie grabbed the saucepan and steamer to get the potatoes cooking.

"You sit, I'll do that," Mike said. "I would have started, but sometimes when you lock up you're home later."

She almost said, "Where's my husband and what did you do with him?" But it wasn't a joke—Mike had vanished months ago.

He turned on the stove, and Birdie opened the fridge and poured herself a glass of tonic water. She'd discovered that if she added lemon she could pretend it was a G&T, which lessened the sad fact that they couldn't afford to waste money on alcohol.

"Lucy said you're volunteering for the Irish festival." Mike sat opposite her. "Why didn't you say?"

"Would you be interested?"

His face tightened with offence. "Of course. We always used to talk about our day."

Her permanent resentment kicked hard. "You haven't asked me about my day in months."

"You don't make it easy, Bird. Most of the time you act like you don't need me and I'm no use to you."

"Need you?" She heard her incredulity whiz around the room. "Of course I bloody need you. I've needed you for months, but you checked out on me, the family, life!"

His mouth twisted but she couldn't tell if it was in anger or remorse. "I nearly died, Bird."

"I know. I was there watching. Terrified." She hadn't touched him in months, but whether it was muscle memory or something else entirely, she found herself reaching out until her hand rested on his arm. "But you didn't die."

"Sometimes I wish I had."

Her breath whooshed out of her lungs and it felt like she might never drag more in. "You can't mean that."

He shrugged. "There've been times when I did."

"But why? Jack and Lucy and the doctors gave you a second chance so you can see Rigby grow and ..." Her heart tore a little. *Spend time with me.*

Sadness ringed him like thick cloud. "I'm not sure I deserve a second chance."

"Don't say that."

"It's how I feel."

She struggled to absorb this news. "Every day?"

"A lot." He gripped her hand so tightly it hurt. "I hate how badly I fucked up everything. If I'd died, at least you'd have got the life insurance money. Instead, I've ruined your life."

She shook her head, not sure where to start tackling his irrational thoughts. "You haven't ruined my life."

One side of his mouth tweaked up. "You're working at the IGA."

"Hah!" It was the first hint of humor she'd heard from him in too long. "Please don't reinvent history, Mike. The truth is we made every Elite decision together. There were so many times we could have said no but we kept saying yes. We both jumped into Fortune together."

"But I should have—"

"No. Stop. I've been there and 'shoulds' are a direct line to misery and blame. I should know—I've been living it for months. And just like you, I've been making most people around me unhappy. 'shoulds' have no value for me anymore." She rubbed her thumbs over the back of his hands. "We did what we did because we believed it was the right thing to do. We wanted to help the kids, and then we wanted the freedom that plenty of money gives. Was that greedy? I don't know. I see people with more than us and no one considers them greedy. But again, those thoughts aren't going to serve us well either."

He stared at her. "When did you get so wise?"

"I've been seeing a counselor." His eyes widened in surprise. "One of us had to and I figured it wouldn't be you."

He flinched. "It's embarrassing. And it won't bring the money back. Oscar—"

"Is tilting at windmills. The police in Melbourne haven't found anything. The longer it takes the more I think Brad spent all the money long before we realized it was missing. If we want any peace, we need to accept that."

"I'm not there yet, Bird."

"Well, I hope you get there soon, because I don't want to be miserable or angry anymore. I want to like me again. I want to like you again."

He stood and put a knife in the potatoes. "They're cooked. I'll mash them with olive oil."

"Heart-healthy."

"Yeah." He smashed the potato masher into the saucepan, stopped and turned to her. "You don't like me?"

She shrugged. "Not lately. And be honest—since the restraining order, have you liked me?"

He sighed. "I found that hard. I blamed you for Bevan not talking to me."

Blamed. Past tense.

"Do you think I'm the only reason Bevan's not talking to you or anyone else?" Birdie said.

Mike grunted. "Lucy said the same thing."

"I have a new respect for our daughter-in-law."

He put the beans in the microwave and set the timer for far too long. Birdie almost said something, but she was starting to wonder if this meal was a peace offering of sorts so she stayed silent.

"They were our closest friends, Bird." Mike's voice cracked and his pain and confusion washed over her.

"I know, and it hurts like hell. But I can't think about the whys or hows of it anymore or it'll sink me. I'm exhausted by floundering. All I want is for the joy to return to this house and drive out the resentment and bitterness that's choking us. But Mike, we can only do that by looking forward instead of constantly lamenting the past."

He plonked pasta bowls onto the counter. "You accused me of sticking my head in the sand. Isn't that the same thing?"

She shook her head. "I accused you of inaction. There are things you can change and others you can't. We can't change the fact we lost our money and it ruined us financially. But constantly revisiting it and wishing it hadn't happened will destroy our lives."

She sipped her drink and lobbed the thought that had pestered her for weeks. "Do you want a divorce?"

Fear leaped into his eyes. "God, no. Do you?"

How did she say what she wanted without making demands and being accused of nagging? *The truth?*

She blew out a long breath and drew in another. "I want to create a new future with the Mike who more closely resembles the man I knew and loved before our world imploded."

He served the meat and poured gravy over the mounds of potato, then added the overcooked beans before carrying the bowls to the table.

When he sat, he tucked in his napkin, then looked at her. "I've wallowed in a blue funk for too long. I'm sorry."

Tonight was a continuous stream of astonishing revelations.

"You had a near-death experience on top of a life-changing one," she said. "Are you starting to feel more hopeful?"

"I'm no longer terrified I'll drop dead."

"I didn't know."

"Yeah, well ... I couldn't say."

She wanted to sigh but forced herself to focus on the positives. "But you have now. It sounds like you've spent a lot of time thinking about dying. Will you talk to Malcolm now so I have one less thing to worry about?"

He chewed his mouthful slowly, then swallowed. "Yeah, okay. He's not bad for a quack."

She allowed a kernel of hope to unfold inside her. "What else is making you hopeful?"

"I'm enjoying making things for Rigby's train set."

"A project's always good."

"Yeah, a project is." He pushed the mashed potato around the bowl. "I thought if it was okay with you, maybe I could volunteer at the Irish festival too. You know, do something together? It's been a while."

She smiled at him. "I'm running the Irish stew kitchen so there's a ton of spuds that need peeling and mashing."

"Well, I've perfected the art."

"Dinner is lovely."

"I overcooked the beans."

"You'll get it right next time."

He nodded, obviously thinking about something. "I rang the trailer company today."

Birdie tried to keep her brows from hitting her hairline. "Oh, and?"

"The bad news is it hasn't sold down the wait list. They've given us a month and then they'll pursue us for the final payment."

"Pursue us?" Old panic scuttled. "We don't have anything to pursue."

"We do unless we declare bankruptcy. I reckon we advertise the van for sale and see how we go. Better that than being dragged through the courts."

She had an overwhelming desire to hide. "Will you handle it?"

"Yeah. I owe you that. I'll talk to Jack about the best online places to list it." He rubbed his jaw. "How long do you reckon the kids will be living here?"

"I have no idea. Why?"

"I was thinking, we could turn the back garage into a granny flat. We were going to do it for your mom, remember? We got the plumbing sorted and then she passed away. We've still got the plasterboard and I've got the time."

"It would give them more space," she mused. "They need it."

"We need it."

This time Mike touched her and old memories stirred.

"We can certainly offer it to them as an idea," she said.

"And when they move out, we can put it up on Airbnb and generate some funds."

She stared at him in stunned delight. "Wow, you have been thinking a lot."

He winked at her. "It's not all just pottering around in the garage, you know."

"I think it sounds like a great idea."

"Good. Doing the conversion will be a good test of what I can handle both work-wise and stress-wise."

She frowned, suddenly cautious he was rushing things. "You're thinking of going back to work?"

"I'm thinking a part-time job is something to aim for, but I'm not rushing it. I'll discuss it with Malcolm."

"Thank you."

"For agreeing to talk to Malcolm?"

She kissed his hand. "For coming back to me."

CHAPTER THIRTY-NINE

LUCY SAT across from Jack at a Laminex table inside the local cheap eats. A flatscreen television hung from the 1980s exposed brick wall, and Jack's gaze kept sliding toward it even though the show was a soap he'd never watched and the sound was muted. She tried not to feel the loss of white linen tablecloths and fine-dining service, and instead sipped the cheap but cheerful sparkling wine, anticipating the always-reliable roast lamb and five vegetables.

She was still reeling from arriving home to find Jack playing with Rigby on the trampoline. He'd greeted her cautiously, as if she was a bomb that might go off if not handled with kid gloves. It annoyed her. Why was she the one being made to feel her behavior was unreasonable when Jack refused to think beyond living with his parents? And why the hell hadn't he called her to tell her he was coming home early when everything about his body language was the polar opposite of delight in surprising her?

When Mike had insisted they go out—hell, he'd almost pushed them out the door—she'd been too stunned to speak, let alone object. Once, time alone with Jack would have been a wonderful treat, but with their communication reduced to short and curt text messages she felt like she was sitting opposite a stranger.

"Birdie will get a surprise," she finally said after they'd sat silent for far too long.

"That I'm home early?"

"That Mike cooked dinner."

His mouth gave a quick twitch. "Yeah, the old man's a bit of a disaster in the kitchen."

"Maybe he's trying to change."

"God, I hope so. Still ..."

"What?"

"We've got years to recover, but Dad hasn't. I just wish ..." He downed his beer.

Lucy changed the subject. "I've volunteered for the Irish festival."

"Yeah?" Surprise filled his face. "On top of work when you're always tired?"

She swatted away the strand of guilt that tried to squeeze her—she did complain a lot about being tired. "I wanted to help Izzy and you never know, it might be fun."

His brows pulled down. "Have you checked with Mom and Dad if they're okay to look after Rigby?"

"No need. It falls on a weekend you're home."

He tugged at his hair that was overdue for a cut. "So what, you work five days and spend another two at the festival?" She nodded. "Jeez, Luce."

"Jeez, Jack. What?"

"I'm only home one week in four and you're going to be busy the whole time!"

She threw up her hands. "It feels like it doesn't matter what I'm doing or not doing, you'll find fault with it."

His shoulders stiffened. "Well, I'm glad we're spending precious money tonight just so we can argue."

She studiously drank her wine. The bell over the door rang and they both glanced at it, desperate for the distraction.

Tiffany walked in with her ten-year-old son, Hudson, and paused by their table. "Hello, Essens!"

"Maa-umm!" her son groaned.

Tiffany handed the boy her credit card. "Say order for Stanley and only tap the card for twenty-five fifty."

As Hudson ran to the back of the shop, Tiffany rolled her eyes. "He's always starving after basketball and he loves Mac's roasts. Anyway, I'm glad I ran into you. Just before I left the office I got an offer on your place."

Hope billowed in Lucy's chest. "Oh my God! Seriously?"

"Definitely. And by some miracle, it's higher than the one you rejected."

Jack grinned at Lucy for the first time that day, then faced Tiffany. "Are you going to keep us in suspense or tell us?"

The realtor glanced around the half-full restaurant. "This town has flapping ears so—"

"Mom, can we go?" Hudson returned clutching a white paper bag.

"I'll text you the offer," Tiffany continued as if she hadn't been interrupted. "You can discuss it over dinner and give me a bell in the morning. How does that sound?"

"They won't back out if they don't hear tonight?" Lucy asked.

"Mom!"

"I'm coming, Hudson." She pushed him toward the door and followed.

Jack rubbed his hands. "A higher offer! *This* is why we waited, Luce."

Despite his enthusiasm and her own excitement, Lucy felt the sting of rebuke. She turned her cell phone over, willing the text to arrive.

Jack pulled out his cell too and they both stared at their devices.

"No phones at the table," the waitress teased as she slid their plates in front of them.

As Jack was forking lamb into his mouth, Lucy said, "I'm too nervous to eat. How long is Tiffany going to take to text?"

"She'll feed that annoying kid of hers first just to shut him up," Jack said.

Lucy was too anxious to muster a laugh.

Jack's cell phone pinged and she tried to read the notification upside down. "What is it?"

Jack shook his head. "Just work."

She nibbled on some roasted squash and then her cell phone vibrated. With trembling fingers she swiped at the screen. Forcing herself to take in every word she read slowly. By the time she had read it twice, her heart had lodged itself in her throat.

"How much?" Jack asked.

Lucy turned the phone around so he could read the figure.

His eyes darkened and he mouthed an expletive as his palm hit the table. The silverware rattled on their plates. Other diners glanced curiously in their direction.

"How the hell does Tiffany get off telling us that's more?" Jack said.

"Technically it is."

"It's offensive when we know how much the house is worth."

"I think it's a sign."

Jack grunted. "Of what? Bastard pricks trying to rip us off?"

She shook her head. "Commerce is all about what the market will bear and what the customer thinks something is worth. With today's interest rates, no one thinks our house is worth what we're asking."

Jack dropped his head into his hands. "God, I'd hoped it was going to be over. But it's never going to be over, is it?"

Something made Lucy request a definition. "What exactly?"

His eyes, red with disappointment and fatigue, sought hers. "This nightmare of losing the house *and* our foot in the market. God, it's not even Melbourne or Geelong and we still can't afford it. At this rate it will be two or three years before we can have another crack and—"

"I don't want to live this way, Jack."

He slumped in his chair, resignation dragging him down. "We've been through this, Luce, over and over and over. It doesn't matter what you want when we don't have a choice."

She leaned forward, keeping her voice low. "That's the thing, Jack. There is always a choice. We need to make a different one, because if we don't ..."

"I thought you and Mom were getting on better." The words rolled out on a sigh.

"Birdie and I are trying hard to make it work, but this isn't about your parents and me. This is about us."

Bafflement creased his features. "What about us?"

"You in WA, me here. You expecting me to put my life on hold every fourth week."

"I don't do that."

"You do! You just got pissed that I'm volunteering at the Irish festival. And every time you're home and I want to discuss our lives, you play the 'I'm only home for a week' card. Then you go back to the mine and play the 'I'm too busy and important at work' card so we never talk about anything!"

"God, Luce, I'm killing myself to keep us afloat."

"And you think I'm not? We're both working flat out. Our jobs see more of us than we do and Rigby's being raised by childcare workers. This was never the plan."

He grimaced. "Neither was losing all our money."

Lucy held onto her exasperation at the circular argument. "But it happened. And I'm worried that if we stick to the current plan, losing the money won't be the worst thing that happens to us."

"And I'm worried if we deviate from the plan, we'll lose what little we've got left."

She spelled it out. "No house is worth losing our marriage."

He stared at her, shock white on his face. "You said you'd never put Rigby through a divorce."

"It's the last thing I want to have happen, but look at us, Jack. All we do is argue or exist in furious silence. Before we lost our money we believed in short-term pain for long-term gain. We accepted the long hours, the time apart, and we had fun when we were together, because ultimately it meant the three of us being together full-time in Glingilly and another baby. But let's be honest, even with an end date we were limping to the finish line. Now we're apart more than ever, Rigby hardly sees you, and there's no end in sight. Clinging to the dream of a house is not worth it, Jack. Not if it destroys us in the process."

"But we were so close!" The words came out on a moan.

"And now we're not." She stood and moved to sit next to him on the banquette, her thigh resting against his, absorbing his bewilderment and pain. "Do you remember our dream?"

"Bloody hell, Luce. It's all I've thought about for four years."

"Say it."

"Why?"

"Please."

He sighed as if she was making an unnecessary request. "Own the house outright, work in Glingilly and cuddle up to you every night."

"And if you could only have one of those three things, what would you choose?"

"Is this a trick question?"

"No." But it was probably the most important question she'd ever asked him.

He placed his hand on her thigh. "To cuddle up with you every night."

Her heart flipped in relief. "And it's mine too. Let's make a choice so that happens."

"We're already making that choice."

"I don't mean in five years. I mean this year. And before you jump in and tell me all the reasons why it can't possibly happen, please can you listen to my idea?"

He sighed. "Okay."

She put her hand over his and interlaced their fingers. "I know this will be hard for you because it's a one-eighty from what we've always dreamed of. We need a circuit-breaker, Jack. A complete change." She tapped her cell. "Let's push for a few more thousand then accept the offer on the house. And before you say it, I know it won't give us what we need to get another loan, but that's part of the new plan. We park a chunk in a low-risk investment and we use the rest to take a year off and travel around Australia."

"But that's always been Mom's dream." He sounded utterly disconcerted. "And you've never suggested ever wanting to do something like this."

"I know, and before everything went bung it wasn't necessary. Now it is. Think about it. We'll be together instead of this half-life we're living. It will give Rigby the stability he needs."

"How is moving around in a camper stable?"

"His parents are with him all of the time. A trip like this will give us breathing space to work out what's really important and how we want to live our lives."

His eyes scanned her face. "You've really thought about this."

She nodded. "Ironically, it was something your mom said."

"About going around Australia?"

"No. About changing a plan when it's no longer working. I love you, Jack, but I'm miserable and I think you are too. Are you?"

He ran his free hand through his hair. "Yeah. I hate being away so much and not having our own place."

"And that's our future if we put buying a house ahead of *us*. I lived through the discontent and unhappiness of my parents' marriage and watched what it did to them. I'm terrified if we keep going like this for much longer, we're risking too much."

"I thought I was doing the right thing for us," he said quietly.

She squeezed his hand. "A year ago we were both doing what we thought was best for us. Now all the goalposts have shifted."

He was quiet for a long time and it took all of her restraint not to push him for a decision. She tried eating some of her dinner, but her stomach roiled with anxiety so she asked the waitress to remove her plate.

Eventually Jack said, "So I'm guessing you've crunched the numbers?"

"Every night for three weeks."

"So what's the plan? Do we deck out a truck or ...?"

Relief thundered through her and she kissed him. "That's something we need to decide on together. There's a stack of YouTube channels and Instagram feeds dedicated to vanning and free camping around Australia with loads of information. Our four-wheel drive might be old but it's reliable so that's a good start."

"And how do we pay for everything?"

"Some people get sponsors, others sell merch to help fund their trip, but you and I have skills that lend themselves to well-paying casual jobs. We can plan our itinerary so we're in bigger towns every three months and stay for a few weeks to top up the coffers."

He picked up her hand again. "Are you sure you really want to do this?"

She heard the earnestness in his voice and knew he was visualizing her dealing with red dust and doing without many of the things she'd once thought she needed to be happy.

"You think I can't live without my hair straightener, but I can. Since Elite crashed and burned, I've learned to live without a lot of things, but I can't live without you and Rigby. You're the most important people in the world to me and we need to be together. Of course there'll be challenges, there always are, but we'll be in the same space and we'll work them out as we go along."

"I'm looking forward to it." He kissed her full on the mouth, his tongue flicking hers with promise. "Let's go home and get naked and then you can show me those numbers."

For the first time since their world had exploded, optimism lightened the brick in Lucy's chest.

CHAPTER FORTY

Izzy was riding high after a successful festival meeting with Birdie and Mike Essen. They'd taken on the organization of the Irish stew and baked potato kitchen, and the catering for morning and afternoon tea as well. Now her biggest headache was chasing up the bands. Musicians loved the idea of performing, but not so much completing their indemnity forms. But that was a tomorrow job after she'd put in some time on her university assignment that was begging for attention. Between the festival and her studies, her brain was kept busy so it didn't have much time to obsess about the ongoing police investigation into Brad's assets.

As she was leaving the hall, she pulled out her cell phone to text Brooke. She didn't want to wait until the next festival executive meeting before sharing the good news about the Essens. She was bringing up Brooke's name when the phone rang in her hand.

"Hi! Have you got ESP?" Izzy said as she answered.

"Why?" Brooke asked.

"I was just about to text you about the festival. I've got the best news!"

"Actually, Izzy, I'm calling on police business. Can you come down to the station, please?"

As Izzy stepped into the interview room, she tried hard not to let the memories of Detective Mitchell and his confrontational interview style haunt her. It wasn't enough to stop her mouth from drying, her heart racing and her fingers rising to the back of her head.

The voice of her counselor played in her mind. *What are some productive ways you can deal with your stress, Izzy?*

Not now, Caroline! Yoga, a run or a warm bath were not going to cut it here.

Brooke followed Izzy and slid a café-made latte across the table. "Here."

"Thanks." Izzy took a deep sip as if caffeine would calm her.

"Can you please stop looking like I've just slaughtered your firstborn," Brooke said.

"Sorry. Being back here isn't easy."

"Yeah, I get it. But today I'm giving you a positive experience."

"The coffee?" Izzy joked.

"Hey, I paid for that myself." Brooke smiled. "Remember last time you were here and I said Melbourne had taken over the case?" Izzy nodded. "Well, I've just been notified that they've concluded their investigations into Brad Quinn's financial activities."

Izzy's breath solidified in her chest.

"There's evidence of fraud in regard to the illegal use of Elite funds to buy property in Western Australia, but there's no evidence pointing to the Noosa apartment being a proceed of crime."

"But ..." She couldn't have heard properly. "Are they absolutely certain?"

"They had Barsky's report as a starting point, and they've spent four months looking into everything with a fine-tooth comb, so I'm taking that as a yes."

"So does this mean ..." Izzy's tongue felt too large for her mouth.

"Are you saying the apartment's mine?"

"That's exactly what I'm saying." Brooke grinned. "Oh, and by the way, I Googled it. Peregian Beach. Nice! Reckon I can get an invitation one day? I could do with some Queensland sunshine."

Izzy laughed weakly as guilt rose to join her confusion. Elite members had nothing, but she owned a 3 million dollar apartment?

She tried to sort her thoughts. "And you're sure it's not being pursued as part of Brad's assets?"

"As far as the police are concerned, it's not Quinn's asset, it's yours. Like I said, there's no money trail from Elite that leads to it."

Izzy thought about the engagement ring in her sock drawer. Just like the apartment, she'd been waiting weeks to lose it and now she was being told the investigation was over.

"What about the engagement ring? It's worth a bit."

Brooke shrugged. "If they'd wanted to seize it, they would have. Fraud goes after the big bucks and in cases like this where millions have vanished, they're not interested in the small stuff."

It seemed wrong that 25,000 dollars was small, but the survivalist inside Izzy wasn't going to argue. "And his cars and other assets? Will there be any money from their sale for the Elite members?"

"The cars were leased and as Quinn defaulted on the payments, they've been repossessed by the dealer. There's not much else."

Izzy should be punching the air, crying with relief, spinning around in joy, but instead her scalp tingled with anxiety and her ears buzzed.

"So it's over? They're not going to come after me later?"

Brooke looked thoughtful. "I guess the Elite members could raise a civil case, but I think they'd be pushing it uphill. The apartment's in your name, and I doubt going after the ring is worth court costs, but I'm not a police prosecutor. Even so, it's unlikely."

"Right ..."

Izzy's hand rose toward the back of her head, but suddenly Brooke was resting her hands lightly on her shoulders and smiling at her.

"Izzy, don't look so worried. Repeat after me: this is good news."

Her heart seemed to be beating in her throat. "This is ... good news."

"That's the spirit."

"I ... it's just ... I didn't expect this. Thanks."

"You're welcome." Brooke walked her to the front of the station. "I'm just glad I got you to commit to the Irish festival or you'd be on a plane tonight and heading north."

Izzy heard herself laugh but inside everything was numb.

When Izzy arrived home, Thor raced from the car, up the back steps and straight to his food bowl. She went through the motions of opening a can, spooning out the contents and refilling his water bowl without being fully aware of what she was doing—her mind fixed on what Brooke had told her.

It wasn't until her cell buzzed with a message from Lucy—*What time tonight?*—that she remembered she'd invited her friend and Cooper to dinner.

She opened the fridge and saw with relief the thawed salmon and fresh vegetables. As she closed the door, she wondered about texting Cooper and asking him to pick up a bottle of champagne. She couldn't think of two better people to help her celebrate her good news.

A sharp pain struck like a stitch and she pressed her hand to her side. Would Lucy see this as good news when she was losing her own house? Izzy tried to look at it from Lucy's point of view and knew without a shadow of a doubt that her new and valued friendship was unlikely to survive this.

She doesn't need to know.

The thought hit as both a solution and a complication.

Izzy had no great desire to move to Queensland—she preferred the cooler climate of south-west Victoria. Perhaps the best decision was to rent the apartment and generate income. It would give her the freedom to start her new career, whatever the heck that was going to be.

She was typing a reminder on her cell to check out Noosa realtors' property management fees when it rang. She checked the caller ID—

Judy. Her finger headed fast to the decline button, but hovered just above it, unable to execute the task. She'd ignored the last few calls from Brad's mother, so she probably should take this one.

"Hi, Judy."

"Izzy!" Judy's voice slurred down the line. "Where are you?"

It seemed an odd question so she countered with, "Where are you?"

Judy laughed. "Glingilly, silly. I told you we were flying in today."

"Right," Izzy agreed vaguely, unable to recall Judy mentioning it. She immediately thought of Birdie and the Irish festival. She crossed her fingers that the Quinns wouldn't stay long. They usually only lasted two weeks in Glingilly before returning to New South Wales and there were still a few weeks until the festival.

"Can you come earlier than six?" Judy was saying. "It's a lovely evening and I thought we could have girls" cocktails on the terrace." She giggled. "I'm working my way through the new cocktail book Bevan gave me."

"I'm sorry, what?"

"You got my email inviting you to dinner?"

"No."

"Never mind," Judy said airily. "Come anyway."

The thought of spending the evening alone with the Quinns made Izzy shudder. Thor trotted over, his head cocked to the side as if checking she was okay.

"I'm sorry, Judy, but I have plans tonight."

"I see." The giggly tone vanished. "Does it have anything to do with that university professor?"

Izzy's hand curled around the back of a chair. "I don't have to tell you what I'm doing, Judy," she said carefully.

"We know anyway. You've been seen with him from Portland to Peterborough."

Izzy's blood ran cold. The Quinns had been out of Glingilly for weeks, and up until her recent breakfast with Cooper they'd avoided being seen together in town.

"Brad loved you, Izzy. He adored you and took care of you. We take care of you. You can't do this to him or to us. You need to go to confession and—"

Izzy cut the call and her trembling legs collapsed her onto the chair.

"This is nothing to worry about," she said to Thor, her voice unsteady. "Judy's drunk and grieving. That's all."

But she couldn't dismiss as easily the fact that Judy knew she'd been fishing with Cooper numerous times on a variety of different beaches. Who was telling them? And more to the point, why?

She ruffled Thor's ears and kissed him on the top of his head, trying to ignore Judy's words about care. "I don't owe them anything."

He licked her face and she laughed.

She texted Birdie and Lucy.

> Sorry to be the bearer of bad news but FYI, the Quinns are back in town. Izzy x

Two thumbs-down emojis came back.

LUCY
> Still good for dinner?

IZZY
> Absolutely!

Izzy checked her watch. She had plenty of time to prepare the coconut salmon curry and make the bathroom as clean as the rust stains on the porcelain allowed before her guests arrived. She stood and connected Spotify to her small portable speaker, turning it up full tilt. Singing and swaying, she kept Judy's vitriol at bay while she cooked.

The so-called five-minute preparation time on the recipe was more like fifteen and it took a while for the heat to permeate the cast-iron pot, so the curry was only just reaching a simmer when she'd finished wiping down the bathroom. As she pulled open the silverware drawer to set the table, she heard a knock on the door.

Neither Lucy or Cooper ever knocked, but she wondered if they were being more formal tonight because she'd invited them to dinner. Whichever of the two of them it was, they were impolitely early, but she didn't care.

Thor beat her to the door, then growled.

"Not this again," Izzy said. "You know you love Cooper and he loves—"

She stopped. Cooper hadn't said he loved her, and rightly so—it was all too soon. And was love even what they were looking for when Izzy was going to leave town next year? No. This thing they shared was simple and straightforward. She was enjoying Cooper's company and he was enjoying hers.

She jiggled the sticky latch and opened the front door. Surprise made her stutter. "B-Bevan."

"Hello, Izzy."

He moved forward and kissed her. Then, whether it was surprise or ingrained manners, she found herself stepping back to allow him entry to the cottage. She stood in the doorway, scanning the garden for Judy.

As if reading her mind, Bevan said, "I came alone."

Another jolt of surprise hit her. When she thought about the times Judy and Bevan had visited Villefranche when Brad had been away, they'd rarely visited separately. Since his death, she'd only ever seen them together.

Izzy remembered Judy's phone call an hour earlier. "Is she okay?"

"She's upset you've blown off her dinner invitation."

Irritation rippled. Surely Bevan hadn't driven here to berate her about dinner?

"I didn't blow her off. I never received the email." *She's drinking a lot.* "Perhaps she thought she'd sent it?"

Thor had backed up and was snarling and barking.

"I see his manners haven't improved any," Bevan said. "Something smells good."

"Curry, which I need to check. Excuse me." Izzy walked to the kitchen, her thoughts jangling.

"Dodgy board or two you've got there," Bevan said as he entered the kitchen. "I could have fixed them for you if I'd known."

The criticism was implied—Izzy was at fault, again.

She stirred the curry, then turned down the heat before looking at Bevan. "Was I expecting you, Bevan?"

He pulled out a chair and sat. "I thought it was time I visited and found out why on earth you're choosing to live in this dump."

Choosing? "That's easy. It's what I can afford."

His neatly trimmed brows rose. "I think we both know that's not strictly true."

"I think I know the status of my bank account better than you do."

"I'm talking about the Noosa apartment."

The caution she'd experienced around Bevan since Brad had disappeared intensified. Brooke had only given her the news about the apartment two hours ago and Izzy hadn't told anyone. Surely Bevan didn't know.

There's no surely about anything, Cooper's voice quietly warned her.

"It's no use to me if the police instruct the receivers to sell it," she said, feigning ignorance.

"Izzy, Izzy." He shook his head at her as if she was a little girl. "Your lack of faith is disappointing. Of course it's not a proceed of crime." His lips curved upwards and for a split second she saw a hint of Brad, but then the smile changed to something far more rapacious. "And that's why we want you to come to dinner tonight. After everything we've been through these past months, we need to celebrate some good news."

Play dumb. "What good news?"

"The fraud squad's released the apartment."

"I don't understand ..." She screwed up her face, hoping it looked like he'd taken her by surprise. "How do you know before me?"

"I've got a mate in the police force. It comes in handy from time to time and he knew I'd want to know."

"About *my* apartment?"

This time his smile was a rictus. "Come on, Izzy. It's never been your apartment."

"It is. I paid half the deposit and made monthly repayments!"

"Yes, but you didn't discharge the mortgage, did you?"

And who did, Bevan?

"My name's on the title."

"And as I explained months ago," he said patiently, "that's for tax purposes."

And they were back to the point of contention.

"That's the thing," Izzy said. "Brad never mentioned it to me."

"I know more than anyone how much grief interferes with memory, but I can assure you, he did. Judy and I were over for dinner when he brought it up and we discussed it."

She raked her memory of the many meals they'd shared and the endless talk of investments. As this was her investment, she was certain she wouldn't have tuned out, but her search came up blank.

"You know what you're like when you're entertaining, Izzy. You're always focused on the food and wine and the decorations."

The words hit with uncanny accuracy and she couldn't deny them. Even so, they didn't sit easily.

"We weren't married and our finances were separate, so exactly how was the tax break going to help Brad?"

Bevan shook his head as if he couldn't quite believe what he was hearing. "That business major really hasn't done you any favors. Over the years, I've bought properties in Judy's name and it's served us well. The tax break comes when the asset is realized."

Warning bells pealed. "Unfortunately, Brad isn't here to realize it."

"No. But I am."

"Excuse me?" Her heart rate thumped so hard it bruised. "You're not Brad, and I have no intention of selling it."

"Interesting moral shift." Bevan stared her down. "Then again, you have kept the engagement ring."

Guilt and fury blew through her, mixing confusion and skepticism. "Are you saying it wasn't mine to keep?"

He gave her an indulgent smile. "Of course not. It's a gift and Brad got a lot of joy designing it for you, chasing down the diamonds and haggling a good deal. Knowing that eases some of my grief. But jewelry is very different from the apartment, which is not a gift. Your mortgage repayments only represent a tiny share of its total value, ergo not selling it is a form of theft. Recently, you've made it very clear what your stand is on theft and embezzlement."

Did Bevan know she'd worked with the local police and Cooper? No! That wasn't possible. Unless ... But her thoughts were trumped by an overwhelming feeling that somehow the Noosa apartment meant she was being used. Her brain lurched and creaked as she trialed different things to say that would gain her more information than she gave away.

"When Brad disappeared, you and Judy told me over and over that he wanted to look after me. This apartment is exactly that."

"Us," Bevan said firmly. "We said he wanted to look after *us*. And to be honest, considering everything that's happened and what he let those bastards in Dubai talk him into, he didn't do a very good job."

Izzy blinked, disconcerted. In all the years she'd known Bevan, not once had she ever heard him criticize Brad.

Bevan sighed. "Look, I didn't want to tell you this because as a father I want you to remember Brad the way he should be. But when things started going crazy, it was all a bloody mess. Brad was hemorrhaging money and I had to step in. I did what I could to preserve some assets so he didn't take us all down with him."

She thought of the Elite members who'd lost everything and ached. "You knew Brad was running a Ponzi scheme?" Her voice rose in accusation. "And you didn't warn anyone?"

"For God's sake, Isobel! Would I have encouraged our friends to invest in Elite and risked my financial services license if I'd known?" He slumped and rubbed the back of his neck. "Until Brad came to me frantic for help, I had no clue what was going on. Then I did what any father would do for his son."

Izzy's mind struggled to make sense of the information, trying to slot Bevan's words into a timeline that was permanently engraved on her. She wanted to believe him—he looked and sounded gutted—but nagging doubts refused to fade.

"Did that include leaving Brad and going on retreat, knowing he might take his own life?"

Bevan's lips whitened around the edges. "How dare you! He was my precious son!"

The pain in his voice echoed her own grief for Brad and the way he'd died. Then it castigated her for distressing Bevan.

"I'm sorry." But questions still lingered, demanding to be asked. She overrode empathy in favor of information. "I need to make sense of it all. Why didn't you tell me what was going on?"

A long sigh rumbled out of him. "The less you knew the better."

"What does that mean?"

"Considering the shitstorm Brad got himself in, I had to act fast and protect the family. Brad, Judy, you. I did what I could and you should be thanking me instead of giving me the third degree."

"Thanking you?" Incredulity roared so loud in her head she put her hands to her ears. "I was treated like a criminal for weeks!"

He threw out his hands. "You think you're alone there, sweetheart? You're not. Judy and I were treated exactly the same. But keeping you in the dark paid off, because the police realized you didn't know anything and now you're free of Brad's poor decisions. I gave you that gift because you're family."

She recalled her overwhelming relief when the police had cleared her of any involvement with Elite and the sense that she'd got her life back. She opened her mouth to thank him.

But was Bevan keeping her ignorant really protection when she'd proven her own innocence by breaking into the cloud?

I had to step in ... so he didn't take us all down with him.

It suddenly hit her that when Brad had told Bevan that Elite and Fortune were a Ponzi scheme, Bevan must have known their friends had lost their life savings. But instead of going to the police and exposing his son as the thief he was, he'd moved to protect their—*his?*—

investments. Did that include moving money? The money no one seemed able to find.

Oscar thinks they shipped our money overseas. They know a lot of people and they have some influential friends with the power to protect them.

Izzy had dismissed Birdie's comments as conspiracy theories. Right now they looked far more watertight. Especially when she added in Bevan admitting to having mates in the police force.

She'd barely had time to consider the full implications when Bevan was saying, "And now the police investigation's finally over, it's time to get things back on an even keel."

He pulled some papers out of his jacket pocket and smoothed them on the table. "In the spirit of family and fairness, I'm happy to offer you a million dollars. It's an excellent return for you, as you only contributed half the deposit and your repayments only covered the interest."

Izzy felt like she was standing on shifting sands. "What are you talking about?"

He sighed as if she was the most difficult woman in the world. "You never did listen very well. I'm talking about the Noosa apartment. You transfer the title to me and you receive a million dollars in return."

Once, she would have considered a million dollars a lot of money. Once, she would have considered Bevan's offer a gift of care and affection from a loving family. But in so many ways Bevan and Judy had abandoned her—both before and after Brad's death.

"Would you give away 2 million dollars if you were me?" she asked.

A muscle twitched in Bevan's cheek. "The only reason you still have the apartment is because of me."

Go carefully. "Do you have proof that you paid for it?"

"I arranged for it to be rescued." There was an edge to his voice.

She'd bet her million dollars that was code for putting a great deal of distance between him and the purchase.

"Rescued it and chose to use my name, not yours or Judy's," she said.

He rolled his eyes. "Of course your name. You were buying it with Brad."

She crossed her arms to reinforce her resolve. "I don't believe you."

"That's your prerogative. But what we're dealing with here is a straightforward business transaction that's in your best interests."

"And that's the thing, Bevan. I think it's in your best interests."

He took a breath as if he needed to keep himself in check. "Don't get greedy, Isobel," he said mildly.

"I'm not—"

"Good. Just sign the papers like a good girl and you'll get the money."

"I'm not going to do that."

"That would be a very unwise decision. One that comes with some nasty consequences." He clicked the pen. "Sign the goddamn papers and then we don't ever have to see your traitorous face again."

Izzy's head jerked back at his vitriol. "I think you've got that back to front. I'm the victim here, not the traitor!"

His eyes narrowed. "The headstone on my son's grave is yet to be installed and you're already sleeping with another man. You might talk the talk about business ethics, but you've always been a gold-digger."

The words lashed her, but she clung hard to her truth. Yes, the money and the gifts had muddied things for her, but she'd fallen in love with Brad well before they arrived. It was his and his family's obsession with money that had ultimately broken them.

"If you've always thought I was a gold-digger, it wasn't very sound business sense to put the apartment in my name, was it?"

His nostrils flared. "Brad said you were easy to handle. Obviously that was his dick talking."

Izzy flinched at the crude description and her dislike of Bevan intensified to loathing. "Legally the apartment belongs to me. Of course you can fight me for it in court, but I feel that will connect you to it in a way you've gone to great lengths to avoid so far."

She remembered Birdie telling her about the man known to have gangland connections being warned off investigating where the Elite money might be. It crossed her mind she was possibly already in trouble, but fury and injustice railroaded wariness.

"Even with your mates in high places, Bevan, is it worth the risk of drawing attention to a mere 2 million dollars when it's got to be a drop in the ocean compared to the amount you 'rescued.'"

He shot to his feet and for the first time real fear planted itself inside Izzy. Thor raced to her side, a low growl in his throat.

"You've always liked talking about things you don't understand, Isobel, but remember this. It's on public record that we all lost money and that I'm as shocked and appalled at what Brad did as everyone else. It's also well-known that I fully cooperated with the police, giving them access to my investments and bank accounts, so this little flight of fancy of yours is just a joyride that will crash and burn before it's even had time to take off." Anger and loathing twisted his face into an ugly scar. "I strongly recommend you don't share your thoughts with anyone."

Her gut wobbled like jelly. "Is that a threat?"

"Judy and I are gutted that Brad stole so much money from our family and friends. We certainly didn't raise him that way. This whole 'poor me' victim thing you've been cultivating in town doesn't wash with us either. If Elite members have a beef with anyone, it lies with you. It's your greed and avarice that changed Brad. You had him on a string, doling out sexual favors in exchange for a lavish lifestyle. The foolish and besotted boy stole to keep you happy. That diamond ring is a case in point. Judy and I plan to say exactly that during our interview on 60 *Minutes* next week. Good luck living in Glingilly or getting a job anywhere after that."

He crossed the kitchen to the back door, then turned. "Of course, we might be tempted to change our minds if you sign over the title."

Her fingers gripped the edge of the counter. "That's never going to happen."

"Good luck then, Isobel. You're sure as hell going to need it."

The door banged shut behind him and Izzy vomited into the kitchen sink.

CHAPTER FORTY-ONE

When Cooper found her, Izzy could barely speak. He wrapped her in a blanket, made her hot, sweet tea and cuddled her close. When the sugar hit her bloodstream, she managed to give him the gist of what had just happened.

"Jesus, Izzy. Get a restraining order against him. Brooke will believe you."

"But will the magistrate? I've got a feeling I'll be the one humiliated in court."

She told him about Birdie and the other Elite members constantly encountering roadblocks when they tried to talk to Bevan. About the protection she now believed the Quinns had inside the police force.

"It's all wrong," Cooper said.

"Corruption is." She laughed, the sound both vicious and resigned. "It's also bloody hard to prove and most civilians get burned trying. Hell, even whistleblowers inside the force struggle. There's no dispute that Brad committed fraud, but the official police line is that the crime started and ended with him and no one else was involved. Case closed."

She leaned into Cooper, appreciating his bulk and warmth. "I feel down to the depths of my soul that the apartment was paid for with

Elite money. But you couldn't find the money trail, and either the police couldn't or they chose not to look. I doubt we'll ever know for sure. What I do know is that Bevan will never publicly admit what he said to me, and I don't have a recording of it, so ... checkmate."

"I can revisit the numbers," Cooper offered. "I might have missed something."

"Thank you. I'm sure everyone in Elite will be grateful even if that bastard has pulled off a bigger scam than his son."

Cooper shrugged, as if spending hours of his own time on their behalf was no big deal. "Right now I'm more concerned about Bevan Quinn's threat to trash your reputation and imperil your future. If he goes through with it, and even if you sue, accusations like that live on the internet forever, giving companies a reason not to hire you. You don't deserve that."

Cooper's face was a mix of anxiety and concern, and it circled Izzy in care. She stroked his cheek. "Don't look so worried."

"Izzy, it's no joke."

"I know." Bevan's threat was a tight corset stifling her breathing.

"So what are you going to do?" Cooper asked.

The lead weights of doom that had been pressing down on her since Bevan's bombshell suddenly felt less heavy. Like the glory of sunlight penetrating dense cloud, it was suddenly obvious what she needed to do.

"I'm going to fight him in a way he'll neither expect nor understand."

The following evening, Izzy stood in the Essens' living room flanked by Lucy and Birdie with a hand in each of theirs. Even so, their support wasn't enough to stop her heart from racing. For the previous ten minutes while the Elite members arrived, she'd felt the daggers of squinty looks and heard the question, "Why is *she* here?"

Birdie had given each person her hostess smile and said, "She's as much a victim of Elite as the rest of us. Cuppa? Cake?"

On Lucy's urging, Cooper and Izzy had spoken with the Essens that morning and the decision had been made to call an Elite meeting that night—the sooner the better.

"The meetings are usually at Oscar's," Birdie had said.

"I think we should host this one, Bird," Mike had said. "It sends a message that we're a united front with Izzy."

"And I can set up a video link for Jack," Lucy had added.

Now that everyone held a slice of apple and walnut cake and a drink, Mike clapped his hands for silence and introduced Cooper.

As Cooper stepped forward, he looked straight at Izzy, his smile saying, "We've got this."

God, she hoped so She hugged the smile, trying to believe it, but like everything to do with Elite, there were always unknowns.

As Cooper spoke, Izzy carefully watched the looks on the faces of the Elite members. Most were impassive but all were concentrating hard.

"Let me get this straight, Cooper," Oscar said. "Despite what the police are saying, you think I'm right. Our money's gone overseas."

"It's a hypothesis," Cooper said.

"I'm the one saying I believe it's gone overseas," Izzy said. "And it's been buried behind layers of company walls."

Twenty sets of eyes immediately swiveled her way and she squeezed Lucy's and Birdie's hands hard so she couldn't pull at her hair.

"So you do know something," Oscar said tightly.

Izzy shook her head. "I only have a gut feeling like you do. But Cooper's kindly offered to relook at the numbers in the hope of finding something, anything. Because without solid evidence we're stymied. Even then ..."

"Quinn was a bastard in life and now he's a bastard in death," Alan Lumsden said.

"Actually, I believe Bevan Quinn is far more involved than he's led us to believe." Izzy took a steadying breath, knowing her next statement would place her in the eye of a storm. "I've inadvertently become the owner of a beachfront apartment in Noosa that I feel was almost certainly purchased with your money."

A series of gasps bounced around the room.

"I knew she must know something!"

"What the hell is 'almost certainly'?"

"You've told the police?"

Their questions hammered her and she fought to keep her breathing even. "I promise you that at the time, I had no idea what was going on. All of you knew the money was missing before I did. But since that devastating Thursday afternoon, I've learned a lot. As for the police, they told me the apartment's not a proceed of crime and that it's free from further investigation."

"Aren't you the lucky one then," Gaylene Hewitson said, her tone ugly.

"Steady, Gaylene," Birdie said. "You might want to listen before you say anything else."

The woman huffed and Lucy nudged Izzy to continue.

"I was never complicit in Elite and I lost money too. It's just recently I've come to believe I'm a pawn in a very complicated fraud that includes the apartment."

"What makes you think that?" Oscar asked.

"The apartment's now in my name only and the mortgage has been discharged, even though I only ever invested 100,000 dollars in it. Yesterday, less than two hours after the police told me it was no longer under investigation, Bevan flew in from New South Wales, insisted I sell it and offered me a deal. When I refused, he threatened to make my life difficult. That bit won't surprise any of you who've run up against him."

Murmurs ran around the room like electricity.

Izzy pushed on. "Legally, I own a 3 million dollar apartment and I have a 25,000-dollar engagement ring."

"That we paid for!"

"Shut up, Jim, and listen," Mike said.

"As much as I want to scream it from the rooftops that Bevan Quinn's a crook," Izzy continued, "There's no evidence to implicate him. If we try to cast doubt without evidence, our lives will become even more difficult."

More murmurs started and she raised her hand like a stop sign. "I'm not suggesting we give up, just that we do things quietly. If we're lucky—and let's face it, justice has let us down so this is all about luck now—Cooper might find a breadcrumb. It may lead to many more and prove that the apartment, the ring, and God knows what else, has been bought with your money. We may never recoup all of it, but there is 3 million dollars of it that I intend to liquidate and share with you all. I've spoken to three realtors and, unlike down here, the market up there is buoyant. They have lists of people desperate for a beachside investment."

"What do you say to that, Gaylene?" Birdie said.

"What about the ring? Is that in the pot too?"

When Izzy nodded, Gaylene said, "A twenty-way split isn't fair when some of us lost more than others."

Birdie sighed. "I was actually pointing you toward saying thank you."

"Why? It's our money!"

"In the spirit of fairness," Izzy continued as the room's antagonism slapped her, "the amount each of you receives will be calculated on the percentage each of you lost from your total investment. A third party will handle the payments. Someone with no skin in the game so it's as fair as possible."

"It's also not open to negotiation," Mike said. "We're bloody lucky Izzy's the honest person she is. Other people would have taken a 3 million dollar windfall and run."

"People like the Quinns," someone said.

"I suppose when you put it like that," Gaylene muttered. "Thank you, Isobel."

Izzy accepted the reluctant thanks as an olive branch. "I know it's not going to restore your finances to what they were, but I hope it helps."

"It certainly will." Oscar rubbed his hands together. "Our next point of discussion is how to make the Quinns' lives so bloody miserable in Glingilly that they move permanently."

As suggestions flew around the room, the Essens, Izzy and Cooper moved to the kitchen.

"You okay?" Cooper asked.

Trembling, Izzy stepped into his arms, grateful for the support.

"You were amazing," Lucy said, joining in the hug. "No one would know you hate public speaking."

"I'm just glad it's over." Izzy corrected herself. "I mean, it's not *over* over. It may never be over if we can't nail the bastard to the wall. But I hope this money helps people start to heal."

"We know what you mean, dear." Birdie frowned as the voices drifted in from the other room. "It's getting a bit negative in there, Mike. Crack open that bottle of bubbles and get them to focus on the positives. They're getting some money back."

Cooper steered Izzy outside. It was a clear night and he pointed out the rising Southern Cross.

"You've done an amazing thing, Izzy."

It didn't feel amazing—just the right thing to do.

"I've made a moral and ethical decision so I can sleep at night. And while I'm in Glingilly I can look Lucy and Birdie in the eye." *And you.*

She suddenly laughed.

He pulled her in close. "What?"

"I'm not sure what's going to piss Bevan off more. The money going back to Elite members or the fact he can't publicly slander me for being grasping and mercenary."

"I just hope he leaves you alone now."

"Yeah. Me too. But it might be too much to hope for."

CHAPTER FORTY-TWO

BIRDIE AND MIKE locked up the Glingilly hall after a practice session in the kitchen. Birdie had wanted to test the commercial stove and work out the best way to serve a hundred people a bowl of stew on mashed potato and a glass of Guinness. Together they'd walked through the process, trying to use the space in the most efficient manner and anticipate bottlenecks.

She linked her arm through his as they walked home. "I enjoyed that."

"Me too. It felt like we were on the same page. You know, working as a team again. I think Izzy will be pleased with our suggestions."

"Every time I see her I just want to hug her."

"Yeah. Let's hope Noosa sells fast."

They let themselves in the back door and were surprised to find Lucy and Jack in a suspiciously quiet house and with lunch on the table.

"Where's Rigby?" Mike asked.

"We asked Izzy to take him to the park for an hour," Jack said. "We'd like to talk to you both without him interrupting."

Birdie glanced at Mike, checking if he knew what was going on, but he shrugged.

"This sounds serious," she said.

"It's nothing to worry about." Lucy sliced a quiche and passed around the plates. "We think it's good news."

Birdie clapped. "You've sold the house?"

"We've sold the house and cleared our debts," Jack said. "But that's not the good news."

Mike's hands paused on the salad servers. "How can that not be good news?"

"It doesn't leave us enough to comfortably handle another home loan."

"What about the money you'll get from Izzy? Won't that help?" Mike said.

"It will, but that's months away and Lucy and I are sticking to our plan."

"Fair enough."

Birdie tried not to sigh, especially as life in Cork Street had improved since she and Lucy had come to understand each other better. Recently Mike had finished the granny flat and the kids had moved out there. It had a kitchenette, which meant Birdie only had to share her kitchen for the evening meal and it had made a huge difference to her state of mind.

"It's not what you're thinking, Birdie. It's a new plan we made the last time Jack was home," Lucy said. "Rigby needs his dad more than one week a month and Jack needs us and we need him. We can't keep living this way."

"So we're going to buy a camper and spend the next twelve months traveling around Australia," Jack said.

For a moment Birdie only heard white noise, and then her heart did something that both hurt and healed. They were taking her trip. She expected jealousy to raise its vicious green head, but when she looked at the happiness on their faces, the only emotion to strike was relief. They were back rowing their marriage in the same direction.

She tamped down her rising worries that they were going to decimate their savings and the chance of another house, and reminded herself they were adults who made their own decisions. This was their life and only they could live it. She was proud they were putting their small family first.

"That's exciting news!" she finally said, meaning it.

"What sort of camper are you looking at?" Mike asked.

"Nothing flash," Jack said. "We've got a really tight budget so we're looking at second hand, but there's not a lot available down here in our price range."

"We're thinking we'll start off camping out of the four-wheel drive until we get into northern New South Wales, then buy something there," Lucy said. "The choice is bigger."

"What's your budget?" Mike asked.

"That's their business, Mike," Birdie cautioned, not wanting Jack or Lucy to arc up when things had recently settled into a much calmer rhythm.

"We have a travel trailer, Birdie," Mike said patiently.

Jack was shaking his head. "That's way out of our price range, Dad."

Birdie suddenly understood what Mike was getting at. "It may not be."

Lucy's silverware clattered onto her plate. "How? It cost more than the average house deposit."

"And we paid for all of it bar the last ten grand, which we don't have. We've had it on the market for months, but it's not a standard design so no one wants to pay what it's worth. If we don't come up with ten grand by the thirtieth, the company will repossess it and we'll lose the lot."

Lucy stared at them "Are you saying that for 10,000 dollars we can use your trailer?"

"Steady, Luce," Jack said. "Dad got the ute customized to tow it. Our old car might not manage it."

"If you wanted the van then we could discuss swapping cars for the year," Mike said.

"Oh my God! I can't believe this," Lucy said.

Jack's grin was reminiscent of when he was eight and had found tadpoles in the pond. "And the ute's got the set-up to get to places really off road."

Lucy's enthusiasm dimmed. "Are you both absolutely certain about this? Sienna might have something to say. I don't want it to turn into an issue that might damage things now the four of us are getting along."

"I doubt Sienna wants to invest 10,000 dollars in a travel trailer," Mike said.

But Birdie knew exactly what Lucy was getting at and this time they would do things the right way.

"We'll both make lists and discuss all the issues," she said, 'then write an agreement and sign it so we're all on the same page. Things like a return date. And you'll need to factor insurance into your cost estimates, which will be more for this van than you've probably budgeted for."

"No problem," Jack said. "If you only want ten grand then you're already saving us money."

A tug of war played out in Birdie's head. Their 10,000 dollars saved the travel trailer so all of them could use it. But it was a small percentage of what it was worth, so if Jack and Lucy paid more it would free up money. But then they'd eat more into their savings, which was their choice but—

"You two saved my life," Mike said quietly. "This is our way of saying thank you."

The debate in Birdie's head stilled. "Mike's right." She put her hand in his. "And when you get back, perhaps it will finally be our turn."

"We'll treat the van like it's ours," Lucy said. "But after a year of use, it won't be brand new when you take it on the road, Birdie. There will be some wear and tear."

"I know, but it's better that than no van at all." Excitement skittered along her veins. Some of it was for the possibility of her own big trip, but mostly it was for Lucy, Jack and Rigby and their more immediate adventures. "And I want lots of photos and video chats when possible."

"Too easy, Mom." Jack kissed her on the cheek.

"And just so you know, as soon as you take off, we'll be turning your flat into an Airbnb."

Lucy laughed. "Is that code for 'Jack and Lucy are not moving in when they get back'?"

Birdie smiled. "It's more notice that if you need to live here while we're away, you'll have to run the Airbnb. I don't suppose there's any chance you're leaving before the Irish festival? Beds are at a premium and I could get three hundred dollars a night."

"If you can cope, we can move back inside for three nights," Jack said.

"For nine hundred dollars, I can cope. Besides, I'll be at the festival most of the time."

"Me too," Lucy said. "Jack will be on deck looking after Rigby and the guests. As for a leaving date, we want to be here for Christmas. But don't stress, we know you'll be crazy busy at work so we'll cook."

"And I'll decorate." Mike said. "Rigby can help."

"And Sienna can wash up," Jack said.

Birdie laughed, feeling lighter than she had in months. "Sounds like a perfect plan."

Birdie sat on the recliner with a decanted can of prosecco and a bowl of salt and vinegar chips on the table beside her. Jack was at work, Mike was playing twilight lawn bowls at the club with Oscar and Alan, and Lucy and Rigby were visiting Izzy. Giddy at having both the house and the remote to herself, she scrolled through the television's free-to-air options. Surely there was something she'd enjoy watching on her own.

She wasn't in the mood for Scandinavian noir—since they'd lost all their money, crime series were too close to home. *Married At First Sight* made her want to reach into the television and slap the contestants, and unless it was tennis, she wasn't a big fan of watching sports. Perhaps she could try reading?

She suddenly thought she heard tapping and muted the TV. She strained but only heard crickets. She'd just convinced herself she was imagining things when she heard it again. It sounded like a key clinking on glass.

No way!

That sound had always been her and Judy's code for "I need to talk."

She pulled the lever and the recliner shot upright, launching her to her feet. As she marched to the back door she convinced herself it was a confused magpie chick tapping on her clean laundry window, but the justification wasn't enough to stop her heart from thumping.

There was no bird on the sill and she opened the door. Judy stood on the back step.

She was wearing her signature colors, but she'd lost weight so instead of the chic tailored look, the clothes hung off her like sacks. A line of gray regrowth clung to her hair, her lipstick was smeared, and clumps of mascara darkened the saggy skin under her eyes. The fermenting scent of alcohol mixed with Chanel. Birdie barely recognized her.

The strands of sympathy trying to form around her heart were instantly neutralized by the restraining order Judy had taken out against her.

"What the hell are you doing here?" she demanded.

"I wanted to see you."

"I don't think so. You took out a restraining order against me, remember. It means I can be arrested if I talk to you and that's not on my bucket list."

Judy turned her palms upwards in supplication. "I miss you."

Birdie closed her eyes for a moment, desperately seeking a kernel of calm. "I find that hard to believe."

"Please. It's true."

The pleading in Judy's eyes took Birdie back in time to when the kids were little. Judy had arrived unannounced at dinnertime. Birdie had called to Mike to serve the kids and she'd gone into the garden and found Judy sitting on the teak bench, her head buried in her hands. Bevan had just confessed to allowing his secretary to give him a blow job in the office.

The announcement had stunned Birdie. "But why?"

"Stress," Judy had said firmly. "Work's been crazy for him lately."

The word had rattled around in Birdie's head, unable to find a place to rest. "If a BJ relieves his stress, why didn't he ask you for one?"

Judy had dissolved into tears, her distress disconcerting Birdie, who'd hugged her and stroked her hair. Between sobs and sniffs, her friend had stammered out the story. It had been a difficult year. Bevan was getting his new business off the ground, money was tight and he was working long hours. Brad, who could add up huge numbers in his head, was struggling to read. He was seeing a private education specialist who was expensive, and all the exercises Brad needed to do took up a lot of Judy's time.

"And," she confessed, "I know I told you I only wanted one child, but I've been trying to get pregnant for two years." Instead of sex being spontaneous and adventurous, it had become something that only happened when she thought she was ovulating.

"It's my fault Bevan fell for that slut's attentions," Judy sobbed. "I should have been more attentive to his needs."

Birdie disagreed, but as Judy had only just regained her breath she didn't want to risk her breaking down again. "Has he sacked her?" she asked.

"He didn't have to. When he told her it couldn't happen again, she quit."

Birdie thought about Bevan at the club—his genial personality, the way he danced with the women whose husbands refused to glide them across the floor, and how he made people laugh. A charmer, but in a good way. And there was never any doubt that he adored Judy—he worshipped the ground she walked on. He showed it in his smile, his gestures and all the gifts—big and small—he showered on her. There were times when Birdie wished Mike was half as attentive to her as Bevan was to Judy.

"What are you going to do?" she asked.

"Be a better wife."

The words sent a shudder down Birdie's spine. "And is Bevan going to be a better husband?"

"Of course he is!" Judy's shoulders straightened as if Birdie had unjustly criticized him. "He's gutted. He's gone to confession and he's promised me over and over it will never happen again." She shredded a tissue. "To be honest, it's the wake-up call we both needed. To remind ourselves what's important and to fight for it. He loves me, Birdie." Judy suddenly smiled. "And we're going to renew our vows. You know how much Bevan loves a party."

"That sounds like a great idea."

Although she and Judy were best friends and they shared almost everything, there were some things about her and Mike's relationship that Birdie held back. It niggled at her now that if Judy was so certain this incident was just a momentary blip and she clearly didn't want to hear any criticism of Bevan, why hadn't she kept it private?

As if reading her mind, Judy closed her hand around Birdie's wrist. "I need you to forget I told you. Promise me you'll never tell Mike." Judy's voice was frantic. "I couldn't stand it if he thought less of Bevan for one silly mistake. And that's all it was. A stress-induced silly mistake not helped by me being obsessed with getting pregnant."

"I promise."

The words came out automatically in solidarity for her best friend, but as Birdie heard them, they grated slightly like an irritated patch of heat rash. As if together she and Judy were burying something that needed light so it never happened again.

But to her knowledge, it never had happened again. Birdie had spent years admiring the way the Quinns had put the incident behind them and gone on to become a stronger couple, successful both at work and home. Now that admiration had gone up in flames with the disconnect between their friendship and the theft of their money, before exploding under the indignity of the restraining order.

"Birdie, please," Judy begged. "Can I come in? I need to talk to you."

Birdie stepped outside into the fading light, but this time it wasn't to protect Judy from the flapping ears of a husband and children, but because there was no way in hell she was allowing her inside her home.

She walked to the now gray and weathered teak seat. "Talk then."

Judy blinked like a startled chick. "So how are Jack and Sienna?"

This time Birdie did a double take. It was the sort of caring question they'd always asked each other about their families. She had no desire to answer it.

"I think we have a few other things to discuss first before we ask about the kids."

Judy flinched and Birdie could have slapped herself. "I'm sorry. That was incredibly thoughtless. I didn't say it to deliberately hurt you."

Judy gripped her hands together, the familiar diamond rings now loose on bony fingers. "I regret the restraining order. If I had my time over I'd never have agreed to it."

"Agreed to it?"

She nodded. "Since Brad ... the medication helps, but sometimes making decisions is beyond me. Bevan was only trying to protect me and he was so furious with you, Birdie. But now I see it was the wrong thing to do."

"I regret hitting you." Birdie spoke the truth.

"Thank you. That means a lot, especially when people are a constant disappointment." Judy's cheeks suddenly pinked. "Like Isobel. She played Brad like a bow. No matter what he gave her, she always demanded more. Once she got her hands on that diamond engagement ring she kept finding excuses to delay the wedding. She broke Brad's heart, then she broke him. I blame her for his death!"

She looked at Birdie with wild eyes. "Do you know the first thing she asked Bevan after Brad died? "What did he leave me in his will?" Thank God Bevan talked Brad out of leaving her anything."

Birdie clearly remembered many conversations with Judy and Bevan about Izzy and Brad. How they'd expressed their hope they'd marry sooner rather than later and give them grandchildren.

"Did you hear Izzy ask Bevan about the will?"

"No. When they told me about Brad, I was so distraught that Bevan was worried I'd hurt myself. The doctor gave me sedatives and I lost a few days."

"But you were at Villefranche with Izzy before the funeral."

"Yes." Judy sounded like she didn't understand the point of the question.

"If you blame Izzy for Brad's death, surely you would have wanted to stay the hell away from her, not be in the same house with her?"

"We had to plan the funeral." As Judy's gaze slipped and slid, Birdie knew her brain was also struggling to focus. "Bevan said it was important."

"What was important?"

"Making sure Brad hadn't been stupid." She shook her head hard. "No, not stupid. My darling boy wasn't stupid, but you know how he struggled. Remember when he went to Melbourne determined to make it on his own? We gave him a year, but at the end of it he was floundering and losing money. Bevan found a way to bring him back without losing face and put him in charge of Elite. He hoped one day Brad would take over, but ..."

Birdie stopped breathing and sent up a prayer of thanks for Judy's dulled senses. Had the woman been sober or unmedicated she'd see the truth of what she'd just said written clearly on Birdie's face. Bevan Quinn ran Elite. Brad was just a puppet.

More than anything Birdie wanted to rush to the phone and tell Mike to call an Elite meeting. Thankfully, reality cautioned her. The ramblings of a drunk woman with mental health issues wouldn't hold much water, but they were a start. Now they knew without a shadow of a doubt that Bevan Quinn had been heavily involved. Had Brad been stupid or had his father set him up as the fall guy?

But her antipathy toward Bevan wouldn't reach that far. She'd never once doubted that Bevan loved his son.

"My Brad tried so hard." Judy's voice cracked. "But it was never enough. Not even the best is enough for Bevan," she said bitterly. "I should know."

The acrimony bit Birdie hard and she had a crazy urge to rub her sternum. Not wanting to kill the conversation with a direct question, she revisited her old self. What would Judy's best friend have said to her?

"Bevan loves you."

"Hah! If he loved me he wouldn't keep having sex with other women." Judy's hand fumbled in her bag and she pulled out an engraved hip flask, unscrewed the cap and drank a slug. "I'm not even sure that time I told you about was his first. Counting the number of diamonds he's given me over the years, I'd say he's fucked at least twenty other women."

Tiny tingles of shock detonated all over Birdie's body. "What the hell are you still doing staying with him then?" she asked.

"I'm not strong like you, Birdie. I never was."

"I'm not strong!" But as she said it, she realized that since Elite she was a hell of a lot stronger than she'd given herself credit for. "You never know what you're capable of until it's demanded of you. You can leave Bevan and start again."

Judy shook her head, misery rising off her like mist. "I've already lost Brad and I'm barely standing. If I lose anything else ..."

Birdie stared at Judy as if she was seeing her for the first time. During all their years of friendship, she had admired Judy and basked in the faint glow that radiated from the spotlight she inhabited. Now Birdie saw beyond the costume of perfection Judy had always worn. She glimpsed a broken grieving woman clutching at the illusion of security with a man who disrespected her and may have sacrificed their son for money or to avoid a jail term, or both.

"That man you're clinging to is evil. He's hiding behind some creative accounting and company laws," Birdie said. "And your comfortable life is paid for with money stolen from people you once called friends. What stories are you telling yourself so you don't sink in shame?"

Judy dropped her head into her hands and her shoulders shook with sobs.

Console her.

But Birdie thought of everything she'd done just to survive the year. How Lucy had let go of her dream and fought for herself and Jack. What Izzy had generously offered. And her hand refused to reach out and touch Judy.

She was deciding what to do next—*Wait it out? Offer a cup of tea?* —when she heard the creak of the side gate. She swore softly. She really didn't want Lucy or Mike involved.

"There you are."

At the familiar voice, Birdie shot to her feet. Bevan was striding across the lawn.

Completely ignoring her, he squatted in front of Judy. "Come on, darling. It's time to go home."

Judy raised her wet face, now streaked with snot, smudged mascara and rouge, and nodded like a child.

Birdie's mind raced, trying to piece things together. Although very late to the party, she knew now that if Judy had told Bevan she was visiting Birdie, he wouldn't have allowed her to come.

"How did you know she was here?" Birdie asked him.

"I tracked her cell phone."

"Do that a lot, do you?"

Bevan pulled Judy to her feet and put an arm around her. Birdie saw through the action and pity almost felled her.

"Remember what I said, Judy. About new starts," she said desperately. "And I'll remember what you said too."

But Judy was slumped against Bevan, her eyes half-closed, barely awake, let alone able to compute Birdie's words.

Bevan glanced between the two women, his face taut. "Since Brad died, Judy's struggled. Her grip on reality slips and she gets confused."

"She was saying some interesting things."

"About Brad and me?" His head dropped and he rubbed the back of his neck. "You think I don't hate myself for not realizing Brad was thinking of ... Every day I wish we'd never gone to that bloody retreat. That we'd been here to stop him. Get him the help he needed. Of course I do. I've lost my son."

His pain reached out and penetrated Birdie's anger and betrayal. She felt her throat thicken and tears threaten.

"And my wife." His voice cracked on the words.

Instead of increasing Birdie's sympathy, it shattered it. "Your wife's standing right next to you."

"Does she look like my Judy to you?"

No. But Birdie didn't voice it. She was too busy questioning if she'd ever truly known Judy Quinn. Or Bevan.

"I've tried hard to keep her out of the hospital," he said. "But she needs more than me to get better. She needs her friends, but this town's turned its back on her."

Birdie crossed her arms to stay the urge to spit at him. "You took her to New South Wales."

"After you hit her and sent her spiraling. She lost her son and then her best friend attacked her. I hope you can sleep at night knowing you're the reason she's under psychiatric care."

The words foamed around the seal Birdie had glued over their friendship. Some oozed in, stinging and burning her with guilt. *Thirty years of friendship and when she needed you, you turned your back.* Her resolve wavered. Had she contributed to Judy's illness?

No! No! No!

Birdie lifted her chin and stared Bevan down. "You've got that round the wrong way, Bevan. You're the reason she's in this state and I think it suits you. You're not just a crook, you're a conniving bastard."

His eyes darkened to obsidian. "I am neither of those things, and you saying it isn't helping Judy."

Birdie refused to play his mind games any longer. "We're going to nail you. Prove you stole our money."

A long sigh rumbled out of him as if he carried the worries of the world on his shoulders. "Brad stole your money and I'm sorry. If I could turn back time—"

"You're a lying bastard too."

His jaw tightened. "I wouldn't be saying things like that if I was you. Not unless you can afford a defamation case."

"Birdie," Judy said. "I—"

"Sweetheart, it's time to go." Bevan ushered Judy forward so quickly she stumbled.

"Judy! You can always call me," Birdie offered, hoping one day Judy would do the right thing and implicate Bevan.

"Bevan?" Mike stood at the gate, his bowling bag in his hand.

"Mike! Good to see you. Sorry I can't stay. Blame the women." He leaned in to Mike like he'd done so often over the years when he was sharing a joke or having a quiet word. "The girls got into another clash and Judy's shattered. I need to get her home."

Mike looked at Birdie. Unlike the day of Brad's funeral, his face wasn't angry or resigned, nor was it confirmation of Bevan's statement. It was one hundred percent concern for her. She surreptitiously raised a thumb, hoping he'd see it and know she was okay.

Mike turned back to Bevan, and Birdie wondered if he'd take his shot—the one he'd been unable to fire since Elite had crashed.

"It's good you're leaving, Bevan," Mike said. "Saves me kicking your lying ass to the gutter. If you ever set foot on my property again I'll call the police. Now fuck off."

Judy's hand shot out, grabbing Mike's arm. "I'm sorry."

"It's time to go home." Bevan peeled back her fingers.

"What are you sorry for, Judy?" Mike asked.

Bewilderment played across her haggard features, as if she had no idea what Mike was talking about. "Brad," she said. "My darling boy's gone."

Birdie held Mike's hand as they watched Bevan bundle Judy into the car. "Feel better you got to tell him to eff off?"

"Little bit. He looked rattled."

"He's worried Judy might have let the cat out of the bag."

"Did she?"

"Yes, but don't get too excited. She told me she can't leave him, and while she stays he holds all the aces. I wouldn't be surprised if he has her committed and she goes into the hospital for a long time. Either way, I bet my bottom dollar they'll be gone from Glingilly by tomorrow. He'll want to keep her as far away from us as possible."

Birdie walked inside and switched on the kettle. "I thought losing our money was the worst thing that could happen to someone, but I look at Judy ... I never thought I'd say this, but I'd rather be living my life."

Mike set two mugs on the counter. "Even if the money's gone, I like to think we'll get Bevan in the end. He'll have made a mistake somewhere and I'm putting my faith in Cooper to find it."

"I get it," Birdie said. "Some of me burns to expose him too, but Mike, I don't want to lose our lives to something that leaves us bitter, twisted and stressed. We've already lost enough. We need to concentrate on the positives—your health, the house, the kids and Rigby."

"And our new Airbnb project." He smiled at her. "I'm with you one hundred percent, Birdie. You can even dust off that planning book for our around-Australia trip."

She shook her head. "No."

"No?"

"A year is a long time and as we know, anything can happen. For now, Let's just live each day in the present."

"This from the biggest planner I know? Might take some practice."

"I know."

"Let's start now then." He leaned in and pressed his lips to hers.

She closed her eyes to the teabags in the sink and the splash of milk on the counter and wrapped her arms around his neck, following the kiss to wherever it led.

CHAPTER FORTY-THREE

TWO YEARS LATER

Izzy was doing a comms check with the lead volunteers and confirming that each festival venue was running smoothly. This was her third Irish festival and she still got a buzz of achievement that rivaled any artificial high. Although the festival retained its early roots with the potato-peeling and soda bread competitions, the "Danny Boy" sing-off and the community parade, she'd grown the music side of things and the food offerings. This year there was the added art exhibition and for the first time every festival ticket had sold two months out.

The walkie-talkie crackled and Izzy responded. "Hey, Rach. All good?"

"No!"

Rach was one of three of Izzy's event management students who were doing a course-required placement at the festival. The positions were highly coveted by the students and Izzy only chose the most capable, because inevitably things went wrong and it was a baptism by fire.

"The Four-Leaf Clovers missed their sound check," Rach wailed. "I've texted them, I've checked the bar tent, but I can't find them anywhere. I even called them," she said as if this was a massive step. "The marquee's full of excited punters and there's no band."

"I checked them in so they're here," Izzy said. Musicians made the festival what it was, but they also caused her the most angst. "Did you try the pubs?"

"Yes!"

Izzy suddenly remembered a small red-haired child hanging off the lead singer's hand and begging him to "hurry up."

"Try the kids' potato dig," she said.

"They're not going to be there." But after a short silence the walkie-talkie crackled into life again. "OMG, Izzy! You're a legend!"

As Izzy stepped out of the communications tent, a tingle shot through her. The main street was closed to traffic and festival flags fluttered in the breeze. People popped in and out of shops, wandered through the market stalls and queued at the food vans, pouring money into the Glingilly community and beyond. This year she was running buses from neighboring towns as there wasn't a spare bed to be had in Glingilly.

Two and a half years since Elite had exploded her life, Izzy occasionally experienced moments of astonishment that she was still living in Glingilly. More surprising, but dearly appreciated, was her happiness living here. The summer after Elite had crashed she'd been determined to leave, especially after Lucy had excitedly told her that she and Jack were heading off around Australia. Izzy had forced a smile and tried hard to be happy for them, but as often as she'd reminded herself that Lucy wasn't her only friend in town, Brooke's company didn't quite match a friendship that had been forged by a life-altering event.

On a hot January day, she'd put aside her own feelings and joined the Essens on Cork Street to wave Lucy, Jack and Rigby off on their adventure. When the van had disappeared from sight, Birdie had turned to her and said, "Mike's out on Wednesday night. If you're not doing anything, I know I'd enjoy the company."

Although Izzy had admired Birdie's organizational skills at the

festival and appreciated her support prior to the other Elite members
trusting her, she wasn't certain they shared enough in common to spend
an entire evening alone together. But the first night was unexpectedly
enjoyable, and over subsequent visits Izzy slowly realized that Birdie
was part friend, part the mother she'd never had, as well as being a font
of wisdom she could plumb.

A couple of months later, after Birdie had recounted a story Lucy
and Jack had shared on a video call, Izzy had said, "I guess it's time I
restarted my life."

Birdie gave her a quizzical look. "Haven't you already done that?"

"Ah, no. I'm still in Glingilly."

"So throwing a festival that put Glingilly on the map and
establishing the Elite trust, not to mention learning how to fish, isn't
restarting your life?"

Izzy had arced up at the veiled reference to Cooper. "I'm never
putting my life on hold for a man again!"

"Good," Birdie said firmly. "I doubt Cooper would want you to.
Has he asked?"

The question had forced Izzy to concede that Cooper made few
demands on her. Actually, was suggesting they "catch up" even a
demand? The few times she'd said no to an invitation because she had
an assignment due, he hadn't made a fuss, just asked when she was free.
But as the months passed, what had started off as casual, giving her the
much-needed freedom of not being tied down, now made her question
what Cooper wanted.

What she wanted.

"The plan was always to change careers using my new
qualification," she'd said stubbornly to Birdie, despite the thought not
filling her with excitement.

Angry with herself, she'd announced to Cooper that night that she
was now actively job-searching. He'd nodded and said, "Good for you."
He'd even sent her a couple of links for jobs in Melbourne with the
message *you'd ace this*. Although both jobs had been closer to what she
was looking for, neither were a fit.

It was Birdie who'd pointed out the newly created tourism job in Warrnambool.

"'Relevant university qualifications, strong communication and strategic thinking skills and a proven ability to translate strategy and policy into deliverable outcomes,'" she'd read aloud. "This sounds like you."

Izzy had sighed. "It would be perfect if it was in Melbourne."

"Really? Do you have a Brooke, Lucy or me in Melbourne?"

"Lucy's not actually here," Izzy said sulkily.

"She'll be back." Birdie had pushed a pen and notepad in front of her. "Write a pros and cons list about moving away from Glingilly and the people who love you. Include the risk of your trich escalating."

"Oh my God! You sound like my therapist."

"She's obviously a very wise woman," Birdie had teased, then sobered. "Izzy, you need to do what you need to do. I'm just worried you're clinging to an old solution to a problem that no longer exists. I know you hated throwing Elite events, but they were just theme parties you can do with your hands tied behind your back. The festival challenged you. This job will too."

Izzy had struggled to come up with one pro for moving to Melbourne other than "more career opportunities." The fact that the perfect job was in Warrnambool had instantly voided it.

One year into her new position, Cooper had sent her a link to a job in the university's business school for a lecturer to teach event management. His accompanying message, *you'd ace this*, gave her food for thought. She hadn't known she'd love teaching, but like Cooper, she'd discovered she enjoyed the perspective the students offered to her real-world experience.

"Izzy!" She turned now to see Cooper jogging up to her. He dropped a kiss on her cheek. "Once again I'm in awe you did all this."

She laughed. "I had help."

"All the best do."

She slid her arm into his and they crossed the road to the hall. "You ready for dinner?"

He grinned. "You buying?"

"I reckon the boss gets free Irish stew for two, but I'll shout the Guinness."

"You're on."

Cooper opened the door for her and they walked into a wall of noise—animated voices, the toe-tapping sound of a fiddle, the scraping of chairs and the clatter of silverware.

"Over here!" Lucy Essen called out. "We've got drinks."

"You go," Izzy said to Cooper. "I'll be there in a sec." She stuck her head into the kitchen. "All good?"

"No dramas at all." Oscar was dumping mashed potato into bowls with an ice-cream scoop. "We're following Birdie and Mike's instructions to a T and we've only got happy customers."

"And Birdie couldn't help herself," Gaylene Hewitson added. "She's 2,000 miles away but she called us from Lawn Hill just to make sure we had enough meat." She dished stew over the fluffy mashed potato and handed Izzy two bowls. "There you go. Enjoy."

"Thanks."

Izzy joined everyone at the table, kissed her friends hello, and stroked the downy head of the baby in Lucy's arms. "How can she sleep through all this noise?"

Jack laughed. "Babies have three settings. Awake and screaming, awake and happy, and dead to the world."

Rigby plonked a green bucket on the table. "I dug six potatoes. Dad says he'll help me make chips."

"Good for you, mate," Cooper said.

Rigby wriggled under Cooper's arm. "We can catch the fish."

Izzy and Cooper had looked after Rigby when Lucy went into labor, and to distract him from missing his parents they'd taken him fishing.

"He hasn't stopped talking about it," Lucy said. "To be honest he was more excited by the fish than his new sister."

"How's the cottage coming along?" Cooper asked.

"You won't recognize it," Jack said.

Izzy laughed. "That's good!"

"Come on, admit you miss it just a little." Cooper slid an arm around her. "After all, we fell in love there."

When Izzy had decided to stay and take the job in Warrnambool, Cooper had asked her to move in with him.

"It makes sense," he'd said. "You'll be closer to work."

"Sometimes sensible isn't always the best thing." She'd flexed her fingers, making fists and releasing them to keep them far from her hair. "I never thought I'd say this, Cooper, but I need to stay in Glingilly."

He'd slid his hands into hers. "I don't care where we live, as long as we're together in the same place."

"I want that too." She'd kissed him. "And central heating."

"Too easy."

They bought a fully renovated Californian bungalow close to the river. Izzy teased him about his obsession with the lawn, but she loved watching him shirtless on the ride-on mower. He set up a permanent stand for her telescope and only joined her to stargaze when she invited him.

After Lucy and Jack had returned from their fourteen months away, they'd decided to rent rather than buy. "We want to have another baby," Lucy had said. "And even if we never buy another house, that's okay. We're never stressing ourselves financially again."

But Gavin Whitehead hadn't been able to re-let the cottage after Izzy had moved out and the overinflated property market had finally settled. So in an unexpected piece of good fortune, they'd used their combined savings and a share of the Noosa apartment money to put down a deposit on the cottage, leaving enough in reserve to make it both safe and no-frills comfortable.

"We're on track to move in by the time Birdie and Mike get back," Lucy said now. "We owe them that. there's no way we could have afforded the renovations without living rent-free for the year in Cork Street."

"It's not exactly free," Jack said. "Some of those Airbnb guests are seriously hard work. I dream of a few days off, but someone's made the district too bloody popular."

Izzy laughed. "I think you can blame Mike more than me for the stellar occupancy rate. That fireplace he built when he added the outdoor living room is pretty attractive. There's something special about snuggling up on a sofa in front of a fire and glancing up to see stars."

"If it's not raining," Jack said.

Lucy rolled her eyes. "My husband the romantic."

"Hey, we had plenty of nights lying under blankets of stars up north, remember."

"And they were magic." She smiled and passed their sleeping daughter to him.

The hall suddenly quieted and Izzy glanced up. Brooke had walked in with another officer. The chatter quickly restarted when everyone realized the police had arrived for their dinner.

Brooke paused on her way to the kitchen. "How's the stew, Izzy?"

"It's not quite as good as Birdie's but it's close."

"Great. I'm starving." Brooke tapped her fingers on the table and Izzy recognized the action. Brooke was about to change the subject. "Do you remember Detective Mitchell?"

Izzy flinched. "Is that a joke?"

"Still too soon?"

"It will *always* be too soon."

"He was just doing his job, Izzy," Brooke said, not unkindly. "And he's got a new one that might interest all of you."

"What's that?" Jack asked.

"He moved to Melbourne last year and he's recently joined the fraud squad."

"Is that a good thing?" Izzy asked.

"I think so," Brooke said. "He never trusted Bevan Quinn, but fraud took the case out of our hands."

Not a lot had progressed on the Elite case. Cooper had found some money that may have pointed to Bevan and they'd engaged an attorney to argue for the reopening of the case. It had been unsuccessful.

"I doubt Mitchell will be able to convince his superiors," Izzy said.

"Well, there's the thing." Brooke smiled. "There's been a big restructure in fraud and a couple of people have moved on."

Izzy's heart leaped and although she kept her eyes on Brooke, she reached for Cooper's hand. "Are you saying Mitchell's going to reopen the Elite case?"

"That's exactly what I'm saying. He's re-examining the evidence and I'm sure he'll be in touch with you all soon."

"Hey, Brooke!" The officer was holding two meals and tilting his head toward a table by the door.

"I better go. See you at the GGSC dinner on Thursday."

Izzy turned back to face everyone. "Dare we hope?"

Jack had his cell phone in his hand. "I texted Mom and Dad and they actually have reception. Mom says breathe and take it one day at a time."

"Good advice," Cooper said. "But I'll be calling Detective Mitchell on Monday morning to set up a meeting so I can wow him with my graphs, charts and spreadsheets."

"Sounds like a plan." Jack stood and scooped up a sleepy Rigby. "We better get these two home to bed and the babysitter so we're back in time for Céilí Clare. Don't party too hard without us."

Izzy laughed. "Professor Barsky's not known for that."

"Neither are you," Lucy said. "Time to face it, Izzy, you're very happy living a quiet life down by the river gazing at stars."

Lucy was gone before Izzy had thought of a pithy reply.

"You want another drink?" Cooper asked.

"Not here, it's too noisy."

They exited via the side door, but instead of walking back to the main street, Izzy crossed the grass behind the clapboard building and stood at the post-and-rail fence. She watched the full moon rise, its white light as bright as a theater spot.

"Light pollution's bad tonight," Cooper teased as he stood behind her, his chin nuzzled into her hair. When he spoke again his voice was serious. "Are you happy with your quiet life?"

"I don't think it's quiet. I think it's full of things that invigorate me, challenge me in positive ways and make me happy. You're a huge part of that."

"I'm glad."

She turned into him. "Two and a half years ago I didn't think being happy was even possible, and then you quietly came into my life and stuck yourself in my corner even when I didn't know if I wanted or needed it. I kept waiting for you to tell me what to do, or pin your needs on me, but you never did. Sometimes I worry you don't ask enough."

He stroked back the strands of her hair the light breeze had flicked onto her face. "I do ask, Izzy. How do you think we ended up buying a house and moving in together?"

"I guess ..."

"What?"

She screwed up her face, a little embarrassed. "It just didn't feel like an ask."

His gaze caught hers. "I like to think that's because you love me."

She smiled up at him. "I do love you."

"I know." He kissed her. "Let's go find a table in the festival bar so when Lucy and Jack get back we can pretend we've been partying hard without them."

"I'm technically still on the clock."

"And we're going to be where the only evening event is happening."

As they walked, Cooper said, "I'm a bit dark on Lucy and Jack for leaving when they did. I was hoping for a baby cuddle."

Cooper had been the third person to hold Willow after Lucy and Jack.

"It sounds like your baby alarm clock's going off," Izzy said.

He shrugged. "Maybe. Is yours?"

"Maybe."

He stopped abruptly and faced her. "Really?"

It was her turn to shrug. "I always thought I didn't want kids because I was worried I'd be just like my mother. No child deserves to be abandoned, but ..." Her hands rose and fell. "Now my life's thankfully very different from my mother's, and I look at Lucy and Jack and what they went through. How they put their family first and they've come through the other side together and stronger. I know to the depths of my soul you'll put your family first too. With you by my side, I've got a chance of being the mother I want to be."

He kissed her. "So we're really going to do this?"

The moonlight captured the eagerness on his face and she smiled. "There are a few things to iron out first."

"Right. Of course. Your job. Well, I get parental leave, which I could take after your maternity leave and—"

"Shh." She put two fingers lightly over his mouth. "We're not even pregnant yet."

"Yes, but it's always good to put expectations on the table."

"You're right. Being on the same page is important." She picked up both his hands and rested them under their chins. "You're the first man I've ever been with where the thought of having a baby doesn't break me out in a cold sweat or make me want to pull out my hair."

"I'll take that as the ultimate compliment."

She wanted to smile but she still had important things to say. "Cooper, you show me you love me in so many little ways, from a cup of tea in bed to still baiting my fishing hooks and a thousand ways in-between. I hope I do enough so you know I love you too."

"Well, you could start baiting hooks," he teased.

"Yeah, nah, never going to happen. How about this instead?" She cleared her throat as her mouth dried. "Dr. Cooper Barsky, will you marry me?"

His eyes widened in surprise. "I thought you didn't want to get married?"

"Me too. But if it comes down to marriage or baiting hooks, it's suddenly a no-brainer."

"Well, when you put it like that ..."

"I think I didn't want to get married because I hadn't met you."

He blinked a couple of times, then cupped her cheeks, his palms warm against her skin, and kissed her.

When he pulled back, she checked, "Is that a yes?"

"More of a 'hell, yeah!'"

She laughed. "Come on, I'll buy you a drink to seal the deal."

The festival bar was filling and Céllí Clare were doing sound checks. Izzy checked in with Rach who assured her, "All good, I've got this."

When she turned around she couldn't see Cooper, but Lucy was waving to her from a table.

"How did you two get back so fast?" Izzy asked.

"We've been gone an hour." Lucy glanced at her. "Did you get tied up troubleshooting?"

Izzy laughed. "You could call it that."

Cooper arrived with a bottle of champagne and four glasses and placed them in the center of the table with a flourish.

"Jack, buzz your parents and see if they pick up," he said.

"Um ... okay."

"What's going on?" Lucy asked. "Did the police call with more news?"

Birdie's and Mike's smiling faces appeared on Jack's cell phone.

"I thought everything was okay in the kitchen," Birdie said.

"Relax, Birdie, all is well." Izzy lifted her champagne glass. "Cooper and I just wanted to check if you'll be home in March?"

"That's the plan. Why?"

"Oh my God," Lucy said, delight dawning across her face.

"Because I just asked Cooper to marry me and now I need a bridesmaid and a mother of the bride."

Birdie's and Mike's congratulations blared through the speakers, Lucy was squealing and Jack was hugging Izzy.

"Our awesome festival director just got engaged!" Rach's voice boomed over the PA system. "Congratulations to Izzy and Cooper."

"Does that mean free drinks?" a wag called out.

Céllí Clare launched into an Irish wedding jig and Cooper caught

Izzy around the waist. The crowd clapped and stamped their feet as he swung her onto the dance floor, romping back and forth until they were both panting for breath.

Once anxiety would have urged Izzy to flee from the center of attention. But here, in the heart of her community, with the love in Cooper's eyes fixed on her and dear friends close by, this was the only place she wanted to be.

She stepped in close and wrapped her arms around his neck. To cheers and whistles, she kissed him long and leisurely. After all, there was no hurry.

She was home.

Thank you for reading ***The Money Club***. If this is your first ***Fiona Lowe*** novel, you have another six to enjoy!

Read an excerpt from them all at
fionalowe.com

Daughter of Mine
Birthright
Home Fires
Just An Ordinary Family
A Home Like Ours
A Family of Strangers

Join My Newsletter
For a free novella, *Summer of Mine;* the prequel of *Daughter of Mine,*
please join my VIP Readers newsletter. Register at
fionalowe.com

ACKNOWLEDGMENTS

This novel was written on Wadawurrung and Eastern Maar land. I pay my respects to the First Nation Peoples of this land as custodians of learning, literacy, knowledge and story.

Many people assume I have experienced every event I write about, but fortunately I have not. However, research helps me walk in my characters' shoes. The idea for *The Money Club* came from the collision of living in a town that's been impacted by a couple of big Ponzi schemes and listening to an ABC podcast. I chose to set the book in the south-west of Victoria only because it has a long history of Irish settlement and horse racing. Oh, and fabulous hot springs I had to try out for myself!

Many thanks to Kerri Coghlan for talking me through the ins and outs of owning a racehorse and giving me an understanding of what's involved in Fashions on the Field. For those who are interested, I based the Glingilly racecourse stand on Camperdown's glorious heritage-listed one.

I spent a weekend at the Koroit Irish festival, soaking up the event so I could write it into the book. What's not to love about great food and toe-tapping music? I was stunned and delighted to take home the winner's sash for the soda bread (non-traditional) competition.

Thanks to Penelope Janu for some legal advice regarding property titles; Dr. Jennifer Hallowes, veterinarian, for information on horses. Wayne Peterken passed on what he's learned about surf fishing; Erica Mansfield added golden information to my limited exposure to Jack Russell dogs and Christine Tomczak was a welcome pair of eyes.

Thanks to Rachael Donovan for believing in the book, and to Nicola O'Shea and Annabel Blay for smoothing out the rough edges. Thanks also go to Norm Lowe and Norma Blake for their hard work preparing this edition for the North American market. If you're not aware, it is not only the changing of the spelling and unfamiliar terms, it is also every single quotation mark as Australian publishing uses single quotation marks for speech.

Team Lowe continue to support me in getting this book into your hands. Thanks to Barton for the cover design for this edition along with all the banners, slideshows and website maintenance. Thanks to Sandon for always being happy to brainstorm book ideas and plot problems and to Gabi for reading the books so enthusiastically. And last but not least, thanks to Norm for the meals, the laundry, being the driver on research trips and always being in my corner. And a HUGE thanks to you, dear reader, for spending your precious time reading *The Money Club*. The choice of books is enormous and the book budget limited, so I appreciate it very much. I love meeting you on book tours, Facebook, Instagram, TikTok and email. Please stay in touch; your enthusiasm keeps me writing.

ABOUT THE AUTHOR

FIONA LOWE has been a midwife, a sexual health counsellor and a family support worker; an ideal career for an author who writes novels about family and relationships. She spent her early years in Papua New Guinea where, without television, reading was the entertainment and it set up a lifelong love of books. Although she often re wrote the endings of books in her head, it was the birth of her first child that prompted her to write her first novel.

Authentically Australian, her stories are often triggered by a secret or a mystery, and explore the themes of family, community and second chances. Described as gripping, thought-provoking, heart-warming and ultimately uplifting, Lowe's books have been praised for their emotional depth. She is the recipient of the prestigious USA RITA® award and two Australian RuBY awards.

When she's not writing stories, she's a distracted wife, mother of two "ginger" sons, a volunteer in her community, guardian of eighty rose bushes, a slave to a cat, and is often found collapsed on the couch with wine. You can find her at her website, fionalowe.com, and on Facebook, TikTok, Instagram and Goodreads.

BOOK CLUB QUESTIONS

*Financial scams have always existed. Do you think a scheme that targets family and friends is more despicable than one that rips off strangers?

*According to research by Relationships Australia, financial stress is the number one cause of relationship breakdown. Why do you think this is?

*When a woman gains a mother-in-law, in many ways she gains a stranger. What are the cliches around mother-daughter-in-law relationships? What strategies are needed to foster positive relationships?

*The impact of financial scams can vibrate through families and workplaces, and some scams are so large they have placed country towns in recession. What are the ramifications when family and work relationships are exploited to this degree?

*The Australian dream of owning your own home is very different from other countries where more people rent than buy. Do you think this dream places too much pressure on people? Does it have a negative effect on quality of life or does it improve it?

*Do you think as a society we place too much emphasis on consumerism? Is it possible to be content with less or is that a drop in living standards?

*For an average-income earner, having enough in a retirement fund is a daunting task now that many people's retirement years number more than thirty. Does the ever-present need for financial security open people up to taking risks?

*Juggling working outside the home and motherhood is an exhausting constant in many women lives. Is there a solution?